For Luca, and Kirsty. 'It is meaningless to just live, and pointless to just fight. You have to love, or you always lose.' A.G Smith

CONTENTS

Here it is, everything I have, everything that has led up to the downfall of the Stronghold. My journey, along with the tales of cursed wartime will reveal all.

They told me there were no rules to this thing, that I could hold the world in the palm of my hand, but at what cost...they never told me the price I would have to pay. They never told me I would have to watch it all burn to a cinder.

I've never forgotten what old King Enzo once said to me, 'You have no right to decide for yourself what is right and wrong. It is your duty to accept the true justice of the King.'

If only I had listened. What a fool I was for thinking I could be a hero.

1. ~ COMPANIONSHIP ~

I entered Lady Senna's training ground. It was as silent as a grave at night. Carved out of an enormous hillside cavern and owned by my most trusted of friends, Lady Senna Stone, it was a mostly unknown destination. She was a very private person.

In the year since I had last entered this training ground, it had changed quite a bit. A pool of crisp water sat in the centre, bubbling as if it were being boiled. Two small rivers seeped away and into the walls, splitting the cavern into two halves, and for each half, there was a tunnel of chambers and underground water channels. Patches of rocky ground, connected by mounds of misshapen stone and short walls littered the cavern.

Lady Senna was already warming up when I arrived. As she stretched down to her toes, a length of long blonde hair began to unravel from the tied bunches atop her head, covering her eyes. My arrival had gone unnoticed, and it would be, so I thought, as safe an opportunity as any to test my stealth. I was a commanding assassin after all.

Creeping around the side of a rocky mound, I positioned my straight-edged and cross-hilted sword to the right of my shoulder and in preparation to strike I peered ever so cautiously over the mound. I watched as Senna, balanced with perfect precision, steadied her entire body weight on only one hand.

I was certain that she had not noticed me, though if she had and was playing me for a fool, then she would be sorry. She had left herself wide open and her wood shafted spear was too far out of useful reach.

This was my chance. I leapt with all my strength and rippling the air with a twist of my sword, I spun sideways over the mound.

Senna was no longer there and before I could put a stop to the motion of my twisted movement, the cold tip of Senna's spear was screeching across the side of my sword arm. Sparks danced overhead and with a sigh, I was smashed to the ground.

'Nice try. I could hear your fat armour a mile away,' Senna said, pointing the sharp edge of her spear to my throat.

'Perhaps you are right.' I brushed the spear tip away.

'You look odd. Have you changed something?' she asked.

'Has it been that long, Senna,' I replied. 'Well, I have been sporting this new look for some time now. As you know, I used to wear a full set of light steals, but it was too loud. It dulled the sharpness of my attacks. I now use Sand steel.'

'Sand steel…'

'I know, I know. It cost a fortune, but its lighter and stronger than my old suit.'

'And what's all this?' she said, jabbing me in the right bicep.

'I have also removed armour from my thighs, my midriff and everything from the gauntlet to the shoulder plate on my right arm.'

'You do go on a bit…well, to tell you the truth, Mace, it looks stupid, and you're probably the loudest assassin I've ever met,' she said, smirking. 'I guess you will be wanting to test it out?'

Senna pointed her spear tip at my throat once again, this time crouched in an offensive stance. Excitement beamed from her bright blue eyes.

'Let's get on with it. I've been warming up for almost an hour waiting for your slow ass,' she continued.

'How did you ever become a lady?' I asked, dropping my stance.

With the flick of my wrist, I whirled my sword around to meet with the tip of Senna's spear.

'I thought you were ready?' I roared, jumping back to gain some distance.

Senna's spear was more than twice the length of my sword and I was not taking any chances. He slashed away from a spear thrust and then charged with wild swings from left to right. Anticipating the movements to follow, Senna struck at my abdomen. Without a moment to spare, I switched hands and turned swiftly into a leg sweep. It caught her ankle and sent her hurtling backwards. She landed with a thud, and sending a spear thrust that almost gutted me, she instantly sprang back up to her feet.

I ran back at her and in ducking to avoid the deadly spear end, I drove the swan-shaped pommel of my sword into the side of her head. She stumbled back, spun to one side and with a well-placed elbow, launched at me. I was left holding my jaw and as I turned, Senna gripped my arm, bent it upright and with force enough to knock the sword from my hand, tripped me to the floor. We were a tangle of arms and limbs as we wrestled for supremacy.

'Give up…you're a scrawny wimp,' she said, slipping away from my grip, and with one arm placed around my neck, she squeezed with all her strength.

'Give up.' She rolled over to lock her other hand around my neck and with one, two and then three slaps to the ground, I submitted to defeat. Senna gladly surrendered her grip.

'For the sake of goodness, Senna,' I said, rubbing my throat in relief. 'You almost snapped my bloody neck.'

'You mean, for goodness sake, I'm guessing. And you would not want me going easy on you now...would you?' She smirked.

'No...of course not.' I surprised her with a mighty kick to the chest, that sent her tumbling across the floor. A groan escaped her lips. She rolled to one side and my face dropped.

'Senna, are you alright?' I yelled, offering a hand.

In seeing the smirk on her face, I immediately regretted my decision to help.

Senna threw out her leg, tripping me over, and on springing up from her hands, she slammed me full in the face with the heel of her boot.

This fight went on for almost two hours and in that time, we exchanged a black eye for a bruised cheek and a limp knee for a dislocated shoulder. It was fair to say that we were left with more than just aches and pains.

From the viewing platform at the edge of the cavern, evenly matched and as breathless and sore as one another, Senna and I watched as a single puff of cloud claimed the emptiness of the sky for its own.

'Mace, if you have not yet heard, I have recommended you as a candidate for Mainland Division Lordship,' Senna said, with a surprised look on her face.

'Are you serious? I said, full of surprise.

'Are you not ready? There will not be another Lord's trial for some time.'

'What if I die, there is a very high chance of death.'

'You can either die in search of your destiny, or you could live in wonder of what could have been. I thought this was what you had always wanted.'

'This all I've ever wanted, Senna. I'm just...I'm scared.'

'Please don't be.'

I did not want to dismiss the confidence Senna had in me, but I was nervous about what to expect from such a recommendation. If selected, I would have to endure the King's trials. Twenty-two very skilled and powerful people, including Senna's previous Dame, Mary, died many years ago during my brothers' trial. It was a gruesome affair.

'You look like your about to cry. Don't worry yourself so much,' she said. 'I would not have recommended you if I did not think you were capable of Lordship, neither would Lord Hawk.'

'Lord bloody Hawk...'

My stomach curled. I had no words and nothing but a forced smile creased my lips.

Having Senna's recommendation was all I could ever ask for, but to also have the King's second seat, Lord Hawk's recommendation was a true honour.

2. ~ INSOLENCE ~

I laid there, over the edge of the hillside cavern, resting almost into slumber, when a voice as soft as falling snow sent my heart racing, 'My Lady…It is time for your appointment with the Police master.'

I soon realised that it was none other than Lady Senna's second in command, Dame Eva Fang, on approach. She was quick-tempered, pale-skinned, and although her amber eyes gave the impression of elegance, she was quite arrogant. She thought far too much of herself.

Two small swords, a pitch blacker than her plaited hair, dangled from her waist sides and above them, pressed tightly against her ribs, a dozen floral daggers shimmered in the dim light of the training ground. She was an absolute pain and I knew very well, that she disapproved of my friendship with Senna. She often called me, clown face or horse nose when referring to me in conversation. I did not take it to heart though. She was from a continent on the Eastern side of the world where women are treated with less respect than stray dogs. She utterly detesting men and adored Senna with more admiration than she wishes to receive.

'Lady Senna…are you hurt?' Dame Eva immediately screamed at the sight of her Ladies blackened and bruised face. 'What has that clown done to you?'

'For the sake of five minutes peace, Eva. I am fine, and I have told you more than once today to cancel all my meetings,' Senna replied. 'If you are going to help anyone, then you can help Commander Mace. He is much worse off than I am.'

'Apologies, my Lady. I must have forgotten to cancel. But that does not change the fact that clown face Mace Black has hurt you. Look at what he has done to you, and to make matters worse, his name is on the list for potential Mainland Lordship.'

I could not help but to chuckle to myself.

'I put Commander Mace on that list, as did Lord Hawk,' Senna snapped. 'Are you saying we were wrong to do so?'

'No…of course not, I just meant that…' She looked around for a reasonable response.

'I will hear no more of your scornfulness towards Commander Mace, nor his potential Lordship. You will obey my commands and assist Mace.'

'Yes, my Lady,' Eva said, pacing towards me with a wave of untamed anger in her eyes.

'Thank you, but I do not require assistance,' I said, jumping to my aching feet with the small amount of energy I could muster.

'See, Commander cock nose is fine. Shall I now assist you, my Lady?'

Eva held her arm out for Senna, who looked through her and said with a sigh, 'Dame, if you truly need to assist me, you can wash my dirty clothes...and Commander Mace's for that matter. As you can see, we managed to get ourselves into quite a mess. I think Mace may have even soiled himself.'

I rolled my eye's as Senna pushed Eva's arm away and began to strip off.

'Shall we, Mace. A dip in my fern hot springs will do you the world of good.'

Senna pulled the cape from off my right pauldron with a single sweep of her arm and intending to have it washed, began removing the rest of my armour.

We adjured then, arm in arm, towards the exit of the training ground, whilst Eva watched on with utter disdain. I could not turn my gaze. Her face twisted into an angry grimace. Her eyes, filled with disapproval, looked straight through me and yet, as she picked up my bloody cape from the pile of dirty washing at her feet, I saw beauty, sophistication and a polished charm that I had not before noticed. Although the young and high-ranking Dame was full of loathing towards me and my clan, I was sure that deep down, she meant well.

'Senna, please do not wind the poor girl up,' I said. 'You know she can't stand me, and you have just asked her to wash my dirty clothing.'

The amused smile across Senna's face turned to a hearty laugh.

'Have some fun will you. If you had not noticed, she likes you and I have just allowed her to see your little friend.' Senna peered down at my waist with raised brows.

Before long, Senna and I had travelled down a winding set of stone steps and had arrived at the fern hot springs, named for the surrounding ferns that grow there and nowhere else in Mangrove. The circular spring in the heart of the hill sat perfectly still under the stalactite cave and yet when entered, the water burst to life with a splash and spilt out over the surrounding ferns.

After only a moment of soaking my aches and pains, I felt utterly refreshed. It was as if the hot spring water had taken my lifeless form and made it new.

A comfortable silence was shared between us. We sat on the rocks of the spring, soaking in the therapeutic magic of the bubbling water. We splashed, we played, we baited and mocked one another until our hands were old and wrinkled.

'My apologies for all your bruises, Senna,' I said sincerely, yet with a hint of mockery that I could not hide from her. 'It was not my intention to cause you harm.'

'Mace, don't make excuses. You forget that you have yet to defeat me in combat.' Senna slipped out of the hot springs and where the ferns were clear, and the air was cool, she sat and shared a cup of water with me.

I was newly invigorated and freshly rested, though my eyes became heavy and the weight of the world, all at once, began to sink away.

'Senna, are you as tired as I am?' I asked, receiving no reply.

She had fallen into slumber. I covered her with a towel, as any gentleman would and was suddenly startled by Dame Eva's presence. She stormed through the thickness of green ferns and to the side of the hot spring, where she said in a vulgar tone, 'Dimwit, your clothing is clean.'

She tossed my cape and perfectly shined armour in my face.

I could not help but to breath in the fresh lemony scent that had soaked through the fabric of my cape. I dressed as fast as I could, though it was not fast enough to avoid Eva's stares. Perhaps she did like me, I thought, not expecting her to have done such a fine job of washing my clothing.

'I must be off,' I said. 'I have matters to attend.'

'Do not bore me with your stupidity, clown face.'

Eva was utterly irritating and wished nothing more than provocation for her actions. I shrugged her rudeness from my shoulders and without a word, began to take my leave.

'Dame Eva,' Senna said. 'You will go with Commander Mace and for today, you are under his watch…Enjoy yourselves.'

Senna rolled over and placed her fresh washing under her head for use as a pillow.

'But, my Lady,' Eva and I said in synchronicity.

'That is an order. Another word from either of you and…and I don't know, but it will be bad.'

Holding each other in contempt, Eva and I left Senna to slumber and the fern hot springs behind us. We ventured down the side of the hollowed-out hillside, through the many miles of the Service Divisions factory work front and arrived late in the day beside the East gate. There, I had some business that required my attention. I explained to Eva that there had been some recent desertions within the ranks of the Assassination squad and that I must show them exactly why they should not abandon their posts. Paying no   attention,   Eva   admired   the   overcast   trees

3. ~ DESERTION ~

The skies opened with a thunderous roar. Rain pelting the ground, turning the earth soft and soaking me through to the bare skin.

'Step lively lads, the Commanders here,' old man Oliver, the most senior member of my assassination squad shouted, alerting everyone to my presence.

They all greeted me with, good day and welcome Commander, as they stood to attention. I acknowledged every one of my men with a slight nod and as I walked back and forth inspecting their attire. I ensured that despite their dampness, they were well presented and ready for the expedition ahead.

'Sorry looking bunch of fools,' Eva said, storming past them all with a face of anger and ahead of rain speckled hair.

'Men, say a single word about her presence here today and you will be running laps.'

'Of course, Commander Mace, but what is she doing here?' Boris the Brawler replied.

Not only was he the smallest and most irritating of my assassins, but he was also the most confident, or as most would put it, the most obnoxious man in Mangrove. I wanted nothing more than to cut his shaven head from his spotty neck. He was pompous and played a risky game with his dry wit. But, for all his faults, he was a good assassin and that was all I needed him to be.

Dame Eva sat under an old oak tree and as a little blackbird perched itself atop her shoulder, she whistled a pleasant tune. The bird appeared to understand her and as she pulled a small piece of wet parchment and pencil from her breast pocket, the bird squawked in time with her tune.

'Commander,' old man Oliver said, scratching some dirt from his beard. 'The deserters were seen heading East, through the Wormwood.'

'Well done, Oliver. Dame Eva, are you ready to depart?' I thrust my sword high in the air and rested it on my shoulder plate.

'One moment,' she replied, writing on her wet parchment until there was no space left to write, and when the bird had finished squawking, she tied the parchment to its leg and sent it flying.

'Commander Mace,' said Boris. 'I mean no disrespect, but I am not going to stand here in this forsaken weather, waiting for some little Dame to finish talking to god damn birds. I'm cold, I'm wet and there is just no good reason for it.'

Eva stood, walked over to Boris and with a fierce gaze, said, 'What is your name?' She placed her petite hand atop his curly brown head of hair.

'My name is Boris. What's it to you?'

'Boris, dear boy, you must learn your place,' she said in a gentle tone of voice.

Blood squirted out from Boris's stomach. He screamed out in such pain that he was sick on his boots and when curling in a ball to hold back the blood, he spat profanities at Eva. Without a hint of caring, she smirked at Boris and said, 'Are all your men this soft. I cut him open with nothing more than a fingernail.' She licked the blood from the tip of her black-painted nail.

'I am ready now, Mace. Oh…and the curly-haired boy should probably visit the medical research Divisions.' She strolled East with a skip in her step and a smile on her face.

'Oliver, Rosen, Mathew, Rider, come with me. The rest of you, take Boris to the Medical Research Division,' I commanded.

I would never admit it, but I was rather pleased with how Dame Eva had dealt with my most insubordinate of assassins.

I picked up the pace and with Dame Eva and four good assassins at my side, I eased into a gentle run. We all followed covered track marks through the Wormwood and after only a few hours of mud-covered and rain-soaked trailing later, we came across an old bungalow. It reminded me of the place where I grew up and the place in which my mother was killed.

In the likeness of my childhood home, the bungalow was old and in pre-war style. Large oddly shaped bricks bulged out from the outer walls. It looked as if it had been rebuilt from odds and ends. An over-scaled chimney, with decorative brickwork and chimney pots, stood slanted on the steep timber roof. Arrangements of windows, some tall and others small, were precariously placed between the bungalow's brickwork.

'It is too quiet out here, Commander,' Rider said. 'Perhaps they are expecting us.'

He was one of the newest assassins. A paranoid and frightened expression lay thick across his young face.

'Calm down and listen,' I said, putting my ear to the air and between the cool breeze, I heard the whispering of voices, the shuffling of feet and the heavy breathing of hidden men. 'Stay back…and stay hidden.'

4. ~ VIOLENCE ~

On approaching the bungalow, tears began to form in the corner of my eyes. I tried to focus on anything but that memory from my past, the memory of my mother's death.

I was but a boy, no older than five years of age. My mother, Sophia, was supportive and loved her family until she was ripped to pieces by the one who loved her most, my father, Hollis Black. He was, as we all have come to be, a cursed man and for a time he kept control, providing strength for our family and fighting bravely alongside his brethren in the Beast war. But one day, my father fell to sickness and began losing control of his mind. Mother never left his side and when inevitably he lost the battle for control, his curse took him. He was transformed, body and soul, into a red-eyed demon and in my mother's fleeting moments, she shouted for me to run. Though as she did, my father, in his demon form, took her in his grip. I wanted to run, but could not move, nor take my eyes away from the image that will forever haunt my dreams. My father took her by the head with one hand and with the other, ripped her in half. The demon, dripping with blood, stood before me and as if I had not already seen enough, he crushed my mother's head in the grasp of a single hand. I was too small and too weak to save her and when soldiers from the Citadel ran in to slay the demon that was once my father, I cowered still and watched on as they were struck from existence.

'Mace…Mace. What are you doing?' Eva asked, with a hand over my heart and an unaccustomed air of sympathy in her voice.

I said nothing in reply and wiping the tears from my face, I drew back my sword and walked up the stone step of the bungalow. The front door, engraved with an eagle, was left ajar and with a cautious step, I pushed it open.

'Commander Mace,' a tall and thin assassination squad deserter said in surprise.

His jaw dropped and his face paled. The man fell back. In a panic, he tried to unsheathe his sword, but it was too late. I punched him full in the face and with the flick of my cross-hilted sword, I split the man's skull wide open.

Wiping a warm splash of blood from my face, I did not hesitate to step inside the bungalow and when I did, two men in white fox masks burst out from the back of the bungalow's dark hallway. Furious war cries washed out the patter of the rain as the masked men, swirling war axes above their heads, caught me off guard. I kicked one in the chest and cleaving the straight edge of my sword on a side angle, I sliced the other across the neck.

Blood spilt out over me. In a continuous motion, I turned full circle and chopped the remaining deserters head clean off his shoulders.

I Jumped backwards out of the bungalow. Two heavily armed fox masked men fell from the slanted roof. I dodged sword swings and spear thrusts. I cut through the front man's defences and with the sweeping of my leg, sent him toppling down the stone entrance step. The next man, with a short and curved sword, was quick to cut up on my face and in a clash of steel, I held back against the pressing force of his sword. Stalling the man's strike, I watched with bated breath as he held the force with the strength of only one hand and with the other, pulled the mask from his face. His lip split as he smirked.

'You have not the strength to stop me, Mace Black,' he said, his blade flashing as he brought it up and with a throaty groan, smash it back down. I dropped my sword, rolled to one side and as the man stepped forward to hold his balance, I struck him with such force to the side of the head, that it smashed wide open.

Rain pounded over the forest, setting streams running and when I heard in the distance, the snapping of a twig, I threw a sleeved knife into the throat of a young masked man. I rushed towards him and before the man could draw his sword, I pinned to a tree. I planted my feet wide and in a squatted motion, wrenched the knife down from his face. Blood bellowed out from the mouthpiece of the man's mask. Only a murmured gargle met his tongue before he fell to his knees.

Old man Oliver whistled from behind an overcast oak tree and gestured with the point of his finger for me to look up. From the top of the overcast trees, the lurking shadows of two black-clad women descended. They slid down ropes and with a dancer's grace, leapt from the treetops.

I blocked a flying wood spear with the back of my gauntlet glove and angling my sword upwards, cut the woman's stomach wide open. She landed beside me with a thud.

Slamming a bone spear down with tremendous force, the second woman screamed out as if a demon had its claws around her throat. I held back the blow and with the hilt of my sword, sent the woman spinning to the flat of her back. As my arm shivered from the impact, I regained composure and slide the flat tip of my sword through the front of the woman's fox mask.

'Mace Black.' A voice belted out from the not so far distance as the woman choked on the blood that burst from her face in time with the last beat of her heart. 'Why have you forsaken us.'

I recognised the voice now. I turned and charging full tilt towards me, was my old comrade from the Mainland Division, Commander Clint. The enormous oaf of a man, lifting a heavy stone Warhammer over his head, stopped before me and braced himself, ready to bear down on me with all his weight.

'This is madness,' Eva said, drawing her sword as she stepped out from behind the trunk of a tree. 'You must not do this alone.'

'Just watch,' Rosen said, swiftly pulling her back in place.

An instant before Clint's Warhammer crushed every bone in my body, I kicked the legs out from under him and rolling swiftly to my left, I dodged the blow of the hammer. A deep groove was left in the damp earth. I swung around and with a sword slice, cleaved the front from Clint's face and left it, as if it were a wet rag, dangling from his chin.

Clint was now in the shadow of death, though he was not yet dead and in a wild rage, he whirled his mighty Warhammer from side to side. I watched on as the man stumbled and fell into the grave made from his savage Warhammer groove.

By only strength of will, the wood spear-wielding woman with a hole the size of a man's head in her stomach stood to her feet. She raised her spear. Launching at me, she screamed some incomparable nonsense from which I had never heard the likes of and as if having her guts splayed was not bad enough, I buried the silver swan-shaped pommel of my sword into the top of her skull.

'Please don't kill me,' she cried. 'I have a family. Show mercy.' She tripped backwards and scrambled away.

'Stand and face your punishment.'

I strolled calmly towards the woman, removed the mask from her face and looked deep into her shallow green eyes. 'You are a fool.'

'Mace, look out,' Eva shouted, tossing out a floral dagger from each hand.

Each dagger stuck firm into the trees either side of me and for a moment, I thought she had gone mad. That was until blood seeped out from the bark and two men with dagger holes in their heads came storming from the hollowed-out trees. Of course, they met a quick death at the end of my sword. Though I could not take my eyes off Eva. Her cunning anticipation had spared the embarrassment of being caught in a trap of my teaching.

A small dagger zipped past my face, skimming the side of my ear and by the time I turned to face another wood spear thrust from the wounded women, I had just about had enough of her. I gripped her face with one hand and with the other, stuffed the flat tip of my sword into her mouth and down her throat until she choked to death on a warm steel drink of her blood.

'How could I have been so stupid. I was almost fooled by my own trick.' I fell to my knees in a fit of laughter and for the briefest of moments, I held Eva's gaze as she squeaked out the sweetest little chuckle.

'That was impressive, Mace. Though I do recall seeing it somewhere before...your style that is. I recognise it,' Eva said, lost in a look of past thought. 'I remember now. When I was a little girl, my father took me to see a demonstration of Elite force skill. They were mostly bloody and violent shows of strength, except for one, a man who moved just like you. The smooth fluidity of his style was enchanting.'

Eva gently stroked a hand across my shoulder. Her face was red and overcome with an awkward shyness.

'Swan Choker,' I whispered. 'The man you remember, his name was Swan Choker. He was my sword master and a loyal friend to my brother. But, one day he disappeared, leaving no trace of himself, save only his famous swan sword, this sword.' The fine smith work was evident, as I held it up to the sky.

'What happened to him?' She asked, leaning in close.

'Well, rumour has it, that for reasons involving his cousin, Lord Hawk, he fled to the South point and joined the cursed King in rebellion. I was only young when I knew him, but he would never join such an organisation. He was the proudest of men. Either way, he would have had a good reason for leaving.'

'He taught you well, Mace.' Eva leant in closer still.

She looked deep into my dark eyes. I did not know what to make of this and for a moment, thought that she was going to kiss me. She did not and instead, seeing my hesitation, moved away. With the fear of what she always thought me to be, a clown, I could not bring myself to do anything more than a smile.

'Men. Burn this cabin to the ground, along with the deserter's bodies and write a report of what happened here today,' I commanded. 'Help yourselves to what remains.'

The rain stopped, and the clouds parted from the light of the white moon. Eva returned with me to the East gate. We remained silent, neither uttering a single word. An intense feeling of passion came over me and I was unsure if Eva was feeling the same strange infatuation. It was as if, after so many years of mockery and hateful scowls, we had at this very moment, met for the first time.

'I am sorry, Mace,' she said, darting off as we approached the stone arch of the East gate. 'Please do not follow me.'

That was the last thing I remembered, for a gloved hand brushed past my cheek, covered my mouth with a cloth of liquid fire and as it burned my throat to cinders, it sent my mind spiralling from consciousness.

5. ~ BRETHREN ~

Twenty-five days ago, ...

Lord Mantis had returned from his year-long travels in the vast land of Manrock, high in the north-west, where the Beast's dwell. He has been summoned personally by King Enzo to attend an important council meeting.

Whenever Mantis returns from anywhere, the grey scaled and over extravagant, Sir James Sand would be on due course to greet him home. James was not a trusted man in the Shadowland, no one had time for his secrets or spying. He could not swing a sword worth a damn, and save from being proficient with the organisation of the Divisions paperwork, he had no discernible attributes. It was hard to believe that he was Lord Mantis's right-hand man, or that he oversaw the three shadow Division squads.

James strolled West, along the outskirts of the Shadowland to great with Mantis ahead of the meeting. He went about his business, whistling a cheerful tune as if the worries of the world held no sway over him.

When he reached the flat brick streets of the Black Manor road, he realised the lateness of his hour and began pacing over the painted turtle pond at such a pace, that by the time he arrived at the entrance door of the Manor, he was soaked in sweat and out of breath.

The Black family crest, the standing snow bear, was engraved into the centre circle of the wooden back door. Two guard's men, wearing yellow robes above their blackened armour and holding very different, yet equally long swords, stood attentively either side of the entrance. In reality, Mantis had neither the use nor the time for guard protection. The men, armed as they might be, merely opened his door for him.

'Sir James. You are expected. Please make your way to the waiting room. The Lord will see you shortly,' the smaller guardsman bellowed out for all to hear.

'Good morning,' James said, politely tilting his head forward as he passed the guards.

In the corner of the waiting room, to James's surprise, was a greying old woman, playing an enchanting tune on a large wooden harp. Beside her, playing along with an equally pleasant, yet higher-pitched flute, was a young woman with an elegant appeal. Engrossed by the pleasant music, James had not yet noticed that Mantis was sat opposite the musicians, smirking from ear-to-ear. He was in the middle of a neck massage from a rather interesting young woman. Ever twitching ears adorning the top of her blood-red hair and a white-tipped tail, like that of a fox, poking out through the back of her slender fitted dress.

'You are late, Sir James,' Lord Mantis said, waving him in. 'Have a seat and enjoy the music. You have already missed your message.'

Mantis stood, followed by a moan from his creaking joints. His incredibly long and unnaturally straight hair swung behind his robe of blue, green and red, as he pulled them up over his back and shrugged them over his shoulders.

In his way, Mantis was quite the colourful character and most amusing of all, was not the way he appeared to float above the ground as if gravity held no sway, but the way he surrounded himself with such bright variety. James rarely saw this extravagant side of his Lord, nor did most for that matter. Mantis was rarely seen outside of the battlefield, where he would wear a suit of heavy golden armour and would enjoy nothing more than a good fight to the death. He was a ruthless man, yet in his private chambers, he favoured the bright colourful comforts of life.

'How are you, my Lord?' James asked, receiving a rather painful handshake. 'You look well...and tanned, have you been somewhere hot, overseas perhaps?'

'I am well, James. And no, I would not risk crossing those damn seas to find a bit of heat. I informed you well in advance of my departure, that I would be travelling to Manrock. And as for the tan, well that is quite the story. You see, whilst training some of the Chieftain's iron rhinos, I was attacked by a demon. It was a big one. Arms like tree trunks, teeth like arrowheads and the heat that rose from it would melt the greyscales off your face, James. I took a step too close and the ugly thing scorched my skin. Naturally, I ran it through with my longsword and chopped it in half.' Mantis burst into a fit of laughter and if only for a pitiful moment, James laughed along.

'Young Kita, you may be dismissed.' Mantis ordered, sliding his cold calloused hands over the young woman's knees, guiding them as he spread her legs apart.

He paused, a teasing smile creased his lips and before the young woman had time to react, he placed three silver pieces in the palm of her hand. She did as anyone in her position would do and simply bow in appreciation of her Lords generosity. Though when leaving the open room, she stumbled and fell into the hard frame of the door. Without a hint of sympathy or word of worry, Mantis laughed deep and heartedly at the woman's embarrassment.

As chivalrous as it might be to lend a hand, Sir James did absolutely nothing to aid the young woman. The disapproving look was as clear as day across his face, but he knew as well as any, that if he disappointed Mantis, he would have to pay the price, and it was a price that he could not afford to pay.

'Is she a Drongan, my Lord?' James asked.

'She is a rare beauty, isn't she? I found her beyond the Manrock mountains. She was scavenging for food and as any decent man would, I fed her. She is now mine and mine to keep.'

'My lord, I thought that all Drongan's were laid to waste in the Beast war?'

'As did James, until I came across young Kita.' Mantis clasped the one-handed grip of the oversized longsword that lay at his feet and as if it was no heavier than a stick of wood, he swung it over his shoulder. 'Come, let us attend this meeting with the King. Although, I cannot say I have missed the oafish prick or the rest of his council for that matter

6. ~ CONDUCT ~

Lord Mantis and Sir James arrived within the Stronghold walls. They were both lost in the glazed sheen of golden sun, that over the Eastern side of the Kings Blood Tower, brightened the dullness of their dark eyes. A heavy covering of low-lying clouds soon dissipated the light of the sun and the Blood Tower, renowned for being the place of the King's justice, was again as bleak and as cruel as the King's very nature.

'Open the door, it looks as if it is about to rain out here and we do not want sir James to rust,' Lord Mantis shouted, followed by a deep chuckle and a steel thudding slap, that sent Sir James stumbling forward.

With a disdainful look in his eye, James smiled and remembered how peaceful the Shadowland had been during his Lords leave of absence.

There was no answer at the door. Mantis became impatient and inhaled a mighty breath, readying himself to call once again for the door to be opened. He did not show it, but Mantis was nervous about this council meeting. He had a tale to tell, but he knew as well as any, that with all the wisdom in the world, King Enzo would not hear him out. Unlike most councils, King Enzo's was more of a meeting place to receive orders, than it was a place in which the King receives council on all matters concerning the Kingdom.

The massive steel doors of the Blood Tower creaked open and from within the darkness, a very familiar voice said. 'I thought that was you, old fool. Where have you been for so long?'

'Dame Lambert Crow. It has been some time. Have you missed me?' Mantis asked, dropping his sword with a crash.

Lambert eyes, bright and red like a demon, emerged from the darkness, as she leapt out and landed perfectly positioned atop Mantis's strong shoulders.

'Have I missed you?' She stroked the line of white stubble that lay across his slanted jawline. 'I haven't missed you one bit...old fool.'

Mantis played with her as if he were playing with a child. He threw her into the air and on catching her, spun her around in circles and tickled the pits of her arms. They were both left in a hysterical state. Neither would ever admit it, but they had missed each other very much.

They had forgotten the time and continued to play and mock each other until Lord Giovanni Hades appeared in the doorway. He shook his head in disapproval. The eight-foot man is his simple button shirt, had a longer beard than the Kings and demanded almost as much respect. He was remorseless, like stone, having no time for jokes or child's play.

'Lord Mantis, Dame Lambert…if you please,' Lord Giovanni mumbled, pointing them in the direction of the tower doors.

Mantis's jaw dropped. He picked his sword up from the cracked surface of the ground where it lay and walked, with a deadly silence under the arched tower doorway.

At the top of the tower, beside the Kings own chambers, was a large hallway, filled either side with Lord Giovanni's infamous grey guard unit. At least, twenty grey caped and heavily armed guards, with helms made in the likeness of goat's skulls, stood to attention as Lord Mantis and the others passed them by.

'Greetings all.' A recognisable northern voice sounded from behind them.

All but Giovanni turned to see Lord Hawk, the black-eyed and grey-haired leader of the elite force, standing there, with a bronze helm under his arm and a bronze Warhammer in his hand.

To his right, Lady Lavender, the elegant and high-class leader of the medical research Division, looked as if she had just come from a funeral. She wore only black. Her hair was long and as dark as night, and her eyes, like cracked ice, were sheened in a mesmerising shallow blue.

Lady Keira poked her orange feathered head of hair around the side of the stairwell. 'Are you all just going to stand about jamming up the halls.'

She was the light-hearted leader of the Naval Division, Queen of the harpies and the apple of the King's eye. With a dark, yet freckled, complexion and the most beautiful set of orange wings that trailed in her shadow, it was clear to see why the King adored her so. She was a stunning beauty.

'Let us have some order here,' Lord Giovanni commanded, silencing the hallway. 'Lord Mantis, please lead the way into the council hall. The rest of you, follow along.'

There is not a Lord or Lady who would dare question him. If they did and he was dissatisfied, there would be serious consequences for their actions.

Almost instantly, every Lord and Lady dismissed their idle chatter and proceeded to the council hall. It was huge, sparsely furnished and poorly lit, with portraits of the old Lords and Ladies scattered around the dark red walls. A grand table with eight chairs and a King's throne stands at the centre of the hall, surrounded by many old suits of armour, and of the many suits on display, there was a tiny set, that belonged to the first-born son of the King. It was particularly eye-catching, engraved with a description, which reads; In memory of the infant prince, Nico of Mangrove. May your soul rest in peace.

The great white lion, Lord Noriega, the sixth seat of the council and the Beast Chieftain, sat proudly waiting for the meeting to begin. His vulture, known as Rain, scraped its black beak across the lions back.

The tall, brown and beautiful, Lady Senna Stone, the fifth seat of the council and leader of the Services Division, sat opposite the Chieftain, brushing a length of knots out of her long blonde hair.

'Everyone is here, what a nice surprise,' Lady Senna said, taking a stand. 'Mantis…it is good to see you again. You are looking well.'

'Shut your stupid mouth. You are disgusting. Did you not have time to brush your hair before this meeting.' Lady Lavender taunted, giving Mantis no chance to reply.

Unfortunately for Senna, Lavender's place was to the left of hers, in the third seat, and although she was professional and would not lose her composure, she would and always has, held a grudge against her fellow Lady.

Everyone was now seated in their usual places around the grand table, save only for the King, who was traditionally the last to arrive.

Silence shot through the hall. The double entrance doors burst open. All eyes watched as great King Enzo of Mangrove made his entrance. He was the last-born son of Roland the relentless, the so-called, King of all Kings. Born into wealth and power, with unmatched arrogance, King Enzo has made quite a name for himself. His actions have not only led to peace between man and Beast but are the single cause of the cursed rebellion at South point. One could say, that for every step forward, he takes two back.

He wears only the finest of furs, although he never looks comfortable with them on, and they are many times more comfortable than his crown. Filled with gems and rubies the size of which only a King could afford, his crown was a marvel to behold atop his head of curly brown hair.

As always, the Lords and Ladies of the council stood to attention on the Kings entrance and as always, the King raised his hand for them all to be seated. But something was not right. The King did not walk in and come straight to his throne seat at the head of the table. Instead, he stood by the side entrance.

'Your Highness, is there anything the matter?' Lord Giovanni asked, from his old wooden first seat.

Without a word, King Enzo shook his head. He was grinning excitably and could not take his eyes away from the side entrance.

'What took you so long, boy.' The King said, an eager smile bursting across his ageing face.

His second-born son ran into the hall. He was finally being introduced to the council. The young boy, at five years of age, has never left the confines of this tower, nor ever laid eyes upon the Lords and Ladies of the surrounding lands. His most frequent company was his guard unit, the barracudas, and his lonely view of Mangrove from the top of the tower.

The King took the boy up in arms, held him in a tight embrace and said with delight, 'I would like to introduce you all to my son and heir to Mangrove, Prince Luca. He will, from now on, be attending meetings with us. As you are all aware, he will one day be King, maybe the greatest of all Kings and it is for that reason, that you must show him the same respects that you show me. It is very important that he learns from you all and makes the most of these meetings.' The King paused and laid a hand on Luca's head. 'Also, I promised the boy, that when he was five years of age, he could make some new friends, so you will be his friends.'

A rare grin stretched out the King's checks. In that same instant, an oddly shaped old man, dressed all in blue, carried in a child-sized throne seat and placed it to the right of the King's throne.

'Do you think this is wise,' Lord Hawk asked in a harsh tone of voice. 'What can a child possibly learn from these meetings, with these savages?' He meant to offend the King.

'You fool. One day you will bow to this boy and call him King. Get used to his presence,' Senna snapped.

'Lady Senna is right. Do not forget your place or disappoint my son, Hawk. I will take what you have said as a joke...maybe you can be the first to introduce yourself to your Prince.'

The King was in an unusually friendly mood.

'My King, I would like the first honour of introducing myself to the prince,' Lord Giovanni said, standing with a pompous salute. Almost everyone's eyes rolled at his sycophantic display, yet not an abstaining word was uttered.

'Would you like that, Luca?' The King asked.

The boy simply nodded. He was too afraid to say a word in these halls, with some of the most intimidating and powerful men and women in Mangrove.

'This is for you, Luca. It was meant for your late brother. He would be proud for you to have it,' the King said, placing a curved sabre in his son's hands. 'Save for the illustrious ruby pommel, it is a small version of my own.'

The boy took his seat and in exact imitation of his father, he placed the sabre atop the table.

'Well, my Prince, I am Lord Giovanni Hades. I remember when I was introducing myself to your father and your grandfather before him, and so on for many generations. I have been in this world for longer than I care to remember and for all my years of protecting your family, from great King Hammond to brave King Graham, I have never seen eyes like yours. Such peace...' Lord Giovanni smiled at the young prince.

'Well, let us not all ramble on like Giovanni. Come, Hawk, introduce yourself,' King Enzo demanded.

'Listen up boy. My name is Lord Hawk Barrington, I command the Elite force, the most powerful force of warriors you will ever lay eyes upon. All my Elites are cursed men and most all my Elites go on to greatness, even legend. I too have a son, his name is Snake and I have a daughter, named Eagle. She is a year or so older than yourself. Perhaps, young Prince, with your father's permission, I will bring her to play.'

'Please father, please can I play with the other children,' The young prince said in a squeaky voice.

'Yes, but Lord Hawk must supervise you,' The King replied.

Hawk gave the young prince an acknowledging tilt of his head. This was an unusual offer for Lord Hawk to make. Though perhaps, in his wisdom, he knew that if he must befriend the future King, then by showing him the kindness of a cursed man, he may show the same kindness to the next generation and free them from servitude.

'This is taking far too long. Look here, Luca. The pretty lady with the dark hair is Lady Lavender Rose. She delivered you from your mother. Next to her, is Lady Senna Stone and next to her, at the end there, on the seventh seat.' The King pointed. 'Is Dame Lambert Crow. She is temporarily taking the place of Lord Brick Bisson. Rest his soul.' The King tilted his head sympathetically towards Dame Lambert, who in return, stood and took a bow.

'Father. What has happened to Lord Brick?' The young prince asked.

'We will get to that, Luca. Now, do not interrupt. To your right, in the fourth seat, with the long silver hair, is Lord Mantis Black. He has recently returned from his travels in Manrock, where the Beasts live. Stood behind him, is Sir...um Sir.'

'Sir James, your highness. Sir James Sand.' Feeling insulted by the King's forgetfulness, James could not bring himself to look his Highness in the eye, nor could he contain the beads of sweat that dripped from his scaled brow.

'Ah yes, Sir James. He is giving a hand over to Lord Mantis of the most recent events. The large white Lion in the sixth seat, with the Vulture on his back, is the Beast Chieftain, Lord Noriega. I am not sure of the vulture's name.'

'Rain,' The vulture squawked. 'Rain.'

'Lastly, the young orange-haired woman to the far right, in the eighth seat, is Lady Kiera. Her wings are magnificent, are they not? She is the Queen of the Harpies and was a very good friend of your mother's. Now, son, you must introduce yourself to my council.'

'Yes, father. My name is Luca of Mangrove and…um, it is nice to meet you all,' he said in a whisper, staring down at his dangling feet.

'That will do, my boy.' The King said, looking around at his council. 'Now, let us get to business.'

By the eager look in Lady Lavenders eyes, she had something to say, and it would take well over an hour for her to say the same thing she says every time this council meat. 'The Medical Research Division is lacking income.'

The King dismissed any notion of increased funds and scorned her for bringing it up.

Sir James then gave a handover to Lord Mantis of the last month's events, detailing the desertion of a dozen assassins. This put Mantis in quite a rage and although he too had something to say, he would first order James to deal with this situation.

Mantis then took his stand and said without expression, 'Whilst in Manrock, overseeing the training of some young Beasts, I came across something extraordinary. I am sure that you will all find this to be more than noteworthy. I have discovered, what I believe to be, a new form of curse.'

'Make it quick Mantis,' the King interrupted, bashing his fist on the tabletop. 'I will not have mine or my councils time wasted with cursed nonsense.'

'As I was saying,' Mantis raised his voice and despite the Kings lack of interest for anything involving the cursed minority, he continued his tale of discovery. 'It is common knowledge that curses are parasitic organisms that live in or around the host and benefit from the nutrients provided. There are three known forms of curse. The two most common, are those attached to either the body or the brain, giving the host advanced physical or mental capabilities to keep itself alive. The third and rarest form is the manifestation, where the curse takes presence as a physical being and provides external protection for its host.'

'This is nothing new, Mantis,' Hawk said, stroking his white beard.

'Yes, you are right. There have, until this discovery, never been any other recorder forms of the curse. I have never seen anything like it in all my life. I call it Ethereal. It was as if a cloud of smoke had taken the form of a hundred men. With my longsword raised, I went to cut them down, though when I did, no mark nor movement was made to my advances. The ghostly figures, as fast as they had appeared to me, were gone and by the morning breeze, blown from sight.'

'Preposterous,' Barked the King.

He walked to the far side of the council hall. No one, save for Dame Lambert, uttered a single sound and when she said, 'That is no curse you saw, Mantis.' The King looked back and for a moment was overcome with worry.

'That is quite enough. Let us finish this godforsaken meeting,' the King roared, standing nervously behind his seat.

He took the crown from his head, held it by his side and let it roll through his fingers. It hit the floor with a crash and caused nothing but silence to ring out through the old council hall.

'Dame Lambert, I am aware that at this moment in time, you are troubled, but I must insist that you give an account of the actions leading to Lord Brick's death.'

'Yes, my King. As you please,' she replied, taking a hesitant stand beside the seventh seat. 'After heading off an assault on the Citadel, Lord Brick and I, along with twenty Mainland soldiers, cornered the East bay pirate known as, Trench War. When we charged him with the orchestration of the attack, he fled. We gave chase and we had him cornered. We thought we did anyway. Dozens upon dozens of pirates dropped from the rooftops. It was an ambush, a setup from the very beginning. Lord Brick and twenty brave Mainland soldiers were massacred that day, all in the name of petty amusements for some thieving pirates. I was spared only to tell this bloody tail.'

Lambert wiped the tears from beneath her eyes and with the utmost haste, stormed past the grey guards and out of the hall.

'Poor girl,' said the King, quickly changing the subject. 'As you are all aware, a Division must have a Lord and before this meeting is adjourned, a candidate worthy of consideration for Mainland Division Lordship must be recommended.'

7. ~ SOLITUDE ~

Present-day...

Turning over on what I thought was my bed, I curled up to a soft feathered pillow and realised that it was no more than a hard stone and when feeling the bed beneath me, I found only damp earth to rest above. I sat up and as I did, struggled with a sudden stabbing pain in my back. I wiped the mud from my face, reached to my side and realised that I was not only missing my sword but also my suit of armour. In its place, was nothing more than an old shirt and ragged pants.

Consciousness came back to my eyes and I saw the lingering fog of the woods, the darkness that danced in the shadow of the moonlight and the living river of small creatures that crawled underfoot. I remembered then, Lady Senna sending Dame Eva with me, the bird with the note and Eva's Hasty exit. The hand that came from the shadows, the taste of liquid fire and Dame Eva, running off as it all happened. It was evident that this was all a set up to begin my King's trial.

Stopping and resting my aching back every so often, I followed some barely visible tracks through the thickness of the woods fog. I stood still for a moment and with a mighty sigh of relief, stretched out my back and relieved the pressure that cracked from my shoulder blade.

A badly decapitated deer lay suspiciously across the track marks ahead. The smell of its fresh death lingered in the air. Although it had a limp hanging ear and what remained of a bottom jaw, it would make a fine meal for a hungry man.

The deer would not cook itself, so I gathered as many dry leaves and twigs as I could for a fires nest. I smashed small stones together and after nursing an ember under the nest with a wisp of breath, flames burst into life, licking the twigs and growing to an immense blaze before my very eyes. Plunging a stick through the backside of the deer and another through its chest, I balanced the carcass precariously above the flames.

I knelt in the dirt and looked towards the end of the path. Smoke billowed out from the fire, setting my eyes streaming. I wished for the comforting warmth of my bed chambers, my loyal assassins in the next barracks and if I would ever need it, my sword by my side.

'Come on, Mace. You are not weak,' I said to myself, slapping my mud-covered hands across my cold cheeks. I clasped a firm grip on the deer's leg and ripping bone from the flesh, I indulged on its juicy, yet slightly charred meat. What I could not eat, I left behind and continued along the marked-out path through the woods.

It was damp, dark and overgrown with green nettled hedges, that edged out like saws to cut the skin.

'Who is there,' I said, startled at the sound of what I presumed to be a woman calling from within the hedges, and after a moment, I realised that it was merely the whispers of the wind playing a trick on my mind.

I was truly in a place befitting a tale of horror. The hedges jerked and rustled as if something stirred within them. The snapping sound of a dry twig sent my heart pounding and my head lapping with wild paranoia. A single cloud loomed overhead, blotting out the light of the white moon.

A shiver crept up my spine as darkness surrounded me. I became uneasy and began to question my sanity, for I had never been fearful of the dark and had always embraced the paranoia within me. It has kept my guard up and saved my life on many occasions.

I paused for a moment, collected my thoughts and a hand full of sticks that were sharp enough to use as weapons and made haste through the increasingly eerie woods. I remained fearful of the tricks and torment conjured by my mind and was now walking with more pace than I had the strength to carry forward.

'kill the girl,' the wind whispered as it howled unnervingly past my ear and try as I might to stay on course, I turned around to find that I was still alone in the dark. Nothing, save for the rustling of leaves and clawing of branches made a sound.

'kill the girl and claim your Lordship,' the wind whispered once more.

'You are just my mind playing tricks,' I shouted out. 'I will ignore you and you will not further disturb my thoughts.'

I was breathing deep and slow to steady the sharp edge of my nerves, to no avail, for a few metres ahead of me was the outline of a man. He was moving towards me. I gaped on in horror. A cold sweat consumed me.

'What is going on here?' I whispered ever so quietly. 'I am the Commander of the shadow Divisions assassination squad. I am not afraid of anything or anyone.'

The volume of my voice increased with every word, if not only to remind myself of who I was but also of what I was.

I composed myself once again, took a deep inhale of breath and realised that the figure of a man before me, was no more than a pile of sticks and stones.

The wind picked up and as it stung my face, it shot through the trees either side of the path and pushed the fog clear. I began to feel safe. My alertness and rational senses returned and with them, the sight of my surroundings. I was not far from the riverside, a mile at best guess. The path had led me through the Deccan woods and no less than a few footsteps ahead were the outskirt of the woods.

A sudden groaning stopped me in my tracks. It came from the path and called me back. It was as if the woods were frightened of being left alone in the dark and without my companionship, they would be just that.

'You do not need me,' I said, feeling somewhat crazy for calling to the woods and as I had expected, the woods would not answer my call. I slapped my cheeks to redness and stepped off the haunted path that has led me thus far.

8. ~ DEPRAVITY ~

I was almost through the Deccan woods when I heard a voice that was quiet and helpless, like that of a little girl, and as I was not the kind of man to ignore such a sound, I ventured off track in further investigation. That was just the way I was, Honourable to a worthy cause.

I followed in the direction of the voice and scrapping trackable marks in the earth, I strolled up the worn wooden steps near the Seadogs riverside and down a long and windy cobbled street, that by the overgrown tangle of weeds poking through the cobbles, had long since been walked upon.

'Is anybody there?' I yelled out and received no reply.

At the end of the street, there was a slug speckled path and at the end of that path, a housing estate stood alone. Lanterns lit up the many half bricked houses, that appeared to be either under construction or half destroyed. Despite it being less eerie than the whispering woods, I remained plagued with unrealistic outcomes of events that may or may not yet come to pass.

'Help me. Please, someone, help me,' screamed the girl once again.

She was not far, nor by the soft tone of her voice was she very old. Though she was, without a shadow of a doubt, very much in need of assistance. My mind ran wild and I put to question many times, whether this had any significance concerning my trials or a circumstance of such unfortunate measure, that fate brought me along this very path to save this girl. Time would soon tell and regardless of what has caused the girl to call for help, I would do everything in my power to see her safe.

Filling with rage at the horrific thoughts of an innocent little girl running from wild rats or worse, demons from the outskirts of Mangrove, I stopped for a moment and composed myself. There was no sense in running into a situation without reasonable thought on my side. So, forcing clarity to the forefront of my mind, I ran with the utmost haste in the direction of the girl's voice.

'Do not worry,' I bellowed out. 'I am on my way'

Fate took its course and all at once, the streets lanterns blew out in a gust of frosted wind. It shed the buttons from the front of my tattered shirt.

It was dark, so dark in fact, that in the light of the white moon, no shadow spread further than the dented front door of the very end house on the estate. Three horseless carriages, side by side, sat out front. I was drawn particularly to one carriage and if it was not much larger and in much better condition than the others, with shimmering gold wheel trims and the blackest of glass windows, I would not have recognised it. The carriage belonged to the infamous, dirty Bill, who was not only a murdering halfwit but the leader of a small gang of thieves. Most recently, he had escaped from the Mangrove penitentiary, which was quite an achievement for an old pervert. Escaping from any prison, let alone Mangroves maximum security facility was no easy feat. It was in all the papers, along with a warning not to approach this man, next to a picture of his ugly mug.

I watched on in horror as a skinny young man, no older than my brother, was tossed from the brown wooden door of the house and left out for whatever hungry creature takes his fancy. Most of his skin was missing, along with his manhood and an unmeasurable amount of blood from the wide-open slit in his throat.

He was long dead by the time his face scraped across the hard surface of the cobbled street, but I could not help but feel sick at the foul condition this man was left in. As for what they might have in store for a helpless little girl, I was not waiting around to find out.

From my vantage point, I ducked behind an overgrown green thorn hedge and looked around for something, anything, that I could use as a distraction. I could not very well barge in with nothing more than pride and a hand full of pointy sticks at my disposal. With haste in my step, I ran to the next house and where I would hope for an attention-drawing plan to form in my mind, there was nothing.

'This should do nicely,' I whispered to myself, as I pulled a stone that was almost too large and too heavy to lift out from under the damp earth.

Sneaking with a cautious step, I went back to the end house and peering through the front window, I saw four grubby old men, drinking to an unreasonable extent. In their merriment, they appeared to be fighting over what to do with the helpless little girl. She was curled in a ball, atop an old-style chest in the far corner, wearing a bright pink princesses dress, and making no such sound as to startle a reaction from the gang.

A tear formed in the corner of my right eye and making a note of the house's layout, I saw that what was most likely a quaint setting for a small family, was now deader than it was alive. Though it was not Bill, nor his gang that had made such a mess of this house, it was the pressure of time and lack of treatment that had left the place suitable for an old gang's shameful acts of cruelty. It was as if the house had no memory of the outside world. Bubbling mould blackened the walls, whilst the air, abandoned of all freshness or flowered scent, lingered with a musk of frightening thickness. The filthy and misused waste that lay across the damp splints of underwood only added to the lack of respect.

Gripping firm to the large stone that I strained with a lack of strength to lift, I smashed it through the side window of Bill's carriage. I felt no better after the release of pent-up rage, so I stomped on the hundreds of glass shards until, beneath my feet, lay thousands of bright reflected pieces of a puzzle that will never be put back together.

'You will pay for your crimes, Bill,' I yelled out, running full tilt towards the dented front door, and with pride in my heart and a spiked stick in my hand, I bashed on the door with such a tremendous thud of force, that it would be heard from the Mangrove Citadel.

Silence shot through the house. Only the slow stepping of feet, that on approaching the door, halted momentarily.

A whirling of frosted wind swept past me and sent a chill up my spine. I took the deepest of breaths and holding behind my back the sharpest of spiked sticks, I held my nerve and halted as the door creaked opened.

'What the hell do you want? Boy,' an old man with half a mouth full of teeth said in an unexpectedly squeaky tone of voice.

His face was gaunt, and the shadow of his wrinkled chin was deep and dark under his mess of long greasy hair. I looked the man over and gaining a sense of his character, stared deep into his bloodshot blue eyes. I remained silent and unstirred.

'Boy, what the hell do you want? If you don't leave this house right now, you're in for a world of hurt.' The old man stumbled forward slightly.

Despite his warning and the throbbing veins in my head, that felt as if a strong heartbeat would pop them open, I remained silent and unstirred. I focused on the old man's cold beady eyes. Without the slightest hesitation, the man grabbed the scruff of my shirt. It was at that moment, with wild cries of exertion and the intentions of a quick death, that I struck hard and I struck fast. The old man's death was not to be painless and by the rolling back of his eyes, he had not the time to watch his life flash past. The very instant that spike pierced the flesh of his neck, he fell to his knees and gurgled his blood. He was not long for this world.

That stick lay clean through the side of his neck. I could not take my eyes off it and although I should not have enjoyed killing him, I relished in it. The release of anger was so exciting, that it was almost intoxicating.

I pulled out the now bloodied spike and kicking the old man to the flat of his back, I ran in through the doorway. My bravery held no bounds, I was full of strength and led only by my determination to rescue the little girl, I would face dirty Bill and end his wretched existence once and for all.

'Who the hell is this kid? And what the hell has he done with Bobby?' Bill said, coughing a lump of black mucus that dripped from his mouth.

'I am Commander Mace Black of the shadow Division, and if you favour your life, you will let the girl go.' Bill laughed, along with the other two similarly scruffy men beside him. He even spat on my bare feet in the process.

'You boy, are a funny one, but that does not change the fact that you are as good as dead,' Bill said, boasting a smirk to his subordinates. 'I like you…I do, so we won't just take your life…No, that would be cruel and I'm not a cruel man. We can have a little fun together, can't we, Commander.'

Maybe it was the congealing blood that had dried my hand to the stick, or the dank lingering smell of old smoke around the room, that caused me to stumble forward. Regardless of the cause, the outcome remained the same, and it was not one moment past, that I was envisioning Bill squealing like a pig to the slaughter and the next, I was vomiting chunks of deer meat over him.

Hiding her face beneath her hands, the little girl looked through her fingers at me and whispering something incomparable, stood from the chest. I did not, for the life of me, know what she was trying to say and having no intention of asking her, I did the only thing I could think of doing. I launched myself headlong across the room at Bill. Though before a single step was taken, a fat and greasy oaf of a man, with more chins than I had time to count, struck me across the back with an iron bar. The smell of him was awful and far worse than any pain he could cause me.

I wretched, again and again, spilling more bile and vomit. If I did not know any better, I could have sworn that badly decapitated dear was poisoned. My consciousness began to slip away. The room blurred, but I would not be stopped. Nothing, save from pain of death, would stand in my way.

I leant up on my elbow, turned full circle and threw myself forward with all my might. I rammed the sharp end of my bloody stick so hard into Bills leg, that he squealed out like the proverbial pig he was. Blood sprayed out over the room and as Bill danced the dance of fools, a smile that was only brought on by a good deed, creased the little girl's lips.

I was so pleased with myself, that I had not given a second thought to Bill's subordinates surrounding me. By the time I realised the error of my ways, the heaviest of steel boots had smashed across my jaw and sent me slamming backwards so fast, that I could not, for all the King's gold, get myself back up off the floor.

9. ~ PRIDE ~

I found myself lost in ties of rope and weary from a pounding head wound. It was not until the fold of cloth that blinded my sight was ripped away from my eyes, that I came to terms with my situation. I was in trouble. A cold bucket of ice water washed over my face and pulled each one of my nerves to the surface.

'Damn it,' I spat, shaking the dripping shards of ice from my face.

Edging closer and closer, Bill grabbed at my throat and with a grin of teeth that were too large for his mouth, said, 'This is what's going to happen. Firstly, I'm going to send an important message to an important person. The King if you must know. You see, we found something valuable, almost priceless, that King Enzo of Mangrove himself, would not turn away.' He paused and winked at the fat subordinate to his side. 'Did you see the naked man outside? The one sleeping in a puddle of his blood.' I nodded.

'Well, Commander Mace,' he continued. 'That man tried to take my valuables from me and when people take my valuables, I take there's from them.'

Bill grimaced. He spat out another throatful of black phlegm and dangled before me, what I could only presume, was the dead man's proverbial ball and chain.

'You are a sick man,' I said. 'I do not want your bloody valuables. I only want the girl. Now please, let her go.'

I struggled to break free from the ropes that restrained me, and as I watched the gang in a fit of hysterical laughter, I doubted very much, that I would make it out of this alive.

'Have you got a bloody screw loose, boy? What bloody girl are you talking about?' Again, he paused and this time, looked at each one of his subordinates.

He slapped me across the cheek and with a fit of bloodshot anger in his narrow eye's, he stood over me and stroked his rough hand through my silver hair. Perhaps he was playing a poor attempt at mind games, but as clear as day, I saw a helpless little girl in the corner of the room and I knew that Bill could see her too.

He pulled a foul-smelling black rag from his back pocket and to my sickening dismay; as if the taste on my tongue was not bad enough, he stuffed it so far into my mouth that it touched my tonsils.

'You see this, boy. This was my fathers.' Bill said, spinning a small, yet surprisingly clean skinning blade around his fingers.

A cheer erupted through the room, along with the smashing of empty beer bottles. I used this distraction as an opportunity and shuffled along the foul-smelling floor as fast as I could.

'What is with this kid,' the oaf of a man said, with his boot firmly pressed against the side of my injured jaw.

Chopping off his manhood and leaving it for the crows, tightening his head in a vice until it burst open, or the cleaner option of simply drowning the fool, were just a few of the imaginative thoughts that swam the dark pool of my mind, as I lay helpless before the hands of Bill and his brutish subordinates.

Suddenly, the deepest of roars boomed in every direction. The very earth beneath our feet quaked violently. It rattled the unsteady oaf onto his hands and knees.

'What in the hollow pit of hell was that,' Bill yelled out, seeing nothing out of the ordinary as he peered out through the window.

Reminding myself that opportunities come little and often, I swung my legs around and planted my right knee so swiftly into the distracted oaf's chubby cheek, that he spat bloody teeth into his hand. He screamed out like a baby without his bottle.

'I'm going to strangle him.' The oaf was now red-faced and raging.

The grip he had around my throat was so strong and so tight, that I could feel my windpipe caving in. He could have quite easily choked me into an early grave, but he did not and instead, hoisting me up from the floor, he threw me against the back wall. I landed atop many shards of glass. I was mindful to not show any sign of weakness, though it was with difficulty, for a chunk of glass the size of my hand was stuck in the side of my leg. I muffled a shriek of agony under my breath.

The ground quaked once again, harder and more violently than it had done previously and shaking Bill to his knees, it was soon joined by a startling display of thunder. The sky was bluer and more alive than I had ever before seen. Birds squawked as they flocked away in the far distance, glass from all the windows and small flaming lanterns, all at once, cracked apart. If only for the briefest of moments, I was glad of what I presumed to be, the god's company.

Bill dropped his skinning blade and looked out at what had troubled the peaceful darkness of the night sky. Never had I seen a man so fraught with fear. He stared out into the darkness with un-blinked eye's and saw a Harpy lady, dressed in dark shimmering purple, with huge black and yellow wings, stood atop the opposing rooftop.

I would like to think that what I saw came from a place beyond ours, where only those pure of heart would soar high above us all, casting their judgement down on the wicked and unjust alike. But I knew all too well, that gods and tales of heroism were only for the weak of heart.

Her hooded robes waved like flags in the wind. Two large swords dangled from either side of her waist and her dark purple armour, shimmering in the dim light of the moon, distorted her form. Her hand reached down for the hilt of her longest sword and as her wings spread wide for impending flight, my heart raced with anticipation.

'Jimmie, pass my crossbow and be quick about it,' Bill screamed.

'Yes, Bill. Right away.' Jimmie ran into the hallway, only to return a moment later with a leather quiver, filled with arrows and an old silver crossbow. He notched an arrow and threw the bow to Bill.

The wind swirled through the house, distorting Bills view of the mysterious Harpy lady and within the blink of an aiming eye, she was gone. Frantically, Bill looked for any sign of the Harpy, but saw only empty darkness and backing slowly away from the window, he made the all-too-quick decision to use me as a hostage. He aimed his crossbow mere inches from my face. I struggled furiously to free myself from those damn restraint.

'Get the hell out of here or I'll kill the brat,' Bill shouted, digging his crossbow into the side of my head. 'And don't think I won't.'

The dark hooded Harpy, in the blink of an eye and with perfect sword placement, jumped through the window and almost split Bill completely in half. It was with incredible force that Bill was sent tumbling backwards. Salty blood sprayed out and over my face.

Piercing a gaze at Bill's thieving friends, all the Harpy lady had to do was stab her bloodied sword into a floorboard and like rabbits to a wolf, they ran in fear for their lives.

They darted hastily towards the front door and when the hooded women pulled three small blades from inside of her cloak, I was not amused, nor when she pinned the heads of the three remaining men to the wall with them, was I pleased. Only for the selfish reason that I wanted their lives for myself. Though there was no doubting her skill. With just one thrust of her arm, the Harpy lady had killed them all and yet still the question remained of who she was and where she had come from.

10. ~ EXTRICATION ~

The Harpy lady, dressed all in dark purple, walked slowly towards the little girl and looking deep into her sad eyes, leant over her. It was clear that the girl was scared and despite the Harpy saying no words of harm or threat, being covered from head to toe in thick armour and wielded enormous swords, gave her a frighteningly haunting presence.

She smoothed the little girl's hair from her face and revealing a bird-shaped birthmark on her neck, the Harpy left her in peace. Turning her attention now to me, she stroked her armoured hand across my face. A small knife, like those buried in the skulls of Bills subordinates, was pulled from her boot. I was unsure whether she meant to free me from restraint or cut me open, and when she sliced the rope that bound my hands, there was no denying the relief of freedom. The first thing to do was remove that disgusting rag from my mouth.

'Thank you,' I said, mustering the strength to keep my face brave.

The Harpy stood and removing the hood from her face, revealed, to my surprise, that she was no more than a teenage girl. She brushed her fingers through her long black hair and with a heart-warming smile, soothed the little girl's fears. It was fair to say that I liked her immediately.

'You must be Commander Mace Black,' she implied, extending out her arm, for what I presumed was a handshake.

With a raised brow, she swung her arm around and slapped me across the side of my swollen cheek. 'What was that for.'

'My name is Captain Kara. I am from the Naval Division and am currently on an important trial, which if succeeded, will grant me the seventh seat on the King's council. You have probably heard of my Aunt, Lady Kiera, Queen of the Harpies,' she said. 'And, I slapped you because you should not be meddling around here, it is dangerous. Now please, go home and get out of my way.'

'Are you not a bit young to be a Naval Division Captain, and I will have you know, that I am also on the King's trail. I believe our mission is to rescue this little girl.'

'Speak for yourself, apart from the old man hair, you look about fifteen years old. Anyway, I have found clues to indicate, that this little girl is not what she seems…she must be killed.'

'I cannot let you do that,' I said. 'I do not care what you or your clues indicate, I will not stand by whilst an innocent little girl is murdered.'

I was unsure whether It was brave or just plain stupid to take sides against such a strong and heavily armed opponent. But with pride of place and haste of heart, I rolled over to the little girl and placing her swiftly on my shoulder, I ran for it. Captain Kara did not follow, nor did she move or lift a finger to disrupt our path of departure. She merely stood cross-armed with a confident smirk on her face and watched my every move.

I ran from the front door and stopped where I thought the girl would be safe from sight. At the end of the darkened road, we hid behind a half-constructed brick wall.

'Are you alright?' I asked, breathless, sore and struggle for words.

'Yes,' she replied simply.

'Why is everyone after you?' She looked through me with a puzzled eye, as if she did not have the slightest clue as to the gravity of her situation.

'It's hard to explain,' she eventually said.

'Do not worry, I will protect you none the less.' I made light of my words with the poking out of my tongue and when the little girl looked up with a smile, I felt a sense of pride.

'Talia, Talia Leaf is my name.' The girl pointed at her face. 'You're so kind and brave, will you be Talia's friend? No one is nice to Talia, no one except for you.'

'Yes, I will be your friend, but first, we must make haste. Captain Kara is still out there. Now, Talia, where is your home, your family?'

Without warning, after appearing overly joyed, Talia looked as if she was about to cry and pulling a piece of folded parchment from the top pocket of her princess' dress, she said with a sob, 'Talia has a picture. She must find her father. He's looking for Talia.'

I grabbed her hand to calm her nerves and as I looked upon the parchments worn image; my heart skipped a beat. It was a small portrait of my father, Hollis Black. Though he was not as I remembered him to be. He looked old and off colour. His hair was grey, and his face was gaunt. But he was no demon.

'How is this possible?' I said, remembering a time long past. 'We will consider this as soon as it is safe to do so, but first, we must get you out of here.'

I took one last look at the parchment and handing it back to Talia, I dismissed it and the memories that ached my heart. I checked frantically at what might be lurking in the shadows and a calm voice said, 'We have been here too long. We must move.'

Talia wiped the tears from her face and whilst nodding in agreement, she peered over the wall. I pulled her back and checked for myself. I saw no threat of danger and gripping Talia's hand; we began to make haste. Though as we did, Talia startled me with a scream.

'Talia is sorry for crying,' she said. 'Her family was killed saving her. Please, Mace, please don't be angry.' Tears began streaming from her green eyes.

'Talia, we must move right now,' I said in a harsh tone of voice.

I had not the time for her tale of sorrow. I had sympathy for the girl, but I could not help her if she would not help herself. She did not appear to understand the danger that she was in and when I suddenly realised that we were no longer alone, a gust of wind blew in from behind the wall.

'Hello again,' Captain Kara said, standing before us with an overly pleased expression on her glistening face of golden complexion.

I squeezed Talia's hand, pulled her behind me and in a voice of uncertainty, said, 'Stay with me.'

Kara pulled her silver sword from its sheath. Silence fell over the night and it was not until Talia peered out from behind me, that the earth beneath our feet rumbled once again.

'Do not hurt Talia's friend,' she screamed out.

Kara stopped and, in her hesitation, looked fixedly between my open chest and Talia's throat. Anger rose from within her, yet she remained hesitant to strike. She cried out with such emotion, that it echoed through the night sky, as a warning for Beast and man alike to be wary this hour. She drew back her sword, spread out her wings and with the twist of her foremost foot, flipped around and floated almost weightlessly above the ground.

I covered Talia with my body and closed my eyes for what I hoped would be a quick death, but no such killing blow was struck. Peering out from the squint of my eye, I saw that Kara was gone, vanished like smoke in the wind. Only a silver dagger remained. I did not know whether to laugh or to cry. Kara had changed her course of action and for that, I will remain ever grateful. However, Talia was not yet safe from harm, and the King would still be expecting her head.

11. ~ ABDUCTION ~

We ventured to the Shadowlands and walking at a steady pace, I became concerned with what I would tell Mantis. My brother had the right to know what has occurred, yet bringing Talia to him, would most surely put him in the way of harm. I was unsure of myself or what the best course of action would be. I decided, that for now, I would keep Talia hidden and tomorrow, in secret, I would inform Mantis of everything and hope that he understands.

Talia slowed her pace and rubbing her eyes from tiredness, tripped over her own feet. I held her up and when I saw that she could barely hold up her head, I put her on my shoulders. I whistled a pleasant tune from my childhood. She slumped atop my course silver hair and drifting into a deep slumber, she began to snore like a Beast with a blocked nose.

Before long, we were safe beside the Shadow Divisions assassination squad barracks, where the Black Manor house towered over the landscape and cast the surrounding land in darkness. My command chambers, built of thick pine planking's and decorated with old rusted weaponry, stood at the end of the assassin's barracks. Shadows crept past the windows. I saw one of my intoxicated assassins stumble out from a side door and stroll off into the night.

Reaching the rear of the barracks, if we hoped to remain unseen, appeared to be an impossible task. Though sneaking was something I did very well. So, with Talia on my shoulders, I crept low across the unlit section of grass to the side of the barracks, ever so quietly behind the path of the pacing century guards and to the old timber door of my chambers. It had the Black family crest, the Standing Snowbear, engraved in its central square.

'Talia, you must stay here, and stay quiet. Can you do that?' I asked, to which, with one finger to her lips, she nodded in reply.

I turned the long silver door handle slowly, yet quietly and as I did; I could not help but feel somewhat foolish for having to sneak into my own home.

Nothing more than an average silver room key lay at the end of my chambers. Someone has been here, I thought, taking extra caution in my step. With a slow and exaggerated approach, I was careful to avoid the creaky boards of floor underfoot, that cracked and groaned with every step.

Considering my lounge as I crept by, I noticed that a grey fur coat was laid next to a half-eaten piece of bread. Peering past the corner of the room, I saw the footprints of large men. They had not long passed through here.

I was finally safe in my sleeping room. It looked untouched and just as I had left it. I slumped to the floor with a mighty sigh of relief and was glad to see my bed, my books and my favourite black scabbard, that I was gifted at the Mangrove combat tournament. I was so pleased to be home that I forgot to lock the door behind me and forgot that Talia was still waiting outside. I pulled up the window and whispered, 'Talia, come here'.

Not a moment later, she poked her head around the corner of the barracks and unaware of the attention she might draw, she ran towards the window with a heavy step. Gesturing for her to slow her pace, I put my finger to my lip. She copied my actions and with an exaggerated stride in her short step, she remained quiet.

'Talia, are you alright?' I asked, whisking her off her feet as I pulled her into the room. She instantly found my stash of fine chocolates. With a smirk, she began to indulge.

'Yes,' she replied simply, making a mess of the chocolates, that were now smudged over her hands and smeared around her mouth.

'I am going to try and get this glass out of my side and clean up little. You can sleep in the wardrobe, or under the bed if it suits you better. I will find you something more appropriate in the morning.'

'Talia hasn't slept for a long time; can she sleep now?' she asked.

'Of course, you can. Good night, Talia.'

I pulled the deeply embedded shard of glass out of my leg and trying not to make a sound from the pain of it, I clenched my fist and bare my teeth. A puddle of blood, with a slurp, sank away down the plughole.

I was not sure if my imagination was playing tricks on me or if I could truly hear Talia screaming in the next room. It was followed by the sound of a struggle. I was certain that she was in danger. Soaking wet, with a bloody leg and nothing more than a towel around my waist, I ran out of the shower to find that she was gone.

'Talia,' I called out, looking for a track to follow. 'Talia.'

Before I could look over my shoulder at the approaching sound of steps, I was pinned to the bed. A sharp stab pinched the skin of my arm and in a fleeting moment, I could not move, nor struggle away. Blindfolds covered over my eyes, metal chains clasped my wrists and I was stuffed headfirst into a large bag.

12. ~ CONFLICT ~

It was sand and it was hot. Accompanied by the unmistakable sound of a cheering crowd and the rank stench of congealed blood, it was obvious where I was. I knew very well, that I was in the Archimedes fighting pit, or as it is more commonly known, the Arc. Named after the great warrior King of the past and first King of Mangrove, Archimedes, it holds pride of place in the Strongholds centre, the King's Cross.

The best seats of the Arc were high on the podium, where raised many metres above the arena, the King and his Lords and Ladies would sit. Three levels of grand circular promenades surrounded the pit. The first of which was reserved for Sirs, Dames and esteemed guests. As the promenades ascended, the dimensions became smaller and the decoration, as well as the soldiers, guards and Mangrove public who sit there, far less grand. Those at the very top, which included the poor and the sick, who were so far from the action, that they could only hear the crowds roar.

As the last remnants, of what could only be poison, lingered in my veins, I felt the grip of leather on my skin, the weight of armour pushing the breath from my lungs and the familiar folded steel of my cross-hilted sword, that I dearly missed, in the palm of my hand. The folds of cloth that blinded my eyes were removed, though I could not, through the penetrating light of the morning sun, see the faces of those daring to bring me here.

I remained still, my head pounded, and the vulgar taste of desert dryness lingered on my tongue. When the dark of my eyes adjusted to the light of day, I could see the outline of spectators, blurring in and out of focus, as they made their way through the grand circular arches. I saw then, the jewelled Mangrove crown, as clear as the sand of the pit was stained red with blood, atop the King's head. I looked upon the pompous glare in his squinted eyes and my heart filled with contempt.

'Mace Black, Commander of the shadow Divisions assassination squad,' the King blurted out, as silence fell over the Arc.

The King, tilting his crown behind the curly line of his hair, stood calmly with a high chin and a proud chest. To his left, dressed in the finest black furs that money could buy and chewing through a roll of soft bread, sat young Prince Luca. To his right, with an unwashed appearance on his gaunt face, stood the ever-loyal, Lord Giovanni.

'Congratulations on passing your trials,' the King continued, raising his voice with every word. 'Now, let us view your skills for ourselves and you may prove yourself worthy of Lady Senna's recommendation…Begin the combat.' The crowd went wild with excitement.

A large set of wooden gates at the opposing end of the Arcs pit swung open with a crash and in walked the Chieftain, Lord Noriega, the giant lump of a white lion, followed by his squawking assistant, Rain.

'King Enzo, please tell me where Talia is?' I asked, silencing the crowd's roar once again.

All eyes, eager for a response, turned to the King. 'Bring her in,' he said, gesturing for his side servant.

A very pale and ghastly thin man, with a well-fitted suit of fine velvet, pulling a looped chain, brought Talia forward from behind the flowing red furs of the King's robe. She was collared around the neck and dressed as a princess in pale blue. Fear was evident in her pale green eyes, yet she held her nerve.

'As you can see, she is safe and depending on the outcome of this combat, will remain safe.'

'Let us get on with it then,' I barked, mostly to the King's lack of a moral code, but also to the Chieftain, as a warning of my readiness.

I slashed my sword through the sand. It was with such speed and strength that Rain, the irritating vulture, in a flustered panic, flapped its wings and squawked, 'Not safe, not safe.'

'What is not safe?' I responded.

The vulture, with a single flap of its wings, perched itself atop my sword hand and again said, 'Not safe, not safe.'

It scratched, with its beak, a line of black onto my gauntlets and with a wild hiss, flew to the top of a nearby pillar. Having neither the time nor patience to ponder on this strange bird nor how it communicates with the Chieftain, I raised my sword and approached the white lion.

The Chieftain roared and scratched at the concrete covered sand beneath his paws. I braced myself for an attack, but none came. Eye to eye, no less than a foot from one another, we stared, as if into each other's very souls. Then the taunting began. I glared at the Chieftain and in return, the Beast bore his fangs and licked the scent of my flesh from the air.

For a time, neither of us made a move and despite his towering size, heightened rank and royal status, the Chieftain was not the type to underestimate his opponent.

I circled the Beast, observing the pattern of his movements. I tried to gain a sense of my surroundings and then, as the Beast turned to the King, I took my chance and pushed forward. The Chieftain retreated and as he did, he swung at me furiously. I dodged away with a side roll.

The Chieftain moved back towards the underside of the King's podium and in a crouched position, with the white hairs of his mane standing tall on end, he grimaced and growled his discontent to the crowd. It was an intimidating display, that much, from the crowd's shocked reaction, was evident. Though I had seen it all before and knew very well from my past time with Maxi, my old Fox Beast, that it was a display most Beasts made before an attack.

I raised my sword high and prepared to strike, for if I did not and waited to defend against an attack from an opponent with the Chieftain's strength, I would be defending against the impossible.

The muscles on the Chieftains foremost legs, as he crouched low in the sandpit, rippled and expanded. I took a step forward, turned into a side sweep and at the very last moment, when all was still, I bore down on the Chieftain with the sharpest edge of my sword. The Beast, with a barrage of well-placed claw strikes, accompanied by the sound of hissing and cheering, ripped through the air and sent my sword, as if it were no less dangerous than a twig, to the flat of the sandpit.

I was now defenceless and as such, I could not help but leave myself wide open. The Chieftain lunged forward and with the slightest scrap from his claws, he sliced a deep gash into the thick steel of my chest plate. Blood seeped through my undergarments, dying the sand red beneath my feet. The Chieftain liked the salty taste of my cursed blood from the underside of his claws. The spectators, standing from their seats, stomped the ground and cheered with wild excitement.

I glanced up at the crowd and spotted Sir James Sand, mocking me with a disdainful smirk and Dame Eva crow, covering her eyes with her hands of deception.

I stood from the red sand and with bated breath, looked over the Arc in search of strategy or anything that could be used to defeat such a formidable foe. Although I found none and when it seemed, in the heat of the blistering sun, that all hope was lost, I remembered something that my most trusted of friends, Lady Senna once told me about the behaviour of lions. She said, that if one should pull on a lion's tail, it will not only become fully enraged but lose its might in muscle, inevitably paralysing its movement.

The suffering pain of my chest wound fell from intolerable agony to an enduring ache. I must attempt Senna's strategy, I thought, for I had none other and there was, save from pain of death, nothing to lose.

The Chieftain, in a show of strength and intimidation, bated me forward, but I would not be moved. Pounding his paws on the sand-swept surface of the pit, the Chieftain charged. He charged as if his life depended on it. He charged as if I was the last meal he would ever come to eat. I waited still for the opportune moment and with a side step, I spun around, drew my sword from atop the dry sand and sliced, with an intent to kill, up at the underside of the lion's main. My sword, that had not only survived every torture of my hands but years of Swan Chockers use, smashed apart on the Chieftains iron fangs. The crowd fell to such silence, that a dropping pin could be heard by every Beast in Manrock.

From the flat of my back, I could do nothing but hold the shooting bolts of pain that rippled, with teeth crunching effect, up and down my sword arm. Every bone in the right of my arm, from the small of my wrist to the large of my shoulder, had shattered under the attacking impact. Dame Eva's perturbed screams, from her standing position on the second row of the first promenade, howled over the volume of cheering crowds. Poor Talia wept salt tears over her silver chained constraints.

The Chieftain, baring his teeth and claws on a slow approach, flung the broken shards of my sword to one side. If I did not know any better, I could have sworn that the great white lion was smiling at me. I had just about had enough of being made a fool of and attempted to stand. I was soon knocked back down. The Chieftain was toying with me and every slap from his un-clawed paw only added fuel to my fire of burning rage.

'Has anyone ever told you not to play with your food, Noriega,' Lady Lavender joked, a rare smile accentuating her sharp jawline.

The Chieftain put the immense weight of his paw atop my chest and slowly motioned his claws to the surface. They cut through my skin and punctured my lungs. From the flat of my back, I was still unable to move. Breathing became a struggle, moving became impossible and the small amount of heart-wrenching strain in my broken arm was less than useless against the Chieftains might.

13. ~ VICTORY ~

Darkness began to wash over my mind and I knew not whether to laugh or to cry, whether die here or whether Talia would ever truly be safe.

'Get up Mace, get up and fight,' my brother shouted.

His voice soared higher and packed more of a punch than any other and when it reached my ears, a mere moment before darkness faded over me, it gave me hope.

It was quiet and lonely in the dark corner of my mind. My only accompaniment was a cursed vision of red light. It called to me. It drew me in close and I could not, for lack of self-control, resist its pull. I could not look away. The weightless world of my mind, although dark and full of tricks, felt like home and I thought, perhaps, that I might stay a while. I was so close to the red light, that I could almost reach out and touch it, but I dared not, for though it was beautiful to gaze upon, the thought of touching such a thing frightening me.

In the darkness, I could hear the lions roar, the crowds cheer and my brother's deep laughter, but when I looked to find them, the red light shot through the darkness and into my chest, illuminating the pitch blackness of my mind. I could once again see, and everything was clear. Mantis slapping his thighs in hysterics, the concern in Senna's bright blue eyes, that when met with my own, faded back to their former glory, and the confused faces of almost every spectator in the crowd, as they silently stared on.

This long-overplayed ordeal, that King Enzo of Mangrove thought wise to trial upon me, was not yet over and although I had awakened from the red lights dream, I was not expecting to be quite as rested and free from harm as I now was. But that was not the only surprise under the light of the morning sun, for my situation, once shrouded in darkness and defeat, had turned in my favour. My hands dripped with the bloody flesh of a Beast, my chest, that fell under easy pressure, was as good as new, and the great white lion, whose victory was once at hand, stared defeat in the eye. His paw was mangled beyond repair and his throat, which bled profusely, hung from a hole in his neck.

'Mace,' the crowds cheered. 'Mace,' Repeatedly they roared, and it was not until the Chieftain stood to his feet and licked his paw clean, did they eventually stop and return to silence.

On approach, the Chieftain hobbled on his only useful legs and with a wide-open jaw of snarling and snapping teeth, he stood tall on his hind legs. It would appear to all that this combat was not yet over and although none could be certain of the outcome, all were still with a silent pause of anticipation.

'Finish it. Finish it,' The less honourable spectators in the higher promenades chanted, and although I was no longer in the mood for killing, especial a high Lord and a proud Beast, I had to end this combat, for Talia's sake.

Sir James smirked incredulously from his point of vantage and Mantis was poised on the edge of his seat.

I charged for the Beast and pulling a small blade from the innermost side of my cuisses, I cut furiously at the Beast's face. I sliced him across the eye and if he had not moved a moment sooner than he did, his face would be mangled to a bloody mess. In a last attempt to finish the combat, the Chieftain raised himself on hind legs and bore down on me with all his weight and might.

'Stop,' the King burst, without a moment to spare.

A second later and the tip of my blade would be in the Chieftains wide-open chest. I tossed the blade to one side and as the Beast came down on me, I moved to my left and heard the snapping of bone as he landed on the rough sand of the pit.

A cheer so loud, that Mangroves peace would be stirred from it, ran through the Arc. The King, in all his magnanimous glory, began a slow clap, that sped with the joining spectators until no other sound could be heard for miles around.

'As promised,' the King said, not that I could hear him over the thundering roars of the surrounding spectators. Though I need not have heard the fool, for I could see clearly what he was doing. He was freeing poor Talia from her chained constraints.

'Mace,' she screamed.

Her face was full of tears and although her tears were not of sadness but relief, they were tears none the less. With arms out wide, she ran as fast as her legs could carry her down the arching steps of the King's podium. I pulled her up in arms and squeezed her in a tight embrace. I knew then, that she would finally be safe. How a life saved can put the pressures of combat into perspective, really was a funny thing.

Not a moment later, at least ten men in white medical research uniforms, stormed into the Arcs pit. They were followed by a white horse-drawn carriage, that was filled to bursting with ointments, potions and the most amazing marvels that medical science had to offer.

In their attempts to stitch and bind the Chieftains wounds, the medics, with all the best will in the world, could not do a thing to help. Their efforts received nothing more than growls of discontent. Lord Noriega was, after all, the Beasts Chieftain and was far too arrogant to receive medical attention. He roared louder and deeper than he had during our battle and frightened the medics, who only mean to fulfil their duty, halfway into an early grave. He remained stubborn and threatful until Lady Lavender said in harsh tones, 'Noriega, you will receive my Divisions attention, or so help the gods, I will feed you to my fish.'

The Chieftain accepted medical treatment and in doing so, unintentionally caused Mantis such amusement, that he laughed himself into a fit of hysterics and fell backwards into Lady Lavender's bony lap. He received quite a clip around the ear for it. Unfortunately for Lavender, it just spired him on.

'Silence,' the King ordered, instantly halting the rabble of chatter and cheer. 'Commander Mace Black, you have now proven yourself worthy of Lordship. You have six hours to clean yourself up and report to my council hall for your anointment. You are, from this day forward, the seventh seated Lord of the Mainland Division.' The crowd went wild, tossing their hats and helmets in celebration.

Bandaged around the throat and foremost right leg, the Chieftain approached me. I was hesitant and thought for a moment, that he sought revenge. I put Talia down and pushed her behind me. The Chieftain did not want revenge, he merely wanted the respect and admiration a proud Beast deserves. He bowed down and accepted his defeat. Though as he did, his bloody Raven, as if from thin air, perched itself atop my shoulder and said, 'Lord Mace. Lord Mace.'

'You are a fine opponent and a great Chieftain. You have my respect,' I said, with a hand on his bloodstained and furry mane.

'Come, Talia, let us rest.' I bowed to the King and my countrymen and adjured to the safe comforts of my chambers.

14. ~ SOLEMN ~

Fifteen years ago, …

On a dark and dreary mid summers morning, in the small riverside village of Low down east, a stone's throw from the Shadowland, I made haste for the market. My fool of an older brother, Lord Mantis Black, ordered for me to collect his order of devil's lettuce, the strongest and most expensive of Mangroves herbal vegetables. I would not usually be at my brother's beck and call, but as it was worth five silver and it gets me out of the house, I was happy to help.

At the end of the market road, I could hear the squawking of seagulls, followed by the chiming of the riverside bell, which only rang at the end of the trading day, or in an emergency.

'Typical,' I said, peering up at the Northerly storm clouds, that cast out the sun and covered the outskirts of Low down east in a shadow of darkness.

An ever-increasing gale of wind whistled through the market stalls and motioned the clap of thunder from the blackened clouds, brushing the merchant ships off course.

'Half-fang, we must find shelter.' A red and blonde coated Fox Beast, who's only purpose in life was to protect and obey me, obediently came to my side.

On spotting a blue crest of bright light bolt across the sky, Half-fang ran around in a dizzying dance of circles, snarling and snapping at the sky. It looked as if she was trying to threaten the damn storm away. Despite her amusing efforts, the storm was upon us. Though this was no ordinary storm, I had seen this storm before. It was many years ago on an awful day, the day my beloved mother was killed. This very storm, it would seem, has plastered a thunderous racket in the sky once before.

There were at least five miles between Low down east and Mantis's Black Manor house, where I lived. It was too far to walk, without getting soaked, and I did not bring any coin, so a carriage was out of the question.

Utterly drenched under the roof of the storm and soaked through to the bare skin, Half-fang and I ran wards the riverside bridge.

On our way, an old keeper of crabs haggled with a merchant over the price of his wares. Half-fang barked at the merchant, startling the man into a backwards tumble. If I had not held her back by the scruff, she would have ripped the frightened look clean from the merchant's face. Something about salesmen dismayed her. Perhaps she could smell a tall tale, or was disgusted by their overly perfumed scent.

We moved on and sat on a large moss-covered slab of stone under the bridge, where we waited for over an hour for the storm to pass, but such luck was not for us, and the storm raged on for what seemed an eternity. Wind rumbled, whirling and slashing its way over the top of the bridge. Flashes of light broke through the clouds, followed by the booming roar of crackling thunder.

I was becoming paranoid, I felt as if I had to get out from under the bridge. The dullness of the dark and the reverberated patter from every drop of rain was driving me mad. I decided then and there, not to further my frustrations by waiting any longer. I would have to endure a thorough soaking.

'Half-fang, come,' I called out, and she came to my side without hesitation.

As we reached the line of rain that ran down the side of the bridge, Half-fang halted and stared out at the raging storm. She growled aggressively. Her long mouth salivated and the orange hairs at the back of her neck stood up on end.

Wondering what could have turned this simple Beasts temper, I looked to the sky and save from a flash of bolting light, I saw nothing out of the ordinary.

At nine-feet, from top to tail, with razor-sharp teeth and a growl that would intimidate the bravest of men, Half-fang had little to prove, especially to a sky of storm-ridden clouds. I stroked the length of her thick frame for comfort sake and in doing so, I managed to calm her. I meant well, but when eventually I moved my hand from the furry frame of her back, she whirled around in a wild madness.

She stopped with deadly stillness and stared at me. It was a deep long stare, the kind of stare one would expect from someone about to pass out from intoxication. It frightened me; it was strange to see her like this. For a moment it looked as if she was considering something, and was not entirely sure whether to do what it was that she was considering.

She winked once, and then again with the other eye. I just stood there, I had no idea how to deal with this, whatever this was.

She snarled at me and snapped her teeth together with lusting slobber that slanted her jawline. It would seem she had finished considering.

Half-fang did not hesitate to pounce and with a wide-open jaw of slobbering teeth, she pierced the skin of my forearm. A feeling of warmth rushed over me as the Beast tore away at my arm and ripped flesh from bone. My screams, along with the booming of thunder, echoed through the underside of the bridge. There was blood everywhere. It was an utter mess.

I cowered away and closing my eyes, I wished that I was safe at home and not meat for my bloodthirsty fox Beast.

'Half-fang it is me, Mace. Stop this. Stop, I beg you.' I whimpered to the Beast I had once loved.

Tears began streaming down my cheeks. I thought this was the end. In a stiffness of fear, I could barely move a muscle, save for the holding of my forearm to stop the endless bleeding.

For a brief moment, I could hear only the pouring of rain, so I peered out through my cowering fingers. To my unwelcomed surprise, Half-fang was standing over me, with a pitiful look in her eyes. It was almost as if she was now in fear of me.

I held her gaze as she crept backwards at a snail's pace. Further and further she sank into the darkness and with a sorrowful squeal, she turned tail and ran into the storm.

I was distraught by what had just occurred. I did not care that she had retreated, nor that she would ever return, though if she ever did, Lord Mantis would most likely have her guts for garters.

'Do not ever come back, you stupid Beast. I hate you,' I yelled out with all the authority I could muster, before slumping back onto the wall of the bridge.

The throbbing agony that shot up and down my forearm was intensely painful. With every beat of my heart, more blood than I ever thought possible to lose poured out over the damp stone surface.

I was cold. The shirt on my back stuck tight to my scrawny frame, and I was so scared and so utterly drained of all hope, that I just sat there sobbing in solitude.

No one would come for me and I could not stay there under that bridge any longer. I gritted my teeth, ripped the shirt from my back and wrapped it tightly around my open wound. I gave thought to the possibility that I would not make it out through the storm, and at that very moment, when I envisioned my demise, the rain stopped and the sky burst to life with a flash of red. It shone through the low-lying clouds, burning a hole in the sky.

I gazed up, amazed at this strange sight. For the briefest of moments, I forgot the throbbing discomfort that set my arm to spasm and my throat to sickness.

I watched as the light increased in brightness and billowed over the sky above. I watched as it folded in on itself and with an intense brightness, descend gradually through the dark clouds. I was in awe of the magnificent beauty before me and drawn like a moth to a flame, I could not turn away.

That was the moment everything changed. Like an arrow from the gods, that bright red light shot down to claim me. I opened my eyes to the sparkle of stars amidst endless darkness, and as I did, a voice from beside me said, 'You're a bit wiry aren't you...but then again, Mace Black, you might just be the one we are looking for.'

I realised then, that I must have been knocked unconscious. I instantly turned his gaze. Beside me, sat cross-legged, was a very large and very tall man. He was entirely bald and had such dark skin, that it concealed the very contours of his face. A curly black beard, that was ribbon tied in two bunches and brushed against the lapels of his ill-fitted suit, revealed the number fourteen mark to the right his neck. It was written in ancient numerals.

It was an unexpected encounter, to say the least, but I was not concerned. I was enveloped in a feeling of warmth and rejuvenation, I no longer cared. I did not care who this man was, nor what he wanted with me.

I held my injured arm up to the light of the moon. It was no longer a torturing affliction of discomfort, but as it had always been. I carefully removed the blood-stained shirt and was taken aback by the condition of my wound. Where once there was mangled flesh, not a mark nor scratch remained, and I could not help but notice that my skin was now as pale white as my teeth.

That's when I knew for sure, and the very thought of it made me sick. The red light from the sky was no coincidence. It had cursed me.

From that moment on, like my brother and my father before me, I was cursed.

'I am sorry for what I must do,' The man beside me said.

He lifted me from the floor and with the motion of one strong arm, swung me over the bulk of his back.

I could see from this high point of vantage, that there was a cobbled street on the other side of the road and on that street, almost completely hidden from sight, save from the dull flicker of candle lamps, was a grey horseless carriage.

On approaching the carriage, black plumes of smoke began to bellow out from what looked like a small chimney on its roof, and as of its own accord, the passenger side door of the carriage crept opened.

I was thrust from the man's back and with unnecessary force, thrown inside the carriage.

'You will remain seated, Mace Black. Everything will be explained to you shortly,' the man said, taking his place in the much larger seat beside me.

The man pushed forward a copper coloured lever and on stamping his foot to the floor pedal, he motioned the carriage forward. It groaned and it roared as it rolled along the flat streets of Low-Down East.

'My name is Lester, but you can call me, Fishbone, most everybody else does,' the man said, in a hoarse tone of voice. 'I was sent by the cursed King to save you from the laws of this land.'

I did not trust a word that came from his lips, yet for fear of reprisal, I did nothing to question him.

Unnoticed by Fishbone, who was busy burning the end of a wooden smoking stick, I turned the handle of the side door and found it to be locked tight. I peered to the back of the carriage in search of an alternative escape route, and to my surprise, I found two very similarly dressed women with somewhat similar faces staring back at me. Both had short blond hair, luminous lime green eyes and on their wrists, they had the same ancient numerical marks that Fishbone had on his neck.

One was marked with the number seven and wore a seamless black dress, matching black boots and an array of orange sparkling jewellery around her neck.

I could not help but notice, that she was covered, almost from head to toe in scaring, and were on the right, a hand should be to match with the left, nothing more than a neatly bandaged stump remained.

The other woman, who had the number four marked on the underside of her wrist, was the highest-ranking and she did not take her eyes from mine.

'Please excuse our unintentional rudeness,' she said, with an air of empathy. 'We mean only to help. My name is Karen Silver, and next to me is my stubborn younger sister, Ella.'

'And how exactly are you going to help me?' I plucked up the courage to ask, for if I did not and remained silent, I would surely regret it.

'You will know soon enough,' Karen said, crossing her arms, as she began whistling an unpleasant tune.

I knew not what this meant, but it appeared that Fishbone did. He motioning the carriage left and with the turn of the steering wheel, sent us all hurtling down the side of a hill. It was with such speed, that before I could sit back, the carriage had burst through a wooden fence and met with the fast-moving traffic of the Mangrove carriageway.

The Oakwood forest was to the right of us, the open plains of Lowdown east to the left, and ahead, in the far distance, the twinkling lights of the Mangrove Citadel led a path northward.

'Is this beady-eyed little brat the one we're looking for, Karen? He's going to be nothing more than a waste of the South point's time and resources,' Ella said, in smug tones, as she smoothed a single finger through the length of her long hair.

'Why do you say such things?' Karen replied, scowling at Ella with eyes of disdain. 'Is there somewhere more important you need to be?'

Ella sighed like a spoilt child and said no more. Though she had already said quite enough, for my brother, Lord Mantis, has spoken of the South point many times before, and on not one occasion has it been with any kindness. From what I can recall, the South point is a powerful organisation that actively defends the cursed minority against King Enzo's cruel military drafting laws.

It was for that reason, that I remained deadly silent. I had to be cautious. I pondered on what to make of my unfortunate situation, and though I knew very little of it, I knew for certain, that if the South point were here for me, then there was no doubting it, I was cursed.

Shifting the copper coloured lever to the far left, Fishbone stomped hard on the floor pedal and brought the carriage to a speed far greater than any horse-drawn carriage could travel. We swerved between one carriage and then another, leaving large plumes of black smoke in our wake, as we rattled along the hard surface of the road. Fishbone accelerated to even greater speeds and on pressing down a switch to his right-hand side, he unlocked the carriage side doors.

He leant over to me, pushed open his door, and watched as the pressure of wind snapped the door from its hinges and sent it hurtling headlong into a cow field alongside the road. I could only imagine what was coming, and as the wind swirled through the carriage, I did something that I never thought I would do. I begged.

'Please Fishbone, please do not throw me from this carriage. You said you were here to help me.' I was fearful of the awfully painful way in which my life would be taken.

Ella laughed hysterically as if crazed with madness, and all I could do was pray. Pray that I was brave. Pray that I could put up a good fight and save myself from harm. But I was just a frightened boy at the end of my short life. There was nothing I could do.

My body was flung out of that carriage like a rag doll. I could scarcely look. The hard surface of the road was speeding up to meet with the side of my face.

'Mace, you fool.' My brother's deep voice roared as if from nowhere.

Within the blink of an eye, Mantis had leapt from the back of a large white stead, and in his famous suit of heavy golden armour, he smashed into the surface of the road. It was a brutal landing, to say the least, but Mantis did not appear to be the slightest bit injured. In that same instant, he caught me in his arms as if I were no heavier than a new-born baby, and with a grin from ear-to-ear, he sliced through the tires of the horseless carriage with his longsword and sent it hurtling off balance. It bounced up, smashed back down and as it carved past a slight curve in the road, it collided with an oncoming cart. Wood and iron scrapped along with the head and chest of an unexpected workhorse. The poor creature suffered, thrashing and jerking, until its last breath. The black horseless carriage continued flipping over and over until it was no more than a ball of blood-covered waste. It was a horrific sight to behold and one that I would not soon forget.

'Silver hair suits you, little brother,' Mantis said, chuckling to himself.

I had not, until that very moment, noticed that my hair colour had changed. I could not help but laugh at my new silver sheen of short white hair. It was, as it has been for every member of my diminishing clan, a sure sign of our curse.

'Dirty bastard,' Ella screamed out. 'You think you can sneak attack me and get away with it.'

She was mangled and deformed from the wreckage. She spat blood and with each breath, gasped as if it were her last.

'It looks as if a slow and painful death is in store for that one.' Mantis chuckled hysterically, smoothing a length of long silver hair out of his face.

'Thank you, Brother,' I said, bursting into sudden tears. 'If it were not for you, I would be dead right now.'

Mantis flung me down atop the hard surface of the road. He took a knee beside me, rested his enormous black steel longsword across his leg, and said, 'Dear brother, remember to take time as you pass…for on the cursed road, there will be need of patience.'

Mantis was not laughing, nor was he smirking. He was sad and, in his despair, he stared into the far distance. He looked lost, perhaps in the memories of a time long past.

15. ~ ANOINTMENT ~

Present-day...

All eyes were on me as I entered the King's grand council hall for my first meeting as Lord of the Mainland Division. Beads of odorous sweat dripped from my brow. I could scarcely tell if it was too hot or my nerves were getting the better of me. All I could feel was the power and intimidation that came from being in the presence of the highest figureheads in Mangrove.

'He is quite handsome up close,' Lady Lavender said, peering at me with a seductive eye, that I could almost feel caressing my mind, and if it was not for the subtle raising of Senna's brow, I would have blushed with bright cheeks.

I was unsure of how best to proceed in such a place, where all who enter demand the utmost respect. Despite my hesitance to step past the doorway, I strolled in as if I were the highest-ranking Lord in all of Mangrove. Though such confidence was not to last, for a feeling of sickness crept up the back of my throat and as I went to introduced myself, a dribble crept from my mouth and dangled down my chin.

'Do not make a fool of yourself, Mace,' Senna said. 'You are now a Lord and hold a seat in this council. Stand tall and walk in with pride. You have earned your place here.'

She was embarrassed by the impression I was making. She did, after all, put her sterling reputation on the line to recommend me, and for that, I will remain ever grateful.

'Take your seat and be quick about it,' Lord Giovanni said, waving me in from the far side of the table.

'Yes, of course.'

I walked over to the only seat that was not yet sat upon and was glad that Senna was beside me. She rolled her eyes in such a way, that I remained silent and made little to no eye contact with any other Lord or Lady around the table.

With a look, more of disdain than of welcome, Dame Lambert Crow of the Mainland Division walked slowly to the side of my seat. She held a folded black robe under her arm. She made me feel very uncomfortable. She showed no delight in having me as Lord in her Division.

'Attention in my halls,' said the King, grimacing as he picked his teeth. Let us begin this meeting.'

At that, Senna shoved the robes, along with a snake patterned silver shoulder plate, into my arms and with a sigh, also slammed a large eight-sided and blacker than night coin atop the table. I placed the robes and shoulder plate to one side and could not help but to admire the fine dark blue stitching along the seam of the robe, that separated the thick cotton from the indented silver lining.

'My thanks, Dame Lambert,' I said, moving my attention now to the coin, which if I was not mistaken, was a rare and old piece of eight.

I rubbed my thumb over its strange octagonal engagements and turning it over, not only did it glow with a pulsating purple light, but it contained the all too familiar image of King Roland's crown. This was no ordinary coin and when I looked to ask Lambert why she had given this to me or where it had come from, she was nowhere to be seen. All eyes were focused on the King in his throne. I immediately put the coin away before anyone noticed its luminous glow. My questions would have to wait.

'Just ignore her,' said King Enzo, clicking his bejewelled fingers together. 'She still mourns the loss of your predecessor, Lord Brick. It may take some time for her to come to terms with this.'

In response to the click, young Prince Luca, who has still yet to leave the confines of the red tower, strolled across the back of the hall. He appeared to be struggling with the weight of a long wooden box.

'This is for you, the new Lord,' he said, presenting me with the box.

'My prince, you must be very strong to lift such a box.' I jested that I could not carry the same weight.

The Prince giggled aloud and on his way to the small throne seat beside his father's, he tripped over his own feet and toppled over. He remained in good spirits and took his seat.

Inside the box, that I had not the patience to leave unopened, was the recognisable shimmer of folded steel. However, this was no ordinary steel, it was black steel; the finest and sharpest material that money could buy. If I worked tirelessly for fifty years, I would still not have the coin for such rare steel.

The weight of the sword, that seemed unnatural for its size, fell from my grasp as I wrenched it from the box. It was a fine piece of smith work, that much was evident, and from the way the surrounding Lords and Ladies admired its form, I could see that it was something special. The blade was flat and almost identical to my previous, except that it was entirely black and had the word, Mainland, engraved in old cursive along the right edge. The hilt was in the shape of a cross and was, without question, the brightest silver I had ever seen. It gave me a sense of something more. It was as if I was a new man, a higher class of people.

'We did consider a fine scabbard to go along with your sword of Lordship,' the King said, with a smile. 'But you, like your brother, appear to carry your sword around as if it were no more than a stick for walking.'

'This is a fine sword. The finest I have ever seen.' I bowed to the King and the young Prince.

'My brother, as Lord of the Mainland Division. Is this a joke?' Mantis said, sniggering in Lord Hawk's ever-listening ear.

'Admittedly he is young. But then again, he did hold his own against the Chieftain,' Hawk replied, unknowingly leading my brother into a burst of laughter, that was directed towards the Chieftain, and although the great lion sat proudly, he was not amused by Mantis's mockery.

Not only was there a wooden splint wrapped around his injured front leg, but he was bloodstained from his mane to the middle of his back. Spraying hot breath and saliva through his pearly white teeth, the Chieftain roared his dissatisfaction towards Lord Mantis.

'The Beast Chieftain, beaten by my fifteen-year-old little brother. You must feel quite the fool, Noriega,' Mantis mocked.

He stood abruptly, bashed the hilt of his great sword against his armoured chest and in a display of strength, whirled the sword from left to right.

'Both of you, desist this foolishness,' the King shouted, crashing his fist atop the table. 'I will have no violence in my hall.'

At that very moment, Prince Luca burst into a fit of tears. This only angered the King. It was not worth risking cruel punishment, not for the sake of a meaningless battle, and so, Noriega and Mantis immediately took their places. They avoided eye contact with the King, who glared at my brother, that was until I broke the mood.

'Prince Luca,' I called out.

Lady Senna shook her head with wide eyes, indicating that my involvement was unneeded. I ignored her looks, pulled a wrapped piece of chocolate out from my top pocket and placed it in the palm of the young Prince's hand. At first, the King looked as if he were picturing my head on a spike. Witnessing the dissipation of his son's tears, he sat back and nodded his approval with a half-smile.

'Let us begin,' the King said, raising a hand for everyone's focused attention. 'I am sure that you are all aware by now of what has occurred. A fortnight ago the honourable Lord Brick Bisson lost his life defending the Kingdom's peace. He fought bravely till his last breath. Because of this, a search began for someone worthy to fill the vacant position. As you are also aware, Commander Mace was recommended by Lady Senna, and the following day his trials began. I, King Enzo of Mangrove, Ruler of Mainland, along with help from Captain Kara of the Naval Divisions surveillance unit, thoroughly evaluated Mace Black in these trials, which he successfully passed. After a final test of combat, against Lord Noriega, we found no shortcomings in his abilities or character. Therefore, I announce that the former shadow Divisions, assassination squad Commander, Mace Black, is hereby promoted to the rank of Mainland Division Lord, and will take the seventh seat in my council.'

'Your grace,' I said, standing abruptly.

'What appears to be troubling you?'

'I am honoured and humbled to be promoted in Lordship and take a seat in your council, but…meaning no disrespect, why was an innocent little girl put through such hardship in the process?'

'I will only explain this to you once, Mace Black,' he said. 'The trials are set to test your character, honour and bravery, which you demonstrated in an abundance. During your trials, you were monitored by Captain Kara, as you are probably aware by now. Using her unique skillset, she blinded you to the truth of things. Bill and his gang's escape from Mangrove prison, was not an accident, nor was there perception of Talia's presence. You are probably wondering where Talia came from, are you not?'

'Yes, your highness.'

'Every so often, we find children wondering the Division streets, normally injured or starving. These children were abandoned for being different, left to fend for themselves. Talia was found raiding through bins outside of the medical research Division, hungry and frightened. Never putting her in any real danger, we used her for your trial, under the capable protection of Captain Kara, who cursed Bill and his band of fools with blindness, allowing them only to see what Kara wanted them to.'

'You used her,' I spat, interrupting the King.

'Such foolish talk! You have no right to decide for yourself what is right and wrong. It is your duty to accept the true justice of the King. Kara was once like Talia, starving on the streets, left to die by those supposed to love her. We took her in and allowed her to earn a living for herself. She is now a highly-regarded Captain, eating the finest foods, and leading a fleet of naval vessels fit for a King. Talia was also allowed to earn a living for herself. She is now in your capable care and about to live in one of the finest Division manors. Would you rather we left her to die on the streets, like a dog.' The King paused. 'Remember Mace, she will never go hungry again.'

'My apologies your grace.' I was ashamed to look in his subtle brown eyes.

'I expect nothing less from you, Lord Mace. Protecting a small child, even against your King, is an incomparable notion of excellence,' the King continued, before adjourning the meeting with a simple wave of his hand.

Moments later, as the night crept in, I cornered my brother under the spine the red tower. I hoped to discuss Talia with him. 'Mantis, I need to show you this.'

I pulled the picture of our father from my back pocket. Mantis was less than interested in what I had to show him. Until he saw it.

'Where did you get this?' he asked in disgust.

'Talia showed me this after I rescued her, saying that it is a picture of her father and that she has been looking for him.'

'What are you trying to say, Mace, that our father, the great Hollis Black, was having an affair, before losing his mind to a curse and killing our mother. You are saying he gave his seed to another woman in secret. Is that right, Mace?' Mantis raised his voice with every word.

'I do not know, Mantis, that is why I am discussing it with you. I have not mentioned a word of this to Talia, but by her age, she was not conceived until after father had lost his mind, and became--.'

'Do not say it, brother. Hollis was a good man,' he said. 'He spent his life working tirelessly for our family. He was a hero, Mace. He made mother happy, until…well, you know.'

'Mantis, please, calm down.'

'No brother, you have said quite enough. Do not think that I will stand here and let you besmirch our father's great name, not for the sake of some stupid little girl and her damn picture.'

'I did not mean anything by it.'

At that, Mantis had just about heard enough and smashed his armoured fist across the side of my face. With one hand, he lifted me, almost effortlessly from the ground by my throat. He pulled me in close, so close, that I could smell the minty freshness of this breath.

'I do not want to hear another word of this, brother,' he said, so distraught, that he dropped me to the floor and spat out his disregard for my honour.

Whilst struggling to catch a breath, I watched Mantis look back in contempt and toss the picture of our father to the wind.

'Do you remember when you were kidnapped, Mace…think about it,' he said, pausing to stare at the sky, before taking a slow step into the night.

He was not laughing, nor scorning me with insult, as he usually would. He appeared somewhat content and strangely reserved. It was as if all the worry of this world had fallen from his shoulders.

16. ~ ACCEPTANCE ~

Upon the rising sun, I entered the Mainland Divisions less than grand assembly hall, that was unfortunately filled with the lingering damp stench of feet.

Wearing blue spiked armour and a white sash under her black robe, Dame Lambert Crow stood to the right of the long wooden stage. She called the soldier units to attention on my approach. Over thirteen thousand men and women stood in the enormous blue and white striped hall. They were lined up in three distinct rows, headed by what I presumed to be their Commanders.

On approach, my stomach knotted with nerves. Dame Lambert glared her dissatisfaction through me and handed over a fresh roll of parchment, that detailed the hierarchy of the Mainland Division. I scanned over the parchment, gaining a brief understanding of what will inevitably come to be second nature.

The first row was infantry. The unit was well known for its brutality. They wore blue spiked armour, possibly to intimidate their adversaries, and carried only swords and spears as weapons. Led by Commander Richard Bloom, a balding halfwit with a stocky frame, they were disobedient and loved nothing more than week women and strong ale.

The centre row was made up of artillery, which consisted entirely of slim built women. They wore black robes, tight fitted blue leathers and brown quivers on their backs, that matched the bows to their sides. Led by Commander Sophia Sundance, Lady Lavender's second cousin, they hold pride of place in the central row. It was fair to say, that I had never seen such an attractive unit.

Lastly, was the cavalry, who also dressed in blue leather, but it was very different from the artillery. It was heavy leather, the type of material that can withstand the same quality of impact as light armour, whilst leaving enough room for manoeuvrability. The cavalry distinguished themselves with a white sash, which I have heard is scented with a fragrance to keep their horses calm under pressure. These proud horse masters are the backbone of the Division's strategy and it is for that reason, the short and dark-haired Commander Snake Barrington, Lord Hawks firstborn son and master strategist, was their leader.

It was more than a little overwhelming to have so many soldiers under my command. They were very different, not only in numbers but in spirit, from the hand full of assassins that I was accustomed to. They were rough and ready, with a lack of posture and use of pronunciation. They were the pawns, the bottom scrapings, the lowest form of life in an otherwise cursed world.

'It is an honour to introduce myself to such a fine group of soldiers,' I pronounced, marching across the stage. 'I am your new Lord, Mace Black.'

Sweat dripped from my brow. The men and women of the Mainland Division paid little attention to my words, and to diminish the last hope of the new day, they whispered cruelties and mockery amongst themselves. I covered my sadness with a false smile. I wanted to march my way back down that wooden staircase from where I came and crawl into a warm bed. But I would not. My will would not allow such an act of cowardice.

With wavering uncertainty, I turned my attention to Dame Lambert for a closer connection. She was, after all, going to be my second in command. Though, after considering the demon red eyes beneath her hateful scowl, I wished no longer to make her acquaintance. None the less, I was not rude, my mother did not raise me that way. I was going to make an impression if it killed me. I offered out my hand, but received nothing, save for further scowling.

'I will not accept this,' Dame Lambert screamed, brushing a length of golden blonde hair out of her spiteful face. 'We haven't had a moment to mourn our true Lord, Brick Bisson and now you're here. You are not worthy to replace such a great man. His blood is still fresh on the streets of Mangrove for goodness sake.'

'Please Dame, I mean no disrespect and will not interfere with your time of grieving.'

'Aren't you an assassin from the shadow Division, the so-called, Black command?' She asked, making an uncomfortable scene for the thousands of onlooking eyes.

'Well, yes,' I answered, wondering what I could have done as an assassin to offend her.

'You are a murderer,' she said, closing the gap between us. 'You spend your time sneaking around, killing people in their sleep. It's cowardly. You are not an acceptable choice to lead this Division as Lord.'

'I fear that you are going too far with this,' Commander Snake butted in.

'Am I, Commander, or am I just saying what we are all thinking. Well, isn't that what you are all thinking,' she shouted towards the silent units, burning with bitterness. 'How can we follow orders from a nobody like him. The only reputation he has is from his brother, Lord Mantis.'

She looked over the hall, hoping that her subordinates were in support of her accusations.

'We will obey him, Dame.' Snake said, calmly sliding his fingers down the shimmering green pommel of his sword.

'Snake is right, Dame. We will obey him. It is not his fault that Lord Brick, rest his soul, is no longer with us,' Commander Sophia said.

This was very awkward. I was standing with the highly-regarded Division leads and they were discussing my future in front of me. Though it mattered not, for whether they chose to accept or dismiss me, I would not stray from my path.

'Have you got anything to say for yourself?' Dame Lambert shouted, grabbing the scruff of my robe.

There was no gesture more insulting than a back turned and when I made no reply, she did just that. She turned her back on me and knew very well what it meant.

'Why do you not react? Mace Black. I have insulted you in front of the entire Division. Aren't you going to do anything? You coward.' She turned and pulled me close.

With her voice raised, she looked deep into the darkness within my eyes. She wanted nothing more than a reaction in front of the entire Mainland Division. I did not react, nor turn from her ill gaze.

'Are you not angry?'

'Not at all,' I replied, grasping a firm hold of Dame Lambert's hand. 'I understand that you are grieving and emotional from your unfortunate loss, but I am, as of now, the Lord of this Division. You will need to get used to that. As for your insults towards the assassination squad, do not let it happen again. They are loyal, brave and my brothers. You would be wise to remember that. Though I do not stand before you as an assassin, I swear my allegiance and loyalties to the Mainland Division from this day onwards,' I looked about the hall and raised my voice for all to hear. 'When I awoke this morning and put on my new suit of armour, coloured in the royal blue of the Mainland, I was no longer a Commander, I was Lord of the Mainland Division.'

I spurred a half-hearted cheer from the units. It echoed through the high-roofed hall.

As the red began to fade from Dame Lambert's face, the grip she had around the scruff of my robe loosened. Expecting the best of outcomes, I smiled at her. At that, she took a deep breath and closed her eyes. I wrongly assumed this to be a sign of calming and without warning, she swung her child-sized fist towards my face. I caught the blow in the palm of my hand. It was unexpectedly powerful for a woman as small as Lambert. She was strong, there was no doubt about it. Though I wondered, how exactly she was in the rank of Dame. Showing such insolence to a Lord was lash worthy at best. I guess rank does not simply change one's personality.

Years ago, when my brother first took his place as Lord of the Shadow Division, I thought for sure that he would learn respect for his fellow man, but as with all things about Mantis, I was wrong. Perhaps that's where Lambert gets it from. They are best of friends after all.

With a look of contempt, Lambert yanked her hand back from my grasp and ran out of the hall as fast as her legs could carry her.

'I do not accept you as my Lord,' she yelled out, slamming the hall door with a thud.

'Mace, ay Mace, some carriages be waiting for ye outside.' Came a familiar voice from the side door.

It was none other than my old friend, Commander Wallis McNealy. As always, his attire consisted of thick furs, mud-covered leather boots and a tartan undershirt. His ragged red beard swung from side to side with every large stride. I was more than pleased with the interruption. He had saved me from thirty or so thousand onlooking eyes.

'Many thanks, dear friend. Allow me a moment to adjourn things here and I will be with you,' I said, waving to him in a childlike and overexcited fashion.

'I forgot that ye be important now, my Lord.' Tilting the heavyweight of his battle-axe over his arm, he chuckled his way out of the hall.

'Wait in the courtyard. The Lord of the Manor will be out to see ye in a mere moment.' Wallace said, his harsh deep voice rumbled in from outside.

'I am now going to lay out the new objectives for the Mainland Division,' I said in my finest Lords voice. 'I have thought long and hard about it. I have considered what it is that we should stand for and that is protection. Protecting the Mainland, The Stronghold, every Division in Mangrove and even the Eastern bay if we must. In two days from now, I will be leading a small expedition through the Mangrove Citadel. I have reason to suspect that some of the foolhardy pirates from the East bay have been entering the Citadel in disguise, stealing anything they might find to be of value, including women. I have heard they take the richest and most powerful citizens from their beds whilst they sleep at night, just for the fun of it. I will hand-select only the finest and bravest to accompany me. That is all...You may be dismissed.'

Making quite the ruckus as they spoke amongst themselves, one unit at a time, the men and women of the Mainland Division, left the larger than life hall, taking the damp stench of old feet with them.

I approached Commander Richard, who was already chomping his way through half a bread roll and said, 'Commander, please bring a dozen of your men out to the courtyard. My furniture has arrived earlier than I had anticipated, and I will require some assistance.'

'Yes, Lord Mace, of course. I have some recruits that would be perfect for the job,' he answered, mumbling and spluttering a mouth full of bread.

'Ben, Franklin, Charley, Alex the boy, Alex the girl and young Toby, get your sorry souls to me…and hurry up about it.'

He pulled a small ruffled up piece of stained parchment from his top pocket and was about to show it to me, but I could bear no more of his mumbling.

'You may be dismissed, Commander.' I made a hasty exit.

17. ~ RELOCATION ~

Five black carriages were lined up by the front courtyard of the Mainland's blue manor, filled with everything I own, along with recently purchased items to fill up the larger than life Manor. I will soon make a home of it.

'What took ye so long...Lord,' Wallace said, admiring one of my old turtle shields from the side of the front carriage.

'Well, I was busy.'

'I be yanking ye chain, Mace. Come on, let's get this junk unloaded. I guess that be your Manor over there?'

'Yes, it is rather grand, is it not?'

'I, be far grander than ye old dark barrack chambers, that's for sure.'

At that moment, Talia came running out from the right side of the Manor, dressed in a fine flowing blue and silver dress, tapered with the most delicate of embroidery work. Shimmering pearls rattled across half the length of her miniature frame, silver dyed leather shoes tapped in the wake of her small step and the smooth blonde of her long hair, that was once locked in knots, was now fresh and flowing. Followed closely by the dark-haired and even darker eyed, Miss Lemon, who wore only the drabbest of long funeral dresses, Talia was lit up with joyful glee. She was happier than I had ever seen her and with Mainland's best nanny at her disposal, I hoped that she always would be. Maybe if I had a Miss Lemon of my own when I was but a boy, the unfortunate ideals of my life would have taken a very different turn.

'Talia dear girl, how do you like the Manor?' I asked, catching her as she jumped into my arms for an embracing cuddle. Though in my heavy suit of thick cased blue armour, I had to be careful not to squash the life out of her.

'Talia likes it very much. It's so big and has so many rooms. How many people will live here?'

'Just you, me and Miss Lemon, though I am sure to have many visitors,' I answered, pulling a piece of chocolate from my robe pocket, that Talia shovelled in so quickly, that she almost choked. I questioned ever giving her another.

'Talia, Lord Mace is busy,' Miss Lemon said, pulling Talia briskly away. 'Come now girl, let us have a look at the courtyard and the gardens.'

I could not help but laugh at Talia's soured expression. She was a handful, that much was clear, but if anyone could teach her how to be a Lady, it was Miss Lemon.

'She is a funny little girl, Mace.' Wallace laughed, slapping my back with a force greater than I had anticipated.

'Yes, she sure is.'

'Can we deliver this damned furniture already? I haven't got all day.' A balding man from the front carriage interrupted, puffing his impatience into on a long handle pipe.

'How dare ye speak like that in front of a Lord,' Wallace threatened. 'Do ye have enough time to lose your wee head I wonder.'

Wallace stored towards the balding man with his great axe held high above his curled red head of hair. He was preparing to decapitate the man.

'Wallace. It is alright,' I said. 'You there, move around to the entrance and start unloading.'

I held Wallace back by the arm and waved the foolish delivery man towards the grand double fronted door of the Manor.

'My Lord, please accept my apologies. My mouth sometimes speaks out before my mind has a chance to tell it what to say,' the man said, shaking as he bowed his head.

'Ye be lucky Lord Mace is so kind, otherwise, your head would be decorating my wall,' Wallace added, slapping the front carriages horse on the thigh, spurring it into a short charge.

Whilst Wallace and I were hoisting a sizable chest of draws from the top of a carriage, Commander Richard, along with a dozen of his recruits arrived in the curved courtyard of the blue manor.

'You wanted help, My Lord, and help is what I have brought you,' he said, chomping through a greasy portion of chicken wings.

'I am glad of the help. Thank you all. Please make a start on this carriage,' I guided them all to the side of the second carriage. 'And be careful, some of these items are incredibly valuable.'

'A home fit for a Lord,' Richard said, burping a breath of foulness from where he leant, relaxed against the side of a carriage.

Usually, I am a patient man. I always have been, but when everybody was pulling their weight and Richard was not, I began to lose my calm. Though I would not put a demand on him, not just yet anyway. This one would need some time, I thought.

'Yes, it is a rather luxurious home.'

It was so much more than just luxurious. Built-in a similar style, yet on a smaller scale to the red tower, it was a sight for sore eyes. High ribbed blue metal walls crept around the outside of the grey brickwork, like great vines growing up from the earth beneath. The internal composition consisted of a large great hall, well-sealed with fine oak, which leads to almost every other room in the Manor. There were fifteen-bed chambers, each containing a worthy bed, stone chimney and wardrobe. To the far east, was the pantry, no more than a stone's throw from the chapel, that I dare not step foot inside, for it was covered with old cracked tiles, oversized engraved figures of demons and an old Alter to a strange god from a past faith. Two grand dining halls ran alongside each of the kitchens, finished with a King-sized table, that was always filled with fresh bread, sweet fruit and chocolate cake for the taking. The newest part of the ancient Manor was the oak shingled granary, an outside building in which the dairy is also contained.

Huge spiked gates surrounded the courtyard and gardens, and the entire Manor was guarded, around the clock, by my men. I would soon find a better use for them.

The Manor would make a fine home for Talia, I thought, marvelling at the building before me. Though I hoped the increased size and age of it would not overwhelm poor her, she was, after all, accustomed to bin picking. Maybe some house animals will do the girl some good, as it did for me when I was just a boy living in my brother's black Manor. 'Commander. Whilst the soldiers carry in my furniture, I will need you to take a message to Lord Noriega, the Beast Chieftain.'

'Yes, of course, my Lord. Though I thought you wanted me here,' he replied, backhanding the grease from his chin.

'The recruits will be more than sufficient, Commander.' I pulled a roll of parchment out from the back part of my chest plate, along with a led tipped pencil and began to mark out a letter.

'I will take it after lunch, my Lord.'

'No…that will not do. I require this to be done immediately,' I insisted. 'It is of the highest importance that this letter reaches the Chieftain as soon as possible.'

He gave me the stare of a simpleton, the sort of stare that would suggest my fairness was unreasonable. I placed a tape seal on the rolled-up letter, passed it over to Richard's grubby hand and continued unloading the carriages. Grumbling as he stood from his leaning position, he was soon out of sight and out of mind.

18. ~ DISCUSSION ~

Meanwhile, Dame Lambert, raging with anger, stormed north through the wide-open streets of the Mainland Division. She passed the grand Arc stadium and the blood-red tower on her way to the calming beauty of the King's cross gardens. A favourite spot for those looking to rest their weary heads or gather a splash of inspiration.

It was filled with bright colourful flowers and thick with smooth indulgent scents. The finest sculpture work in the land surrounded the golden apple trees at the centre. Though it never really drew my attention. There was always something to ruin my mood in those gardens, be it an advancing swarm of buffalo bees or an army of pollinated plants to set my eyes itching. No matter the time of day or season of the year, I could not bear to waste a second, let alone hours, indulging in those disappointingly famous gardens.

'Damn it, damn it, damn it all to hell,' Lambert screamed as she marched across the freshly cut garden grass.

She was so stiff in her tense way of walking, that she looked unwell and rather uncomfortable. Her fingers left marks on her palms from constant fist clenching. Her step staggered from side to side, like that of an old arthritic woman and her face was so creased with discussed, that she could quite easily be mistaken for a demon.

She slumped beside a nearby wall, that was made entirely of uneven stones and sharp-edged rocks. She went from resentment to sadness in a matter of moments. She was alone with her thoughts, or so it would seem. The truth is, there was always a watchful shadow lurking around the King's cross gardens.

Lambert cried out her sorrow, she cried out for the loss of her old Lord, she cried out because it was all she could do when her mind was no longer able to comprehend the pain of her aching heart.

'What is with that sour look on your face?' Lord Mantis whispered, surprising Lambert as he looked down at her from the top of the very wall she sat below.

'What does it matter to you?' she replied, wiping the tears from under her eyes. 'Stop your smirking and leave me alone. I'm not in the mood for your jests at this moment in time, Mantis.'

'Pathetic,' he answered. 'You are a Dame…not a very good one, but a Dame none the less and you should not be seen in such a way.'

Mantis was no longer atop the misshapen wall, where Lambert had expected him to be and as fast as the changing wind, he was beside her, smirking as he stared at her with an untamed wildness in his dark eyes.

'For goodness sake, Mantis, stop arsing around.' Lambert was aware of the silly games Mantis liked to play and he liked to play them more often than was funny.

'I guess you've heard the rumours?' Lambert said, scowling. 'If you think you can come here and mock me, Mantis Black, I will beat you to within an inch of your life.'

She did not blink, nor look away from his penetrating stare of sarcasm. Mantis was more than twice her size and had power beyond her imagination, but she would not be crossed, not today. She meant every word of her conviction and would not be made a fool of when she felt like this.

'And why would I do something like that?' Mantis replied 'I was just enjoying the view from the top of this ugly wall when my peace was disturbed by your whimpering. To be honest Lambert, I really could not care less about your Division or the rumours surrounding your old Lord.'

'Could you not have just left me alone, instead of making me feel worse than I already do.'

'I was going to tell you something about my little brother, but…oh what was it now. I appear to have forgotten.' Mantis smirked with a sarcastic grin.

'What is it Mantis? Stop playing games and just tell me will you,' she snapped.

It was easy to see that Lambert was not the most patient of Dames, but when it came to obtaining information about her new Lord, she was downright demanding.

'Just be careful, Lambert. I have been watching you act an absolute imbecile ever since my brother became Lord of the Mainland. Do not get me wrong, Mace is weak-willed and he does not appear very strong, but he has power. Deep within him is an uncontrolled strength, that left unchecked could spell the end for us all. You are too weak to understand, so you will just have to trust me,' he said, squashing the point of his nose against her cheek. 'His power scares me, Lambert.'

'What was that?' Lambert said, disturbed by a rustling in the rose bush across the path.

'How long do you plan on watching us?' Mantis roared, pointing the tip of his enormous sword towards the bush, but there was no answer. 'I am growing impatient.'

Mantis strolled casually towards the rustling bush. The way my brother walked, was not only very haunting but quite majestic. He appeared weightless above the ground, like a cushioned blanket of air was always beneath his feet.

When Mantis was close enough to cleave the rose bush in half, along with anyone hidden inside, a plume of smoke rushed out. More and more smoke rose to the surface and as it floated above the bush, it began to form into the figure of a woman. Mantis gaped on in horror.

'This is it, Lambert...Ethereal,' he said, reaching out to the ghostly figure.

'Why do you look so pleased with yourself, Mantis?' Lambert stepped to the side of him. 'I do not exactly know what it is, but it is no curse. I have seen them for many years. They dwell in the far north, floating around without purpose.'

The Ethereal woman reached out to Mantis and as a strong gust of wind whirled through the gardens, it ripped the woman apart.

'You cannot leave. I have not finished with you,' Mantis said, as he dropped to his knees.

'It will return. It is following you.' Lambert paused and reached out to feel the last remnants of smoke pass through the air. 'Many years ago, in the northern farmlands, I was followed by one of those Ethereal figures, as you like to call them. At first, it frightened me, then I became fond of it and after enough time had passed, I came to understand it.'

'What is it then?' Mantis could not contain his anticipation for an answer.

'It is a spirit, Mantis. It is the living figure of lost life. These Ethereal figures have an unfished business and are unable to rest in peace.' Lambert looked to the vast emptiness of the sky. 'That woman has unfinished business with you, as my dear brother once did with me.'

'Let me get this straight...you, my most trusted of friends, believes that a dead woman has taken the form of grey smoke, and is following me around because I am something to do with her unfinished business.' Mantis gave Lambert a look of dissatisfaction, the same look he gave to simpletons. 'You are a fool, Lambert. Everything out of the ordinary in this world is cursed or under the effects of a curse and to think otherwise is ignorant.'

'How dare you.' Lambert pulled her curved sword from its sheath.

'I am sorry, Lambert. Perhaps I have overstepped the mark,' he said, as Lambert slid the sharp curve of her steel sword back into its blue sheath. 'Your knowledge of the Ethereal form is invaluable and will shed some much-needed light on my research.'

'Mantis, please tell me more about your brother?' Lambert asked, receiving no reply.

Mantis stared ahead, lost in thought. This annoyed Lambert. Like most people, she did not respond well to ignorance. She closed her eyes, took a calming breath and realised, after counting down from five, that he was gone, vanished like a flame on a winter's wind.

19. ~ CONTENTMENT ~

Lambert was no longer in any mood to be sat in the King's cross gardens, nor was she willing to be distracted by any further foolishness or misfortune. She wanted her Commanders and her new Lord to see her clearly again.

She returned to the blue manor, which was at the furthest end of the Division, overlooking the outer wall of the south gate. After a brief stroll through the Manor gardens, she walked up to the end carriage of the courtyard.

'What is all this?' Lambert asked, smirking in my general direction.

This was very much unexpected. Lambert never smiled, nor did she grin or look pleased in any way. For a moment, I thought she had turned over a new leaf, but when I saw how she tentatively held the hilt of her sword, I knew I was being drawn into a false sense of security.

'Those be the looks of a woman scorned, or in need of some affection,' Wallace said, strolling casually to my side.

'Why is every member of the bloody Shadow Division on my case today.' She glared at Wallace. 'And what the hell is going on here?'

She glared at the recruits and carriage drivers. She glared at everyone, except for me.

'We be unpacking for Lord Mace. He moves into the Manor,' Wallace answered.

'What bloody move?' Lambert screamed.

Wallace was so unconcerned at Lambert's lack of conduct, that he answered in his usual upbeat attitude. 'Haven't ya heard, young Lord Mace be taking residence in the blue Manor today. I would have thought everyone knew that a Lord must live in a Manor.'

'Yes…indeed.' She snorted in disgust.

'You look thirsty, Lambert. Have some water,' I said, offering her a drink from the large canteen bottle beside the end carriage.

I half expected her to slap it from my hands, but she did not and for that, I thought a little better of her.

'It is nice to make your acquaintance, Dame Lambert,' Wallace said, holding his hand out to Lambert. 'I must be attending to other matters now.'

She looked away with a snort of derision.

'I think she likes ya, Mace.'

'She has a funny way of showing it,' I said. 'Thank you for all your help, old friend. You are always welcome here.'

Wallace laid a hand on my shoulder and took his leave.

'Don't speak to me like I'm not here, Mace.' Lambert yelled out. 'What have all you infantry recruits got to say for yourselves. Well, out with it.'

The recruits were too nervous to answer.

'Out with it, I say.'

I was just about to interject when a brave soul stepped forward and said in a soft tone, 'Lord Mace is moving into the blue Manor today, my Dame. We are simply helping him.'

He was young, brave and incredibly tall, with a strange knot of hair that sagged over the side of his shaven head.

'What is your name?' Lambert asked as she approached the nervously twitching recruit.

'My name is, Franklin.'

'Leave the poor boy alone, Lambert,' I said, leaning back on the yet to be unloaded end carriage.

She immediately forgot about Franklin and turned her aggression towards me. 'You, Mace Black, are no Lord of mine. This entire situation is beyond me. Just thinking about you moving all your belongings into Lord Bricks home makes me sick to my stomach.'

As I watched her pace across the courtyard, I wondered how long I should endure her insolent and childlike tantrums before I punished her. It was within my power to do so, but I was hesitant. I did not want to worsen her suffering. Besides, she was now my Dame and the Mainland Division have come to love and respect her. There must be a way of getting through to her.

'I am moving into the Blue Manor, Dame Lambert. You know that...I know that, and every man, beats and woman in Mangrove knows that I am moving,' I said. 'I asked some of the infantry recruits for assistance. Do not get me wrong, I do feel bad for asking, but as you can see, there is no real way I could have managed to move all of this on my own.'

She stood with a vague expression on her frowning face. She was not impressed.

'I will not accept this. You are in Lord Brick's home for pity's sake.'

'Pity has nothing to do with it, Lambert. You have lost someone very close to you. I understand your pain, I really do. But this is now my home, just as it has been for every Lord of this Division and every Division that has ever had, or will have, a Lord or Lady in command.'

'I understand completely. I just refuse to accept you as my Lord.' She drew her curved sword and aligned it with my throat. 'Don't just stand there, do something…coward.'

She snarled, pushing her sword closer and deeper into my throat.

'I will not raise arms against you, Lambert,' I answered, wishing that my new sword was not halfway across the courtyard. 'You will just have to kill me.'

Lambert did not cut my throat, nor did she stab or sever any part of me. Instead, she sliced, again and again, into the thick black wood of the last carriage on the courtyard. With every slice of Lambert's savage sword, the carriage became less sturdy and less able to hold the weight of its load. Eventually, the carriage caved in on itself. Ancient pots smashed over solid copper pans, antique wooden spears snapped under the weight of stone carvings, and the metallic bowl, from which Maxi used to drink, fell to my feet. Luckily, the bowl was unharmed. It held more sentimental value than any other treasure in that carriage.

The well-worked steed, after being jolted back by the caved-in the carriage, stayed surprisingly calm. It was as if the poor horse had seen worse and was not at all phased by the fast swings of Lambert's sword or the loud crashing sounds that came with it.

'Carriage driver,' I called out, ignoring Lamberts immature acts of aggression.

'Yes, my Lord,' he answered, hid behind a low wall on the other side of the courtyard.

'Please accept my sincerest apologies for the destruction of your carriage. Will you accept this as recompense.' I threw a small purse, containing no less than twenty gold coins, across to the man.

As he jumped to catch the purse, he tripped over his own feet. From the flat of his back, he looked inside the purse and beamed with joy. 'That's too much, my Lord. This is only a carriage. It cost me four gold when it was new and that was eleven years ago.'

'You are pathetic, Mace Black. Pathetic,' Lambert said, sheathing her sword as she strolled off into the distance.

Yet again, I took no notice of her.

'That gold is not for the carriage, it is for the horse,' I said to carriage driver.

'He isn't worth half a silver, my Lord. He's as blind as a bat and as slow as a pig. But if it pleases you, my Lord, by all means, have him,' he answered.

'That is exactly what I will do. This blind carriage horse is braver than he looks. He can now frolic in the blue Manor gardens and ride Talia around to his heart's content.'

Commander Richard approached at pace, holding a small Snowbear by the lead. 'My Dame…Dame Lambert.'

He stepped up to the courtyard. He was concerned about Lambert. She did not answer his call, nor at the very least, look back at her loyal Commander. She just walked away.

'Where is she going?' he asked.

'Do not worry about her. She needs time.'

I admired the little Beast cub that crawled by my feet. It was perfect. A Snowbear, even as a cub, is one of the strongest Beasts this side of the great ocean, and from Richard's struggle that was clear to see. Not only would the cub make for a great house Beast, but was also the crest of the Black clan. It was the best choice of Beast.

20. ~ EXPERIENCE ~

Talia spent her first night of blissful slumber in the Blue Manor. She was more than comfortable in her very own duck feathered bed for the first time in many years. It was a luxury she had only ever dreamed of. At first, the silence of the Manor was strange and haunting in the dark of the night, but after a few hours of well-deserved rest, she felt right at home.

I sat with Talia this morning, overlooking the beauty of the Mainland gardens. She was loving her new life, especially when she could make daisy chains in one of the finest botanical gardens in the land. The thirty acres of natural beauty was a little slice of paradise in this hard and bloody world. There were thousands of plant species, in colours that would make a rainbow appear dull, growing around the central woodland trail. Ancient sculptures, depicting the Beast war, surrounded the outskirts of the gardens, giving it historical merit.

Soldiers walked by, offering their greetings and jesting with Talia. One friendly old gardener, hunched and grey, played with her for a while, until she became tiresome and snuggled under my arm.

'Mace,' Talia said, looking up with her bright eyes.

'What is it, Talia?'

'Have you found Talia's father?' she asked, pulling herself up on me.

I did not know what to say to her. I have been thinking long and hard on the matter, losing sleep and concentration over it and I was no closer to an answer than I was on the night I met her.

'Dear Talia, I am sorry. I have not yet found him,' I answered, stroking her freshly washed and cut blonde hair.

'What a shame,' was all she said.

I half expected her to be sad at this, but she smiled, then hugged me. It was as if she was thanking me, for putting every effort into the search for her father. I felt guilty and dishonest. I could not keep lying to her, I thought, watching a couple of small black birds fight over a small stick in the distance.

'Nice weather we are having,' Commander Richard said, surprising Talia and me, as he sat down beside us. He was with a rather large and hairy soldier, who remained silent and nervously nodding in my direction. I was curious as to what he wanted.

'Nice and s…sunny, my Lord,' The large man stuttered, spitting on every word of his struggled pronunciation.

'Yes, it is rather pleasant,' I answered.

'Where are my manners. Lord Mace, this is private Frances. He's a big fan of yours and one of my infantrymen,' said Richard. 'Well, he was, until he suffered a nasty blow to the head. He now spends his days in the rehabilitation ward at the medical research Division.'

'And why are you telling me this?'

'He's not got long for this world, my Lord.' Richard moved in close. 'After seeing you in combat against the Chieftain, he's been eager to meet you. I wish only to honour him with your presence if it would please you, my Lord.'

I smiled and laid a hand on his shoulder. Richard, it would seem, was an honourable man after all.

'I hear you are a fine soldier, Frances,' I said, feeling sorry for the large man's suffering.

Frances laughed and became childishly shy.

'My Lord, Frances is not the only reason I am here,' Richard said. 'May we speak privately?'

'Talia, will you please run to the Manor and let the cub out,' I asked. 'Oh, and ask Miss Lemon to arrange some lunch.'

She skipped happily towards the glass doors at the rear of the Manor.

'My Lord, the men are talking,' Richard said. 'Rumours have spread of an assault on the South point and they are frightened.'

He appeared nervous just mentioning the South point. Though he was right to be nervous. Any venture through the cursed mountains, that lead to the South points rebel headquarters and the ancient city of Whiterun was a suicidal mission at best. It is said that the walls of Whiterun have never been breached and all those brave enough to attempt it, have never returned.

'Please Commander, do not believe everything you hear. Yes, there will be an assault, but it will be carried out by the Elite force and only after thorough surveillance. It is a task far above the training and rank of Mainland soldiers. Now, on a day like this, I plan on enjoying the peace of this world. One should, after all, be able to relax and enjoy life.'

'Yes, my Lord.' Richard was relieved.

He began to chuckle, as did I until I noticed Frances looking up at the sky with glazed eyes. He fell to his left, groaning as he jerked his arms and legs around furiously. I jumped up in shock and Commander Richard lifted him into an upright sitting position. Saliva foamed from his mouth. He went pale and struggled to breathe. As the jerking motion slowed, his arms, wrists and fingers curled up and went stiff. A moment later, Richard slapped the man's cheeks, bringing his eyes back from there glazed form and colour back to his pale face.

'I am, so s…sorry,' Frances said, before wiping the rank dribble from his chin and slumping back into Richard's arms.

'What the bloody hell was that?' I abruptly asked, reaching for the golden pommel of my sword. 'Is he losing control? Because if he is…if he becomes a demon, I will not hesitate to kill him.'

'He has a condition, my Lord. Its disturbers the function of his brain…Look.' Richard tilted Frances's face to one side, showing many scars atop his greying head.

'I will ask you again, Commander.' I held my sword high, ready to strike. 'Is he losing control?'

'No, he is not losing control,' Richard answered in a panic, throwing himself between Frances and the tip of my sword. 'Please, my Lord, put your sword down.'

Frances faded into a deep slumber. I threw my sword to the earth, leaving it standing vertically. Calling for the guards, I pulled Richard up from his crouched position by the crease of his chest plate.

'If he turns, I am going to kill you,' I whispered, nose to nose with Richard.

He could not look me in the eye. I dropped him to the flat of his back and as I did, three guards arrived, clanking as they ran in blue and white armour.

'Guards, take the sleeping man to the medical research Divisions rehabilitation ward. Commander Richard, please join me for a drink and some lunch in the seating area.'

We sat on a long and curved bench. It was finely engraved with leaves and plants. I was enjoying the sight of Talia running around with the snow bear cub. It walked to the side of a small rabbit, lifted his back leg and let his bladder loose over the innocent little rodent. It turns out it is a male.

Richard and I sipped on cold ciders, whilst Miss Lemon brought out tray after tray of the finest meats and bread. Richard must have eaten his body weight. He slapped his belly and burped after fully indulging himself. He gained a scornful look from the very prim and proper, Miss Lemon.

'Please excuse me, my Lord,' Richard said, crunching on a leftover morsel of pork rind. 'We have been relaxing for quite some time now. Is there no business to attend?'

'Enjoy your downtime. It is not as if we are on alert or in wartime,' I raised my glass for the overindulgent Commander to clink with his own.

'What the hell are you both doing. Why are you lounging around when there is work to be done?' Dame Lambert screamed as she stormed over to spoil the mood.

'Good afternoon, Dame. Will you join us?' I asked, shewing the snow bear away.

The Beast was already sharpening its claws on the wooden bench and left quite a mess in the downstairs meeting hall. I was hesitant to let him near Lambert.

'You are a lazy oaf. What the hell are you doing?' Lambert shouted.

She frightened Talia to tears and caused her to run into the Manor, closely followed by the cub.

'Miss Lemon,' I called out.

'Say no more, my Lord.' She followed Talia into the Manor.

'To answer your question, Dame. I was relaxing, enjoying the peace and beauty of the gardens. Such serenity is a treat,' I said, remaining calm.

'You are both sitting here being Lazy and setting a bad example for the soldiers.' Lambert stood with clenched fists.

'Dame, please. I asked Commander Richard to join me for Lunch.'

'Yes, Richard.' She pointed her curved sword at him. 'You should know better than to indulge in this laid-back approach to life.'

He slurped the last drop of cider from his glass and nervously wiped the moisture from his brow.

'During a lifetime, one must enjoy a moment to relax and ponder on life, for it is short,' I said, taking an uninterested approach to this ongoing situation.

'You're far too relaxed to be a Lord. You're going to ruin this great Division, aren't you?' Lambert was red in the face. 'I have made it very clear, that I do not accept you personally as Lord of the Mainland Division. If deep down, you want the best for this Division and its reputation, then you must prove it.'

She pulled her curved sword from its scabbard. Richard looked on in shock. He was unaware of what to do, as this situation was well above his rank or skill level.

'Very well, Dame. If we must,' I said. 'You have dishonoured me and challenged me to combat. I will accept, only if the form of combat is hand to hand. There is no need to bloody ourselves with blades.'

'Fair enough.' Lambert smirked.

As Lambert and I entered the centre of the gardens, opposite the woodland trail, Richard and, at least, twenty other men, including my guard unit, began to form a ring around us. I untied the scruff of my robe and removing my blue chest plate, I revealed the scarring on my pale chest for all to see.

'Let's do this,' Lambert roared, spinning full circle and kicking at the empty air.

Spectators filled in around the edges of the gardens. They were all eager with anticipation. Traditionally, one would bow to their opponent, showing respect, so I did. I made sure not to take my eyes away from Lambert. She looked away with a snort of derision. She was either showing her inexperience in the ways of traditional combat or just lacking in respect altogether. The very next moment, she was running towards me.

'You know what it is that you must do,' I said to myself, lowering into a sturdy defensive position.

Lambert launched herself forward and jumped high into the air. Doubling back on herself in mid-air, she extended her left leg and in readiness to break my jaw, she curled her body in a downwards motion. She put on an impressive display, especially for such a small woman.

If I had not reacted at that very moment, I would be laid out on the flat of my back. I put one hand up to block her leg and with the other, I flung her across the garden. She landed on her feet. I smiled at her and made sure that she was watching every move I made.

I ran at her, lunging towards her throat with a wide elbow, that if followed through, would leave her with more than just a bruise. Fortunately for Lambert, I did not make contact, nor did I ever mean to. I stopped my attack at the last conceivable moment and left myself wide open. I made no effort to block her advancement. She stuck her knee into my gut and punched up at my face, splitting my lip wide open. I was knocked to the soft earth. She looked down at me with a puzzled and confused look in her eyes. She was unsure of what to make of my actions.

'He didn't even try. He is so slow. What a pathetic excuse for a Lord,' whispered the circle of spectators.

I smirked at Lambert from the side of my bloody mouth. She turned and ran through the woodland trail, leaving her sword and scabbard behind.

'Are you alright, my Lord?' Asked Richard, kneeling beside me.

'I am fine, Commander.' I flipped up from my back and onto my feet in one swift motion.

I hastily departed into the gardens, avoiding eye contact with the onlooking spectators.

I strolled alone for some time, pondering on the spectacle I had made of myself until I noticed Commander Snake in the distance. He stood solemnly beside a blueberry bush. He was watching me. I could see the gleam in his shallow green eyes.

'Commander Snake. Are you well?' I asked, waving in his general direction.

He said nothing and smiled with a sense of gratitude. I knew from this singular gesture, that Snake had witnessed my short combat with Lambert and knew very well, that I allowed her victory. Though I do not recall seeing him in the crowd. Either way, I had not the time nor patience to dwell upon Snakes whereabouts during the combat, nor why he chooses to stand alone in the Manor gardens. At this moment in time, my thoughts were on Lambert. I thought about how stupid I had been and if gaining her respect was worth a split lip. I could have easily defeated her, but I spared her from embarrassment. At the very least, I felt pride in myself. It was the sort of pride that only comes from doing an honest bit of good.

21. ~ REALISATION ~

The night was drawing in. I took Talia up the steep, winding staircase of the Manor and into her bed-chambers. In one corner of the bright pink room, lay a pile of stuffed animal toys and a few princes dolls, half-chewed and slobbered on by the yet to be trained snow bear. A white bunk bed stood tall next to the double-paned window, with a pink and puffed up sofa adjacent, layered with an array of Talia's strange drawings. Some of these drawings were of horned horses and sunny beaches. Others were more ominous. Red-eyed clawing shadows, heads on spikes and the most concerning of all, was of a bleeding woman, hanging out of a carriage wreck. It was just as it had been all those years ago when I first encountered the agents of the South point.

Talia was growing on me and in the short time I had known her, she had become so much more than a mere companion. She had become a friend. She had become family. I would be proud to call her my own. She was not an ordinary little girl, that much, at least, was clear. There was something rather unnerving in the way she stared with empty eyes and in the way that she always seemed to know where I was, even when I meant to be unseen.

'Mace,' Talia said.

'Yes, dear Talia. What appears to be troubling you?'

'Talia wanted to name the Beast. Is Talia allowed?' she replied, with the look of a lost puppy dog.

'Well, yes. I do not see why not.' She put her arms out for me to pick her up.

I pulled her up and held her at arm's length. She smiled curiously, and I wondered what sort of strange name she would come up with. 'What did you have in mind?'

'Fishbone,' she said.

'Why that name?' I was abrupt with her. 'Where did you hear that name?'

'Talia saw the Beast eating fish bones from the bin. It made Talia laugh.'

She was so innocent and unaware of those names meaning. I was glad that it was only a coincidence and she meant not to name the young cub after a long-dead rebel from the South point.

'Perhaps...another name. Do you have any others in mind?'

'Ice cream,' she said.

'Ice cream,' I repeated, with a raised brow and a half-smile.

'Talia wants to call him, Ice cream. He licked Talia's Ice cream today.'

'Undoubtedly a delicious name, but perhaps we could compromise and call him, Ice. I would feel rather a silly fool shouting, Ice cream, whenever I mean to gain the snow bears attention.' Talia exaggerated her nod in agreement. 'When the cub wakes from his sleep, I will tell him that his name is now, Ice. But for now, it is bedtime. Good night, Talia.'

She put her arms out and I gave her a quick hug, before adjourning to the living room.

The warmth of the fire hit me as I opened the creaky door of the living room, which momentarily disturbed Ice's slumber. He saw that it was I and rolled over, flopping his tongue out of one side of this mouth.

Miss Lemon sat comfortably with her legs up on the corner sofa of the living room, sipping on a cup of fresh-smelling tea. A black blanket covered her legs and a plump pillow cushioned her back.

Just after pouring myself a cup of tea from the pot on the centre table, I sat gently on the sofa opposite Miss Lemon. I raised my cup to her in thanks for brewing the pot.

At that moment, three tremendous thuds echoed at the front door. Ice jumped up in shock, ran over to the living room door and sniffed deeply for any scent.

'Allow me,' Miss Lemon said, slowly edging herself upright.

'No...I will go. Keep Ice in here.'

'So, you are called Ice now,' Miss Lemon said, smiling and clapping her hands together.

That was how she taught him to come to her and without a second thought, he did just that. He was appearing to gain more obedience with every passing day.

Mantis and two of his guards were glaring back at me through the glass square at the top of the front door. They all looked rather serious. Mantis wore his usual extravagant attire. A purple and fur-lined poker dot robe, over clunky golden armour. His sword was in one hand, and with the other, he held a marionette puppet up to the glass.

His house guards, who were almost as brightly coloured as he was, wore yellow robes over their black leather jackets. One was tall and balding, whilst the other was short and hairy. They both carried long swords over their shoulders.

This was an unpleasant surprise. Mantis always finds a way to stir up trouble and I doubted that this would be any different, though he was my brother and I could not turn him away, nor his guards.

'Hello brother. What do I owe the pleasure?' I said, lifting a huge metal lock to one side and pulling open the double oak doors.

'You do not seem too satisfied to see your dear older brother,' Mantis said, with a hint of sarcasm, as he handed over the marionette and strolled in like he owned the place, guards in tow. 'I have been thinking about our little conversation. I may have acted unreasonably and am now ready to talk.'

'Greetings, Lord Mace,' the tallest of the two guards said, as he ducked under the door frame.

'Lord Mace,' The smaller guard said, bowing as he walked past.

'Do not pay any notice to those two. The tall one with a baby face is, Marko and the small unshaven one is, Grey. They are merely escorting me. They are good company...more than useless at almost everything and as weak as cats, but they do make for good company,' Mantis said, laughing as he always does.

I do not think that it has ever occurred to him, that he can be quite insulting. Though the guards did not help themselves. They just stood there, blank-faced and only smiling when Mantis made eye contact with them.

'Come, sit in front of the fire and help yourselves to some tea. Miss Lemon has just brewed a fresh pot.'

I placed the marionette on the corner table of the hall.

'Brother, I must insist that we speak in private. Only for a moment,' Mantis said, pulling my arm back as I opened the living room door.

'Yes, of course. You two can sit in the lounge. Enjoy a cup of tea and show Miss Lemon the same courtesies that you would show me.' I turned my attention to Mantis. 'We will talk in the side office, brother.'

I opened the living room door and Ice came running out, sniffing at the legs and feet of Mantis and his guards.

'A fitting pet, Mace. It has been a long time since I have laid eyes upon a snow bear. He should make for quite the house guard,' Mantis said, feeling the muscles along Ice's back legs and up to his jawline until Ice ran back to the lounge.

In my office, I sat on one side of my black glass and curved desk. Laying my arms relaxingly across the top of it and peering into my reflection, I realised that my silver hair was getting long. It was due to be cut.

Mantis sat opposite, looking around the book-filled and boring room. 'We may both be Lords now brother, but you need help with your décor. There is not a single ounce of life in this room.'

Mantis chuckled to himself. He laid his claymore across his lap and randomly pulled a pink rose from his pocket, which he placed in my quill pot.

'What do you think of little Lambert Crow?' Mantis asked, leaning forward.

'She is a pain,' I replied.

My brother burst into a fit of laughter. For a moment, I joined him. I was not sure why, as Dame Lambert was no laughing matter, but I could not resist. Mantis was finding everything very amusing until he stopped laughing abruptly and began staring deep into my eyes.

'Listen, Mace. Lambert was very close to Lord Brick. He was like a father to her. Witnessing his brutal murder took its toll on her. It changed her. You will find it as hard as stone to win her over.'

Mantis looked sympathetic. There was no more humour in his cold eyes, nor laughter in his sharp and featureless face. This was serious. Mantis cared about Lambert's well-being and how our relationship if ever there could be one, was going to blossom.

'Did you know, that Dame Lambert was given her manly name by her father, against her mother's wishes,' Mantis said with a serious tone in his voice. 'Shortly after Lambert's birth, her mother was found at the bottom of the sea dog's river. Her father, at the time, was the Commander of the Mainland Divisions Infantry unit. At the age of five, she was trained in the most ruthless of martial arts and survival techniques. At ten, she was shipped overseas to a prestigious military school for boys, where she was mercilessly raped and beaten. At twelve, she ran away. She ran to the jungle and after surviving alone for many years, she decided it was time for revenge. She set that military school on fire and killed everyone unlucky enough to have survived the blaze. After that, Lambert sailed home and for a short time, she lived a normal life. She worked her way up the ranks of the Mainland Division and fell in love with a young cavalryman. Despite her father's disapproval, she planned to marry the man and on her wedding night, her world was changed forever…Her soon to be husband was found floating down the of the sea dog's river. She knew very well, that it was her father's doing and when she confronted him about it, he struck her. That was the last thing he ever did. Lambert wrapped her slim little legs around his throat and squeezed and squeezed until no breath reached his lips.'

Mantis was very serious. His words came with an air of warning.

'Why are you telling me this, brother?' I asked, pouring Mantis a tumbler of rum.

I could not stomach a drink after hearing such a story. The miseries of my life were pale in comparison to Lamberts.

'Well, I should not really be telling you any of what I have. Though, I feel you need to know. I feel you need to understand Lambert if you are ever to gain her respect.' Mantis gulped his rum and slammed the tumbler down.

'After she had murdered her father, she hung herself and would have died, if it were not for Lord Brick Bison. He cut her down and took her under his wing from then on. He educated her, respected her and showed her the etiquette of a Lady. Now that he is dead, she may once again resort to her suicidal tendencies. Mace, I keep a few friends and even less family, so please be careful with her.'

Mantis continued to drink until my decanter of rum was half empty. He smoothed the hair from his face and revealed the tears that ran down his cheeks. He was deeply saddened at the thought of Lambert killing herself. I had no idea that he felt compassion, nor that he would ever express his feelings in my presence.

'She is taking my promotion quite badly and from what you say, I can see why,' I said. 'I have done what I can to get along with her, to no avail. She continues to challenge me at every turn, yet I cannot bring myself to punish her. I believe there is a better way of getting through to her, but it seems that no matter what I do, I will never win her over.'

With tears wet on his face, Mantis began to chuckle out loud. He was either trying to mask his emotions with humour or was feeling the early effects of the rum.

'Are you really giving this your all, little brother. I certainly am no expert when it comes to Dame Lambert, but as a man, who has sat Lordship for over fifteen years, you should hear me out.' Mantis leant back in his chair.

'Yes, go on. I am listening,' I said.

'Those chosen to command should sympathise with those who serve,' he said. 'Do things as you see fit, Mace and if it turns out that no one follows you, then perhaps you are not suitable to lead.'

'Since when have you been the type to care about how others feel,' I replied.

'Ever since they made you a Lord.'

He looked me up and down like he knew something that I did not. He stood up, crossed his arms over his claymore and peered out of the window, into the ever-darkening night.

'Why does my Lordship concern you?'

'Why does anything happen, brother? Why do you have a little girl now? Why does she have a picture of our father? Why has the King given you a bloody Lordship in the first place? It all seems far too convenient…doesn't it.'

'I am afraid of what to say. I have no real answer, except that Talia and I are connected in some way.'

'May I see her,' he asked.

'Well, I do not see why not. Just be quiet…she is sleeping.'

I was hesitant. I was unsure of his intentions, but I trusted my brother, more than I trusted myself. He has, after all, saved my life and been there for me when no one else has.

The house was silent. Not a word was uttered from the lounge and when Mantis and I walked past and up the staircase, we assumed there was an awkward silence between Mis lemon and the guards. I thought nothing of it and continued up the stairs. Mantis followed close behind, making quite a racket in his full suit of armour.

At the top of the stairs and towards the left, was Talia's bed chambers. A pink stencil of her name lay fresh on the top of the door. I gently pushed it open and put my finger on my lip, gesturing for Mantis to be silent.

'At least she has a splash of colour on her walls,' Mantis whispered, holding his laughter in his hands.

He walked past me and picked up a small bear-shaped toy from the floor. He admired it and held it up in front of the dim lights that lay across the window sill. He placed the bear gently next to Talia's head and leaning down with his ear to her chest, he listened to her heartbeat.

I waited by the door and assumed that he would only take a quick look at her, but he continued to examine her, feeling her skin and smelling her breath for some time. Mantis was a strange man, who did strange things, so I thought nothing of it.

'Grey, Marko,' Mantis shouted, staring at me without expression.

As I went to shut him up, wondering why he would act so carelessly, I was stopped. The guards had a grip on my arms and they each had a long sword to my throat. Talia woke from her sleep and let out the mightiest of high-pitched screams. She did not move nor make another sound. She was frozen with fear.

'Mantis, what the hell are you doing,' I shouted.

I struggled and struggled to free myself from the guard's grip, but I could not move and the harder I tried, the deeper their swords cut into my throat.

At that moment, Mantis grabbed Talia by the front of her face and with one strong hand, yanked her up. She struggled to breathe. She could not get free and scratched at my brother's arms with all her might.

'Mantis...stop,' I shouted, blood dripping from my throat and tears streaming down my face.

Mantis did not stop, nor did he say a word in reply. He stared at me with a disappointed look on his face. It was as if I had done something to displease him and he was punishing me for it.

Mustering all my strength, I pulled my head back and away from the guard's longswords. I wrenched my arm free from the smaller and considerably weaker guard, breaking his nose with the back of my head as I did so. An explosion of blood shot out from his nose. He dropped his sword and fell to his knees.

Turning back on myself, I swung around and smashed my elbow into the taller guard's ribs. I struck hard and I stuck fast, but it had little effect. Though it did distract the man enough for me to slip my arm free.

He turned to me, swinging his sword wildly from one side to another. I easily dodged every swing of his sword and punched him repeatedly in the gut, until he bent down, holding his stomach. That was when I punched him in the throat. He fell to his back and began gasping for breath. He dropped his sword and as the last ounce of life fled from his eyes, he spat blood and a throatful of bile into my face. I was in such a rage, that I bent down and continued to punch at his throat until I was soaked in blood and nothing more than flesh remained in the cracks of the floorboards.

Suddenly a stabbing pain shot through my chest. I could barely move. All I could think was how stupid I had been to forget the second guard. I looked down to see the point of his longsword sticking out of my chest and dripping blood into my hands.

'You fool,' Mantis shouted, sliding across the floor with Talia in hand and effortlessly chopping his own guard's head off.

The man's head rolled out in front of me and as his lifeless body fell back with a crash, he landed next to his fellow guard.

'Mantis, why are you doing this?' I mumbled, barely able to make a sound.

My head was light, and my body felt so weak. I was almost unable to take a breath. I pulled on Mantis's armoured leg, but he booted me to one side like I was nothing more than a feeble infant.

'You have not learned a single lesson of my teaching, brother,' he said, swinging his sword across Talia's body with a tremendous force, splitting her in half at the belly.

'Mantis, no…' I screamed, choking on blood as I tried with all my strength to get up.

Looking on, dizzy and traumatised by what my brother had done, I saw Talia's body, lying lifeless before me in two halves. There was no blood, just a black and oily substance squirting out from under her rib cage. No organs were spilling out, just some coloured wires and copper piping in the shape of bones.

'Mace,' Mantis said, leaning down beside me. 'How many times are you going to be fooled, Brother? I have been watching Talia ever since our last conversation, studying her movement's.'

He paused. 'She is a marionette, brother. She is a robotic puppet and I believe she is being controlled by agents of the South point.'

Mantis wiped his claymore clean on one of Talia's blankets. I tried to speak, but just mumbled some incomparable nonsense, whilst blood dribbled from my lip and down my chin. I could barely hold my eyes open. They blurred with glazed vision and became heavy.

'You are probably wondering why I did not just tell you, are you not?' Mantis continued, somehow knowing exactly what I was thinking, as I laid there, no longer able to hold open my eyes. 'It is because you are a fool, Mace. You are so consumed with emotions, that you would never listen to reason. If you knew what I had in mind, you would make efforts to keep me away from Talia. You have always been the same, letting your emotions get the best of you and cloud your judgement. Anyway, you do not seem in the mood for idle chatter, so I will not keep you any longer. And please, for pity's sake, take time as you pass. Think about every move you make before you make it.'

Mantis walked away in a fit of laughter, leaving a trail of bloody footprints in his wake. I could not help but feel an absolute fool. My brother was right. He always was, I thought, remembering that cheerful little girl, who meant so much to me, in such a short space of time. Those thoughts soon turned to hatred and soon drifted from my fading consciousness.

22. ~ REAWAKEN ~

I was surrounded by empty darkness. There was nothing to hear, nothing to feel. As I reached for something, anything, to grab hold of, I fell, but there was no ground to catch my fall, no way of telling which way was up or down. I did not know what I was doing here, but I knew that I did not belong and had to get out.

A cold breeze hit my face, bringing with it the unmistakable smell of strawberries. I tried as hard as I could to move towards the smell, but I had forgotten how to move. I wondered what else I had forgotten. I wondered if I could open my eyes, but had no way of telling in this darkness. I tried to speak, but heard no sound and realised, that I was not breathing. Panic fell over me as I gasped for air and when none came, I tried to scream.

'Help. Help me. I am trapped in here,' I shouted, repeatedly.

There was still no sound and no hope until I heard a voice calling back to me. 'Mace, it is just a dream. Wake up.'

The voice became louder and louder, with that smell again; strawberries. Just as I was giving up hope, I tried to clear my throat and take what I thought would be my last breath. I coughed to clear my throat, hearing the echoing rumble travel up from my chest and out of my mouth. I took my breath and with it, came the hard feeling of a cold floor, the harshness of bright light and the warm comforting feeling of arms being wrapped around me, holding me close.

I took breath after breath, filling my lungs as if it were the last time I ever would. I struggled to make sense of where I was and how I came to be here until it all came flooding back to me.

I felt my chest, where the sword had penetrated. There was nothing for a moment, then a searing pain, that sent a shock rippling through my body. I tried to move, yelping as I did so, but I was too weak to lift my weight. The arms around me became tight and I was hoisted up and onto a white, blood-stained bed, that I must have fallen from.

Looking around from my laid down position on the bed, I saw the refreshing sight of Dame Eva Fang. She looked more beautiful than I had ever remembered. Her black hair was long and flowing, giving off the strong scent of strawberries, that brought a smile to my lifeless lips. She was not in her usual armour and robes, instead, a tight blue dress, that accentuated her breasts, showed every curve of her toned physique. Her sharp-featured face, from the amount of makeup she wore, now appeared rounded and almost plump.

'I am so glad that you are awake,' she said, perched on the edge of the bed, waving her hair in a manner that was most unlike her.

'You look beautiful Eva,' I whimpered, and she considered my dark eyes with the same look of longing, that she considered in the Wormwoods.

She held my hand between hers. 'I am so sorry, Mace.'

'For what?'

'For running off that day in the woods. I was told to do it Mace and I…'

'I do not blame you, or anyone else. I know that you were following orders.'

Peering around the room, I noticed instantly that I was in one of the wardrooms at the medical research Divisions hospital. The white plain room was empty, save from a large cabinet in one corner, a table next to my bedside, filled with colourful flowers and a glass bottle on the ceiling, that was upside down and filled with bright purple liquid. It dripped into a long cord, that to my surprise, was attached to my wrist.

'Mace, please leave it in,' Eva said, full of concern as I tugged on the cord.

I pulled it out anyway, squirting purple liquid over my chest. At that moment, I realised that I was completely naked. Eva's cheeks reddened as I pulled a corner of the bedsheet over myself, covering my manhood, which unfortunately re-opening my wound and soaked my bandage with even more blood than it was already stained with. I coughed up a lump of black phlegm and spat it to the floor. I would have preferred it if Eva had not seen that.

'Eva, that moment we shared in woods, I felt something. I thought it was real at the time, but I am concerned that it may have just been part of your orders to seduce me and inevitably get me to my trials.' I suddenly remembered what Mantis told me and thought that I should be more cautious with to whom I trust.

Her hand was now on top of mine and our eyes fixed on one another. 'No…not at all.' She hesitated. 'I can't stop thinking about you Mace. I have been here for days waiting for you to wake up.'

'What do you mean days? How long have I been here?' I coughed up another rank ball of mucus.

'Five days.'

'Five days,' I yelled out.

She lost her balance, ending up with her arms pressed against the wall behind my head and her face looming inches over my own. I was lost in her passionate brown eyes. The closer she came, the more I wanted her. She closed her eyes and tilted her head. She was going to kiss me, but before any contact was made between us, the door swung open with a crash. Eva jumped up in surprise and without warning, ran out of the room. She wobbled clumsily in her heeled shoes.

In walked the ever-extravagant Sir James, watching Dame Eva leave with a look of puzzlement on his face, whilst bashing his large golden spear on the hard surface of the floor. He put his hand inside of his robe pocket and pulled out a rolled-up parchment. He waved it in front of my face, tut-tutting as a father would to his disobedient child.

'There is no need to get up, Mace. I have been sent here by Lord Mantis with a message from the King, that must be read aloud.' He allowed the parchment to unravel in his hand.

I could not look him in the eye. His grey scaled face was a mess to behold. Flakes of shiny skin dangled from his nose and chin, whilst patches of raw flesh left his pointy featured face unsightly to look upon.

'After many years of addressing you by rank, please do me the same honour,' I said. 'Sir James. I am, after all, in senior ranking command.'

'You are not my senior. I only answer to your brother.'

'I have not the time or patience for this. Do not challenge me, James. My honour or my ranking is above your disrespectful grasp. You can either address me by rank or leave.'

'Lord Mace,' he replied, with a hint of sarcasm. 'I do not seek to challenge you, not today anyway, nor do I wish you any ill will. In fact, your health is in my best interest.'

The hint of a half-smile, that I could not bring myself to trust, lay thick across his scally jawline. He has always thought much less of me. He assumes all my honours have been handed to me on a silver platter.

'You have never seen a man from the Red sand shed his skin, have you?' James asked, changing the subject and nervously running his hand through his sleek black hair. 'We shed once a year, give or take. The older Sandmen shed less and have thin red scales, whereas the women have a hint of blue in their scales. It is a very attractive feature.'

'Must you always come with less than interesting facts about your desert people.'

He tut-tutted once more 'I will read you this parchment, for that is the reason I am here.'

'Yes, please get on with it,' I said.

'It reads; Mace Black, Lord of the Mainland Division and the seventh seat of the King's council. A situation has been brought to my attention, concerning the young girl in your care. I understand that you were unaware of her true nature, as were most on the first contact with her. Lord Mantis Black of the shadow Division, who made this startling discovery, has reason to believe that the South point is behind it and have previously taken an interest in your wellbeing. Therefore, I have no choice but to put you under investigation and as a result, strip you of all your wartime privileges, until you have proven yourself worthy of them. As you may not be aware, the blue Manor has been thoroughly searched, with no suspicions that will require any further action. Miss Lemon has been relieved of her duties and has been sent to the Mangrove Citadel for further questioning. As for your Snowbear, Commander Snake has kindly offered to watch the Beast, until you return from your absence. Kind regards, King Enzo of Mangrove, Lord of the Division lands.'

James held back his smirk. He rolled up the parchment and as he placed it on the small bedside table next to my flowers, he tossed a wax-sealed envelope into my lap.

'That is all it reads. Oh, and this is from Lord Mantis, for your eyes only,' he continued.

'Why were you, of all people, sent with this news?' I asked in harsh tones, annoyed by the King's unjust words.

'I am sorry for your suffering, I am. This letter was going to be read by Lord Mantis. Though after he explained, that you would not be pleased to see him, I offered my services in his place.' James paced around the room, swinging his spear from side to side and appearing overly cheerful.

He began whistling, as he always does. 'Must you Sir James.'

'My apologies, my mind wonders from time to time. I was just thinking about how cruel your brother can be sometimes and how this meeting would have gone quite differently if he were here.'

Surprisingly, James's presence was a relief. He knew the emotional darkness of my brother and understands the pain he causes others. 'You are right about my brother. In the years I have known him, I have yet to understand him.'

'Lord Mantis once broke my arm for being late to supper.'

'That is nothing. When I was ten years of age, he made me tame a Beast bull. He only did it to prove to his friends how strong I was. I barely escaped with my life and for it, I spent three months in a body cast.' We chuckled for a short time.

'Here, take this,' James said.

James handed me a vial, of what looked like thick brown liquid. I took it from him, looked it over and wondered what this strange goo-like substance was. I sniffed it and instantly wished that I had not, for it stank of rotten eggs.

'It is a healing potion, made from the sap of an elder tree. Rub it on your wound and before you know it, you will be fighting fit,' he explained, laying a hand on my shoulder, before walking away.

I opened the envelope from Mantis, finding a ripped piece of parchment and an old foreign coin inside, not unlike my own. After closer inspection, I realised that this was no ordinary coin. It was a piece of eight, though it did not glow with any light, nor look half as luxurious as my own. Each coin had an eight-piece diagram on one side and a crown engraved on the other. I had to assume it belonged to one of the four pirate captains of the East bay, for they were well known for collecting such treasures.

The short message that was scribbled on the ripped parchment reads; dear brother, a gift awaits you in the Baron Dwell. Regain your honour and speak no word of my involvement. Yours faithfully, Lord Mantis Black.

I knew immediately what this meant and had a plan, which would involve Dame Lambert and be the perfect opportunity for us to bond. Though I was hesitant and concerned that this could all just be another one of Mantis's cruel tricks.

'James,' I called out, hearing his spear bashing along the hallway in time with his walk. 'Before you go, would you please assist me?'

James stopped at the end of the hallway and twirled on his toes. Moments later, he opened the door and his half-shed face was pocking through.

'Of course, anything for a Lord.'

'I need you to send word to Dame Lambert, with instruction to meet me in the Mainland hall at first light.'

'It will be done,' he said, tilting his head as the door slammed behind him.

I was alone with my thoughts. Confused notions of my infatuations for Eva, rekindled after only a moment in her company, swam the pool of my mind. An ever-growing hatred for the cowards at the South point, that has turned every trust I once had against me, pulled away at the last remnants of my rational thought. One way or another, the South point will pay for what they have done to me.

23. ~ OBEDIENCE ~

The day was at dawn and the first light was shining through the edges of the curtains, reminding me that I was overdue to meet Dame Lambert at this very moment in time. Slumping out of bed and slowly pulling on some cotton pants, that swung high over my ankles, I noticed that my bandages were not stained with patches of blood. James tree sap was working, just as he said it would. Though I must have been visited by the nurse during the night, as fresh bedding, bandages and a bag of white cotton clothing had been left for me, along with a bowl of chicken casserole, that was still warm and steaming on the bedside table.

I removed my bandages and applied a generous amount of the tree sap, ahead of putting on the cotton top, that was too small for me and stretched over my chest, leaving a revealing gap around my mid-section.

After devouring the bowl of casserole, I made my way out of the medical research Division, losing my way several times in the busy white corridors, that all looked similar and came with an overpowering scent of antiseptic. The sick and injured crowded the corridors. Some were diseased and discoloured, whilst others were missing limbs and sat dead in wheeled chairs.

The Blue Manor, which to my surprise was in better condition than I had remembered, was the tainted memory of Talia. I was filled with an overwhelming sense of sadness.

As I opened the front door, I noticed my armour and robes were freshly cleaned and laid out on the floor, along with my shimmering sword, which was neatly laid across the top of the robe.

Feeling refreshed and rejuvenated, I put on my leathers and armour. I struggled to reach the clasp at the top of my chest plate and so, I swung my furred robes over one shoulder and left the chest plate dangling. I picked up my trusty sword, enjoying the feeling of the flat of the blade and the cross of the hilted handle. Encumbered by my heavy suit of blue Mainland armour, I used an old wooden spear, along with my sword, as a crutch to balance my uneasy step.

I looked towards the top of the staircase and remembered every second of the horrific scene as if it were happening all over again.

In my weakened condition, despite being late for the arranged meeting with Lambert, I took a slow and sluggish step. When I eventually arrived at the mainland hall, the light of the sun illuminated Lambert's bright red eyes, whilst the wind rustled the white bow in her short blonde hair.

There was a noticeable difference in her armour. She was no longer covered with spikes of intimidation and only one, smaller and streamlined spike, sat on each of her shoulder plates. I wondered if the Mainland infantry had also changed their armour to fit in line with Lamberts. All three of the units share a uniform with the Dame. The infantry has spiked blue armour, the artillery has black robes and the cavalry has white sashes. Lambert always wore an aspect of each.

'Why are you so late?' Lambert asked, cross-armed and impatient, as she stood waiting outside of the Mainland hall watching my slow approach.

'Dreadfully sorry. I overslept.' I was pleased to see that she had not dismissed my command.

We entered the hall. 'I haven't got all day,' she said. 'What do you want with me?'

She was as sour-faced as ever, showing no sympathy for my injured state, not that I expected as much. Though, in a strange way she appeared to be calm and rather relaxed.

'You will accompany me to the Baron Dwell,' I commanded, pointing in the direction of our travel.

'But, why?' she paused and crossed her arms. 'I will not go. I will not accept orders from the likes of you.'

I stared into her demon red eyes and pulled my sword to one side. I scrapped it across the surface of the wooden floor, leaving a deep split in the wood. Lambert stumbled backwards, startled by my irregular actions. Before she had a chance to mumble something in her confused panic, I slammed the hilt of my blade into the top of her head, knocking her onto the flat of her back.

She groaned, holding her head with one hand and drawing her curved sword with the other. 'What was that for?'

A line of blood dripped down into her eyes, momentarily distracted her from my next action. She swung her silvered curved sword towards me, or at least where she thought I would be. Where her sword would have met with my face, there was nothing but empty air.

'You disobeyed my order, Dame.'

Turning swiftly back on herself and letting out a scream of annoyance, Lambert found that I was not again standing where she thought I was. Amused that she was unable to follow my steps, I mockingly coughed and taped her on the shoulder. When she turned again, her look of aggression quickly turned to concern, as the flat tip of my sword was touching the soft skin of her neck. She was embarrassed and unable to look me in the eye. She knew very well that I had easily outmatched her.

'Dame Lambert Crow, you have been ordered to accompany me to the Baron dwell,' I commanded once more. 'Do you refuse?'

Instead of disobeying my orders, she sighed and reluctantly strolled towards the direction of the dwell. I was feeling confident about our upcoming journey together. Despite how unreasonable and aggressive she was, I believed there to be good in her. She could one day be a trustworthy and reliable ally.

When Lambert was not looking, I coughed a chunk of bloody mucus into my hand. It had been tormenting my throat for some time. I felt so weak and stared into my hands, knowing that moving around as much as I had been was far too much for me right now. My energy levels and strength were not coming back as fast as I had expected. I struggled to breathe from the amount of blood in my lungs and my head ached slightly more with every passing hour.

'Are you coming or not,' Lambert shouted, many paces ahead, shaking her head and tapping her foot with impatience.

'Yes, of course, I am.'

I wiped my hand across the side of my robe and using the old spear as a walking aid, I followed Lambert in the north-westerly direction of the Baron dwell.

24. ~ PLOTTING ~

Not a single word was uttered as we strolled along the cobbled streets of the Mainland Division, through thin alleyways that required us to walk in single file and down the steep and winding steps that shortcut the Medical Research Division.

A set of long steps, ten men wide and leading deep into the pitch blackness of the Baron dwell, awaited us in the darkest corner of the shadow Division.

The ominous and dark hooded figure at the bottom of the stairs was a famous guard, known as Commander Skull. His robes were long and black, covering every inch of his body, save from the tips of his skeletal fingers and the lower half of his scarred and steel-plated skull of a face. Behind him, was an enormous steel door, rusted at the edges and covered in thick wiry cobwebs.

'His name is Commander Skull. He does not speak, nor allow a single weapon to enter into the dwell,' I said, reaching the very last of the steep and oversized steps.

The cold of the dwell shot out through the cracks of the entranceway and brought an unwelcoming chill with it, that sent a shiver up our spines. Lambert pulled her robe around to the front of her and held it tight to her chest.

'It's freezing down here,' she said, staring at the eerie and skeletal, Commander skull, who had not moved an inch in our presence.

'Greetings Commander. If I did not know any better, I could have quite easily mistaken you for a statue,' I said, placing my blade and spear on a rock to the left of the large stone door.

Without a noticed movement from Skull, who just stood completely still and made an unwelcome atmosphere, Lambert stepped forward. 'What is he?'

'I am not exactly sure what he is, but I have heard his tale. Rumour has it, that hundreds of years ago before man stepped foot in Mangrove, he was an honestly paid swordsman and a sea explorer. He and his family were on the first expedition to these very lands. Though to the dismay of his wife and children, he went hunting and was cut to shreds by a Beast.' Lambert gripped hold of my arm. 'As the story goes, they honoured the man with a cremation ceremony. But during this ceremony, something horrible happened. He woke from death, on fire and confused. He ran north and fell down a deep hole, which eventually became this Baron dwell. He has remained here ever since and will remain here for all eternity, as Commander and guard of the Baron dwell. It is quite the horror story, is it not.'

I almost laughed at Lambert. She was shivering and unable to look away from the Commander's scared skull.

Suddenly, the Commander moved. He let out the most deafening of high-pitched screeches. It was like swords scraping against one another. He put out an arm and began moving towards Lambert. She pulled herself closer to me. There was panic in her eyes. She screamed and cuddled into me, whilst the Commander took her curved sword from its scabbard and threw it to one side. He instantly moved back to his original position.

'Pull the lever and open the bloody door,' I impatiently commanded, hoisting Lambert up into my arms as I strolled past the Commander.

He had not deserved a hurried command, but I could not allow Lambert to stay frightened any longer in his presence. I was trying to win her over and this was not helping.

As I had requested, he pulled the lever down and stood back in his usual unmoving position.

Whilst waiting for the door to slowly creak open, I was almost sick. A spider crawled from the Commander's eye socket and back into his mouth. I could not help but feel sorry for the cursed man. The burdens that he must have suffered throughout his everlasting life are not worth living through.

The further we ventured into a scarcely light underground cave, the deeper and darker it became. It was warm in the cave. Some of the spiders here were close to the size of a wild dog, and as lambert had a phobia of the nightmare creatures, she would not take her grip from my arm. I had no idea that she would be frightened of such things, especially after her confident and fearless display in the Mainland Division.

'If you tell anyone that I jumped into your arms...I will kill you. That's a promise,' she threatened, still holding my arm and flinching every time she saw a movement in the shadows.

'Whatever happens in the Baron dwell, will stay in the Baron dwell,' I replied, reassuring Lambert of my secrecy, and trying not to laugh in the same breath.

She slapped the back of my arm and laughed along, which was unanticipated, but none the less a relief. She was finally appearing to be comfortable in my presence.

There were small inconsistent holes along the damp, moss-covered walls of the cave, containing even smaller fires within. I often stopped to admire the colourful crystals of the rock wall, that sparkled in the dim light of the path. At times, I would gaze for longer than I should, to the dismay of Lambert, who would hurry me along.

Halfway down the path of the cave, we came across a neatly stacked pile of old skulls and bones, cobwebbed under a layer of insect carcases.

'Who died?' Lambert joked, assuming they must belong to the dead prisoners of the dwell.

I gave a polite smile but did not see the funny side, and neither would Lambert, soon enough. We came across more bones, and then even more until they covered every patch of every wall. The fires that once lit the way, where no longer in holes along the wall, but inside of some of the larger skulls, watching our every step with eyes of fire.

The path began to open up into a wide room, filled with a sea of skulls, that were piled so high, they touched the hanging stalactites of the cave ceiling.

'Are there really people locked down here?' Asked Lambert, stepping carefully to avoid standing on the skulls that weren't neatly stacked up, but left for the underside of an unplaced foot. A haunting reality for those confined to this Baron dwell.

'I guess it is cruel to keep people down here,' I said. 'But then again, it is also cruel to leave them up there to cause harm to the innocent.'

I staring into the corner, momentarily distracted by a skull that was much longer and larger than the others.

'Dame, do you see that skull?' I asked, pointing into the distance.

'Yes, what of it?'

'As you know, most who have been cursed do not change their physical form from losing control, just their minds, making them what we call demons. When a strong soul, like that of a Lord, loses control, they also change physically, into creatures we call monstrosities. It is a very rare occurrence, but an occurrence none the less. That skull, with its long-spiked edges and oversized jaw, belonged to one of those poor souls,' I explained, sparking Lambert's interest.

She did not taunt me, nor did she appear aggressive or agitated by my voice, but calm, and rather interested in my knowledge of the cursed world.

At the end of the skull filled room, there was a small door that leads to a small room. Two rather short and chubby men sat at a table playing a game of cards and smoking long pipes. The men looked almost identical, both having short beards and wisps of curly hair at the sides of their balding heads. They wore identical brown armour, that matched their similarly dark skin. The only discernible difference between them was the number of spots and boils on the face of the man to the right.

'Fredward, we have company,' the short man to the left with the spotless face said, tapping the ash from his pipe onto the side of his boot, whilst the other man filled another pipe with tobacco from his pocket.

'It appears we do, Edward,' Fredward said, standing up and striking a match for his pipe.

'I am Lord Mace Black of the Mainland Division and this is my Dame, Lambert Crow,' I said. 'Would you gentlemen be kind enough to open the door for us.'

'We are the guards of the Baron dwell and by the look on your face, we can assume that you haven't been here before, have you Lord?' Edward Asked.

I was not looking at her, but I could tell that Lambert was becoming impatient with these foolish men.

'I came here once when I was a boy. My brother Mantis brought me down here. My hair would have been black all those years ago but I do not remember you two being here,' I approaching the short men.

'Did you say Mantis,' Fredward said. 'As in Lord Mantis.' He looked at Edward with worry.

'Yes,' I said, looming over them.

'My Lord, I am... we are so sorry, we didn't know,' Edward said, full of concern. 'We are not the guards of the dwell... we were just joking. Please take the key.'

Fredward grabbed a large bronze key from a bag to the side of his chair and handed it to me.

'Why are you here?' I asked.

'Well, Lord Mantis caught us sleeping on duty and said that we were too ugly and incompetent to be part of normal society,' Edward said. 'He gave us a choice, either we fight to the death, so one of us can be proven worthy and the other can have an honest death, or we stay down here and keep the fires of the dwell alight.

'Please Lord Mace, show us mercy, we mean no disrespect,' Fredward begged. 'We just wanted to seem important is all. Don't tell Lord Mantis...please.'

'You are both incompetent and deserve whatever punishment Lord Mantis sees fit to give you,' Lambert said, booting Fredward full in his spotty face, bursting his nose wide open.

Edward put his hands in front of his face, expecting the same, but Lambert broke two of his fingers instead. I stepped between the men, who cried out in pain, holding their injuries.

'If I said a word to Mantis about you fools and your incompetence,' I said. 'He would literally rip your manhood out with his bare hands...so I will not. But, if I hear that you have been anything but pleasant to the visitors of the Baron dwell, I will feed you to my snow bear.'

I walked past the little men and opened the thick metal door in front of me, struggled to push its stiff frame.

Inside, there was a blinding light, that squinted our eyes and made it hard to see, but soon enough our eyes adjusted to the brightness, noticing immediately that it came from the thousands of fireflies that littered the ceiling. I locked the door behind us, putting the key safely inside my breastplate.

Looking on we saw that this was no mere prison, but an ancient, multi-levelled underground city, large enough to shelter tens of hundreds of people in the carved-out rooms along the walls, along with their livestock and stores of food. Each floor of the dwell was closed off with large stones, and as the height of the levels increased, as did the danger of their residents. Only a crippling jump separated the levels. Amenities, such as oil presses, cellars, storage rooms, refectories and even a chapel to an un-worshipped old god were located all around the dwell.

Between the highest levels, the fifth and sixth was a vertical staircase leading to the fighting pit, were the most dangerous of prisoners can fight as they please. The ventilation shaft, that ran up the back wall was used as a well, gathering water for all levels. Our destination was a staircase in front of the back wall, which leads to a lower level, where those too dangerous for the civility of the dwell reside in solitary confinement.

As we passed through, many prisoners in the central area played chess on wooden tables, exercised on old wooden machines and fought amongst themselves.

All eyes were on us, especially on Lambert, as women are a rare sight around here and wouldn't last a day with these prisoners, with their white sheets tied at the waist with a rope. All were cuffs around the ankles with thick metal chains to weigh them down. Cross swords were branded on their right cheeks, save from those in solitary confinement. It would take a brave soul to brand their faces.

Disgusted at the looks she was getting, Lambert stayed close to my side, keeping a close eye on the movements of the prisoners, that mostly whispered amongst themselves.

'Be careful and keep your wits about you,' I said, as we approached the centre of the dwell. 'They are well known for attacking, especially when a female is around.'

'What have all of these people done wrong?' She whispered innocently.

'Most of them are rapists, the rest of them are thieves and murderers. The worse the crime, the higher the level. A rare few, however, have not done anything wrong, except for display behaviours that some would consider demon-like.'

Looking up, Lambert noticed a man on the third level making strange repetitive noises and appearing to smear faeces across his chest and face.

'Just like that man up there,' I said. 'Do not worry, it is said that when someone here becomes a demon, they are instantly massacred by the other prisoners.' Lambert put her arm around mine as if a spider was nearby.

'As for our destination, well those prisoners are a different matter altogether. There are three types of people in solitary confinement, firstly are the rich, belonging to high family's, secondly are those who have done great dead's in their life, and lastly, the demons.'

'There are demons down there?' She was shocked at the very thought of a place like this existing.

'Yes, there are. Remember Dame, every demon is just an unlucky and unfortunate soul.'

'Mace, I am not moving an inch until you tell me exactly who, or what we are going to find down there.' Lambert threatened, stepping away from me, appearing rather angry at the thought of there being demons here.

I pulled the new piece of eight from the top pocket of my robe, noticing that it was now tinged with a strange green light. 'Do you know what this is?

'Isn't that Lord Brick's coin?' She said, holding it up to the light of the ceiling for closer inspection. 'No, this coin is different. I don't understand, what has this got to do with anything?'

She rubbed the eight-sided octagonal engravings on one side of the coin and flicked the crown on the other, checking its authenticity.

'There are only eight of these coins in existence and four of them belong to the East bay pirates,' I said, taking the coin back. 'The owner of this coin is one of those pirate captains. The reason we are here is to question the man, and if it is at all possible, form a truce with them. We cannot keep this pitiful, eye for an eye, blood feud going with the pirates.'

'You have got to be joking,' she backed away from me. 'You have had one of the pirates down here the whole time and didn't think to do anything about it. We should go and kill him now.'

'It is more complicated than that. You see, the four pirate captains control the oceans, and between them, they have enough power to rage war on the Stronghold. There would be bloodshed the likes of which you have never seen. It would make the Beast war look like a children's fight. Think of the hundreds of thousands of lives, needlessly lost.'

'What about the ambush? What about Lord Brick's death?' She shouted as prisoners began to gather around.

'If we kill him now, what do you think will happen?' I slapped Lambert across the face and pulled her in close. 'Lord Brick's death will be for nothing if we kill this pirate in revenge. We would be no better than them for goodness sake, and I have no doubt, that it would start a war, dooming us all. That is why the pirate is here, and not impaled on a spike. Dame, give me a break, I'm doing my best.'

'However much I hate those bloody pirates, Lord Brick would not want a war, just for the sake of revenge,' she said, crying into my arms.

Lambert had a heart after all. Wanting her long-awaited revenge, but for the good of all, showing understanding. I really could not fault her.

'Thank you, Lambert, your actions here today will have helped to prevent one of the greatest disasters of all time,' I said, using my thumb to wipe the stream of tears from under Lambert's eyes. 'I tell you what, if a truce is not possible, you can kill the pirate captain as slowly and as painfully as you see fit.'

Turning to continue on our path towards the lower levels, we were shocked at the number of prisoners surrounding us. They were intently watching our dispute and also watching Dame Lambert, who for the prisoners, was an irresistible site, even when she was covered in thick armour.

All of a sudden, a large bald man, who dwarfed over every other prison, came storming through the crowds behind Lambert. She went to grab her sword, remembering at that very moment, that it was with Commander Skull at the dwells entrance. She was not strong enough to form a defensive position against him and had not the time to move away.

The man, who could barely fit into his white sheets, was on top of Lambert, seconds away from crushing her like an ant. She closed her eyes and braced for an attack, but none reached her and when she looked up to see why nothing had happened, I was standing between her and the man, with one arm gripped around his neck, and the other inside of his stomach. There was blood everywhere.

He screamed when I pulled my arm out, along with his small intestines. When the life had faded from his eyes, he fell backwards with a tremendous thud, that spooked most of the surrounding men into fleeing. The twenty or so men that remained were seething with anger, ready to jump in at a moment's notice. None, however, appeared to be brave, or stupid enough, to make the first move.

'Lambert, watch my back,' I whispered, slowly dropping into a defensive position.

'I've got you,' she said confidently, and louder than I had expected her to.

She put her back to mine and positioned herself accordingly. I couldn't help but smile, although, I was still suffering from a pain in my chest and had just killed a giant-sized man. That attack took its toll on me.

The first man brave enough to come at me was a short muscular man, with long ponytailed hair and a patch covering his left eye. He soon lost the use of his good eye at the end of my elbow, which sent him stumbling back into the men behind him. The bravery of the ponytailed fool was enough to muster a reaction from the surrounding prisoners.

A sweaty oaf of a man was charging from the right, drawing back his fist, for what would be a predictable punch. Bending down and turning full circle, I swung upright, towards the underside of his jaw. I took him off his feet and sent his glass like jaw crumbling.

I noticed Lambert in the corner of my eye, spinning and flipping her legs and arms at the men twice her size. Two, three men at a time, she knocked them to the floor.

'That is four for me,' I cheerfully shouted, twisting the head of a skinny prisoner until it snapped and he dropped lifelessly on to his face. 'How are you doing Lambert?'

She was not answering my jest. She was concentration, cursing only at those daring enough to attack her.

At that very moment, three men came at me together, all of a matching height and baldness, appearing rather proficient in their unnecessary display of martial arts skills. Taking a deep breath and swallowing a mouth full of blood, I readied myself for whatever they might throw at me.

They came at me together, all three of them jumping and kicking. In one swift move, I countered the attacks of the first two men, slamming their heads together with an echoing crunch. Unfortunately, I was not fast enough to block the third man, who kicked me in the side of the temple, sending me stumbling off balance. He took this advantage and kept his attacks flowing, kicking me over and over again in the face and head, until I was on my back with a split lip and a black eye.

Suddenly, Lambert flew over the top of me, taking the man by surprise and knocking him off his feet with a backheel to the jaw. I struggled to regain my composure, coughing up large amounts of blood. I was off-balance with blurred vision.

Noticing that more prisoners were surrounding us, I looked for a strategy in our surroundings, which were little to none. The only real advantage we had was the space, as the prisoners were bunched together and must wait for their attacking turn.

Backing off towards a wall could be our best option, I thought, unsure of myself in this almost helpless situation.

'Mace,' Lambert screamed, as she was dragged away and stripped of her armour by half a dozen perverted prisoners.

My blood boiled at the sight of it, and as I ran to aid her, a large and hairy arm reached around my neck from behind and squeezed into my throat, pulling me backwards and choking me.

Prisoners began to gather in front of me, blocking my sight of Lambert, who continued to scream in her attempt to struggle free. Summoning as much strength as I could, I pulled the man's arm away from my neck and broke his nose with the back of my head. I flipped the bloody nosed man over my shoulder, breaking his arm and putting him on his ass, where he belongs.

Two more fell under a leg sweep and one with a chin-splitting punch. I quickly jumped into the gathering prisoners, sending as many elbows and knees into their faces and necks as I could. Four men, bloodied and broken by the force of my attacks, fell to their knees. But, inevitable, as any man as heavily outnumbered as I was should come to expect, they stopped me in my tracks. They held such a tight grip around my chest, arms and legs, that I was barely able to draw a breath, let alone move a muscle. All I could do was listen to them cheer and boast amongst themselves.

'Hold him still,' said a long-bearded and gaunt-faced man, with an incredibly large forehead.

'Now you're in for it, posh boy,' a voice whispered in my ear.

A chant began, getting louder and louder 'Head butter, head butter, head butter.'

I could only assume that the man stood before me with a forehead that took up the most of his face, was going to head-butt me. The man then grabbed me by the sides of my head and smashed me in the face with a nose bursting head butt. Tears streamed down my face. After another three butts, my face was a bloody mess and the man's forehead was dripping with my blood. Whilst the so-called, head butter, tilted back for another strike, that would have finished me off, I coughed up a lump of bloody mucus and to his discussed, spat it into his eyes.

'Little bugger,' he shouted, wiping his eyes clean and readying himself for another strike.

Tilting back further than he had previously, he swung his head forward with neck wrenching force and smashed his forehead into my nose. It hit me like a ton of bricks, but I felt no pain, nor did I even feel the contact, or hear the usual cheer from the other prisoners. I could see clearly now.

Visions of the cursed red light came to me. The light was pulsating like the beating of a heart. It was my heart.

I stood up with ease, unsure whether or not I was dreaming, for the red light beamed from the back of the dwell. I was instantly drawn to it, unable to look away. I could scarily see the kicks and punches that were being attempted on me, as I continued towards the warm irresistible red glow. Soon I could see nothing but the light, pulsating with warmth and calling me in closer. I answered the call. I walked towards it, losing every sense of my surroundings. I was no better than a moth would be to a flame, unable to look away, until stopping me in my tracks, was a faintly recognisable voice.

'Help me,' whimpered the same voice again, but this time, louder and easy to recognise.

It was lambert and I knew that she must be answered before the call of the red light. As hard as it was to turn around away from the intoxicating light, I did, for Lambert's sake. I was not going to fail her.

'Lambert, I am here,' I shouted.

Everything became slow, almost unmoving. At a snail's pace, all eyes slowly turned to me. The man that is known as the head butter, who smashed my face in, was stood in front of me. Almost motionless, he drew back to punch me. I had caved in his unprotected face before he could move an inch to stop me, and yet strangely, I did not feel the contact, only a numb feeling that shot through my arm.

I realised then, that my face no longer hurt, nor did my chest wound, and so I ran for Lambert. I ran as fast as my legs could carry me.

She was half-naked and had been beaten to a mess of her former self. She was surrounded by prisoners. One of them had their hand an inch from her breast.

I showed no mercy. I furiously snapped the arms and necks of every unmoving prisoner foolish enough to have crossed my path this day.

I reached out to the last man, the man with his hand to Lambert's breast, and in one fluid motion, I removed the man's hand and stuffed it down his throat. In only a short amount of time, I had left a trail of bloodied and broken men in my shadow.

After caving in the faces of another dozen or so men with little effort, I took Lambert's half-naked body into my arms. I sat with her for a moment, holding her close. A sorry feeling of incompetence came over me. Looking down at the bruised and bloody condition of my Dame, I wished that I had not commanded her to come here with me. She was my responsibility and I let her down.

'I am so sorry,' I said, tearing up, with my head next to hers.

I went to kiss her on the forehead, and as I did, time began to move at its usual pace, as did Lambert, who jerked up and banged her head into mine.

'What happened?' she asked, holding her head with one hand and her broken ribs with the other.

'I, I do not know how to explain it,' I said. 'The red light, it came to save me. For a short time, I felt as if I was a giant amongst babies, a bird amongst worms. I felt like a god.'

'I should never have brought you here,' I continued, standing up with Lambert in my arms.

'It is ok. Thank you, Lord Mace. I do not know why, or even understand how you saved me, I'm just glad that you did, and that you are here with me,' she said, smiling. 'I saved you as well, remember, and without making quite as much mess.'

I could hardly believe what I was hearing, she called me Lord for the first time, which somehow was not as gratifying is, I would have hoped.

'You do not need to address me as Lord, we are more than a mere Lord and his Dame,' I said, as she pulled herself closer to me, looking deep into my eyes in a way that I had not before.

'Mace, let's finish this,' she said, pressing her plump lips to my cheek.

I assisted with her armour, unable to keep my eyes away from her slender body as I helped her attached the chest plate to her shoulder pads.

An awkward silence remained with us along the final course of our journey. My arm was around Lambert, keeping her steady as we ventured into the darkness of the solitary confinements floor. The air was thicker and flowing less freely down the almost pitch-black staircase.

Every so often there would be a wild scream or crashing sound at one of the steel doors, at the levelled-out parts of the staircase. Red glowing eyes peered out of the small slits in some of the steel doors.

At the bottom of the staircase, there were two large bronze doors, neither of which had the glare of glowing red eyes, but instead, the bright light of a fire shining out. The first cell contained a faceless little girl in a blue princess's dress, reminding me of Talia.

'Who the bloody hell is he? And why is he dressed in Lord Brick's armour?' Lambert asked, peering into the cell and seeing something different than I.

'I do not know and I do not want to find out. My eyes do not show me Lord Brick's armour or a man at all. All I can see is a faceless girl, dressed in one of Talia's princes' dresses,' I explained, pulling lambert to the next cell, holding her close for comfort's sake.

Looking into the last room, I could see more than a few luxuries. The bed to the right of the cell was fit for a King, next to a full and spacious table and chairs. Towards the far of the room, a brown leather chair was turned to face the warmth of the fire, and to the left corner of the cell, there was a plain ceramic bath, a matching toilet and a basket for a cat or small dog.

'Hello there. I've been expecting you for some time now.' A deep voice sounded from behind the chair.

A tall, dark and thin man stood from the seat, holding a rather large black cat in his even larger hands. His hair was black and curled above his unshaven face, that looked half bruised and swollen on one side. He wore a three-piece suit, which I thought was rather extravagant for a pirate.

'I am Mace Black, Lord of the Mainland Division,' I said, curious as to why he was smiling as he strolled towards the cell door, and why Mantis would allow him a cat, of all things. 'I presume you are one of the four pirate captains from the East bay?'

'You are the spitting image of your brother, apart from having a friendlier and younger face,' he said. 'Yes, I am one of the East bay pirates, but we prefer to be called sea Lords. You can call me Dusk, Dusk Stone. And who is the young lady.'

I nudged her and made an exaggerated face, which she knew implied that I wanted her to say something, anything.

'False Lord,' she muttered.

'Better than nothing,' I whispered. 'This is my Dame, Lambert Crow.'

'Some call us false lords...yes, maybe they do,' he said. 'By the way, what has happened to you both? You're covered in blood.'

I was unsure whether he was a genuinely friendly man, or being friendly to trick us into a false sense of security.

'We fell. Anyway, it is nothing to concern yourself with,' I answered.

'How very modest of you, Mace of the Mainland,' he laughed so hard that his cat leapt from his shoulder and landed with a squeal in the unemptied bathtub. 'Though It seems you aren't as light-hearted as your dear brother, neither are you as violent. Speaking of brothers, how are mine?'

He looked through the slit of the door with somewhat innocent brown eyes, that did not suffer the coldness of a killer.

'If by brothers, you mean the other false Lords,' Lambert snapped, stopped by my hand over her impatient mouth.

'Well, the other sea Lords were causing quite a lot of mayhem, murdering, thieving and raping in and around Mangrove, including the murder of one of our Lord Commanders,' I said. 'However, recently they have been quiet, probably biding their time in search of you.'

He laughed. 'That sounds like them alright, most likely Arc and Sand, murdering and such. Those two are rather bloodthirsty. Trench would never leave the protection of his battleship, not for me, and not for all the gold and glory in Mangrove. Just a word of advice, if you don't mind, about my brothers bidding their time. Arc and Sand would never bide their time, nor would they hesitate to charge in here with ten thousand men. I do not believe they are aware of my disappearance.'

'Listen, I do not know whether you have a genuinely kind nature, or you are playing me for a simple fool. I am not as trusting as I once was...so we shall get right to business. I am here to discuss a truce, a peace treaty of sorts. Your freedom, in exchange for a simple promise of peace. Agree to my terms, and on my honour, I will set you free.' I proclaimed, almost eye to eye.

'I would be more than happy to oblige you, although I cannot say the same for my brothers. All I want is to be home with my wife and children,' he said, with his hand on his heart. 'I grow weary of this lonesome cell. The truth is Mace, I have never killed a single soul, it's not really for me, but I am loyal to my brothers and my code of honour. I, Dusk Stone, Captain of the leviathan Battalion and Lord of the ninth bridge, swear on my honour, that for as long as no harm befalls my brothers or my men, no blood shall be spilt by my hand.'

'He is lying,' Lambert shouted, thumping the thick bronze door of the cell.

'I believe him to be sincere Lambert, not that we have much choice in the matter,' I said. 'If and when the other pirates come for him, it will be too late for any course of reasoning.'

I put my arm on Lambert's shoulder. 'Thank you, Captain Dusk, you are a kinder man than I had expected, though your word is only part of the solution. I will need the word of the other sea Lords. I will return soon, and we will pay your brothers a little visit,' I said, tossing his piece of eight to him.

'Wait, you hold onto it...for now anyway. It will bring you luck,' Dusk said. 'Mace, a few things that might help...before you get yourself killed trying to reason with my brothers. They both believe in the old laws and they do not fight with armour, or with more than one opponent at a time. They respect the strength of a man, so prepare yourself for a fight. Whatever happens, I truly wish you the best of luck.'

I took the coin back from him. It was ice cold.

'Oh, please give my regards to my little sister,' he continued, with an eerily grin.

'And who might she be?'

'I here that she has become a Lady of the Stronghold, her name is Senna.'

25. ~ PERSUASION ~

Dame Lambert currently recuperates in the comforts of the Medical Research Division, whilst at a leisured pace, I roamed East, freshly showered and cleanly dressed, towards the Services Division.

Commander Snake, after returning Ice, my snow bear, requested to accompany me. I gladly accepted, as there was a somewhat trusting nature in his green eyes. Though I will not divulge any information about the sea Lords to him, or anyone, save from Senna.

For most of our stroll, Snake remained silent and appeared oddly nervous, as if he was eager to ask an uncomfortable question. Nothing was said through the Kings-cross, neither was it amidst the buildings of the Services Division nor up to the hills path of Senna's hall. It was not until we were outside the guarded black door of the hilltop hall, that he finally said something.

'Lord Mace, we have some recruits for you to meet,' he said, nervously. 'When you have a moment, of course.'

'Is there something you want to ask me?' I replied, well aware that he was not simply going to ask what he was nervously eager to.

'My Lord, one of our young recruits is...well, he is very powerful, so powerful in fact, that it's frightening.'

'Why exactly is he so frightening?' I asked. 'We need all the strong recruits we can get'

I knelt beside Ice and held him still. He was becoming very playful and distracting my concentration.

'I wish to send him to my father, Lord Hawk, and be under his watch...with your permission, my Lord.' Sweat dripped from the brow of the normally calm and calculated Commander.

'Why exactly would we not want a strong recruit for ourselves?'

'My Lord, blood constantly drips, like tears, from his colourless white eyes. There are always wasps on or around him, and he is strangely powerful and too experienced to be a recruit,' he said, unable to look me in the eye. 'He easily outmatched me, and every other recruit during combat training.'

'I see. How old is he?' I sympathetically asked, as two heavily robed guards approached, dressed head to toe in red leather.

'Lord Mace, can we be of service?' one of the guards asked.

All of Senna's guards were female and carried double edge spears on their hilltop patrol.

'Please inform Lady Senna of my arrival. I request her privacy in an important matter. I will be but a moment,' I said. 'Now…what was a saying.'

'You asked me how old the recruit was,' Snake said, clearly embarrassed. 'He looks no more than ten years of age, my Lord.'

'The poor boy, he must be cursed.' I had to decide on a course of action.

'Here is what you are going to do, Commander,' I said, with an air of authority in my voice. 'Take him to Lord Hawk, explaining to him exactly what you have just explained to me. He will most likely try the boy in combat. If he fails or if Lord Hawk decides against taking him on, you have my permission to do as you see fit with him, be it on your head, Commander.'

I turned away from Snake and made my way to the hilltop hall.

'My Lady, Lord Mace has arrived,' a well-spoken service man pronounced, rushing into Lady Senna's Grande hall. 'And his Beast.'

'You are a stupid man, aren't you?' Senna said, standing from her cushioned throne. 'I can clearly see him for myself, and that little Beast has a name, doesn't it, Lord Mace.'

'His name is Ice. Do not worry, I am sure he will behave,' I said, grinning at first and then trying to control my laughter, at the contorted faces Senna was making at me.

I gave Ice a small bone from my pocket. He sat calmly, making a dribbling mess in the corner of the hall.

'My apologies, Lady Senna,' the serviceman said, bowing his head and taking a seat on a floor mat.

I could not help but notice how luxurious the hilltop hall was. It was almost as grand as the council hall. It looked like it was built to last and used more stone in its construction that most other Division Halls. It had a great view of the surrounding land and looked impressive alone atop the hill.

Inside there were large mats instead of chairs, bookshelves instead of weapon racks, and most unlike common halls, it had a golden back wall, half-filled with the names of service division dead.

Dame Eva sat to the right of Lady Senna, on a curved out red leather cushion. She was no longer dressed up for my sake and wore her usual black leathers, red wrist guards and thick red robes, that matched with Senna. Two small swords and two large daggers lay to her side, and a pile of marked out parchments were sprawled out over her lap.

When I saw her there, sifting through papers and purposely ignoring my presence, I was reminded of that strong and fearless woman, the woman who fell for me in the woods. The longer I stared at her, the more I was noticed doing so. She looked up at me, apprehensive and red-cheeked, with a coy smile. My hands went clammy, my heart sank into my chest and my stomach grumbled. Although Senna was frowning at me, and the twenty or so other people in the hall watched on in silent confusion, I was lost in Eva's eyes, unable to look away from her beauty.

'Shall we leave you two alone?' Senna mocked, with a raised brow.

We immediately acted as if we hadn't the slightest clue as to what Senna was talking about. Eva nervously sifted through paper, as I began to meticulously examine the furs of my robe.

'She is not for your eyes,' a finely featured and well shaven young man blurted out.

The man stood from his floor mat on the left side of the hall. He was staring intently at me.

'And who might you be?' I asked, taking the measure of this aggressive man.

Dropping his overfilled brown bag, he approached, wearing a tightly fitted red and brown tweed suit, with short curls of blonde poking out from his barrette.

'I am the postmaster, Argyle Armstrong,' he said waving his finger around. 'I know exactly who you are, scumbag.'

'You had better explain yourself, postmaster,' Senna yelled, as she slammed the butt of her spear onto the floor.

'I saw this white-haired pretender carrying Dame Lambert in his arms,' he said. 'And she had her arms around him.'

Eva looked at me with discussed.

'How dare you,' I said, shoving past Argyle and kneeling before Eva.

'Eva, this man has his facts wrong,' I said. 'Lambert is my Dame and I was taking her to the medical research Division. She could barely walk. She is having her broken ribs put back into place as we speak.'

'Don't listen to him,' the postmaster said.

Eva dropped her lap full of papers and stormed towards him.

'You know how I feel about you,' he said. 'I am just trying to protect you.'

She reached out, smoothed her hand across his chiselled jaw and caressed his neck. 'I have told you before and I will tell you again,' she said, face to face with the postmaster. 'I am not yours to protect. From this day, until your last, never address me directly, never come to this hall or this Division. You are no longer the postmaster.'

'But Eva.' He grabbed her hand.

'You are not welcome here,' she said, punching him in the throat.

'This is your fault, you've turned her against me,' he said to me, catching his breath.

Drunk with love, he pulled a dull pocket knife from his trouser pocket.

'Do not bloody my halls,' Senna said, leaning over the edge of her seat.

'You are a fool,' Eva said, sweeping the postmaster's legs out from under him, sending him to the flat of his back.

His knife hurtled through the air, only to land inches away from his embarrassed face.

'What is wrong with him?' I asked, turning my back on the man for insult's sake, and raising a confused brow in Senna's direction.

'Better to have a knife and not need it, than to need a knife and not have one,' Senna said, bursting into laughter.

'Lady Senna, you can't allow this,' the postmaster said. 'I have been postmaster for seven years. This is my life.'

'Guards, seize this man, he is no longer welcome in my Division,' Senna commanded. 'If he resists, you have my permission to kill him.'

The guards, who appeared to all be female, approached from each corner of the hall. The postmaster fled, falling into the seated members of the hall as he did so.

'You will pay for this. You will all pay,' the postmaster shouted from the door of the hall, moments before he ran for it.

Ice ran out, leaving a trail of dribble in his step. 'Ice, Stop. Come back here,' I called out, to which he turned back, looked at me and ran out anyway.

Eva dropped to the floor. She began to cry.

'Eva, I only have eyes for you,' I said, as the guilt of Lambert's kiss played on my mind.

She hugged me in a tight embrace and rested her head on my chest, letting out a sigh of relief.

'I trust you, Mace,' she said, rubbing her eyes. 'Dame Lambert is lucky to have you as a Lord.'

There was a scream from outside, followed by Ice's unmistakable roar. Had the postmaster been caught, I thought, expecting the guards to be dragging him in at any moment.

Two guards burst in, holding the postmaster firmly between their arms, whilst Ice, bloody-mouthed and excitable, had a firm grip around his ankle.

'Lady Senna, we have apprehended Argyle,' the taller of the two guards said, with her arm around his neck. 'The little Beast slowed him down. He is quite fond of ankles it would seem.'

'Good boy, Ice,' I said, wiping some of the blood from around his mouth.

Laughter echoed throughout the hall.

'Thank you, girls. Please take him to the dwell,' Senna said, smirking from ear to ear.'

'Lady Senna, may I have a moment of your time,' I asked.

'Leave us please,' commanded Senna. 'You too Eva.'

When all of the service members had left the hall, along with the Eva and the guards, Senna offered me the Dames cushioned seat. I tossed a bone out to Ice. He ran after it, jumping in circles, still excited from his earlier actions.

'What is it, Mace?' Senna asked. 'You never want my privacy, except when losing in combat.'

'Senna, I need your help. I am planning to form a truce with the sea Lords and put a stop to the ongoing violence once and for all.'

'Sea Lords,' she said, almost falling from her throne. 'You mean pirates. Don't You? And how exactly are you going to do this?'

'One of the four is currently in solitary confinement,' I said. 'He has agreed, for his part, on a truce. Surprisingly, he is quite a gentleman.'

'Are you joking.'

'The problem I am going to have, it would seem, is with the others. One of them will not step foot on land. The other two, however, are quite aggressive.'

I handed Senna the piece of eight, which no longer shone green.

'This is madness, for even you Mace,' she said. 'And what exactly do you need with me?'

She began pacing back and forth, shooting a confused glare with each step. I reached out to grab her clammy hand and held it in a tight grip. I looked deep into her bright blue eyes.

'Senna, I need your strength, your loyalty and most of all, your friendship. This truce must be kept between our ears only. I will form a squad of my strongest warriors. They will accompany us on a surveillance expedition.'

'Would you lie to the subordinates of your Division?' she asked. 'Would you allow them to confront pirates without telling them why?'

'They are loyal to their Division, but not to me...not yet anyway. They would not understand what I seek to do. Most would take their revenge at the drop of a hat. If anyone had even the slightest idea that a Sea lord slept in the dwells beneath their feet, all hell would break loose.'

'There would be war,' Senna interrupted, releasing my hand and turning her back.

'I will help you, but only as a backup. You must approach them alone. I will form up with your squad and await your signal in the shadows. Iron out the details, select your squad, and keep me informed of the time and place.'

'Thank you, Senna. I owe you one.' I impulsively jumped up.

'You owe me indeed, Mace Black,' she said. 'A black steel spear will do nicely, for the meantime.'

'Whatever you want, it is yours, however, there is yet another matter I must discuss with you.'

'What...more?' she said, exasperatedly slumping back into her chair as if all the life had been drained from her.

'The pirate in the dwell, his name is Dusk, and well, he asked me to give his sincerest regards to his sister. You, Senna.'

'Half-sister,' she said welling up, staring gormlessly into the middle distance.

Perhaps I should have stopped after the surveillance plan, I thought, putting my hand on her shoulder for comfort sake.

She turned to me, slowly and full of sadness. 'As part of the Mangrove workforce, the origins of the services Division pre-exist the King's council, and even the eight Divisions lands as we know them today,' she said. 'The Stone family have run the services Division for as long as people have needed our services. We are, as you know, one of the most powerful families in Mangrove, and with great power, sometimes comes an over-indulgent and pretentious nature.'

'I know all this, Senna.'

'Just listen. My father, who was the previous Lord of this Division, was a money-hungry tyrant, with a, do whatever you want and get away with it attitude. Unbeknown to my dear mother, he had many affairs and many families, which bore many children for him. Two of his sons were born cursed. The poor boys were sent straight to the King and had a dreadful time of it. Those boys, my older brothers, Arc and Dusk, grew to form part of the most powerful rebellion alliances in history.'

'Senna, are you alright?' I asked, concerned that I had opened some old wounds.

'Mace, my brothers murdered my mother, my father, and half of the Stone family. I was a little girl, so I don't remember a lot.' She burst into tears, burying her head into my shoulder.

'Why have you never spoken of this?' I asked.

'I need you to promise me that you never will mention their names in any relation to me ever again. I will not have my name besmirched by those false Lords.'

'I promise, I will never utter a word of this to anyone, although I am surprised that you agreed to help me, after what they did to your family.'

'Do I look inconsiderate or stupid to you?' She said, appearing offended. 'I have been the Lady of this Division for over ten years now and have a pretty good idea of what is best for the longevity of it. I would rather not have my friends or what is left of my family suffer a war, nor would I like to continue hearing about those bloody pirates terrorising the Citadel any longer.'

She was returning to her usual, bright-eyed and cheerful self.

'I don't want to hear any more of this pirate talk, not until you have arranged for our little expedition anyway,' she continued. 'Oh, and are you planning on bringing Dusk with you?'

'Yes, I was thinking that he could be chained to the inside of my carriage'

'Make sure he is double-chained and blindfolded. I do not want him to see me,' she said.

'I understand, it will be done.' I mockingly rubbed the black smudged underpart of Senna's eyes, before adjourning our meeting, followed by Ice, who was still chewing through his bone.

'Mace, take care,' she said, smirking with confidence.

26. ~ CONCEITED ~

Later that day, after a showering display of heavy rain, I sent Ice home and made my way north in search of Snake, who by now should be at the Elite Division with the recruit. Remembering the alarming way in which Snake had described the capabilities of the recruit, I could not help but wonder whether or not he had the skills necessary to best Lord hawk in combat, which is something, not even my brother could do.

Across the Mangrove landscape, the beginning glow of the midday sun broke through the low-lying clouds, followed by the brightest rainbow I had ever laid eyes upon.

I travelled down the stone plated road alongside the Surveillance Division and came across the path of the Elites, which was more luxuries than I had ever remembered. A marble staircase led to a ridged silver path below, with the names and honours of the bravest Elites inlaid with fine gold. The first name was John Cougar, defender of the crown, then Sean Belmore, champion of briarwood, and after that, Sir Volcano, slayer of leviathans. It went on like that for a while.

Stood either side of the entranceway, were two silver warrior statues, touching swords overhead. The Elite Division was perfectly structured with beautiful architecture. I felt like a stray dog or an unwelcomed guest as I strolled, heavy-footed, amongst the surrounding tranquillity.

Everyone smiles and bows, without a hair or piece of clothing out of place. The Elites are a unique force, not just in their strength and skill, but in the way they conduct themselves. From the moment they wake, they are devoted to the perfection of whatever task they have yet to fulfil. Making a cup of tea becomes an artist's performance, swinging a sword, becomes as natural as breathing, and finding absolute completeness in every aspect of their lives becomes a way of life. Every blade of grass was cut to a perfect uniform length, with every house exactly thirty-three feet from the last, and every grain of sand in the Elite fighting pit was smoothed to an even level. Never have I witnessed such discipline, such as loyalty in servitude. Undeniably, it is a warrior's paradise.

Past the reservoir, where the silver manor sits centrally above stilts, reflecting the blinding light of the sun, and past the perfectly presented pit of sand, was a circular slab of rock. It stands five feet tall and fifteen feet wide, with the ancient marks of the old world inscribed across it. That slab of rock was Lord Hawks place of preferred combat.

Gathered around it, knelt more than twenty, long-haired, grey-robed and silver armoured members of the Elite force, along with Sir James and Commander Snake.

Lord Hawk and the recruit warmed up for the third round of their combat, wearing only cotton pants, and using wooden longswords as weapons. The small, dark and long-haired, Sir Ronald Redgrave, second in command of the Elite force, conducted the combat.

When I approached, the warriors of the Elite force all bowed in synchronisation. Sir James, who slumped over the side of the old slab, fixed a squinted, yet emotionless, gaze towards me.

'Lord Mace, over here,' Commander Snake shouted, waving me over to him.

'How is the boy fairing,' I asked.

'He is not quite a match for my father, but he has landed several strikes, and caused him to perspire a little.'

'Have you discovered anything about the boy?' I asked, curious as to the history of such a child, with such skill. 'You know, family, friends, place of birth, at least a name.'

It would be an understatement to say I was excited. I could count the number of people able to break Lord Hawk into a sweat on the fingers of one hand. I was impressed.

'The boy's name is Brandon Brooke, or so he tells me, but he has no recollection of any time before he woke up in the Warding woods, two days ago.' Snake answered, twiddling his fingers anxiously.

Sir Ronald Redgrave blew his curled longhorn, signalling the third round of combat. The bruised and bleeding, Brandon, ran at Hawk, screaming with his sword lifted high. Hawk made no move, nor did he keep his eye in the direction of the boy. Only as the tip of Brandon's wooden sword reached the side of Hawk's face, did he move.

Pulling his elbow around to meet the blow, Hawk splintered Brandon's sword to kindling. This must not have been the first broken sword of the day, I thought, watching the ease in which it was broken.

'Lord Mace, how are you feeling?' James asked, from the other side of the slab, remembering his rank, and manners in my presence.

'Much better,' I replied, unable to look away from the combat.

Brandon was then grabbed by Hawk and launched over my head. Hawk rubbed his jaw. Was he hit?

'Can you believe this boy, that's the fourth punch he's landed,' James said, smiling incredulously towards me.

He was right to be impressed, not only did the boy manage to strike Lord Hawk, he made no sound, not even a whimper at the pain inflicted upon him.

'Excuse me,' Brandon said, holding the cut on the back his head.

I stepped aside, letting him run for the ring. He jumped and flipped with a kick towards Hawk's head. Though the boy's leg was easily grabbed and he was slammed into the hard surface of the slab.

'That will do boy,' Hawk said, offering his hand. 'You are the strongest child I have ever seen. Who trained you?'

'Yes Lord, thank you,' Brandon said, bleeding from his white, lifeless eyes. 'I'm sorry, but I don't remember being trained.'

'Your face, is there anything you can do with it?' Hawk asked.

'No, my Lord, I'm sorry.'

'Don't be, it is just a shame,' Hawk said, stroking the long grey hairs of his beard. 'Mastiff, bring some water for the boy.'

'Right away, my Lord,' the blonde-haired man known as Mastiff said, immediately pacing away to follow orders.

'Lord Mace,' Hawk said, stretching his overly muscular arms behind his head. 'With your permission, I will give my verdict on the boy, as you requested.'

'I am curious, Lord hawk, but this is Commander Snakes task, and it is under his permission, not mine,' I answered.

'Yes father, I mean, Lord,' Snake said. 'I do give my permission.'

Snake jumped hastily onto the slab, where he stood, eye to eye with his father. They shared a height and a hairstyle, but Lord Hawk outmatched him in pure strength. As strong and as stocky as Snake might be, next to his father, he looked infantile. It humoured me to think about Snake growing a beard to match his father's.

'This boy is strong, fast and could probably best most of my men in combat, but unfortunately, he has not, and will never reach the perfection necessary of an Elite. I'm sure that he will make a fine warrior, and one day, maybe even a Lord. It's his face you see, it lets him down,' Hawk said, with a hand on his sons' shoulder. 'Sir Ronald, ensure the boy is given no less than fifteen gold pieces. I am sorry son, but that is all I can do for the poor boy.'

Sir Ronald strolled away so leisurely, that he was almost floating, and a moment later, after searching through a pile of folded clothing, he returned and tossed the boy a small sack full of coin pieces. The boy was speechless at this kind gesture

'I am thankful that you would do the boy such an honour,' Snake said, bowing as he comes back to my side.

I could not help feeling sorry for the boy. He was unwelcomed with the Mainland and with the Elites. If the poor boy is found unwelcome with the other Divisions, he would either be an outcast or placed in the Baron dwell. The Stronghold divisions are the only honest place for a cursed boy in Mangrove.

'I will take the boy,' Sir James shouted, approaching fast and smirking under his sharp uneven teeth.

'And what do you want with the boy?' I asked, confused and unsure of James intentions.

It was a grand gesture for James to make, and a life-changing opportunity for the boy, but what purpose would he serve. I did not trust James, not one bit.

'I was thinking of making the boy Commander of the assassination squad, after sufficient training of course,' James replied. 'His face does not bother me.'

'Sir James, you are welcome to the boy, however, do not insinuate that I am a cruel man for demanding perfection in my ranks,' Hawk said, displeased with James.

'I mean no disrespect, but I am confused as to how you can turn away such a fine warrior, with so much potential.'

'Nula, come to me,' Hawk commanded.

'Yes, my Lord,' the incredibly beautiful young women answered, standing tall before her Lord.

'You see this girl,' Hawk said, holding her by the forearm. 'She is one of the least perfect members of my Division, yet she would sink a man's jaw with a single glance. The boy will never obtain beauty, neither will you, James. This does not mean you cannot go far in life; it just means that you must take a different path.'

'What of your face?' James said, bashing his spear down in irritation. 'It is not perfect or pleasant.'

'Watch your tongue, unless you wish it removed,' Hawk ragged, gesturing for Nula to return to her kneeling position. 'Beauty is in the eye of the beholder, and I hold all of the bees. Now, get out of my sight. I've lost my appetite looking at you. Where on earth is Mastiff with that water?'

James remained silent, giving no more than a frown and a slight tilt of his head. I can see where my brother gets it, I thought, looking around at all of the long-haired, perfectionist members of the Elite force.

'A hundred apologies my Lord, there was a blockage in the pipes,' Mastiff explained, running over, carefully holding a ceramic jug of water. Lord Hawk laughed, as did the boy, who's bloody tears ran heavier than they previously had.

'Brandon, come with me,' James commanded. 'I will show you to your new barracks.'

'You will go far in this world boy, just watch this one,' Hawk advised, tapping the boy on the back and swilling down a mouthful of fresh water, before handing it to the boy, who almost choked attempting to drink as much.

'Thank you, Lord Hawk,' Brandon said, taking a knee. 'Thank you, everyone, for your kindness.'

'You can learn something from that boy, James,' Hawk said, peering through the corner of one eye.

On return to the Mainland, Snake and I came across a homeless boy, sifting through the bins at the Kings cross. Exchanging a look of remorse, we gave the child a few gold pieces each and carried on our way. What would the King have in store for this child, I thought, as the ill forgotten memory of Talia crept to the forefront of my mind, begging for sorrow.

'Commander, I have a mission which involves you,' I said, scratching my head nervously. 'The mission is a surveillance expedition at the Mangrove Citadel. We will pass through the Oakwood Forrest and over moat bridge. There, we are going to search out any signs of the sea Lords. I will be dressed as a commoner, to arouse less suspicion, whilst the rest of you will be my backup, led by Lady Senna.'

'What is my role in all this?' He asked.

'You will choose ten of your best men, inform Sophia that she must prepare ten of her best, and ensure everyone is at the north gate, mounted and ready to leave on the second fall of the sun. Oh, and have a four-horsed Mainland chariot ready for Lady Senna.'

'Yes, my Lord, of course. By the fall of the second son, do you mean tomorrow night?' Snake asked, running his fingers across the red brick of the King's tower as we passed beneath its arch.

'Yes, isn't that obvious.'

'Well...I guess so my Lord, forgive my ignorance.'

'Do you trust me, Snake?' I asked.

I pitifully counted the number of trusted friends I had. Three girls, two of which I have had somewhat familiar relations with, one aggressive northerner and one giant Lion, who could only speak through a nit-picking gibbon.

'Yes, my Lord. I believe you to be trustworthy.' He had a somewhat confused puppy dog look to his always squinting eyes.

'Good,' I said. 'I too feel that I can trust you, so when we are not on official duty, you may address me as Mace.'

'Yes, my Lord, my Mace...I mean, Mace.' His face went as red as a tomato.

I was now left with the difficult task of figuring out how exactly I was going to get Dusk to the Citadel, without my men knowing and without him being aware of Senna's presence. There was also the exchange with the sea Lords, which could go wrong. Even if they agree to a truce and stay out of the Citadel, they will probably have demands, and Dusk will then have to be exchanged in full secrecy. I wish this situation was simple, I wish for the sea Lords to accept my terms, and most of all, I wish for a moment of peace in my otherwise unsettled life.

27. ~ FAILINGS ~

The next day, between the rising and the setting of the sun, I ventured yet again into the dark pits of the Baron dwell. There, I was more welcomed than I had previously been. The prisoners hid, silent in their huts, terrified from a repeat of my previous bloodshed, that remained stained on the cave floor. Dusk was kind enough not to struggle as I cuffed his wrists, chained his arms, stuffed his ears, and blindfolded his eyes. The back of my carriage will be his home for the next few days of our expedition.

From my bed chambers, I could hear the front door to the manor creek open. Curious and nervous as to who would be brave or stupid enough to walk uninvited into my home, I hurried to the top of the staircase. Peering down, I saw the bandaged, bruised and limping, Dame Lambert. She smiled up at me. It was as if, for the first time, she was happy. It was the happiest I had ever seen her anyway. Maybe I just missed her.

Without hesitation, I ran to greet her. I gave her the slightest of hugs, that was not hard enough to hurt her, yet hard enough for her to know that I cared.

'What is that awful smell?' Lambert said, holding her nose. 'Mace, that is horrible, it's making me gag.'

'It is aftershave, and it is a very expensive and sort after fragrance,' I said, defending the pungent scent that wafted from me.

She stood there, blankly staring, before bursting into a fit of laughter.

'And why are you dressed like that, you look like a carriage salesman,' she joked, unable to contain her laughter until it pained her.

I went to assist her, as she was clearly in no fit state to help herself, but she was too proud to accept it. Expecting anything less would be an insult to her.

'I will be going to the Citadel, to make a truce with the sea Lords,' I said. 'I do not want to draw any unwanted attention to myself. So, I have chosen to suit up.'

'Why did you not inform me. I need to get ready. When are we leaving?' she was worried that she would delay our departure

'Lambert, you are not fit for travel. I need you to stay and recover. If you are bored, maybe you could take Ice to the Beast Division for some training.'

I laid a sympathetic hand on her shoulder. She stepped back, staring at her feet, appearing to take my kindness as an insult. A hot flush ran through me and reddened my cheeks. After what I had been through to gain her respect, I did not want to see a repeat of the hot-headed and aggressive Lambert, that tormented me at every turn.

'I understand,' was all she said, pulling me down by the scruff of my shirt, only to plant an unexpected kiss on my lips, that yet again, lasted longer than it should have. I began sweating profusely.

'Lambert...'

'Say no more,' she interrupted, stroking her hand across my chest, before limping to the living room, where she lay next to Ice, who slept soundly in front of the fireplace.

'You are welcome to stay here whilst I am gone,' I said, grabbing the cross hilted handle of my sword. 'Help yourself to any of the luxuries the blue manor has to offer, just please try and rest, Lambert.'

She said nothing and just laid there with her back to me, stroking Ice as he slept. For a moment I stared, taking in the sight of her with my loyal Beast. This could be a comfortable living arranging. As fast as those thoughts had come to mind, they were gone, replaced by a guilty feeling of betrayal. I betraying Lambert and Eva's trust.

'I will make this right,' I said, not meaning to speak my thoughts aloud.

'What did you say?' asked Lambert.

'Nothing, nothing at all.'

I did not say goodbye, nor did I give a second look, I just took a deep breath and departed. I rested my weary head on the outside door of the Manor, hoping to regain my lost composure. I was not ready for this expedition, but I was not going to be late either, so I began the short walk to the north gate.

Lady Senna, dressed in her usual black leathers, with her shimmering blonde hair tied in bunches, sat cross-legged above a black four-horsed chariot. Her traditional silver spear lay across her lap, with a new grey fur attachment, dangling from a hole in the front section.

Commander Sophia, whilst horse backed, checked the condition of the arrows in her quiver. Her long brown hair flowed with the wind, as did her black robes.

Just as I had commanded, ten of the artillery unit were mounted and ready to depart, as were Snake's cavalry. He was busy pulling the last fastenings around the saddle of his white steed, that dwarfed over the other horses.

'Mace, the sun appears to be set,' Senna said, standing atop the chariot, smirking strangely.

I rode the blue Mainland carriage out from under the cover of an old oak, and Senna's smirk turned to laughter. For a moment, I wondered why, but then unrealized she was laughing at the sight of my suit.

'Yes, Senna, I am wearing a suit. It is very amusing I am sure,' I said, smirking back sarcastically. 'Commander Snake, lead the way. Sophia, you will follow. Senna and I will take the rear.'

Senna laughed so hard that she almost fell from the top of the chariot, until she focused her attention on the carriage, realising what must be inside. She looked to me and then to the carriage. The windows were blacked out and it was double-locked on all sides. Appearing saddened, Senna swung her spear around and jumped into her chariot, where she remained silent.

Under the arch of the north gate, we met with the overgrown mystery of the Oakwood forest, that was particularly haunting in the dull light of the moon. The crunching of twigs and the soft pounding of hooves were the only sounds to accompany us for miles around, save from the occasional wildcat growl or wolf howl.

The trees loomed overhead, appearing to scrape the sky, with arms that clawed out. An array of different smells crept from every direction. Sweet oak to the right, damp moss to the left, and every so often a whiff of faeces would linger in the air. The bells from the clock tower could be heard chiming in the twentieth hour of the day, and the twinkling nightlife of the Mangrove citadel was a guiding light in the far distance.

This forest was strange, almost eerie. It made normal life seem like a far distant memory. After several hours of travelling, we had not gained much distance. We had a long way to go, and the men, to keep their spirits high, sang merrily away. Their song was so droll, that it was met with the howling of wolves I could not help but laugh. They clapped and cheered at the end of every verse, as did Lady Senna, who could be heard singing along from inside of her chariot.

Overcome with excitement, she leapt to the top of the chariot in a single swift motion, and waving her spear around, she danced and sang for almost an hour, until she was tired and decided to jump over to my carriage.

'Do you have everything you need in your carriage, Mace,' she said, slumping herself down beside me.

'Yes...I have everything I need.'

'So, tell me, how are you and Eva getting along?' she asked, resting her head on my shoulder. 'I've heard a lot about you two, more than I could honestly be bothered to listen to. The way that she goes on about you is more than enough to handle. It would make the soppiest of little girls sick.'

'I feel very strongly about her,' I said, blushing from embarrassment.

This was not the sort of thing I ever spoke about with anyone, even Senna. Usually, our conversations were about who could kill who in a fight, or which weapon is better against another.

'Don't give me that rubbish,' she said. 'How long have I known you, seven, eight years, maybe more, and in that time, I have never seen you so much as look at a woman. You love her, don't you?'

'You might be right…as always. I do feel love for her, but not in the way you might think,' I said. 'When she is with me, I feel like the only man in the world. I become lost in her beauty. My only fear is that we may not be compatible.'

Senna jolted upright. 'For goodness sake, you are so bloody soppy. I feel a little sick. But seriously, it amazes me that you are not into men.'

'That is rich coming from you,' I said, laughing. 'Whenever Eva and I are together, our nerves get the better of us. Maybe we do not have as much in common as I would have hoped. She is beautiful and that is great, but what happens when we have nothing to talk about. What happens when we are spending as little time together as possible, just to avoid an awkward silence.'

'You are getting a bit ahead of yourself. Don't you think.' She looked me dead in the eye. 'I Shouldn't be telling you this, but she has very similar concerns about you. My advice to her was the same advice I now give you. If it is not meant to be, then it will not be, and you must move on.'

It was sound advice. More than anyone, Senna knew about heartache. Her first love was killed when she was very young. Her second love betrayed her and so, she killed him. As for her third, well, she was a woman, and she did not share Senna's feelings. This is why I do not jest with Senna about her love life, nor ever really speak with her about it.

'Thank you, Senna.'

'And another thing. Don't be so bloody nervous, you are both ruthless killers, and have never been nervous about that. When we get home, I would like to hear that you bashful children have made some effort,' she said, closing her eyes and curling her arms around me. 'Oh, and Mace, if you like another girl, then you must choose only one before somebody gets hurt.'

28. ~ UNKNOWN ~

We had travelled throughout the night, guided only by the distant figure of the Citadel, that grew ever closer on our slow approach. We were an easy hour ride from the moat bridge, which leads directly to the heavily guarded main gate of the Citadel.

Resting her head on my lap, Senna had slept the entirety of the journey, waking only as we stopped for some well-deserved food and rest.

The dawning sun of a new day danced behind slow-moving clouds in the distance, whilst the moon of last night strayed further from sight. The cool chill that once freshened the air became warm and filled with the annoyance of swarming insects.

'Mainland division, we will stop here and wait for sundown,' I said, pouring some water for the horses. 'Sophia, you and the artillery hunt for some fresh meat. Snake, gather some wood with the cavalry.'

A sudden high-pitched and defining squawk sang in the distance. All eyes attended, considering where the sound of a large bird was coming from.

'That sounds like a pheasant, and a large one at that,' one of the women from the artillery unit said, pulling her bow from around her shoulder and an arrow from her quiver.

Again, the squawk sounded, louder and more defining than the last. The women, eager for the hunt, notched the arrow to her bowstring. Sophia and the rest of the artillery also notched their bows, ready for the large pheasant to pass overhead.

'Take cover. Hide,' Senna shouted in a flustered panic, pulling the four-horsed carriage containing Dusk under the cover of a nearby oak tree.

Stricken with paranoia, everyone drew their weapons, save for I. My beautiful cross hilted and flat-bladed sword was always drawn and by my side.

'Senna, what is the matter with you?' I asked, watching her with confusion.

She was shaking as she gripped her spear and watched the sky.

'Are you all deaf,' she yelled out. 'I told you to take bloody cover.'

Moving quickly, I ran behind the carriage next to Senna, where a wide oak-covered over us. All the units, along with their horses, hastily left the path, taking cover in the surrounding oaks.

The squawk echoed yet again. All eyes attended upwards and all hands covering their ears from the deafening sound. A harsh brightness illuminated the sky, overpowered the sun and heating the surrounding air. The leaves of the wide oak trees began to dry out and shrivel up as the earth shook with hot sweeping gusts of wind. It seared my skin and burned my throat.

'What is this?' I asked, struggling to catch my breath.

Senna had no words, only a clammy hand to cover my mouth, and an exaggerated finger over her lip, gesturing my silence.

Coughing and choking came from many hidden members of my Division, whilst the horses lay exasperated in the dirt with their tongues flapped out. I had no idea of what to expect and was in no hurry to find out what sort of nightmare was scorching the air. Like snow from hell, black ash fell from the burnt leaves overhead.

Of all the winged creatures I had ever seen, none was as beautiful, powerful or as wondrous. It was a bird of fire. It was breath-taking, to say the least, not only in the way it inspired awe but in the way it soaked up and destroyed its surroundings. Being larger than any house only made it more ominous and mystical. Orange, crimson and deep yellow shone from its feathers, that consisted entirely of flame. Although it was narrow, and in the traditional style of a large bird, its beak was rigged and as black as night. Sharp enough to skewer a pig, its talons had three curved claws to the front and one crooked to the back. Most of all, its deep-set yellow eyes caught my attention, with their unrelenting look of intelligence. It was as if it was not of a bird, but a man.

Within seconds it had passed by, leaving a rain of ash and a trail of destruction in its wake, that followed to the Citadel. Needless to say, I was shaken up, but amongst everything, I was sure that it had caught my gaze, I was almost certain.

'What was that creature, and why was it heading towards the Mangrove Citadel?' I asked as long-forgotten fresh air filled my starved lungs.

Catching her breath, Senna looked at me with a sense of panic and urgency.

'It is the pirate, Arc,' she said. 'Well...the manifestation of his curse anyway. The bird of fire.'

Senna moved to the centre of the path, where she was joined by the Mainland units. Their frightened eyes were directed at me, for advice, for orders, for comfort maybe. Unsure of what to say, I looked towards Senna, who knew more than I.

'Men and women of the Mainland Division, what you have just seen was no mere bird. It is a curse...a manifestation of one of the sea Lords curses to be exact. I would love to tell you not be frightened, but that creature would turn a man to ash with a single flap of its wings, however, it is not unstoppable,' Senna explained, turning her attentions to me. 'Mace, if these fine soldiers are going to risk their lives, they must know why.'

She laid a hand on my shoulder. I took a deep breath and held my head high. An eerie silence ran through the forest, as the last of the ash fell around us.

The thought of telling the pirate-hating men and women of the Mainland Division, that they will play a part in forming a peace treaty with the very people they hate, made me feel sick to my stomach. I wished this was not my task, I wished that we could sleep this out in a warm bed, and most of all, I wished that Lambert was here. She would know what to say, she would hold their loyalty.

Sticking the flat tip of my sword into the cracked dry earth beneath my feet, I turned to my units. 'My loyal Mainland Division, I will not sugar coat this. I have lied to you, betrayed your trust, and did not believe that you would be understanding, or accept me for doing what I must do. Before I go on, I want to say that I have done this for the greater good,' I had to take a breath, my nerves were in tatters. 'Tied to the inside my carriage, is the infamous sea lord, Dusk Stone. I mean to form a truce with the sea Lords, who still rape and pillage the once peaceful Citadel of Mangrove. A trade will take place, following the agreement of my terms. Our peace for their brother.'

Some looked away in shame, others retained their frightened expressions, but most stared deep into my eyes with a disdainful look of hatred.

'Those bastard pirates killed Lord Brick. How could you betray us like this? We trusted you,' Snake screamed, angrily throwing his sword into the side of a nearby oak, where it lay deep in the wood.

'I am sorry, to you all. If a truce can be formed, then no more lives have to be lost in vain. Do you not think that this blood feud has gone on quite long enough?' I said, taking a knee.

'We should kill him now. Get him out of that carriage so we can give him a slow and painful death,' one of the clean-cut cavalrymen shouted, followed by a cheer from rest, save for Senna and Sophia, who oddly gave a look more of understanding than of hatred.

'I cannot let you kill him. Please, think about what will happen if he dies.'

'I don't care what happens,' Snake said, ripping his sword from the tree and storming towards the carriage.

'I cannot allow this,' I said, leaving my sword in the dirt, as I stepped over to the carriage ahead of them with my arms held out wide.

'My Lord, please get out of my way,' he said, preparing to attack. 'There is no reasoning to be had with those bastard pirates.'

'What is your plan, commander? What will you do when the sea lords, with a bird of fire and worse, come knocking on the North gate, asking for their brother? What is the plan, for when hundreds of thousands lay dead?'

'I will fight them and kill them all,' Snake roared, bearing down on me with his sword that shimmered in the light of the fresh sun.

Before any strike was made, or any blood spilt, an arrow knocked the sword off-target and slammed into the side of the carriage with a thud.

'Stop this madness,' Sophia screamed out, notching another arrow on her longbow.

'But Sophia...'

'But nothing, Snake. Have you gone mad?' she interrupted. 'You mean to murder Lord Mace in cold blood, just to kill a pirate. You will be tossed from the red tower for treason, along with the rest of you idiotic fools. Put down your swords and think about what you are doing.'

She held Snake in her aim, tilting her bow as she stretched back her arm. With a sigh, he dropped his sword.

'I like this one,' Senna said, from her relaxed and cross-legged vantage point atop her chariot. 'She is feisty.'

Rather than slitting my thought for dishonesty, Snake punched me in the side of my jaw, which surprisingly, did not hurt, nor feel like any contact was made at all.

'Commander, are you alright?' I asked as he hunched over, holding his hand tight.

'Damn it, damn it, damn it,' he droned on, holding his hand, which was not broken, dislocated somewhat, but not broken.

'Listen to me,' I said. 'I mean only to do what is right, for the greater good, but I cannot do it alone. Dame Lambert, who as you all know, did not take kindly to me, is now resting in my Manor. She understands what must be done, and if anyone has the right to kill the pirates, it is her, but she has not. I do not expect you to risk your lives for this cause, and I do not expect you to continue this journey with me, however, I hope it does not come to it, but if it all goes wrong, I cannot fight the pirates or a giant bird of fire on my own. I need back up. If you are with me, then please stay and if not, then you may leave. I swear that no punishment or further course of action will befall you.'

Snake was the first to walk off, pulling his horse by the reins. He was followed by the entire cavalry unit. They were loyal to him.

'I am and will remain loyal to my Division, Lord Mace, but I will not die for a cause that I do not believe in, be it a worthy cause or not. I wish you a safe return,' Snake said, showing his pride as a warrior.

Sophia decided to stay, as did four of the artillery unit. The rest departed without a word, only giving a slight nod to Sophia, as they walked off with their horses. Although this was not part of the plan, the expedition will continue, with my honour intact and my conscience clear.

Lady Senna, with her arms behind her head, slumped back onto the dry ground next to an old oak, whilst Sophia and the other gathered wood for a fire.

Initially intending to help with the fire, I was side-tracked by the indulgent smell of fresh meat. I followed the smell along the path north. To my luck and surprise, the bird of fire had cooked a flock of gulls. They were slightly chard, but hot and steaming and ready to eat.

Sixteen gulls were gathered in total. I could not help but wonder if the others had found such luck on their way home. I stuffed my face with gull meat none the less.

Waiting for everyone to fall asleep, as not to attract more unwanted attention, I gave Dusk two whole gulls and a bucket full of water. He had spent all night tied, gagged and blindfolded in the back of my steaming hot carriage. Despite how uncomfortable it must be in there; he still met my presence with a smile and my gift of food and water with thanks.

29. ~ DECEIVE ~

At the foot of the moat bridge, Lady Senna and I, along with Commander Sophia and the four remaining women of the artillery unit, stood gazing up at the grand wall of the Citadel. Maybe it was the thrill of an unfolding adventure or the pride one gets from fighting for the greater good, but these brave women were all cheery and ready for whatever lay ahead.

We gathered the horses, carriage and chariot, and made our way up the steep incline of the moat bridge. For obvious defensive purposes, the bridge had no sides, nor was it very wide. Single file was the safest approach.

The closer we came to the Citadel, the more we could see. There were buildings so tall, they looked as if they were scraping the sky. Enormous cranes soared overhead, swooping between the inordinate amount of Mangrove flags on the outer wall. Each flag portrayed a soaring Crane, holding a spear in its beak, on a half blue and half gold backdrop. It was an odd-looking flag, to say the least, but as the Crane was the highest populated animal in Mangrove, and spears were the most popular item of trade, it made for a sensible point.

Forty or so guards stood in front of the large, black and over-scaled entrance gate, moving into a triangular-shaped strategic position on our approach.

'Who goes there?' a small and ill-spoken man asked.

He wore a cumbersome looking suit of old-style armour, probably made of iron, and he was holding a spear that was twice his height. He stood at the front of their triangle of identically dressed men and being the only of them wearing a blue barrette, I guessed that he was the man in charge.

'Greetings. I am Lord Mace Black of the Mainland Division, I am here with Commander Sophia of the Mainland artillery, along with four of her unit, and Lady Senna of the services Division,' I said, pulling my carriage up beside the small man. 'We are here on a surveillance expedition.'

'I've never heard of a Lord Mace Black,' he rubbed his moustache curiously. 'Mantis Black, now I've heard of him. Not you...no, I have never heard of you.'

'What is your name, guardsman,' I asked.

'Henry is that you,' Senna butted in from the back of the group. 'Henry Livingston, you little oaf, where is your father?'

'My Lady, he is sick. He's got the flower flu…or some such thing, and left me in charge.'

He looked nervously at Senna and went bright red in the face. Senna jumped down from her chariot and stormed over to the small man. He immediately took a knee, as did the forty or so men behind him.

'If your father saw how utterly incompetent you were, he would send you to wash the public toilets,' Senna yelled at the top of her voice. 'This is Lord Mace Black, Lord Brick's predecessor. Everyone who is anyone knows about him. Get up, and great a Lord in the way a Lord should be greeted and stop wasting our time.'

Senna stuck her tongue out at me like a little girl and strolled cheerfully back to her carriage.

'Lord Mace, I am so sorry. I meant no disrespect, honest I didn't.' He was barely able to look me in the eye.

Unsure of what to say, after Senna's outburst, I simply gave a tilt of my head and waited silently. Being a Lord was a strange concept and one that will take me some time to get used to. I never really knew how to act, nor did anyone know how to act around me.

'Open the gates,' the small man said.

For some reason, his name immediately left my thoughts as soon as I had heard it. I was annoyed with myself for not remembering it.

'Opening the gates,' another voice echoed from behind the gate.

'The gates will be open shortly my Lord. I hope you have a nice stay,' the small man said.

'Thank you,' was all I could think of saying, irritated and distracted by the thought of his name.

Unlike traditional gates, these enormous black ones did not swing open, instead, they slowly rose with a roar. The guards all proceeded through the gates in double file and piled either side of the inner wall, assumedly for safety's sake, as trying to squeeze through would surely cause a few guards to tumble off the bridge.

Through the gate, we were immediately surrounded by a circle of stables, and in the centre of the stable, there was a life-sized and horse backed statue of King Leopold, founder of Mangrove. His sword was pointing to the night sky. On one shoulder a Crane was perched and on the other, a cloak hung to the ground, giving the old King a strong and worthy appearance.

'Give your father my best wishes, Henry,' Senna said, smiling as she passed him.

'Henry, of course,' I said, completely out of context.

I acted as if I had not just made an ass of myself and casually cleaned my sword. Thinking that I was talking to my sword, the woman all shrugged their shoulders. Senna and Sophia shared a look of confusion for a moment and then chuckled aloud. I paid no attention and carried on cleaning my sword until I could not help myself. I giggled and snorted in a fit of laughter. Everyone was in hysterics, save for the guards, who just thought we were crazy.

'It will cost a silver per horse and two apiece for the chariot and carriage,' an old, well-shaven man with grey-hair said, holding a pen and parchment pad close to his chest.

'That's almost a gold piece for the lot, bit steep wouldn't you say?' answered Senna, jumping from the chariot to approach the man. 'Can you not give a discount for multiple horses?'

She united her long hair and elegantly brushing it through her fingers. The old man blushed.

'I, um...maybe I can give you a group discount,' he said, engrossed with Senna. 'Fifteen…no, twenty percent off.'

'You are too kind. Mace, pay the man,' she said, stroking the man's shoulder and giving him such a look that it caused him to drop his parchment pad.

Raising my brow to Senna, I pulled my satchel bag from the side of the carriage and gave the man eight silver pieces, leaving twenty gold, twelve silver and fifteen copper pieces. The man scribbled something on his parchment pad in unreadably fancy writing.

'I will have the stable boys take your horses. They will be cleaned, fed and watered. You will find them stored between stable eleven and fourteen. Here is your receipt, enjoy your stay.'

Poorly dressed and underfed stable boys gathered in from every direction to tend the horses.

'Boys, eleven to fourteen,' the old man shouted, walking towards a small building to the side of the gate.

Strolling with a strangely elated sense of excitement, I realised that Senna was not with us. It appears that she had no intention of joining us, nor did she even look in our direction as we left.

'Senna,' I said, suddenly realising that Dusk was in the carriage and she was going to stay and guard him.

'What is it Mace, do you miss me already.'

'I will blow my signal horn on our return, or if we need your assistance.'

'That's nice Mace. Are you sure you don't want me to hold your hand?' she mocked, turning her back to follow the carriage to the stable.

Through what felt like miles of narrow streets, nooks, crannies and deadens, we found our way to the central province, and what a sight it was to behold. The exquisite stonework detail of the buildings stretches high into the sky. The lights from every office block, every wall and every amusement were blindingly bright, giving it the appearance of being almost alive.

There were so many people from all walks of life, monks from the far south, harpies from the great tree, and even bulky clan folk from the jungle regions. This truly was a marvellous place.

'My Lord, that night tavern across the way, the howling wolf, is where you are most likely to find the pirates,' Sophia announced, pointing to the old-fashioned tavern, with the howling white wolf on its sign.

'Then that is where I shall go first,' I said. 'Sophia, you and the others find a suitable vantage point on the surrounding rooftops. Fire only on my signal.'

Spreading out, they hurried up the drainage pipes of the surrounding buildings, where they remained hidden from sight.

A cool breeze past through the central province, wafting out the odourise smell of my unwashed clothing. I should have changed when we arrived, I thought, sniffing the pit of my arm as I strolled casually on my way to the tavern. At least at the tavern, there would be smokers, drinkers and the smell of sickness to mask my stench.

'How about that crab of yours, you reckon he can hold up,' a tall skinny man said, bumbling out the tavern with his friend.

'He had better do. I got three silver on him...or was it four, I forget,' his friend said, almost falling down the single step in front of the entranceway.

'The odds are ten to one John and that's the last of your coin.'

'You doubting me sonny,' his friend replied, stumbling over his feet and into me. He fell to the ground with the sound of ripping clothes.

'Watch where you're going, bloody rude you are. I ripped my god damn trousers.' He slipped over again in his attempts to stand.

'My apologies good sir. He's drunk, had a bit too much ale and knows not what he says,' the skinny man said in defence of his friend.

'Not to worry,' I said, ignoring them as I continued into the tavern.

To my surprise the men ran off, laughing and cheering amongst themselves, and appearing soberer than a moment ago. Thinking nothing of it, I swung open the entrance door and was greeted by a large lump of a man.

'Three bronze pieces,' he said.

'Excuse me.'

'Can you hear me boy?' he said, leaning in. 'Three bronzes for entrance.'

He held his hand out with an ugly grimace. I went for my coins but found none, nor my satchel bag. In a panic, I frantically looked around, wondering where my satchel full of coins could have gone.

'Those thieving bastards,' I said, feeling stupid.

How could I have been so ignorant not to have realised that those men were sneak thieves, I thought, rushing back into the street holding the grip of my blade in a tight grasp.

30. ~ SACRIFICE ~

The sneak thieves were long gone, but the street was not empty. There was one man. He was staring at me from the shadows across the way. His eyes glistened a fiery red. He had a longsword in one hand, which looked somewhat familiar, and on the other hand, swaying back and forth, was my satchel bag.

In the blink of an eye, he was gone. It was as if he was never there in the first place. It did not matter who he was, nor why he had my coin, I would not fall into a trap and end up like Lord Brick.

With a cautioned step I followed the man, defensively positioning my sword as I crept around a dark corner and down a winding stairway, leading to the corner of a bloodstained alleyway.

'I've been expecting you, as were these thieves it would appear. You should be more careful,' the man said, stepping out of the shadows and throwing the decapitated heads of the two thieves to my feet.

A look of fear remained across their faces.

Now that I could see the man clearly, I was immediately sure it was Arc, Dusk's brother. There was no denying it. Not only did he have a peg leg, but he was tall, dark and had a head of thick afro hair.

'You must be Arc?' I said. 'You need not have killed those thieves, a good beating perhaps, but not death...not a beheading.'

'Just a boy,' he said, taking a piece of gold from my satchel and flicking it into the air.

It was a distraction. As the coin spun and I glanced up, the man was gone, vanished from sight.

'Yes, I am Arc. I believe this belongs to you,' he said, stood beside me, jingling my satchel bag.

I turned fast, nervously swinging my sword, but there was nothing to meet my strike, nothing but thin air. Predicting the same move would be used again, I spun full circle with a barrage of swings and slashes, each parried with an arm rattling crunch of steel.

'The shadow dance,' I said. 'That is my brothers move, how do you know it?'

My eyes were fixed on his sword, which was a perfect resemblance of Mantis's, except for the grip, which was clearly for two-handed use.

'Your brothers move, the bloody cheek of it...is that what he tells you,' he said. 'I can see from your silver hair and dim wits that your Mantis Blacks brother. Am I wrong, Lord Mace of the Mainland?'

'How do you...'

'How do I know,' he interrupted. 'Word spreads fast around here young Mace. Your name is known across the seas.'

He was smirking with ominous intent, that reminded me instantly of Mantis, who always gives me the same look. This man was so familiar to me, in so many ways, yet I had never met him before in my life and only heard his name last week. Some questions needed answering, questions that I believe my brother would already know the answers to.

'Now, let's get to business. Where is Dusk? And don't lie to me, I could smell him with you in Forrest,' he said, with a gleam in his fiery red eyes.

'What...you could smell him?'

'Yes, through Kane. He had you all cowering under the trees like frightened little bunny rabbits.'

'Kane...your bird of fire? He is called Kane.' I stared blankly with a confused interest.

'He is more than a mere bird. He is the Manifestation of my soul, he is my curse, my heart, and most importantly, he is my power.'

'How does that work?' I asked, still none the wiser.

'You don't know much about curses, considering you are cursed,' he said, with raised brows. 'Essentially Kane and I are one being and share one mind. When he watches, I see, when I speak, he hears and what I think, he thinks, with one united mind.'

I still did not quite understand, but then explaining my curse would not exactly have made much sense.

Arc was appearing to enjoy our conversation. We had some common ground. He knew Mantis, maybe even better than I did.

'You've had me distracted long enough, boy. Now, I will not ask again, where is Dusk?' He approached, scraping the tip of his sword along the alley wall.

'Are you not at all curious as to why I have him in the first place.'

'Not really...but Sand will be watching the crab fight for at least an hour,' he said, pausing 'I suppose I have some time to kill. Indulge me, please.'

'Dusk was found placing flowers over Lord Brick's grave,' I said. 'There, he was captured and taken to the Baron dwell. I agreed to release him, on the agreement of his and the East bay's terms of peace, which he gladly obliged to.'

Arc burst into a fit of deeply exaggerated laughter, attempting to speak between laughs. He took a few deep breaths and rubbed his eye's clear of tears.

'He is such a little bitch. You know that Dusk could have just walked out of that dwell, or your carriage, at any point. He's just scared of a little fight. Trench is the same, a bunch of girls.'

'He did seem rather placid,' I said, casually leaning on my sword. 'He told me that he had never killed. If that's true, and I have no reason to believe otherwise, then why on earth is he a bloodthirsty pirate.'

'If you want this conversation to continue, do not insult me,' Arc said, uncomfortably close to me. 'We are not mere pirates…we are sea Lords. You got that.'

'Yes, of course. I meant no offence.'

'And what was Dusk doing putting bloody flowers on Brick's grave, for pity sake has the world gone mad,' he continued, no longer laughing, but full of annoyance at his brother's lake of whatever he expected him to have, a savage nature, a cruel intent, a murderous rage perhaps.

'I can only assume that he was paying his respects to the dead, maybe he thought Lord Brick did not deserve to be murdered in a savage ambush.'

'Wait a minute, murdered like what…an ambush. I thought you would all be happy that we killed that traitor, and there was no ambush, he fled and we gave chase,' he said, twiddling his fingers. 'By the look on your face I can see you haven't figured it out.' he couldn't help but to laugh once again.

'Figured what out?' I said.

'The funny thing is, your brother would have known about Brick the entire time.' He began laughing hysterically.

He was so much like my brother and this was my chance to find out a few things, why they both laughed at inappropriate times, why they shared a sword style, and why my brother never spoke of them or any other parts of his life for that matter.

'Will you tell me about my brother,' I asked. 'Will you please tell me how you know him.'

I pulled Dusk's piece of eight from my pocket and flicking it to Arc, who despite his apparent skills, dropped the damn thing.

'These coins are priceless you know,' he said, smirking as he picked up the coin. 'I like you Mace, more than I like that brother of yours anyway, so I will tell you our past, on one condition. A fight…to the death.'

'To the death…really.'

'Yes,' he said, in all seriousness.

'Alright then. I agree.'

'You best be as good as they say you are, young Mace. I've wanted to fight you ever since you defeated the Chieftain. I heard he needed new teeth after your little scrap.'

With an all-mighty grin, Arc paced up and down, stretching his arms and legs out. He had an excitement about him, it was as if he lived for the thrill of a fight.

'Right then, where do I start…at the beginning I guess,' Arc said. 'Dusk, Sand, Trench, Mantis and I, along with our dead but not forgotten companion, Elinor. We were all children, around the same age, give or take. We all had two things in common, we had very powerful curses, and we were all slaves under the King Richard's rule, King Enzo's father, the man who instigated the first hunting of Beasts. He started the Beast war, a foolish and unnecessary war that cost thousands of lives, man and Beast.'

He sat down and made himself comfortable, placing his sword across his lap, just like Mantis.

'Anyway,' he continued. 'We were the King's secret weapon if you will. He sent us on dangerous and almost impossible missions. Mantis, Sand and I would fight on land, Trench, Dusk and Elinor would fight at sea. Trench had such power over the sea, that Dusk and Elinor never had to lift a finger.'

'Why has Mentis never mentioned any of this?' I asked.

'Do you want to hear this or not?'

'Yes, sorry. Go on.'

'Thousands were massacred at our hands, including a creature called Vends, the oldest and most destructively powerful Beast ever to Walk Mangrove. This creature was an eighty-foot, twenty-tonne salamander dragon thing. King Richard made us fight him one day, us and two hundred men. Two bloody hundred men Mace. We did it, but it was the last thing we ever did for the King. That Beasts took my leg and took Elinor's life. Mantis finished it off, inevitably ending the war. He will deny it to his grave, but your brother saved Mangrove.

'I cannot even imagine…'

'Do you want me to stop, seriously…I don't need to tell you this.'

'Sorry, sorry, please continue.'

'I should take your bloody head,' he mumbled under his breath. 'Where was I… your brother. The problem was, your brother loved Elinor. The day she died was the day he left Mangrove. We didn't think he would ever return.'

A thousand question jumped around my mind as I imagined my brother in great battles, ending wars, and even falling in love. It was hard to believe, as I had never known my brother to love anything, save from himself.

'When the war was over and your brother was nowhere to be found, we had no thanks, and no glory,' he said, lying back, gazing up and the night sky. 'We were chained up in a solid dark cell, with nothing but abuse, uncooked food and Lord Giovanni as our guard. I wouldn't wish that life on anybody. To our luck, the founding members of the South point, including the so-called, cursed King, assassinated King Richard, for his crimes against the cursed. They rescued us, took us under their wing and brought us into their ranks, unfortunately, we were still ordered to kill. For a time, it was good. We saw the luxuries of life, travelled the world and murdered the curse hating Kings of the world one by one, but enough was enough, after almost a century of taking orders, we had to leave and lives, so we took to the seas in search of the peace we had always dreamed of. The South Point has been on our tail ever since that day. Even Lord Brick was after us. Believe it or not, he was their agent number eight and he gave his life to cause strife between us and the Stronghold...That pretty much sums it up.'

A tear crept from his eye and rolled down his cheek.

'I am so sorry,' was all I could say, feeling for the man, who I now find myself trusting.

'For what...if it wasn't for you, I doubt Mantis would ever have returned,' he said. 'Mantis still walks our path and we know that when the time comes, he will be ready and waiting.'

'When the time comes for what?'

'We don't know yet, but we know it will change the world. We are always watching...always.'

'I just have to know, why has no one ever suspected Lord Brick, and why was it said that Brick died stopping pirates from robbing the Mangrove bank. It's all a bit elaborate, don't you think?'

He raised his brow and gave an amused smirk.

'Keep up Mace, I've heard you were naive, but seriously. It takes more than strength and skill to become a Lord, it used to anyway,' Arc said, strolling around. 'Lord Brick was never really a Lord, he just pretended as one. His loyalties were to the South point, as are many of the cursed individuals in the Stronghold. We were set up, made to look as if we had robbed the bank, and when Sand and I were trying to enjoy a peaceful pint of cider, a barrage of arrows flew at us. Naturally, we gave chase and found Lord Brick in an alleyway. He came at us with an axe in each hand, ready to kill or be killed, and well, the rest is history. The Mainland, witnessing the finishing blow, also attacked us. There was no reasoning to be had, so we killed those who tried to kill us first. Self-defence you could say. All but one young Dame made an attack, and all but one young Dame survived. She just sat on the hard ground, traumatised in fits of tears. The so-called Lord Brick made a fool of us all, and he was not alone.'

'Dame Lambert, the young woman you speak of, is my Dame. Her name is Lambert Crow. She was and still is fooled by her love for Lord Brick, but what you have said changes everything,' I said, full of seriousness.

'It changes nothing,' he shouted. 'Don't you understand, Mace. If you go running off to the Stronghold, preaching our word against the death of a Lord, they will have you tossed from the tower. They only call us pirates because the South point made us out as such, which means you cannot be seen affiliating with us unless you want the same title. You need to be smart about this and bide your time. Remember, your brother loathes the South point…more than anybody. Knowing him as I do, he's probably been plotting and planning since he left, all those years ago.'

'I understand,' I said, not truly understanding at all.

I was unsure of my next course of action. I must now fight this man to death, and I did not fancy my chances, but I gave my word, and I will honour this combat, even if it is my last.

'I wish I could form a truce with you, I truly do, but more of the South point will come for us and more blood will have to be spilt. I am sorry,' he said, slowly approaching me, slicing his sword from side to side. 'If it's any consolation, I can promise that we have never, and never will, kill an innocent, you have my word on that.'

I made myself ready for what I assumed would be a devastatingly powerful attack. I dropped into an almost crouched defensive position. Again, and again, his sword crashed into my blade with such force that it took the breath from my lungs. The nerves in my arm began to tingle, the shock of impact ached my shoulder and the speed of his attacks made it almost impossible to reposition.

'Aren't you going to fight me,' he screamed, laughing with almost lusting insanity.

His attacks were not weakening, nor were they slowing down, somehow, they appeared to be getting stronger with every crashing impact. I had to do something, I thought, as numbness crept up my arm and towards my neck. Timing his swings, I rolled left, missing the main blow, and only sustaining a slice to the leg. Having no time to dwell on the pain, I jumped at him, turning a full circle with a swing of my blade. Stepping back, he parried, not expecting my leg to continue rotating around to meet with the side of his head.

'That's more like it,' he said, crashing into the alley wall, where he steadied himself and repositioned for an attack, appearing to be thoroughly enjoying himself.

He was excited, ecstatic even, like a child on his birthday with every toy he could have wished for and more.

A strong offence was my only option against an opponent as strong as Arc. I could not keep up a defence against him and by the look of it, he had no intention of defending my attacks. With the definition of his biceps bulging under the tightness of his shirt, he held his sword high in the air, ready for a back-breaking attack. Matching his stance with strategy, I held my blade low to the right, carefully watching every movement of his body for the opportune moment. With a fire in his eyes and an unrelenting grin across his face, he charged, as did I. High pitched was the sound that stopped him in his tracks, almost like the sound of a horn, but none that I had ever heard or recognised. Unable to stop the force of my blade from swinging up to his rib and seeing no intention of a block or dodge, I made contact. As my blade sliced up the side of his ribs, which under normal circumstances would cleave flesh from bone, it merely ripped his waistcoat and shirt up the side.

'That's Sands horn, he needs help. Mace if you want this peace treaty and want us to stay away for a while, then help me now. If Sand has blown that horn, then it's bad…really bad,' he said, pulling off the ripped shirt and waistcoat to reveal the size of his muscular arms, which were inconsistent to his slim, yet scare covered build.

A strange mark was left where my blade sliced, steaming with a bright glow of orange, like molten steel.

'Lead the way,' I said, accepting to help the man, who I found myself trusted.

I somewhat enjoyed his company, except for his unnaturally enthusiastic lust for fighting to the death, which I was sure would happen at some point.

Nodding with a wink, he scaled the back wall of the alley with only one hand, whilst holding his sword in the other. I followed, with my blade between my teeth. I noticed that the orange steaming mark was now gone from Dusks back and, in its place, a small brown scar matching his many others remained.

We ran across rooftops, dodging chimneys and almost falling as we flung ourselves over them. Sophia and the others, assuming I was giving chase, went to follow. Unnoticed by Arc, who by the looks of it had made this run before, I gestured for them to stop, which they understood. After a few minutes of running with death-defying leaps of faith, we made it to the crab fighting pit, known as the Hatch. Normally lit up for all to see, as a symbol of unity in modern culture. It entertains the world's rich and prestigious, with the ranking crab fighting championships, from scorpion to mint, and even coconut crabs.

What we saw was nothing shy of a disaster, a massacre, a death sentence for the spectators involved. Walls caved in around piles of dead bodies, loose running crabs, some over ten-foot-tall, clawing people in half, and the most haunting of all, were the white-masked men, screaming in a high pitch, pulling people's insides out only to eat trusted.

'Demons,' I exasperated, overlooking the carnage on the edge a four-story-high rooftop.

'But how…there hasn't been a demon in the Citadel in years, let alone, four, five, six by my count. And why are they all masked?' asked Arc, full of concern, with a twitch in his fiery eyes as he looked for Sand.

I had no words in mind, no explanation to rationalise, and no idea as to what the best course of action would be.

'Sand…Sand, where are you,' Arc shouted, growing increasingly concerned and paranoid as to his friend's whereabouts. A loud, harsh squawk cried out in the not so far distance, signalling the approach of Kane, the enchanting yet monstrous bird of fire.

'Arc, don't just stand there, help me. look at this damn mess, bloody crabs killing people, demons running around with masks on. It's madness. I lost thirty gold pieces on these crabs,' Sand said, punching a hole in the side of a five-foot scorpion crab with his steel dusted knuckles.

The small stocky man, with a shaven head and a shaggy ginger beard, had more power than he looked to have. He too, like Arc, wore spat shoes, but unlike Arc, had on a full, three-piece grey suit, with the most unnaturally large lapels I had ever seen. Paying no attention, with a dropped jaw and lost look on his face, Arc stared longingly at a young blond woman, who, despite her small stature, bravely ushered the remaining spectators to safety.

'Arc, are you even listening to me,' Sand continued, as Arc snapped out of his lustful stare.

'Sand, you sorry-looking son a sneak thief,' Arc said, jumping from the roof, chuckling as he split a demon clean in half with an almighty swing of his sword that left a deep gash in the concrete beneath.

'Who is that girl?' Arc asked, looking through the chaos to meet her pale green eyes.

She was a small thing, full of confidence, wearing tight fitted trousers that matched her less than concealing sparkling top and high boots.

'Where?' Sand replied. 'look, over there by the entrance, with the golden glasses.'

'That's the crab keeper's daughter, Kristal. She introduces the crabs before the fights and has quite a violent reputation, as does her father. Can we please do this another time, if you haven't noticed, a lot is going on.'

'Who's your friend?' Sand asked, palming the sweat from his brow.

I jumped from the rooftop at that, rolling as I landed to take the pressure off my legs, which I had not noticed was still bleeding on the right.

'That's Mace Black, can't you tell? He's here to help, so long as we take a holiday for a while,' Arc said, putting his hand on my back with a smile.

'The little Lord, he looks just like Mantis doesn't he, how interesting. Wait, what's this about a holiday, what have you agreed,' Sand replied, looking me over with concern in his eyes.

'It's a long story and one I will explain soon enough, but trust me, he is a very useful ally,' Arc said, as yet another, even louder squawk cried out in the distance.

'Ye, ye, whatever, I'm choosing our destination if we are leaving for a while.'

'Lookout,' I interrupted, as a huge coconut crab put its claws around Sand, who just laughed at me, as did Arc.

Drawing back for an attack, as the crab's claws closed in around him, I was stopped by Arc.

'Just watch,' he said, finding my concerns hilarious.

With a simple touch of his hand, the crab went still, began to foam at the mouth and within seconds had fallen lifelessly back on itself.

'I forgot to say, don't ever touch Sand. The strength of whatever makes contact with him is absorbed. His curse is powerful, yet quite a burden,' Arc said, raising his sword high into the air. 'Let's do this.'

He began running towards the Hatch. Sand followed, punching a crab on the route towards a spike-covered demon, who just moments ago, had ripped the skin from a screaming woman's face. There are seven crabs and five demons remaining, and as the other two concentrated on the later, I would take out the crabs.

A big, boggle-eyed thing, that I had never seen the likes of, edged sideways towards a posh couple that huddled panicked in the corner. I would not make it over, not before the crab clawed them to pieces anyway. Without a hesitating thought, I Launched my blade through the air, and although it was not used for penetration, it sliced cleanly through the crab's larger left claw.

'Don't just sit there, run,' I shouted, jumping atop the crab, where I tore its boggle eyes off with my bare hands.

Rolling off the crab, I grabbed my blade and sliced through its underside, leaving it dead and gutless. As I ran for a small mint crab near the entrance next to Sand, I noticed that Arc had killed another demon, but was struggling, unarmed with two others, that appeared to have him pinned to the ground. Sand, bleeding quite profusely, was still attending the spiked demon. Quickly slicing the mint crab through the middle, leaving five crabs, I ran over to help Arc, who looked bruised and battered.

'Mace, help her,' Arc screamed, as the sky illuminated with the flapping of the fire bird's wings.

The young Kristal, that Arc appeared to be infatuated with, screamed and struggled as a largely built demon held her upside down by the ankle. With a precise aim, I Launched my blade through the air once again, impaling the demon's chest, which had little to no effect.

Soaring with speed and squawking with a deafeningly high pitch, Kane left a trail of smoke in its wake, burning the very air I breathed. Luckily the spectators had either managed to flee or were lying dead around us. Struggling for breath as the surrounding area was penetrated with an overbearing heat, I forced my blade upwards in a twisting motion, which between the demon's heart and lungs should have killed him, at least pained him, but it did neither. For my efforts, I was pounded several times to the jaw, nose and temple, which blurred my vision. With one hand the demon crushed Kristal's ankle with a sound that rattled my nerves, whilst continuing to pound my face with the other. The screams that poor girl made soured out, farther and more heart wrenching than I could bear to hear.

'What are you waiting for…end it, Mace,' Arc screamed, full of rage at the sight of his infatuation being held at the hand of a man-eating demon.

A cut and bloody Sand, who had snapped the neck of the spiked demon, was now angrily punching holes through another.

Scorching the surrounding area, which crisped the unfortunate dead bodies, landed Kane, next to Arc, who was laughing insanely as he held the demons still. The heat from the flames that danced high and rippled into the air, blackening the flesh of the demons until they were crisped and lifeless. At the same moment, my heart pulsated hard in my chest and despite the lack of air, I could breathe reasonably clearly. The strikes to my face no longer hurt, in fact, I no longer felt them at all. Wishing I knew how to control this power inside of me, I saw it, the red light. Learning from my last encounter in the Baron dwell, I knew that however beautiful, I mustn't be drawn in. The world slowed, almost to a standstill and the rush of adrenaline that surged through my veins felt amazing like I was a god amongst ants. Needless to say, I liked this power, it was addictive and I wanted more. With ease, I pulled my blade upwards, cleaving the demons head, as his blood turned black and burnt up in the heat. Catching Kristal, who screams of pain rang through the silent numbness of my mind, I placed her gently onto the ground.

Ascending into the night sky, Kane had served his purpose and would allow us to breathe again. The destructive power of Arcs curses still amazed me, yet at the same time, it was frightening.

Moments later we gathered around the destruction, none of us happy or smiling, yet all of us thinking the same thing. The South point. There were so many questions to answer, but where to begin and how to conduct an investigation without raising suspicions.

'You are a good one Mace,' Sand said, pulling his jacket sleeve over his blood-soaked hand, which I hesitantly oblige to shake.

'Listen, somewhere between stables eleven and fourteen by the front gate, you will find a black Mainland carriage, containing your brother, Dusk.

It has been a pleasure meeting you both,' I said, looking between them both, as Kristal snuggled herself into Arcs arms.

'Mace, take care of yourself, and if you ever need us, you will always find our men in the East Bay. Tell them who you are and they will find us,' Arc said, smiling with a missing front tooth, as he turned his attention to Kristal. 'Kristal, will you come with us.'

'Although you are cute, I don't even know who you, or even your full name…but,' Kristal sighed. 'There is nothing left for me here. All the crabs are dead, the building half-destroyed and my father was the first to fall when the demons attacked. His last words were, be brave, and so I was.'

She burst into tears, enclosing her face into Arcs chest.

'I have no interest in whether this is right or wrong. All I care about is executing the orders given to me. Those who get in my way are considered enemies and will be slain.' A young voluptuous woman screamed from the opposing rooftop.

I recognised her as one of Sophia's artillery, but why was she screaming, and why did blood drip from her noticeably fresh arrow wounds. Leaving nothing to the imagination in a shimmering skin-tight outfit, the number twenty-seven was marked on her shoulder, as a symbol of the South point and a reminder of who the true enemy it. Although she was a young woman, her seemingly ordinary brown eyes beamed with wisdom, like that of a woman far beyond her years.

There was something to her side, something large, that I had never seen before. Its appearance was long golden and in the shape of a tube, that encased the woman's right arm as she pulled it above her shoulder, to form a shield that covered the side of her face. The entire thing was twice her size and was made up of a large pointed cylinder with ancient inscriptions covering the base.

'Mace, stop her,' Senna shouted, pulling herself up the side of the rooftop where the woman stood eagerly grinning, followed closely by Dusk.

'You are too late,' she screamed, activating what I assume to be a weapon and aiming it high into the sky, where the only target, despite his increased distance, was Kane.

Small fins extended from numerous points along the side of the weapon as it rumbled and smoked. Before Senna could reach her, or I could scale an inch of the high rising wall, she fired. It knocked her back into a thick cloud of smoke. Earth rattling displays of flaming gold, flew faster and louder than anything I would dare to dream, leaving a trail of smoke in its wake.

Pulling the woman up by a tuft of hair, Senna revealed the lifeless face of the woman, who amongst everything, had infiltrated the Mainland Division, under my very nose.

'Who the bloody hell is that that woman,' Sand asked, with the same confused look that lay across all of our faces.

For a moment, there was silence, like the earth had ceased to rotate and time itself stood still. With an explosion that cracked the sky and rippled the air, the silence was broken, as was Arc. Collapsing with a scream of stomach curling pain, he dropped Kristal and fell to his knees.

'Arc,' Sand shouted, kneeling to comfort his friend.

'It's Kane…he's dying,' whimpered Arc from his curled-up position.

Wishing for this to be a terrible dream, that I would soon wake from, I could not help but blame myself. If it was not for my actions that led the South point woman here, none of this would have happened.

With an agonising cry from Arc, the sky lit up with a flash of immense brightness, that if not only for a moment, blinded me, but not enough to stop me seeing Kane, diminished of flame and as black as ash, plummet to earth.

With a crash, Kane landed atop the Hutch, lifeless and unmoving. He radiated with a pulsating heat. Across the half-destroyed remains of the Hutch, Arc made himself stand, off-balance and ill-tempered but standing none the less.

'We need to get out of here, right now. Pick her up quickly,' Sand exasperated, as Dusk and Senna fled the scene without a second's hesitation.

Hurriedly, with a deal of force greater than I had anticipated, I hoisted Kristal up onto my shoulder.

'Careful,' Kristal said, grimacing in pain. 'What about Arc, we can't just leave without him.'

Sand began to run in the opposite direction. There was nothing I could do to help, nothing I could feel but guilt, and after witnessing a man's curse stripped away in the blink of an eye, I could think of nothing but revenge. Revenge on the South point.

'Arc will be fine, he cannot burn, we, on the other hand, need to get as far away as possible,' Sand explained, red-faced and panting.

He appeared to be running as fast as he could, which was not as fast as I had expected from someone with such power.

'This should be far enough,' Sand said, a few hundred feet away from the scene, where we stopped and caught our breath.

In that same moment, before I had a chance to put Kristal down, an earth-quaking explosion roared from our previous direction. Smoke billowed through the entirety of the central province, followed by a rain of falling debris. A flame, the likes of which I had never seen, towered over the tallest of buildings and licked the sky, before descending to nothing more than a pile of ashes. An eerie silence, that lingered across the sadness of the Citadel, was all that remained.

31. ~ INJUSTICE ~

'I have to say, that's quite a story, but what I can't seem to get my head around, is why you would trust a good for nothing group of pirates. I understand that Lady Senna and poor Commander Sophia, who may never walk again, by the way, have given sworn testimonies against the South point. But without evidence, without undeniable proof, there is nothing I can do. My hands are tied,' King Enzo said, after hearing my tale, slouched back in his throne seat, with an unamused expression across his face.

Six long days had passed since the unfortunate events at the Citadel. Finally, after many drawn-out and sleepless nights, I have confronted the King, who has extensively evaluated the situation, only to have done nothing about it, save for providing construction funds.

'But your highness, although they still hold territory over the East bay, the sea Lords have left Mangrove. The only threat left to face is the threat of the South point, and they are at our doorsteps, in our homes, and probably planning their next move as we speak. We cannot sit idly by and wait for an attack. They have weapons, the likes of which could level a Division with the single press of a button. Your highness, we must act before it's too late,' I pleaded, from my usual seventh seated position of the table, where all the members of the council watched on with eager intent.

The Chieftain was not in attendance, he was busy sieging land from the western clans, neither was Lady Lavender, who supervised the medical relief of the Beast battalion.

There was not a shred of doubt in my mind as to the worthiness of the cause we must fight for, and fight we must, like our lives, depend on it like the sun would cease to rise if we did not. Getting my point across to the King was not going to be easy, nor was it going to bode well for my already stricken record. I would need the council to plead my cause, and I hoped, for all our sakes, that I am not alone.

'Did you hear nothing of what I said, are you not aware of who you are speaking with,' the King roared, leaning on the edge of his seat with an unreasonable look in his eye, as he smashed his tightly clenched fist atop the table.

'My King, are you not aware as to the gravity of this situation,' I said, regaining my composure.' If you would just allow me the opportunity to gather an advantage. I would not make a move against your will; you have my word. I only wish to protect our lands, our people and most importantly our future.'

'Is it truly your wish to disrupt the peace. Do you believe that your personal vendetta takes precedence over the mass justice of the world? Take him away Giovanni, I want him lashed for his insolence,' shouted the King, more violently and full of rage than I had ever witnessed.

'Daddy please, maybe we should help him,' prince Luca squeaked from the side of his enraged father, whilst Giovanni, well known for his loyalties and never disobeying an order, hesitated to move.

With an unsure look on his face, suggesting his doubts in the King's decision, Giovanna, the most powerful man in the Badlands, was for a moment, unsure of himself.

'Why are you disobeying my orders, Giovanni, have you a reason to doubt my decision...have you all,' blurted the King in a manner unbefitting of his stature.

'Daddy,' prince Luca said, pulling on the back of his father's robes, who unintentionally swiped his arm around with a point making force.

'What...' screamed the King, as the back of his hand made contact with the boy's cheeks, knocking him to the flat of his back.

Prince Luca screamed with such volume, that the grey guards, the high guards and even the King's administrator's burst into the Grande Hall. Birds flocked from the tower top, and not a single council seat was left unstirred at the King's appalling behaviour.

The poor boys face swelled up with a veiny redness. His eyes, like an unstopped faucet, streamed with tears, and his screams of pain were so emotional, that only a mouth full of sick could put a stop to them.

With one hand on his head and other against his lost, but not forgotten first son's coat of arms, the King's heart could almost be seen sinking in his chest. Prince Luca ran from his father, who full of tears, attempted to pull him into a comforting embrace. Of all the Lords, Ladies, guards and Beasts in that hall, the boy ran to me.

Kneeling as the boy buried himself into the folds of my robe, I did what the King could not, and comfort his son. Although it may have been accidental, it will hold a grip on the young Prince for the rest of his days.

'Maybe you should rest awhile, my King,' Giovanni said, with a hand on the back of the empty, expressionless King of Mangrove.

'Yes, maybe you are right,' the King said, pausing as he glanced a sorrowful eye across the hall filled with his loyal subjects.

'Why are you all here...get back in line,' Giovanni said, aiming his attention towards the guards, who moved back to their attentive positions without a second's hesitation. 'This meeting is now adjourned.'

'Wait,' the King calmly said. 'You all deserve an apology...my boy most of all. I am sincerely sorry. I do not know what came over me. Luca, my son, you are right, I should help Lord Mace.'

'My King...'

'It is alright, Giovanni.' the King waved him away. 'Will you please find it in your heart to forgive me, Luca.'

Keeping his face hidden beneath my robe, the Prince exaggerated a nod but restrained himself from meeting his father's ill-deserved gaze.

'What can I do to make things better my son.'

Not a word was uttered, not a slight nod, nor shuffled movement. He remained under my robe, still and silent, as if it shielded him from his father, from this tower, and this cursed world.

'Your highness, might I be so bold as to suggest the Prince spend the evening with me. He can play with Ice, eat chocolates and enjoy some time away from this tower,' I said, with no consideration for my own sake, only for the boy.

'The nerve...' King Enzo stopped, inhaling his concern. 'Is this what you want, Luca?'

He stood before prince Luca and I, with a smirk that could almost be mistaken as incredulous.

'Please daddy,' whimpered the prince.

'Have him home by nightfall. I assume you are aware that my son is the Prince of Mangrove...be it on your head if anything should happen to him.'

'He will be safe in my hands.' The boys excited, yet swollen face, lit up, along with the atmosphere of the hall.

'Your highness, meaning no offence, but can you take such a risk, leaving your only son with Lord Mace. He has, after all, been affected by the South point on more than one occasion. He is a target my King, and I'm not saying anything will happen, nor am I doubting his abilities to protect the prince, I'm just concerned about the level of risk involved.' Lord Mantis said, overexpressing himself for the sake of what appeared to be amusement.

'I agree. Perhaps I should go along and ensure the safety of the prince,' Lord Hawk said, having a similarly expressive way with his words.

Those two were playing some sort of game, that much was clear.

'Yes, do what you must, just have him back before nightfall. Do I make myself clear?' The King said, removing his crown as he slumped back into his throne seat.

Placing the shimmering symbol of his rule atop the table, he ran his fingers through the thickness of his brown curls.

'Lord Mace. Tell me something...that pirate, Arch was it.'

'Arc your highness,'

'Yes...Arc, what exactly happened to him?' the King asked, eyes strongly fixed on my own.

'Well, despite the South points and their attack, and despite the destruction of his curse, Arc just walked through the smoke, naked as the day he was born, skin glowing from the intense heat. In his hands, no larger than a peach, in a blaze of blue flames, was his bird of fire, reborn from the ashes. That's when the other sea...pirate, Sand, made his promise. He gave me a piece of eight and took for the sea, without waiting for his friend, who by the looks on his face, was best left alone. I returned to The Stronghold, but not without first tending to Sophia and the other artillery unit's injuries,' I explained, hoping that for all our sakes, they would one-day return. 'I have a feeling that before the end, we will need them, and in our darkest hour, I fear we may come to rely on them.

'How can you be sure the pirates will keep their promise?' Kiera asked, after remaining silent during this, and most all of the previous council meetings. Although she was the queen of the Harpies, and only usual spoke when spoken to, she had a good point, that I had no answer for.

'They only gave their word...and this,' I said, pulling the purple-tinged piece of eight from my robe pocket, which Prince Luca, who casually sat on my lap, looked over with intrigue.

'That's all well and good Mace, but how can we trust their word?' she said, with kindness in her questioning.

'She is right, words and coins are not proof enough. Even if the coin is worth more than every ship in the sea,' the King expressed.

He looked sad all of a sudden as if all the thoughts that had once haunted his mind had returned. That's when it came to me. That's when I felt most foolish for revealing the coin. It once belonged to one of his seven brothers.

'My King, if I may...the word of those pirates means a great deal to them. I knew them when they were just boys before they became what they are today. They pride themselves on two things. Honour and violence,' Giovanni said.

'What is your point Giovanni,' the King spat, shooting an evil stare at him.

Usually, Giovanni would not accept, or receive such a look from anyone, save for those willing to lose their heads, but he knew the significances of the coin and would play his next words out very carefully.

'I meant to say, that we can trust them, my King. We can trust their honour. Besides, we will know well in advance if they intend to return.'

Without any explanation, my brother got up from his fourth seat and walked out of the hall. I guess by the time the pieces of eight were brought up, he had just about had enough of this meeting.

'Lord Mantis, where do you think you are going, you have not been dismissed,' the King said, to no avail.

Mantis just walked on out of that hall.

'Did you not hear me, Lord Mantis,' the King shouted, standing so abruptly that he knocked his throne seat backwards.

'My King, I will deal with Lord Mantis's ignorance after the meeting, we have more import matters at hand,' Lord Giovanni said, noticing that prince Luca, yet again, hid in the folds of my robe.

'You are right Giovanni. None the less, I want him disciplined. A Lord should know how to act in the presence of his King.'

'Yes, my King.'

'Now then, Lord Mace, what exactly do you suggesting we do as to the South point situation. Bear in mind, that we cannot simply fall into open war,' the King said, twirling a golden ring around his little finger.

'May I interject,' Senna said, sparking my interest and the interest of everyone in the hall. 'War is not a solution, not for us, nor I doubt for the South point, whose walls, as we all know, have never been penetrated. With their defensive advantage, we have no option but to draw them out. First, we must gain intelligence on their ongoing infiltration, their advanced weaponry, and their apparent demon manipulation.'

'And how, if you please, Lady Senna, are we going to gain this intelligence?' the King asked, full of doubt.

'Mangrove is the heart of our economy. They make our weapons, account for our finances and provide necessary materials. Without Mangrove, we stand less able to defend ourselves against an attack. The South point has and will again terrorise our great Citadel. I suggest constant surveillance of the outer walls, by those capable of such a task, considering the situation.'

'I agree. The defence of Mangrove should be paramount. I believe only those of command rank or higher should take up the cause,' Lady Kiera said, in her ever so pleasant voice, that I found myself drawn to.

'Or an Elite,' Lord Hawk burst with a grin. 'It has been quite some time since I've had a good fight. With your permission, my King, I would like to volunteer the services of my Division.'

'Are we all in agreement?' the King asked, gauging the response of each member of the council, starting with Giovanna, who simply gave a nod.

'Of course,' Hawk said, the King glancing in his direction.

'Agreed,' Senna said.

'And Lord Mace,' he said with raised brows.

'Gladly, my King,' I responded.

It was as good a plan as any, and who better than Lord Hawk to execute such a plan. He is, after all, the leader of the strongest group of warriors The Stronghold has to offer.

Lastly was Lady Kiera, who gave a closed-eyed tilt of her head, which lit up the King's face with a perverse smile.

'If we have no further business to discuss, I shall take my leave. Have Luca back before the fall of night,' the King said, putting an end to the meeting.

From the highest balcony on the red tower, taking in the Easterly views of Mangrove, which overlooked the services Division.

Prince Luca and I waited patiently for the overdue arrival of Lord Hawk. The Prince, wearing his best brown robes and holding his favourite toy bear, was so excited, he could barely keep still, or hold a rational conversation.

'There he is, there's Lord Hawk. And that must be...' the prince paused, gaping with an open mouth.

'Eagle, her name is Eagle,' I interrupted, taken aback at Lord Hawks daughter, who I thought would be energetic and playful, not strapped into a wheeled chair, with twisted arms and a slanted jaw.

'Lord Mace, why is she like that?' the Prince innocently asked, with a look of concern on his face, that was now stricken of all excitement.

Seeing nothing like it before myself, I had no answer for the boy but felt that I must say something.

'She is...well, she is a brave young girl, who appears to have suffered a lot. When we go and play, please do not mention that there is anything wrong with her, for sympathies sake.'

'I will not,' he said, rushing through the red metal balcony door, along the top half of the tower and into his bed chambers.

I followed, passing the two grey guards, who almost jumped out of their skin at our presence.

'What is the matter, my Prince?' I asked, bursting into his room through his name labelled oak wood door.

The Prince did not answer, nor did he look back or appear to notice that I was speaking at all. He was fixated on the large wooden box in the corner of his room, where he rummaged through hundreds of toys. Beyond the front sleeping area of the room, with a bed larger than my own, was a brightly coloured playroom. A leather sofa, with soft armchairs and beanbags for comfort, were precariously placed around the room. The curved right wall, which was large than a ten-man barracks, was filled with books, none of which looked as if they were for children. To the far end, under a raised glass ceiling, was a play area in the shade of sculptured pine trees, all for himself. A climbing frame, set on rubber tiles was attached to a swing set, a trapeze bar and a see-saw. Monkey bars circled overhead, alongside climbing ropes and a slide, that twirled into the sandbox.

'Here it is, here it is, Lord Mace,' the Prince said, pulling a fluffy fox toy from the bottom of his box, which was the spitting orange and red image of Half-fang.

Such a long time had passed since I had thought about my old companion, and despite the passing years, missed her no less. It makes me sad to think of her alone in the woods, without a friend in the world. I hoped she lived a full life, I hoped she was happy, and although she will be long dead by now, I hoped that she thought of the times we spent together and the adventures we had.

'Mace,' the Prince said, pulling on the sleeve of my robe to snap me out of my memories of a time long past. 'This is for Eagle; it was my favourite and most comfortable toy.'

'That is a lovely gesture, my prince.' I looked at him there, with kindness in his heart, and understanding in his eyes, which for the first time in years, gave me hope for the future.

At the bottom of the Red Tower, under the arch of the spine, Lord hawk, unarmed but in full armour, grinned as we approach through the large steel doors.

'Ah, Mace, and my Prince. I would like to introduce you to my daughter, Eagle Barrington. She is a little shy,' Hawk said, stroking his daughter's deadly straight brunette hair.

She Jerked her arms back and forth, with a slight dribble that soaked into the chest of her slim pink and white dress.

'Hello, Eagle. My name is Mace Black, and I work with your father.'

'Don't humour her Mace, she may be disabled but is far from stupid. She knows very well who you are and what you do,' Hawk said, grinning with pride as his daughter began to chuckle hysterically.

'He is quite funny isn't he,' Hawk continued, with an echoing laugh.

'I'm Luca, and this is for you.' The prince bowed his head and handed her the fox toy, which was received with an almost incomparable mumble of words from Eagle.

'She says thank you,' Hawk said, pulling a tissue out of his pocket to clean the saliva from his daughter's chin. 'let's not stand here all day, and miss out on this Sun. Mace, you could do with some colour on that pale face of yours.'

The kind young Prince offered to push Eagle's wheeled chair to the Mainland Division, whilst Hawk and I walked a few passes behind. Following the scenic root, we stumbled across a family of ducks, which Eagle thoroughly enjoyed, as the prince pushed her to the pond just outside of the Mainland Division. Becoming thirsty from a short walk around the pond, that involved an extraordinarily large and territorial goose, we made our way to the cobbled streets leading to the Blue Manor.

From the not so far distance, I could see the figure of what looked like a woman walking around the gated courtyard. Walking in front of Luca, I took a closer look, and to my surprise, Dame Lambert, with Ice at her heels, ran towards me with arms out wide. Embracing her with a squeezing hug, I felt at home.

In a shimmering new suit of jagged-edged, spiked armour, under her usual white sash and blue robes, gave her a presence of power.

'It has been so long... you look amazing. Even your hair looks longer,' I said, running my hands through her thick locks of blonde hair.

Despite Ice jumping up and licking the side of my armoured leg, I pulled Lambert close and kissed her with more life and vigour than I had expected to. When her soft, wet lips closed around mine, and her hand pulled around to stroke the back of my neck, I knew that she was the one. Gently pulling away, I looked deep and longingly into her wide red eyes, that I could not draw myself away from, lost in her beauty, her strength and in the way she filled my mind with lust and wonder.

For the briefest of moments, I forgot the world around me, until I saw her, Dame Eva, staring back at me with a look that could kill. Unnoticed by Lambert, which made my brow hot and my hand's throb, Eva watched for a moment, tears streaming down her cheeks.

'Mace, what is it? You look as if you've seen a ghost,' Lambert said, looking back, to see nothing but the Blue Manor and the surrounding environment of the Mainland Division.

Within the time of a blinking eye, Eva was gone, but not forgotten, and although I cared for her, I wanted Lambert. Something deep inside was pulling me towards Lambert.

32. ~ PARANOIA ~

The ever-impulsive Lord Hawk, above all things, lacked patience in virtue, but never so much as when suffering a defeat at the hands of his daughter, in a game of war board no less. The idea of the game is simple, each player, with one hundred game gold and a castle, would roll a dice to determine their position on the map shaped board. Players can spend their gold on recourses, in the form of battle cards, including siege weapons, warships, and many various warriors rank in the thousands. With each roll of the dice, a player receives a further five gold and can move across the board in any direction, placing cards by their strategies. When another player comes in contact with placed cards, they can use their remaining handheld cards to battle, leaving the land and cards for the victor's claim. The winner is the last player with a standing castle.

When all the fun and games had come to an end and the sun began to dwindle behind the far East Bay, we escorted the young prince, as promised, back to his lonesome abode before the fall of night. Five heavily armed high guards stood to attention at the door of the red tower, awaiting the arrival of young Prince Luca. They had no greetings for the boy, nor a friendly gesture, only a quick check of his physical appearance, before being hoisted up those tower stairs faster than we could say a farewell.

Despite playing Childs games and eating nothing but chocolates, Dame Lambert stayed the course of the evening, only to fall asleep across a precariously placed floor cushion, moments before our departure. Needless to say, I left her there, with a cushioned sheet for comfort and Ice curled up beside for company.

'Goodnight Lord Mace, I depart for the Citadel in the morning. We in the Elite do not use birds or such feeble methods of communication, we speak only when the time comes for words, and that is all. I expect no more than a month's evaluation of the area will be necessary, during which time my Elites and I will secure five main base structures around the Citadel's outer walls,' Lord Hawk said, stopping beside the innermost left-hand pillar of the red tower, sheltering Eagle from the cold wind that spiralled through the Kings cross.

'If you don't mind me asking, when exactly did you plan all of that,' I said, almost too close to the great man for my comforts.

'Just now…of course,' he answered, seemingly nonchalant, although in retrospect he has been a war merited Lord for a long time. 'If you feel the need for news, then send only someone capable and trusted to the foot of the Citadels main entrance, that's where the mother camp will stand.'

'Thank you, I have someone in mind.'

'Oh…and who might that be?' he asked, leaning in closer than my comforts could take, so close in fact, that I could feel the rough end hairs of his grey beard tickle against my chin.

'My Dame, Lambert Crow. She is the strongest and most trusted person at my disposal.'

I doubted myself the moment those words left my mouth. Something about the way Lambert made me feel, tore a rift in my mind. One side, following my duty as Lord of the Mainland, with Lambert as a subordinate, and the other, denying my rank and all that I have to guard her safety.

'She is a fine Dame, indeed, as fine as they come. I shall answer only to her and expect no other than her. Is that clear.'

'Thank you, Lord Hawk.'

'It has been pleasant young Mace, but I must get back. Dear Eagle here is far overdue her bedtime,' he said, with a hand on his daughter's thin jerking shoulder, that never ceases to remain still.

'It has been a joy to make your acquaintance Eagle,' I said.

'She is only five years of age Mace, not fifty. You do have an odd way with words.'

'Well…I.'

'Have a good night, Lord Mace,' he interrupted, strolling off into the shadow of night.

'Yes, goodnight to you too,' I replied, curious as to whether Hawk was jesting, or if he thought I spoke strangely, either way, I could not help but admire the man.

For all Hawks power, rank, and reputation, he was in truth, a kind-hearted and companionate father to his daughter, who did not deserve the hand that she was dealt in life.

'Oh, and Mace, don't disappoint that young Dame of yours,' Hawk said from afar. 'Some birds are not meant to be caged, and although you mean well to keep their beauty safe for your own eyes, they are far more magnificent in flight, soaring high above the world, doing what makes them feel most alive.'

Half an hour had passed. I strolled through the large double fronted doors of the blue manner, expecting to find Lambert sleeping soundly under the blanket where I had left her, with Ice curled underfoot. Unstirred by my approach, without a greeting, slight growl, or hint of frivolity whatsoever, Ice was most solemn, and his eyes, full of tiredness, focused somewhere far in the distance.

She must have awakened to discover an empty house, save for a slumbering lump of a furry snow bear, and departed for the comforts of her self-contained barracks. That was my first thought.

Making my way up the stairs, which lingered less of Talia's memory, I heard the ominous creak of an ungreased door or misplaced floorboard.

'Lambert…is that you,' I said, with Ice immediately to my side, sniffing the air as I approached the unlit landing.

Again, and again, the creaking continued. The hairs on the back of my neck stood to attention. I tightened the grip I had on my sword.

'Who is there?' I shouted, turning right at the landing, to find the end window, which I could not for the life of me remember opening, wide open, with curtains fluttering in the breeze.

Loud footsteps echoed from Talia's old bed Chambers, causing Ice to bare his teeth and growl.

'To me Ice, quietly now,' I whispered, whilst slowly edging the end window to a close.

Drawing no unwanted attention, with an untrained understanding, Ice crept over in an almost exaggerated fashion. Encouraging the fine young Beast further was unnecessary, as was spending too long here in hesitation.

'This is your last warning. Be it on your head,' I shouted, as the sound of something heavy was heard dropping to the hard wooden floor of the chamber.

It was not Lambert, nor was it anyone else that Ice could distinguish by scent, otherwise he would not be making such a fuss. My instincts were leading to only one conclusion, which was that another of the South points agents had infiltrated my home.

Moving quickly, yet cautiously to the door, I kicked it wide open, snapping the corner of the handle as it swung to a halt. Nothing was there, no scent to be found in the air, no object broken or out of place, nor sign of intrusion. Bounding to the far wall, Ice buried his nose into the seal of the window and inhaled with all his might, only to find nothing, save for a look of clear desperation in my eyes.

'What is going on?' I whispered, knowing that Ice understood me, but lacked the communicate to reply.

Yet again the eerie sound of stepping feet curled my stomach in knots. This time from the hallway, where we had been stood not a moment ago. Without a pause, or second thought, surrounded by a deadly silence, I ran as hard and as fast as my legs could carry me into the landing hall. Readying myself for a strike, I positioned my flat-bladed sword low and sloping, for a high and unexpected upswing. I launched from the bed-chamber, only to find that my impending target was none other than Dame Lambert, dressed in one of my black button shirts.

Time appeared to slow of its own accord, as my body stiffened and jerked to adjust the destination of my up-swinging blade. I had never been so frightened in all my life, not from the lack of control I had over my sword, nor from the impending meat cleaving blow that would cut flesh from bone, but from the look of pure fright that I had put across the face of the woman I sort to protect. Covering her eyes, she did not attempt to scream, or block the attack, she just dropped to the floor in a silent ball of heart-wrenching tears.

My sword missed her, cutting only a single strand of her golden blonde hair as it sliced halfway up the opposing wall. Although she suffered pain, it was not from a wound or anything external for that matter, but from having her safety stripped from her in the blink of an eye.

I held her, embraced her, did what I could to calm Lambert's nerves, but all that I received in return was an Il tempered gaze. Haunting thoughts of a South point infiltration escaped from my mind, along with any sense of paranoia. All my attention, although unaccepted, was focused entirely on Lambert. The more I pulled her in or squeezed her close, the more she squirmed away and kicked out. She wanted to be alone, that much was clear, but for some reason, I did not leave. In all honesty, like cutting off a finger to spite my hand, I could not do it, I could not move from her side. Something about Lambert drew me in and kept me close. She went still and silent, taking deep, heavy breaths, that sent Ice into a strange frenzy of squeaks and barks.

'Lambert, I, I did not mean to startle you. Footsteps and noises were coming from…'

'You stupid, good for nothing, weak excuse for a Lord. What bloody game you are playing? You nearly cut my head off. You frightened me half to death,' she interrupted, with the same anger and velocity that she used to show me.

'I am so sorry,' I replied, pulling her up to her feet, where she remained in silence, piercing as if through my soul.

'Go ahead. What will my punishment be?'

I Knew that saying that was a bad idea, but it is the only way to speed up the inevitable process of her temper. We would discuss this rationally at some point, I was sure of that, but as of this moment right now, she must release her anger.

She stood up to me, face to face, nose to nose. Expecting an impending broken jaw or back snapped knee cap, I braced for impact, but none came. I could not help but flinch when her soft hand reached out for my face and slowly caressed my cheek. Staring down at her outstretched hand, that made its way to my chest, as the moonlight danced in her wet red eyes, I felt such relief.

'You owe me,' she said, pulling me close by the chest pocket of my robe, which for a moment, seemed like a gesture of peace, a kiss maybe, but I was not so fortunate.

It turns out, Lambert was leading me into a false sense of security. With a slight twitch of her small but broad shoulder under my ribs, I was jerked up into the air. Splintering wood stuck into my back as I landed hard and heavy onto the floorboards of my landing. In a squealing escape, Ice darted past me and down the stairs. Although he is not able to communicate his thoughts or give a reason for his actions, it was clear to see that he was just as frightened of Lambert's rage as I was.

'I am off to bed now...your bed to precise, my Lord,' Lambert said, with a sarcastic bow. 'Before all of this unpleasantness I would have treasured the company of your warmth, but now, I will expect only the pleasured warmth of breakfast in bed...with extra bacon.'

'But Lambert...' I said, reaching out with my cold and callused hands.

My mind wandered with all manner of life-affirming images, some sexual, others noble, but all regarding Lambert, and a life spent by her side. Kneeling to where I sat on the splintered floor, she remained silent and pushed her face into mine. She was so close that my heart began to pound hard in my chest, so hard that I feared she would hear the very beating of it. I closed my eyes, tilted my head upwards to feel for her lips, but felt only a wet press against the side of my cheek.

'Goodnight Mace,' she whispered, softly tickling my ear, before calmly adjourning to my bed chambers.

I watched every step of her muscular, yet slender legs as she walked the length of the landing. I was left alone in the dark, with the haunting thoughts of a South point infiltration swirling around my aching head once again.

33. ~ AMBUSH ~

A humid and musky fog enveloped the Mangrove Citadel as Lord Hawk and Sir Ronald pondered over a map of positions in the mother tent. Five main structures surrounded the Citadel, with the main tent made of a reflective silver material, developed by Lady Lavender to cool or heat the interior as appropriate. Four Elites manned each tent, except for the mother tent, which contains five, including Lord Hawk, who was in high sprites despite the overcast fog.

'They will only strike from this side of the Citadel, which means our defences are lacking in the main entranceway,' Sir Ronald said, running his finger across the map markings, whilst sweating under the weight of his silver Elite armour.

'Ronald, I'll have you know, that our defences are stronger than the entire Mainland, Beast and Naval Divisions put together. Never again question my authority on the matter of placement,' Hawk replied, gesturing with the endpoint of his larger than life bronze Warhammer, which somewhat matched his full suite of inscribed bronze armour.

Understanding Hawks decisions, let alone question them, was something very few men were brave enough to do.

'Yes, my Lord…I could do with some air. Do you mind if I step out for a moment?' Sir Ronald asked, wiping the beads of sweat that ran from his brow.

'Of course,' Hawk replied, far to indulged in his map to look up.

As the day drew to a close and the last light of the red sun retreated far beyond the Citadel, Mangrove and the stillness of the North Sea, Lord Hawk was disturbed by heavy laughter.

'Who is disturbing my work with that racket,' Hawk shouted, slapping the map marking off the table.

'My Lord, it's only me,' an intoxicated voice blurted out from the not so far distance, followed by a cheer.

'Peterson. I should have known,' Hawk muttered.

'My Lord, Peterson is drunk and, well…he has a woman slumped over his shoulder. What are your commands on the matter?' the red-haired and overly feminine, Sargent Pilton asked, poking his head through the silver curtain flaps of the mother tent.

'Two warnings have already passed that fools ears before now, and he continues to undermine my authority. You will do nothing at all Sargent,' Hawk said. 'I will attend to the matter myself.'

'Yes, my Lord.'

The Sargent backed out of the tent, closely followed by Lord Hawk, who was not amused with the lack of respect shown by the overly intoxicated subordinate.

Lord Hawk, in his very nature, is a man of perfection. He has plain and clear rules, which he adopts to set his force of Elites apart from the other Divisions. So Long as an Elite has their hair cut to an exact specific length, the cutting of which is organised by Sir Ronald. So long as an Elite Performs every task to the over expectations of normal quality, the training of which is conducted by Lord Hawk. And, so long as an Elite does not consume alcohol or perform any acts of fornication within the grounds of their Division or whilst on duty, they may enjoy the rich rewards of life, which are far greater and more luxurious than any other Division can afford to offer.

Sir Ronald, along with Sargent's, Nula and Pilton, stood to attention several feet from the mother tent. They all wore their uninformed silver and grey-robed suits of armour, save for Ronald, who's armour along the right arm and sword pommel, was a shimmering bronze, matching that of Hawks.

'I found me a girl…but she passed out drunk in the casino,' Paterson laughed, before tripping over his foot and landing atop the girl, who awoke only to vomit across Paterson's Elite armour, as an added gesture of insult. 'Why are you just stood there, Hawk. Help me up.'

At that moment, with a fury in his eyes, Lord Hawk approached Paterson. For those very stupid few, such as Paterson, who has angered the great unmovable man, will receive only their last words and death.

'My Lord, lend a hand, would you. I cannot seem to get myself up,' Paterson said, belching a breath of foulness across the fresh air of the Oakwood forest.

Every step Hawk took, like a pin drop in absolute silence, range out through the ever-darkening night. The wind howled through the forest trees, buffeting the robes of the attending Elites, who all took a knee with a hand over their hearts.

'You are too kind my Lord,' Paterson blurted, with slurred words as he held his hand out to receive Lord Hawks apparent gesture of goodwill.

Without a word, Hawk pulled the man to his unbalanced feet and took a final measure of the man. Despite being strong and highly regarded in combat, Pilton was unfit for Elite ranking.

'Do you have any last words,' Hawk asked, without a glimmer of remorse or hesitation for what he is about to do.

'Hang on...wait,' Paterson said in a panic. 'My Lord...you are joking, aren't you?'

'I should not have to tell you once, but I have given you two prior warning about your drunk and disorderly nature. You have shamed the Elite name,' said Hawk, lowering his frighteningly large Warhammer from off his shoulder. 'Now...I will not ask again; do you have any last words?'

'Please...show mercy. Please, my Lord,' he begged, gripping around Hawks legs with a pitiful display of regretful tears.

'You may find honour in the next life...go in peace.'

In preparation for execution, Lord Hawk held his great Warhammer high into the air. The wind, as if it ruled in the presence of death, swirled wildly from every direction.

'Wait, I do have a last request...if I may,' Paterson bumbled, through his mouth of phlegm and cheeks of tears.

Although Paterson dishonoured himself and creased irritation across Lord Hawk's brow, he was, with the simple nod of the head, granted his wish of a final request.

The man stood with his chest out and his head held high. As Hawk lowered his Warhammer to his side, the man turned heel and fled into the forest. With a disappointed sigh, Hawk turned a full circle with a two-handed swing of his Warhammer and sent it roaring through the woods. Before the dishonoured man could feel the penetration of impact or scream with the pain of death, the entirety of his head was crushed between the solid wood of an old oak tree and the flat end of Lord Hawks Warhammer. The sound of wolves could be heard howling the cry of a lost soul throughout the forest, whilst the three kneeling Elites, who did not turn or move an inch to witness the death of their former comrade, bowed their heads in a moment of honoured silence. Despite a man's flaws in life, Lord Hawk would most always honour death with a word or two, but for Paterson, Hawk did nothing but spit on dry earth.

'Will someone please have my Warhammer cleaned and have that girl taken to the steps of the Citadel,' Lord Hawk commanded, as he adjured to his tactical planning in the mother tent.

'You heard the man...' Sir Ronald said, looking back at the Warhammer, that despite its unruly weight, remained firmly embedded into the side of the old oak tree.

After only a moments peace in the mother tent, yet another sound disturbed the silence of Hawks map reading. It was like the pounding of a thousand horses, the falling of a hundred trees. High pitched wailing sounds followed the racket. It was like that of a Beast, pelting through the forest.

'Bal Log,' it roared. 'Bal Log,' it screamed. 'Bal Log,' over and over again, with every earth rattling step of the approach.

'What in the blue blood of an old god's name is that,' Hawk shouted from inside the mother tent, that despite being protected from the wind, was shaken to within an inch of standing. Yet again, with a look, of more disappointment than anger, Lord Hawk left the comforts of the tent to see what was making such a disturbing racket. Staring up into the distance, Nula, Pilton and Ronald had not moved more than a few feet in their efforts to follow orders.

'Why are you all just stood... oh, I see,' Hawk mumbled, as he saw what had caused his subordinates to stare out in silence.

This was not a demon; it was too large for that, neither was it a Beast; it too little control and looked too human. The creature on approach is one that has not been seen for hundreds of years. This creature is a Monstrosity. Its hands alone were so large they could crush a man in a firm grasp. Its face was so disfigured, that not even Hawk could mangle it to such an extent.

'Bal Log,' it screamed in pitches of high and then low, showing its teeth, that were far and few between its wide gaping mouth.

It smashed through the thickness of trees and turned grass coverings into barefoot prints.

'Well, well, this is a surprise. A Monstrosity,' Hawk said, almost unable to contain his excitement. 'It would seem that young Lord Mace was right about the South point after all.'

'Don't just stand there gaping at him, form up and attack. I will be right with you, I must first retrieve my Warhammer,' Hawk continued, skipping away joyfully.

This Monstrosity could quite easily kill a man or smash through the walls of the Citadel. This meant only one thing to Hawk. Wartime privileges.

'Nula, Pilton, flank the Monstrosity, I will attack head-on,' Sir Ronald said, taking his breaths deep and hearty, as he drew his sword and steadied himself for the attack.

'Yes, Sir,' the Sargent's both said in synchronicity, with a hasty charge for the cover of trees either side of the Monstrosity, which was no less than a hundred meters from the mother tent.

As the untamed wind cooled the perspiration that descended the nape of his neck, Sir Ronald checked to his left for Lord Hawks watchful eye. The man was less afraid of facing a Monstrosity of unimaginable strength and size than having his Lord notice his fears. None the less, without a glance of interest from Lord Hawk, he charged head-on. His pale disposition gave away his overwhelmed lack of courage, which was not like Ronald. He had faced opponents of an unbeatable appeal before.

Seconds felt like minutes, minutes like hours as Ronald charged through the thickness of the forest. Reaching inside his robes, that waved in his wake like a buffeted flag, he pulled two small knives from his inside pocket. He held the inner grip at the edge of the blades between his thumb and index finger. With a twisted flick of his brawny wrist, they span and curved high into the air and land under the Monstrosity's chin. Although it was not enough to put the Monstrosity down, it was enough to distract it.

The monstrosity's redraw eyes remained deeply focused on Ronald as he ran, sword drawn, between its legs of towering proportions. He sliced furiously, again and again, as fast as his arms allowed him to cleave flesh from the side of the Monstrosity's foot.

'Ronald move,' Nula screamed, notching three arrows to one bow, which she fired with the expected precision of an Elite.

Stumbling back with his larger than life hand over his bulging eye, the Monstrosity roared from the pain of Nula's piercing arrows. With no time to spare, Ronald did as Nula said and moved, but as he did, the haste of his movement caused him to drop his sword in the direct line of the Monstrosity's giant foot.

'Bal Log,' it roared, quacking the earth in a rage of stomping feet and flailing arms.

Whilst the Monstrosity remained distracted, Ronald pulled more thin blades from the inside pockets of his robes and fired them, almost aimlessly at the Monstrosity.

Taking advantage of this opportunity, Nula, who did not appear to fear nor stir away from the Monstrosity's presence, sent a barrage of arrows, three, sometimes four at a time. With more in bravery than he had in sense, Pilton swung from the branch of a nearby tree and stabbed his hook edged silver knuckle claws into the Monstrosity's wildly moving left leg, before ascending with effortless strength.

'Bal Log,' again it roared, with wild swings of its hands.

The attacks fell across Nula's path, forcing her back. She was pelted with spikes of broken oak and chippings of rock stone. Despite being cut to ribbons by fast sweeping debris, and having air stricken from her lungs by the indenting of armour around her ribs.

'Damn it,' barked Ronald, as he ran to the aid of his injured comrade.

The path was not clear, nor was it safe. The second swing of the oafish Monstrosity's hand was moving with such haste in his very direction, that Ronald, who's time was now very much of the essence, could not afford to make a single mistake. Pilton's brave efforts to stab the Monstrosity's chubby spinal column were in vain, Nula's injuries needed attention and Ronald could not move an inch to help them.

His courage and spirit, that time and time again throughout his Elite ranking career, has been witnessed, admired, and even idolised, was wavering.

'This is it...this is my time,' Ronald whimpered, looking deep into the Monstrosity's eyes, which for all their intimidation, were taut with fear.

The last bleating thoughts of Ronald's life flashed before him in the beat of a heart, that most unexpectedly brought a smile of joy to his pierced lips. He was no longer in fear, no longer wishing for the time needed to aid his comrades, but ready to face his end. It was as if Sir Ronald had wanted this, had wanted a way out, an end to the thoughts that haunted his mind. With a face grimaced for impact and arms spread out like the wings of a Harpy, Ronald breathed his last breath of humid forest air, closed his eyes to the world and faced his impending death.

'Bal Log,' was the last thing the mighty Sir Ronald Redgrave thought he would ever hear.

Thoughts of meeting his late wife showered over the deepest corners of his mind.

'What has gotten into, Ronald,' Hawk said, without a shred of fear or doubt in his voice, as he slapped the forceful impact of the Monstrosity's hand away with the solid strength of his Warhammer. The Monstrosity tipped forward off balance.

'My Lord...'

'Keep your mouth shut, Ronald, you have shamed yourself. Never admit defeat...it will admit itself to you when the time comes,' Lord Hawk pronounced, staring through Ronald with a pitiful disdain.

'But my Lord...I no longer wished to live. What is wrong with me?' he composed himself and rubbed the wet from his eyes.

'When an Elite faces death, he laughs and fights through it, he does not wish death upon himself.' Hawk paused and watched the Monstrosity stumble and fall, elbow first onto the mother tent, crushing it, along with his maps and markings, to a level flatter than the forest grass.

A moment's silence rang trough the surroundings, as the leaves of a thousand trees fell to rest and those who stood closest, juddered under the strain of quaking earth.

'I guess my map reading is out of the question,' Hawk chuckled. 'Listen, Ronald. I need you to be an Elite right now...help Nula and take cover.'

Lord Hawk look around, a puzzled thrown lay thick across his brow.

'Where in the cursed world is Pilton?' Hawk asked, looking deep into Ronald's eyes for the answer to the rather serious question.

'I last saw him on the back of the Monstrosity,' Ronald whimpered, before rushing over to Nula, who despite holding her ribs in pain, was far too proud for any assistance.

A roar of pain shot out from beyond the moat bridge.

'Pilton, is that you?' Hawk shouted. 'Are you hurt?'

'I cannot feel my legs,' Pilton replied, from the flat of his back to the right of the moat bridge, with a raspy croak in his voice, before passing from consciousness.

Moving with haste, Ronald ran to Pilton's aid. He hoisted Pilton up, but it was of great concern. His legs were crushed, his arms were broken and he was bleeding out. Ronald carried the brave soul out into the thick covering of forestry.

'Bal Log,' roared the Monstrosity, as it rose from the indented ground beneath.

Lord Hawk, swinging his Warhammer with every forward step, approached the untameable appetite of the Monstrosity's destruction.

'I realise that you have lost control, and I understand that it has probably got something to do with those rebellious sly worms at the South point,' Hawk said. 'But you have injured my Elites and must now meet your demise.'

He looked up at the oversized Monstrosity, who loomed over him within a rage.

'Do you have any final words?' Hawk asked, expecting no response, but honouring the former man none the less. 'I expected not...'

Raising his Warhammer high above his head, Hawk smirked at the Monstrosity, who raised his foot to stomp the proportionally ant-sized Hawk to a parchment's thinness.

'Bal Log,' was the last roar of the monstrosity, that had not only crushed Pilton's legs to an unworkable extend but had crushed the Elite spirits.

It was up to the Kings second seat, Lord of the Elites, Hawk Barrington, to finish what his skilled subordinates had barely started. Although Hawk did wonder, after all the destruction, why the other four Elite camps did not even sound a horn, let alone come to aid.

As the great foot of the Monstrosity blotted out the light of the moon, Hawk did not move. As several feet turned to close inches from impact, Hawk did not move and would remain unmoved up until the point of no return. With a swift right step and a roar mightier than any walling Monstrosity had the voice to carry, Hawk smashed the solid bronze of his Warhammer so furiously through the Monstrosity's large foot, that it shattered its ankle to splinters.

'I hope you find peace in the next life,' Hawk said, taking exactly two steps back and twelve steps left.

The Monstrosity, grimacing a mouth full of inconsistent teeth, fell to the flat of his face, which happened to be at Hawks bronze armoured feet.

'I am sorry,' Hawk said, arching his back as he pulled the weight of his Warhammer up and over his head.

With a mighty swing, that for all his strength, rippled through the stock of his muscles as it made contact with the temple of the Monstrosity's head. Like an egg to a rock, the monstrosity's head cracked open and leaked over the forest floor.

'Ronald,' Hawk echoed through the undisturbed tranquillity of silence, that drew out like a flame in the night. 'Come, let us discuss your situation. Maybe we can agree on some terms of measure.'

Hawk leant sideways, like a toppling tower, but saw no movement through the thickness of tree cover. It might have worried a normal man, having no response from his subordinates, but would only think of scorning their insolence.

A loose hanging flap of grey material hung from the long twist of a tree branch, which was, as clear as day, from an Elites uniform.

'Ronald, Nula, Pilton, will you not answer me,' Hawk shouted with such velocity, that it would stir the citizens of Mangrove from their beds.

Something was wrong, very wrong, it was in the air, he could feel it now.

In his heavy set of bronze armour, with his Warhammer, soaked in the blood of a Monstrosity, who can now rest in deserved peace, Hawk took a large stride in his step towards the foot of the moat bridge. For reasons unknown to Hawk, the moat bridge was not built over a moat. The bridge itself was more than useless and played only the part of a meeting place for travellers.

With a watchful eye, Hawk peered through every nook and every cranny. With a highly-strung ear, he listened out for the slightest of unnatural sounds, but for all his perceptions he found no sign of his subordinates.

'Lord bloody Hawk,' whispered past the tip of Hawks ears in the shallow breeze.

He turned quickly, anticipating more violence. For anyone brave or stupid enough to challenge the great Lord, they would presumably meet the same fate as the Monstrosity. A fool, maybe, but naïve, Hawk most certainly was not. He could smell a distraction from a mile away and has played out every trick in the proverbial book of warfare. None the less, with a cool head and an easy step, he backed away to the underside of the bridge. It was all Hawk could do in this almost unbearable terrain of uncertain outcomes.

For all the steps Lord Hawk remained ahead of the game of war, nothing quite prepared him for the bloody massacre that lay before him.

With pale lifeless disposition across their faces, all three of Hawk's remaining mother tent party, with eyes as wide as their gaping mouths, sat bodiless atop poorly carved spikes of wood.

As bewilderment turned to hatred, and the hollow hole in Hawks heavy pounding heart filled with sorry, he was beyond the point of rational thoughts. Despite the blood boiling in his veins and the shock of witnessing his Elites in such a way, he felt it honourable to give them, at the very least, a burial. One by one, he closed the eyes and removed the heads of his loyal subordinates from the spikes they came to rest on. With his bare hands, he ripped up chunks of damp earth from under the bridge. He buried them there, deep enough for them to remain unstirred, yet not so deep as to prevent them from finding peace in the next life.

'For all that is good in this world, I will avenge you, I swear it,' Hawk shouted, as a single teardrop fell from the corner of his right eye.

It was the first time his eyes watered since the birth of his daughter, and he hoped, for the sake of Mangrove, The Stronghold and all that he holds dear, that it would be his last.

'Look at the state of your perfect Elite force,' a familiar young voice said, rattling the nerves deep in Hawk's very core.

At that moment, when all that made sense in the world seemed a distant memory, the cold steel of a small sword punctured through Hawks throat. An amount of blood that Hawk did not think possible to have, leaked out over every patch of bronze on his armour.

'You disrespectful little...' Hawk gasped, as he came face to face with none other than Brandon Brooke.

For all his former acts of innocents, he had found a way to best the great Lord of the Elites.

'It is I... remember,' Brandon said. 'The ugly boy is I. I guess you are wondering why I did this, well it's simple really.'

Before the boy, who now dressed in the finest leathers, and wielded the thinnest of black steel blades, could say his next unworthy words, Hawk rippled his Warhammer through the air, dislocating his arm in the process. With the speed of a flaming arrow and the solid strength of a mountain, it took Brandon off his feet and dragged his body through the thickness of an old oak tree, instantly crushing the life from his colourless cold eyes.

With a firm grasp around the gaping hole in his throat, Lord Hawk, against all odds, struggled his way past the moat bridge. He stumbled and fell beside the open cracked head of the Monstrosity. He then crawled his way, with a lack of blood and breath, over a mile, to the foot of the Citadels entranceway, only to collapse under the strain of death.

Heroes come in all shapes and sizes, but none with the pride of Lord Hawk, who amongst all things, wished only for peace and perfection in an otherwise cruel world. Tales of his legend and acts of valour will be told from every corner of the land. There is hope for peace in the next life. Hawk will shine a guiding light of strength in the bleakest hours of the darkest nights.

34. ~ DEPARTURE ~

Meanwhile in the safe comforts of the Mainland Divisions blue Manor. The events continue to transpire on the outskirts of the Citadel. Dame Lambert Crow, in her full suit of blue spiked armour, prepared to leave for the Elite force mother tent, where she would hope for any news on the situation at hand.

Regardless of the struggle that Lambert and I have previously endured, and the scare I gave her a week's night ago, she has, despite her stubborn nature, become very close to me. Closer in fact than any woman has ever been. She blessed the hateful thoughts from the darkest corners of my mind. She perceived to only have eyes for me, and for what it's worth, she has made me a better man.

The last week, not only for my lacking duties and newly revived love of life, was one of the best in all my life. Lambert and I, with Ice at our side, walked hand in hand across the north-westerly hills overlooking the land. We dined with my brother in the Black Manor, which was, for all but the hours of mockery I endured at their childish hands, quite a pleasant endeavour. And, under the setting sun that fell beyond the westerly planes, we made Love for the first time. It was like magic. I had never felt anything quite like it. At first, we just kissed and held each other in a close embrace of twisted arms and legs. Then, we lost ourselves in the moment and fell into a spell of infatuation and yearning, which for my part, was rather clumsy. Lastly, in the heat of the moment, when all the lights of the world had gone out, we gave in to our urges of temptation. It was a night to remember, and one that I will look forward to repeating. Lambert and I, because of it, are closer than ever.

Although everything appeared to be working in order, and peace seemed more than just a midnight's dream, it was not all kissing and kindness. We argued and bickered something fierce at times. It was not as if there was anything worth hassling ourselves over, I mean, we had everything we could want. I guess with great power, sometimes comes great stubbornness. Lambert would quite often point out that I have become very arrogant as of late. Of course, I denied the accusation but have kept a close check on my actions and how I present myself, just in case. None the less, we resolve our differences in the way of combat, which was the best possible way and drew the least amount of unwanted attention. Sometimes, it would be a sparring match, or a running race, when other times, we would sit over a calming board of war.

'Here, this is for you,' I said, handing her a sparkling purple box, which due to its curved edge and lengthened size, most obviously contained a sword.

'What is the occasion,' she replied, looking over the box, before taking it from my hands to feel its surprisingly light weight.

'I do not need an occasion.'

'Well, it is very nice of you…but.'

'But nothing. Open the damn thing already,' I said, as Ice burst through the front door with a crash, that almost knocked us both over.

He does this quite often. Now that he is larger than any hound and almost the size of wolf Beast, he has the tendency to pick a fight or two, which for a Beast, is normal adolescent behaviour.

'Will you please be careful, Ice. You nearly took our legs out from under us.'

He rubbed his head across both of our legs, receiving nothing from me, but a squeezing hug and forehead kiss from Lambert. She has taken quite a liking to the young Beast.

'You are just in time to see Lambert off, Ice. For at least the next few weeks, she is going to be in the safe company of Lord Hawk and his Elite force,' I said.

Lambert lifted the sparkling lid from off of the box and gazed with amazement at the fine smith work of her new curved sword. Atop a cushioned sheet of black velvet, lay her new, ridge-edged and curved sword. The blade, like my own, was made of black steel, for a light pull of power. The pommel was golden and made in the shape of a snow bear, with rubies for red eyes, and silver for claws. As an added touch, In the style of her old sword, I had the grip made from brown bull's leather.

'It's beautiful Mace. No one has ever been so kind to me,' Lambert said, stroking the length of the sword, from pommel to tip. 'This must have cost you a fortune.'

'Don't just stand there, try it out.'

With that, she pulled the sword out, using more strength than she had anticipated for the lightness of the black steel. She swung to the side, half stepped and twisted with a flurry of light-handed jabs. She paused and gazed deep into my blacker than pitch eyes, which I met with a smile and an extended wet kiss.

'Here,' I whispered into her ear as I pulled away, only to surprise her by tossing the sword box to the air.

In what looked like the single twist of her dainty wrist, she sliced the box into three equal parts. Ice decided to tear the rest of the box, along with its velvet inserts to shreds. Almost in sync, Lambert and I burst into a fit of hysterical laughter.

'May I leave this with you?' she asked, pulling her old sword from its sheath.

The fitting of laughter ceased its hilarity and slowed to a meek chuckle. Ice, with all the grace of a mad dog, continued to shred the velvet to ribbons. Inevitably I would have to clean up after his mess.

'Yes…of course,' I answered, taking her old sword.

Despite its small size and thin steel, this sword was not only heavier than her new one but noticeable bent at the grip. I cannot imagine, with such tailored mastery of the curved sword, as to how much this new steel will impact on her ability. At least, I can rest assured in the knowledge that I have improved on her safekeeping, not that my Dame is in much need of safekeeping. The expense paid out for black steel, which unbeknownst to Lambert, cost more than her entire Dames barracks.

'You are too kind, Mace. Now, I must make haste, try not to miss me too much,' Lambert said, ruffling the hair on Ice's thick back, before walking away.

The blue Manor will be lonesome and sad without Lambert.

35. ~ CONFRONTATION ~

As I began drawing up plans for an assault on the South point, confident that Lord Hawk would have some useful evidence to back my claim, Dame Lambert approached the North Gate, which for a moment, was almost frightening to pass through. Maybe it was the prospect of danger lurking at the Citadel, or maybe the thought of spending time apart from the Mainland, that stopped her in her tracks.

With the shimmer of sunlight cascading across the bright blue of her armour, Lambert pulled the new sword from her old sheath and marched forwards under the high archway of the North gate.

'You must be the famous Dame Lambert Crow of the Mainland,' a soft voice whispered in the wind. 'I have heard so much about you.'

Clenching the grip of her sword, Lambert hurried an eye over her surroundings. There was no one there.

'Who is there?' Lambert said in a confident tone of voice, as she braced her sword arm. 'Show yourself.'

'Do you not recognise my voice,' again the voice whispered in the wind.

Lambert hurried a glance, but this time, as if appearing from the thinnest of airs, Dame Eva Fang was sat cross-legged atop the arch of the North gate. She stroked the length of her smooth black hair with one hand, whilst twirling a small black sword with the other.

'I do recognise your voice. I've been to enough Service Division conferences to know who their Dame is,' Lambert said. 'What seems to be the problem?'

'Oh, there is no problem…not yet anyway,' Eva replied, as she leapt with a flip from the top of the North gate, landing face to face with Lambert.

She circled Lambert as she hummed with an uncomfortable grin, which did not seem of pleasure or happiness, but pure spitefulness.

'Mace Black is not for you,' Eva threatened with an uncomfortable closeness. 'He is mine. He has always had eyes for me. What could he see in you? You look more of a man than a woman.'

'I am warning you only this once, get out of my face, or I will rip that pretty little head from your scrawny shoulders,' Lambert threatened, with a sneering pierce of sudden hatred. 'My relationship with Lord Mace has nothing to do with you or anyone else for that matter.'

The thick silver padded leather of Dame Eva's suit stretched and shrank under her red robes as she laughed in Lambert's face.

'I have had just about enough of you.'

Lambert pulled back her sword. It hissed as it swept the open air.

'Oh, poor Lambert, I am not here to fight you. I would not want to ruin my nails. I've just had them done to match my robes,' Eva said, flashing the sharp points of her nails across the beaming light of the midday sun. 'Oh, they match your eyes perfectly.'

Eva smirk, as she pushed slowly against the curve of Lambert's sword with the silver palms of her leather gloved hands.

'Listen closely, Lambert…I mean you no harm, I just know that Lord Mace does not love you, nor ever will. He loves me,' Eva continued.

Lambert gripped the thick steel of Eva's short sword, noticing the other slightly shorter black sword to her side, and the daggers that dangled from the back of her robes.

'Why do you think about this?' Lambert asked, switching suddenly from pent up rage to suspicious concern at the thought of being betrayed by her Lord. She was hesitant to give her trust to at first but now cherished it, relied on it, and has come to find comfort in it. A betrayal would break her will.

'It does pain me to be the one to tell you this,' Eva said calmly. 'Mace has kept a terrible secret from you, that did not bother him to detail in front of the seated Lords of the King's council. The late Lord Brick, who everyone, especially yourself, thought was quite an honourable gentleman, was a traitor. He was an infiltrating agent from the South point. He made a fool of everyone, especially his Division, and especially you…poor little Lambert.'

'shut up, shut up, shut up,' Lambert screamed.

'Along with that, Mace and I have shared many moments. You should see the way he looks at me. You can almost taste the lust in his loins.'

Before another hateful word could be uttered, Lambert's eyes flooded with tears. Tears that have not fallen upon her cheeks since childhood. Lambert, without hesitation, smashed her fist into the full of Eva's face, knocking her to the flat of her back.

'Rotten little bitch,' Eva screamed, as a flock of blackbirds landed atop the North gate. 'I cannot believe Lord Mace was seduced by the likes of you. Even your name is of a man. It would not surprise me if you had a cock under that wretched black robe.'

Eva spat a mouth full of bright blood over the white of Lambert's sash.

'Lord Mace and I have something special, that your ugly man's face will not steal away,' Eva said, drawing the second of her short swords from there scabbards.

Wiping the tears from her eyes, Lambert leant full tilt with a high sword. Both Dames were strong, and both had skilled combat experience. If she was only able to concentrate past her lusting for Eva's blood, Lambert would have the strength advantage in close combat.

Just as the black of their steel swords inched closer to contact, the great and powerful Lord Giovanni, with nothing but the bare of his hands, took the impact from both of their attacks.

'This is unacceptable behaviour from Division Classed Dames,' Lord Giovanni said, in his deep rumbling monotone voice. 'This example of foolishness will not go unpunished. Your Lords and Ladies will be hearing of this.'

Giovanni towered between the Dames with an emotionless gaunt appeal. To the likes of Giovanni, who's power sours beyond natural bounds, both Eva and Lambert were no more than infant children to his eyes, and little did he have the time for their petty squabbles.

'But Lord Giovanni,' Eva moaned, fluttering her eyelashes in a tease.

Finding her sycophantic display to be rather inappropriate, Lambert mocked Eva with a look of exaggerated sickness.

'That will be double the punishment for you, Dame Eva Fang. Let this be an experience for the both you…Now take leave from my sight,' Giovanni said.

Eva and Lambert shared a glance of true hatred as they passed one another under the looming frame of Lord Giovanni.

Spitting blood as she walked, Dame Eva made haste for the hilltop hall of her Division, whilst Dame Lambert continued on her northbound venture into the Oakwood forest. She was usually brave, highly strung and unable to bend to the will of others, but Dame Lambert is now in a very fragile state.

36. ~ DECISIVENESS ~

I find that I cannot sit in stillness or hold any thoughts, that are not of my beloved Lambert, in my mind. I find my days are drawn out with distracting absence, and my nights, even more so, are overplayed with dreams of death and demons.

There is not a day that goes by when Lambert is not at the forefront of my mind. She had a grasp on me, that I never wish to be released from. Although we were separated by distance, our fates were now deeply entwined, for Lambert did not only brighten the day with her presence but she brightened my heart. The very soul of the Mainland thrives on her kindness and everlasting loyalty. She was not the Dame we deserved, but the Dame we needed. Without Lambert's love and respect, I would scarcely be seen as a competent Lord, and that plays heavily on my conscience. We needed her, I needed her.

As the minutes turned to hours, and the hours to days, I sat to my dark oak wood desk of study. Higher and higher it piled with papers, that I mean to work through, as I always did on a midweek's morning, but hadn't the mindset for such a task at present. The more paper that piled up, the less eager I was to work through it.

My mind wandered, as did my eyes around my study of books on shelves, parchment rolled maps in stacks, and a half room of yet to be unpacked boxes of odds and ends, that stretched almost to the ceiling.

Whilst I gazed an easy eye over old Mangroves maps, Ice, my ever-growing Snowbear, slept underfoot. After a week in the constant company of Dame Lambert, I could not think a moment past the last elusive daydream, or pull my ill will away from the sounds and sights of normal life. This caused me to be unusually distracted. Instead of task managing next seasons lead duties for Commander Snake and Richard, I pictured Lambert in all her glory. Instead of signing waivers or permissions for the training of recruits, I would long for the cold press of her hand on my heated chest. It was fair to say, that I missed Lambert. We did, after all, spend the entirety of last week attached at the hip, and now separated from the one person that I wished never to be separated from, I cannot bear the dull melodic bore, that is my own company.

'How do you feel about a nice walk around the Beast Division, Ice? I asked. 'It has been some time since I have ventured across their paths.'

Ice struggled to pull the tired lids from his eyes.

'Ice,' I said again, louder this time.

He bolted like a shot from an arrow, stumbling into the frame of the door, and the edge of a casing, which rattled a few precariously placed books from the top shelf.

'Where in blue blazes are you going?'

Ice was running at full speed through the Manor, taking little notice of his size, or surroundings, as he smashed past cabinets and ornaments alike. I wanted more than anything to ignore his behaviour, but I followed the clumsy Beast.

A few moments later, I heard the haunting sound that had set Ice to panic. The sound that serves as a call to arms for men and Lords alike, and keeps all those who do not relish in the glory of warfare hidden from sight. The sound of the war bells, that echoed a cry across The Stronghold. It has been two decades since the last bells rang for wartime, and all those, like my brother, Lord Mantis, who have answered the call, understand the gravity of the situation. Even Ice, with his lack of experience and years of life, is panicked by the thought of war.

But why have the bells chimed, what could Hawk have discovered on the outskirts of Mangrove, and will my lost privileges of war, that are key for Mainland moral, be worth consideration. The next course of action must be played out with a careful caution on my part, as without my wartime privileges, and Dame Lambert's authority, the Mainland Division, with all their strength, will be leaderless. Though worst of all, I will be branded a coward.

I Picked up the pace and focused my attention. A steady footslog across the sizable maze of corridors along the right of the Manor turned swiftly into a quick dash. I jumped over smashed pieces of mirror glass, dodged ornaments and arrived in the wide-open entranceway. Ice had his nose deep in the corner of the double-fronted entrance door.

'Ice, here is what you must do,' I said. 'Run back to my study as fast as you can, and bring my sword to me...we may need it. Then come to the Mainland hall. Do you understand?'

He barked out his acknowledgement and went with haste. I cannot remember the last time my flat-bladed sword was not in hand, and yet, at the signal of war, I had left it behind.

As I braced myself up against the double-fronted entrance doors of the Manor and took one last look to the top of the staircase. I could hear the expected panic of preparation outside. I swung open the doors, and to my dismay, walking up the path in high spiked heels, was Dame Eva Fang. I had not the time, nor the patience to deal with her right now, yet the black smudges under her teary eyes told a story, that I must, for pity's sake, hear out.

'Oh, Mace, you look...tired,' she said on her seductive approach.

Although she looked a picture of perfection in her slim-lined black dress, that accentuated her figure, she was a lot thinner than I remember her being. Her hair was not plated as usual but left flowing like a wave in the light breeze. Though It did not matter to me how she looked, or why she was here. Nothing, save from death, could tear my heart away from Lambert.

'Good morning Eva, should you not be making preparations for wartime?' I asked, taking note of the hundreds of Mainland men and women rushing around in a fluster behind the Manor gates.

The unarmed ran to the surrounding barracks for arms, whilst the fully suited rushed to the Division hall, where they would surely be expecting my presence, and of course, a plan of action.

'I could not very well go to war, knowing that I might not ever see you again,' Eva said.

'Listen, Eva...I am sorry to say this, but I have fallen for another.'

'I thought you might say that. I saw you kissing that boy of a girl, Lambert Crow. She has her claws deep in you, doesn't she?'

'But, Eva...'

'No, you will listen to me, Mace Black,' she screamed, pulling close the gap between us. 'I am yours, no matter what comes between us, and you know that. I know that you want me. I can feel it.'

My legs went to jelly.

'I love you, Mace,' she continued, almost jumping to land an ill-gotten kiss.

'Dame Eva, please. You must understand,' I burst in harsh tones, only to calm immediately after. 'I did have feelings for you, but I believe I have found love. Can we not just be friends, Eva.'

Her face reddened, her mouth sloped in at the sides, and her eyes welled up with sadness.

'I am so sorry, Eva.'

'Oh, it is alright,' she sobbed, wiping the underside of her eyes clean with her forearm, before taking a deeply paused breath, that worried me somewhat.

She was love drunk, that much was clear.

'One way or another, you will love me, Mace...you will.'

At that, she turned away from me, stroked a gentle hand through the length of her hair and, in the blink of an eye, she had vanished. Inevitably, she would return once again for my heart.

All words had escaped my thoughts, as well as the concentration to conceive what she might have in store for me, or worse, for Lambert. Poor Lambert has done nothing to deserve Eva's wrath. It tore a knot in my guts to think that I have scorned her so. I am such a fool and must do something to redeem myself. When I have a moment, I must discuss this with Senna, she will know what to do.

Just as Ice came storming through the Manor with my blade between his tight-jawed grip, Commander Snake, horse backed and armed to the teeth, galloped across my path.

'Commander, the time is at hand, we must discuss our next course of action,' I said, without a hint of notice taken.

'Commander,' I said again, this time with a sense more urgency.

'If it was not for your meddling, none of this would have happened. This is your doing, Mace, you and those forsaken pirates,' he accused, holding the reins of his sturdy black stead.

'I do not understand.'

'You, Lord Mace, have taken everything from me,' he spat, turning circles on the spot. 'One day you will know my pain, and on that day...'

'I have little time for your moral compose to find its point, Commander Snake, now where in the bloody hell, do you think you are going?' I interrupted in such a rage, that even Ice dropped my blade with a clang and fled inside the Manor.

How many must be hurt on my behalf, how much can I bear to hold a grasp on this reality.

'Snake, answer me?' I said in a temper.

'You have said enough.' Commander Snake said, with a firmly knotted brow and a look of despair evident across his face. 'The next time I see you, Mace Black, I will end you. I promise you that.'

He turned tail, dragging up a mound of Manor lawn in his galloping wake. The future of the Mainland Division hangs in the balance, and with an unworthy Lord such as I, to lead them through the storm, hope will be hard to find.

Under Division law, the Lord of the Mainland must authorise the security of Mangrove in wartime, or any situation for that matter, which has been deemed as peace threatening. So, with a disposition far calmer than the stress worthy thoughts of my mind, I called Ice to heal and went with haste to the Mainland hall. I hoped for a worthy audience of willing warriors. What I found was a different matter entirely. Of the thirteen or so thousand able-bodied men and women of the Division, there were less than half, and of that half, none were unstirred.

Stood at the front stage of the unadmirable hall, was Commander Richard, stuffing his face with sugared sweets.

Although in his way, Richard was quite bright, he hadn't the faintest of ideas when it came to holding an audience. He did try, and for that, I applaud him. There was, at least, one loyal Commander left in the Mainland it would seem.

Regardless of my feelings and the many faults within the Mainland structure, I strolled up on to that stage with an unmatchable presence. There is a fine line between confidence and arrogance, that I had fully overstepped. Lambert did say I had become rather arrogant as of late, maybe she was right.

'Silence,' I roared, halting the thousands of outbursts that were left unchecked.

They were an embarrassing ramble to look upon. Do not get me wrong, there all fine warriors, every one of them, they just lack the harsh disciplines of wartime. I could see the fear in their eyes.

'It is Wartime,' I said. 'We must all unite, now more than ever. We must not fight amongst ourselves, or point blame. Our enemy is to the South. You will be wise to remember that.'

Regret washed over me. It was as if all the lost moral of the world had resurfaced itself within the heart of the Mainland, every man and woman of my Division, in all their rough handed glory, cheered and stomped a thunder through those old halls.

During all the war talk, a young man, no larger than the boy prince, charged through the front entrance door of the hall. With a strangely tilted drag to his walk, he was by far the most unconvincing service boy, that Lady Senna has ever recruited to her Division.

'Lord Mace, please report immediately to the King's red tower council hall for an emergency meeting,' the boy shouted as loud as he could. 'I repeat, please report immediately to the King's red tower council hall for an emergency meeting.'

Despite his careless lack of decorum and look of recklessness abandon, he spoke clearly and delivered his message direct. That much, could not be faulted.

'What is your name, boy,' I asked, taking some attention away from the thousands of curiously watchful eyes.

I knew, despite their cheering and stomping, that the men and women of the Mainland would not merely be satisfied with a boost of morale. They wanted answers.

'My name, Lord. My name is Timber, Charles Timber. Everyone calls me Dash.'

By his ever-changing tone of voice and lack of formality, he knew little to nothing of a hard time, let alone wartime.

'You serve your Division proud,' I acknowledged, feeling as if somehow, the boy could do with some good graces. 'Why do they call you Dash?'

'My Lord, they call me Dash because I'm fast. Well, my curse is fast. Lady Senna said I could beat a horse in a race, though I have yet to try.'

'She believes in you, boy. Do not disappoint her.'

With a dignified bow, the boy left in a hurry.

'My Lord, for the sake of the Division, tell us what is going on?' Richard asked, gloomily ascended the wooden stairway of the stage, as if expecting the worst.

'I am afraid you are right,' I said to him, as I looked over the wide-eyed worry of the Mainland force. 'Listen close. You are the front-line defence of the Stronghold and the backbone of the King's military. You have a right to know what you are fighting for. As soon as I return from a meeting of Lords, you will have your answers. For now, prepare yourselves for any eventuality.'

37. ~ DESPERATION ~

'This is an emergency,' the King announced, straightening himself as he entered the grand council hall, where all of the Lords and Ladies, save for Hawk, sat in perfect silence.

As this was an emergency meeting, many Sirs and Dames were in attendance, some of whom I had yet to meet. Sir Archibald, the black wolf, the Chieftains second command, sat on hind legs behind his master. Dame Alice, of the harpies, stood beside her Queen, with a look of bitterness slapped across her freckled face. Of course, Lambert was not in attendance, neither were, Sir Ronald or Sir James, for that matter.

Young Prince Luca was nowhere to be seen, neither was his child-size throne seat. I would have thought this meeting to be a good experience for the boy who would one day rule as King. Perhaps his father felt differently.

Without further ado, the meeting was in full swing, and all who attended, in one way or another, had their suspicions, as did I.

'According to a report from the Elite Division camp, Lord Hawk Barrington has disappeared from the mother encampment,' King Enzo said, with a coldness in his bright brown eyes. 'The headless bodies of Sir Ronald Redgrave, Sargent Nula Wild and Pilton Tracer were discovered alongside the body of a Monstrosity. The reasons are yet unknown and until we have further investigated, assume the worst. The Monstrosity is currently in the medical research divisions forensics department under examination. As you are all well aware, Monstrosities are very rare. This situation, will not be taken likely.'

He stopped for a moment, as still as a rock. He looked as if he was playing some notion or another over in his head, which was most unlike the man of many words.

Lord Giovani stood and pressed a cool hand atop the King's armour bound shoulder. The King simply gazed at the back wall of the grand hall.

'My King,' Giovani said, with a look that showed nothing but pity.

I guess, for a man as old and as powerful as Lord Giovanni, who fears no man, the only worry in his world, where his loyalties to his King.

'Yes Giovanni, what appears to be troubling you?' the King asked, snapping back to the reality of his council hall.

'Nothing, my King.'

'As of yesterday, this was no more than an external investigation into the Citadel incident,' the King said. 'But now the pride of peace depends on getting to the bottom of this situation. For this reason, after careful consideration, I have chosen a select task force of Lords to investigate the scene of the disappearance...and bring Lord Hawk back to us.'

Just then, as I spotted Dame Eva from the corner of my eye, gazing longingly in my direction, the entrance doors of the hall swung open with a thud.

'You are late, Sir James,' Giovani spat, standing abruptly to stare a sense of fear through James.

Stepping into the hall, panting like a wild dog, James had no words.

'James, take your place, immediately,' Mantis said, looking over his Sir with contempt.

'Yes, my Lord, please accept my apologies.'

Clanking his golden spear to the hard surface underfoot with every other slow step, James had the attentions of every man, woman, Harpy and Beast in the hall, yet he seemed rather indifferent about the keeping of his time. It would have shot red-faced embarrassment through the highest-ranking Division Lords if they were to interrupt a wartime meeting. Why was he so calm, what had he been doing to cause his tardiness, I thought to myself? James was not a bad man, not really. He has served his Shadow Division proud on countless occasions and has given my brother no doubt in his loyalties, yet for some reason, I do not trust him, I never have.

'Let us continue without further interruption,' the King said, exaggerating his raised brow towards the snake-eyed Sir James, who now stood with bated breath behind his Lords seat. 'The chosen task force will consist of four Lords, along with a company of combat-trained medics to be on standby. Lord Noriega, Lord Mantis, Lady Senna and Lady Lavender, will make up the team. Lavender will also oversee and supply the medical accompaniment for any eventuality. Do I make myself clear?'

'Yes, my King,' all the Lords and Ladies said at once.

'I wish to go, my King...please may accompany the team,' I said, nervously meeting the King's gaze. I was determined not to look away and I did not, not even when his face dropped, or when his eyes fell to a squint. I never looked away.

'No,' he replied, calmer than ever.

'Dame Lambert is out there alone. You must let me go' I shouted, knocking my seventh seat back as I stood with aggression that should never be shown in this hall, let alone directed towards the King.

'Mace Black,' Lady Senna screamed through the grandness of the council hall, determined to stop the fool I was making of myself. 'You should be ashamed of yourself. I thought you were a man of integrity. Do you not understand how much you are insulting your Dame right now? She is far more capable than the lost little girl you make her out to be.'

Senna was right, Lambert is strong, smart and more than able to look after herself.

'Lord Mace, you are lucky not to be punished for your outburst,' the King said, with confidence. 'Do not forget your place again. You have not the privileges to determine any course of wartime action, or have you forgotten. You must remain within your Division walls until the end of wartime, or until I see fit to dismiss your stricken privileges. Do you understand?'

I wished to ignore him, I wished to anger him, I wish to make a fool of the King, who relies too heavily on his Lords and Ladies to even step foot on the field of battle.

'Lord Mace, do you understand?' he said once more, this time with a look of disgust across his sharply pierced face.

'I understand,' I finally said, only to avoid distancing myself further from my cause, which was, for all the good it would do my dear Lambert, an honourable one.

'Now then, so that we are all clear, Beast Divisions Lord Noriega, Shadow Divisions Lord Mantis Black, Services Divisions Lady Senna, and Medical research Divisions Lady Lavender, will make immediate haste for the Elite campground. The rest of you will take wartime measures to defend the Stronghold.'

Moments later, under the spine of the red tower, where all the Lord and Ladies of the land went their separate ways, I sat on the smooth cold ground, contemplating my next course of action. Should I stay, obey the King's rule and keep my bonds strong with the Mainland, or should I go to Lambert's aid? Even if it means disobeying the King, which in its self, is an act of treason, I wanted Lambert to be safe. If she were here, she would know what to do.

When all despair had clouded my better judgement, the most unexpected thing happened. Lord Giovanni Hades, in his simple way, sat beside me and laid a heavy hand across my forward arching back.

'It will be alright, young Mace,' he said, in is deep-set monotone voice. 'Lambert is stronger than you know.'

All eight foot of Giovani's muscle-bound frame, despite being sat cross-legged on the floor, toward overhead in a manner that most would find intimidating.

'Do not look so worried, I have lost everyone I ever held dear over my many years of existence,' he continued. 'And the one thing I have learnt from it all is to have faith.'

38. ~ FATE ~

The open silence of the everlasting night sky, one by one, blossomed with the most beautiful twinkle of starlight to humble my patch of lonely darkness. Like all small things, the light from the furthest stars, under the strain of the full moon, was drowned out.

For the mourning Elite Division, who wish only for the safe return of their Lord Hawk, a candle was placed in every window of every barracks, house and hall in the land as a symbol of solidarity. The distant dancing flames, the flicker of hope on this most gloomy of nights, and the few brave clouds daring to dwell across the moon's path brought no peace to my soul. There was no hush to the violent beating of my heart.

I sat precariously balanced atop the sloping brown tiled roof of the Blue Manor, watching over the empty streets below my feet. I was higher than any Lord of the Stronghold this night, and yet in myself, I felt low. Many thoughts plagued my mind this night, but none so much as the decision of whether to risk everything in search of my dear Lambert or to obey my King and risk life in regret. Despite that, the reason I wish to sit above the Mainland was not for the sake of self-pity, but in the hope that my half-melted candle flame would somehow reach Lambert far off gaze.

Looking down at the curved courtyard of the Manor, where my blue carriage is parked opposite a stone carved bust of a bare-chested woman, I prayed to the old gods. Maybe they were false, maybe I was stupid to pray on the slightest chance of faith, but it was worth a shot.

And so, I prayed, 'please, if you can hear me, and you truly care for the good and honest members of mankind, I implore you, not for my sake, but for the Lambert...please keep her safe. Please guide her home.'

As expected, when a man addresses the gods through the twinkle of distant starlight, there was no answer. Though in that instant, when my doubting faith began to resurface, the brightest of blue lights blotted out the night sky and illuminated the Division in all its daytime glory. It was a sign from the gods, an answer to my prayers, I thought, as I stood in awe of the magnificent sight before my eyes. Although I knew exactly what the blue light was and where it came from, I did not believe it was a mere coincidence. I believe it truly was the gods.

Many years ago, after my curse day under the old bridge, Swan Choker, the greatest sword master of our time, told me about curses and how they were, for a lack of a better word, eternal. He said, 'whenever anyone is cursed, their curse would have come from the light, be it a blue light, like the one before me, or red like my own. Only someone who is already cursed can see the light. When the time is right, the light will choose a worthy host and they will be cursed until the day they die. But sometimes the curse is too strong for the host, causing what we know to be, the demon.'

I thought often of Swan Choker, and how he used to always impart wisdom my way. Wherever he is in the wide-open world, I hope he found what he was looking for.

As fast as the light had appeared to every cursed eye in the land, the bright blue light of the sky was gone and the night sky once again returned to its former star-speckled glory. Though from this day, until my last, I will have faith, I will for the first time in my short life, believe in the gods of old.

One by one, each candle across the Stronghold burnt out, and with less light to shine through the night, the darker it became. Though it has been said, that the most magical of things occur only on the darkest of nights, and although something magical has occurred on this night, I held out little hope for something that can help me bring Lambert home.

Just then, like all things on this god affirming night, fate took its course.

'Mace is that you,' a recognisable female voice cried in the not so far distance. 'Lord Mace.'

Although I recognised the voice, I could not think who could belong to. And, even if I could, I would not very well be able to see them in this pitch blackness.

'Who is there?' I answered, gripping hold of the high chimney breast to steady my balance across the top of the tall sloping roof.

'Above you,' the woman cried in a panic.

I looked up and saw that the panicked woman was none other than Captain Kara. Her enormous eagle spread wingspan could not hold her weight. She was falling fast, and in her sharp-edged suit of dark purple armour, she would fall heavy.

'Hold on,' I said, dropping my sword to the courtyard below, where it ran through the concrete with ease, leaving nothing but the golden hilt poking out from the ground.

Hundreds of yellow-tipped black feathers fell from the sky, some stained with blood.

'Take my hand,' I said, testing the strength of the chimney breast against the firm grip of my hand. 'I will catch you.'

She was a second from landing, and if I missed her hand, or misjudge the swing I hoped to slow her approach with, she would most certainly be injured.

With one last straining push from her battered and bloody wings, she ever so slightly decreased the speed of her approach. Without a moment to spare, I grabbed hold of her forearm, swung her around to the opposing side of the chimney breast and let out a long overdue sigh of relief. There was no doubt about it, she had met the many-layered brick chimney breast with force. She may have even broken a rib or two in the process. Though it could have been much worse, she could have fallen to her death and I could easily have fallen along with her. By the half-smile across her face, I knew that she was grateful.

'Kara, what in the world are you doing here, and what has happened to you?' I asked, edging my way over the thin gap between the chimney base and the sloping roof edge.

'The King, he…he is dead,' she cried, spitting a full throat of sickness to her side.

I sat her up, leant her over the side of the slope and steadied her, with my arm around her steel-plated waist.

'I am going to need more information than that.'

'At the beginning of wartime, I received a message, ordering me to guard the King, but remain unseen with my curse of blindsight. So, I did and was paid handsomely for my secrecy in the matter,' she said pausing to spit out a lump of sick that was stuck in her throat. 'About an hour ago, I was sat on King Lucas balcony, watching as he grunted and snorted in his sleep. Then…it's hard to even say it. I sound mad. A fake King walked in and snapped, the real King's neck.'

She screamed in agony as she closed her widespread wings inward and began to sob her sorrows away at the fearful thought of failure.

'A marionette,' I said.

'Excuse me, a what?'

'A marionette. Just like Talia, the King is a robot, a puppet being pulled by someone else's strings.'

'You believe me?'

She sobbed, brushing the thick of her hair away from her face to look up at me.

'And why wouldn't I, you have no reason to lie to me,' I replied, almost losing my footing. 'There is more to this story, and I will need to hear it. First, we must get down from here and get you checked over.'

With a few expected growls from, Ice, we descended the dusty loft ladders and made it into the Manor. On closer inspection, Captain Kara was not in as bad of a state as I had first thought, nor was she quite as intimidating as I would have once believed her to be. I still would not underestimate her, not for a moment. She was, after all, one of the most highly regarded of all the Harpies.

'Let me help you out of those blood-stained robes,' I said, not expecting her to jump back and pull the hood of her black robes over her head in a defensive display.

I have seen the same look before. I know that she wishes only to keep hold of her pride.

'I was the same when I was younger, not that I am old. I'm only twenty-five after all,' I said. 'I felt such shame whenever someone tried to help me, until I realised, that I can't do everything alone...no one can. Having a helping hand only gives you a greater sense of satisfaction when you come to repay the favour.'

I slowly pulled the hood from her innocent young face, wondering when I had become such a wise man like my brother. She said nothing but allowed me to assist her all the same.

After a short time, I had checked her over, with Ice's distracted assistance and constant wound licking, that turned out to be surprisingly helpful. I had forgotten that a Beast's saliva is full of healing properties.

Apart from some bruising, the tearing of her wings, and a dislocated shoulder, that Kara barely flinched at when I popped it back into place, she was relatively unharmed. There was nothing that some rest and a bottle of wine wouldn't fix.

'Kara, tell me, if you will, what happened after the King was killed by the marionette?' I asked, needing to know, for the sake of the Stronghold.

'I was conflicted at first, I wasn't sure exactly what to do in that situation,' she said. 'And when I eventually decided to confront the false King, I was held back. It sounds crazy, it does.'

'Please Kara, I need to know everything.'

'A cloud of grey smoke in the shape of a man pulled me back off the balcony and before I could loosen my wings in flight, it was too late. I was tumbling down the side of the red tower, scrapping every iron spine as I fell. At the last second, when the hard earth was almost in front of my face, I spread my wings and flew away as fast as I could. I must have cleared two hundred miles in an hour. Then I saw you on the rooftop.'

She began welling with tears once again. She planted her head in my chest when I sat beside to comfort her.

'It is going to be alright,' I said, lacking the right words.

'I was scared Mace, I know I shouldn't have run, but I...I didn't want to die,' she mumbled into my robes in a fit of tears. 'It's all my fault, I've let everyone down.'

'Captain Kara,' I said, holding her shoulders up as I looked into the sadness of her hazel eyes. 'This is not your fault. This has been planned. Everything has been planned since day one. For all we know, they planned on you coming to her tonight. We need to have our wits about us and take nothing for granted.'

I needed her to be the cool and collected Captain Kara that I remember. I needed her skills right now if we are to stand any chance of stopping whatever the South point has in store. All I knew for sure, was that confronting the false King as we are, without a plan or any backup, was suicidal at best.

'You're going out to look for her, aren't you?' Kara asked, pacing up and down the length of my lounge.

'You mean Lambert…well, I have not yet decided on my next course of action,' I answered, staring glumly down at my blue steel boots.

'It looks to me like you are,' she said. 'Why else would you be in full armour at two o'clock in the morning.'

'I guess you are right,' I laughed.

It was the first smile to crease my lips since Lambert was here, and for some reason, I could not stop.

'What is so funny,' said Kara, laughing along.

'Hold on a minute,' I burst, putting a stop to the hysterics. 'How did you know I wanted to look for Lambert?'

I felt a fool accusing the innocent young Harpy of being untrustworthy, yet I was in no mood to be fooled, not again, not after Talia. My heart could not take much more betrayal or misdirection.

'Mace, please…I was at that meeting. I was stood beside the King. You just could not see me. I used my curse. You were blinded from the sight of me.'

'What is your point, Kara. Do you mean to stop me?'

'You saved my life tonight,' she said. 'I do not want to stop you; I want to help you. Besides, The Stronghold is on full lockdown. You will need my help if you want to get out unseen.'

'Let's move out. We have no time to spare,' I said, quietly confident about our upcoming expedition. 'Ice, come we are leaving.'

Although I was Lord of the Mainland and tasked with the protection of many, I would cut down anyone who stands against me.

39. ~ PERSEVERANCE ~

Whilst Captain Kara, Ice and I, easily escaped through the heavily guarded North gate, and the special task force of Lords and Ladies made haste to the sight of Hawks disappearance, Lambert was on approach to the moat bridge.

The sky's over Mangrove opened up and poured over the land. Puddles began to form around the soft forest floor, which Lambert, who's steel boots were speckled with air pockets, avoided like a plague. She was more than a little unwilling to wet a single foot. She wanted to survival, and she knew that footrot was one of the most common excuses for failing a mission, for it would slow the bravest of men to a standstill.

A shelter must be found, she thought to herself, but there was no sign of the Elite mother tent, nor any of the fabled Elite force. A nearby oak tree, that was far more cast over with sheltering leaves, would make do for a moment of dryness.

Lambert Scanned over her bleak surroundings for any sign of life but found none. The Oakwood forest was always brimming with wildlife, but there was not a single bird in flight or squirrel racing across the treetops.

Suddenly, amidst the splatter of raindrops, Lambert heard something in the direction of the moat bridge. Rustling leaves, splashing water, and the sound of teeth snapping together. She looked to the bridge, but could not see anything on or around it. Again, she heard the sound of something stirring in the darkness. Perhaps it was under the bridge, where it was too dark for average eyes to see.

With a slow and carefully placed step, Lambert crept ever so slowly over to the bridge. There was something hunched over, sniffing the air around the underside of the bridge. What she saw was no man, nor was it a Beast. It was something out of a nightmare, a horrific sight.

She could barely breathe at the sight of what stood before her in the darkness. Claws scratched against the stone on the underside of the bridge as it pulled its way out. It roared and rolled its almost human-like head from side to side. Stepping towards Lambert, it sniffed the air. She could not move an inch. She could only watch as the creature closed the gap between them and became more visible with every step. Its skin was stretched and ripped across the top of its head, just like the skull of the Monstrosity Lambert saw in the Baron dwell. Every bone in its body, especially those along the curve of its spine, stuck out of its skin like thorns sticking out of a rose stem. Then she saw it, stuck tight around the creature's midsection. The engraved bronze chest plate of Lord Hawk.

'A Monstrosity,' Lambert whimpered, looked into the wide gaping mouth of what was once an admired Lord of the Stronghold.

She could not believe her eyes. It was Lord Hawk. Although his face was now severely misshapen, it still somewhat resembled Hawk. He was no demon, he was worse than that, he was a Monstrosity.

The former Lord of the Elites, who's once white teeth were now black fangs, was so close, that Lambert could smell the blood on his breath.

She placed a hand atop her sword pommel. Lambert then did the only thing she could think of doing at that moment in time, and run. She ran as far and as fast as she could.

The monstrosity gave chase. She could hear the pounding of its vaguely human feet and Beast-like roar behind her. She pulled her sword, slipped low and swung for it. But it was gone. Fear encased Lambert as she frantically looked and listened for any sign of the monstrosity. It had an evil about it, an ominous presence that fed on the fear of its victims. Lambert felt as if a sharp edge was pressed against her throat, cutting her with every breath she took.

She was frozen, wishing for her Lord, wishing for Mantis, wishing for anyone to bear witness to what she was facing alone in the dark.

Heavy breaths brushed past the back of her neck. It was behind her, but it was not attacking. It was waiting, but for what, Lambert thought, finding it in herself to turn and face the fearful monstrosity. Their eyes met. Lambert searched for a hint of humanity within them, but as she had expected, there was none. A killing machine was all that remained where Hawks honour once ruled.

The monstrosity had waited quite long enough it would seem. It leant back on its hind legs and bore its fangs for an attack. Lambert raised her sword, but she was too slow. The monstrosity's massive black claws would have snapped her sword in half if it was not made of black steel. Instead, her sword was sent flying into the distance.

Lambert was not the type of woman to give up without a fight, so without a moment's hesitation, she darted for her sword. The monstrosity moved so quickly that within the blink of an eye it was in front of her once more, snarling and snapping like a Beast before its pray. Lambert looked to her sword, and then back to the monstrosity that blocked her path.

'Damn it,' she said, realising that her only option was to run.

But even if she could somehow outrun the thing, where would she run too. The Mangrove Citadel had been on lockdown ever since the Hatch was destroyed by demons, and the Stronghold was too far away. She would have to hide.

Taking one last look in the direction of the Stronghold, Lambert waited for the opportune moment.

'Make a move,' she whispered. 'Make a move you bastard.'

The monstrosity simply stared at Lambert with hungry red eyes. It stomped back and forth, sniffing the air around her. The Monstrosity did not attack, instead, it did something completely unpredictable.

'Run,' it groaned in a ghastly hiss of sound, as it turned away from Lambert.

It swung at a tree with a clawed hand, striking hard enough to tear out a chunk of the solid oak trunk. It was Hawk, she was sure of it. He was in there somewhere, doing all he could to stop himself from ripping her limb from limb.

'Thank you, Lord Hawk,' she said, darting off as fast as her little legs could take her through the forest.

The monstrosity howled, leant back on its hind legs and pushed off after Lambert. That was the last of Hawk's strength. He was gone now, but not forgotten.

Hearing the monstrosity's pounding approach, Lambert began to climb up an overcast oak tree, hoping that she would not be followed up. However, the monstrosity did not need to follow her up.

With a thunderous boom that shook the forest floor, the monstrosity hurled itself into the tree. Bark splintered off in every direction. Hundreds of wet leaves scattered overhead. Lambert toppled halfway down the tree, hanging onto a thin branch for her life. She could only imagine what an attack like that would have done to her.

Suddenly, the tree began to groan and snap. Lambert could feel it move, but she kept her grip on the branch. It was not until the tree was an inch from the floor, that Lambert eventually kicked herself off. It was just Lambert's luck. She had intended to land on the rain-softened forest floor below, but she had severely misjudged her landing and popped her shoulder out of place atop a moss-covered stone. She did not scream, nor did she make a single sound.

The monstrosity would not allow her to sit and suffer the pain of a dislodged shoulder. It charged at her once again. She whirled to her feet and tried to run, but she could not. Her robes were caught on the same unfortunate stone that almost shattered her shoulder.

'Damn it all,' she screamed in a panic, ripping her robes free.

The monstrosity was closing in. She pulled herself free and fled as fast as she could. A moment sooner and Lambert would have been no more than a light meal for the former Lord.

She put the entirety of her strength into every step as she dashed off into the darkness. The only strategy Lambert had for survival was amateur at best. She would make use of the tall oak trees that littered the forest, or so she thought, flying right, and then left, between broken branches and bulky tree trunks.

A roar echoed through the forest, but Lambert did not look back, she could not. Instead, she focused on the ground before her feet, on her movements, and on the trees that she darted between.

She came across a wide opening, where Citadel tree surgeons must have claimed a hundred trees for firewood or furniture making.

The monstrosity was on her heels. She could not turn back, but if she continued forward, without enhancing her distance, she would be as good as dead. There was no alternative. She would have to risk the opening.

Moonlight poured over her from behind a parting cloud. The rain was subsiding, she noticed, as the last dribbles of a downpour landed atop Lamberts knotted blonde locks.

She ran across the opening like there was no tomorrow. She threw every foot forward as if the ground crumbled beneath her. All the while, the monstrosity's hot breath, sent a chill up her spine as it closed the gap between them.

The monstrously hit Lambert's back legs with the full force of its charge. She had left herself wide open and should have expected as much, but somehow, she thought she could outrun the thing. She tumbled and rolled across the thick muddy floor until she skidded to a halt. Before she could figure out which way she was facing, the monstrosity smashed its heavy-handed claw into her chest, launching her across the opening. She heard the scraping of nails departing steel. All the wind in her body was knocked out at once. She tried to scream, but there was no sound. Bile and blood seeped out of her mouth.

Lambert eventually landed on her back in the middle of the moon swept opening. The monstrosity pounded its way over to finish her off.

'Breath,' a voice cried out. 'Breath you fool.'

She did not breathe; she could not breathe. She let go of life and let herself drift into darkness.

'Breath,' again the voice cried, this time with feeling, with passion.

She found the strength to sit up, cough out a throat full of bad blood and breathe again. It was a short and agonising breath, but a breath none the less. She realised, that the voice was her will, it came from within her.

Lambert was still coming to terms with her surroundings when the monstrosity leapt for her. She lunged forward with all her might but moved less than an inch. Then, with the luck of a thousand lifetimes, she was saved. It all happened so fast. She only had time to see the killer instanced in the monstrosity's red eyes and a blur of its stretched-out human skin before the figure of a man drove a sword through its neck. But it was not enough to stop the likes of Hawk, let alone what he had become. The man was instantly slammed to one side like a rag doll.

Lambert had lost all awareness of her surroundings. She could not take her eyes away from the brightly illuminated red eyes of the monstrosity as it thrashed around in pain. Green blood, that stank of all things rotten, ran from its throat.

Lambert looked at the man, and then at the monstrosity. It was hard to believe that the creature before her was once Lord Hawk, the legendary second seated leader of the Elites. But even harder to believe, was that a man, who appears harmless, was able to injure it. There were so many questions that needed answering. Who was he? Why had he come to rescue her? And, where did he come from?

He was not tall, nor was he short. He was not fat, nor was he overly thin. He was completely average in every way, save for the number twenty-one that was marked by the South point under his left eye. A strange sweep of white curly hair, that had almost receded entirely from his head, waved like a flag in the breeze. He looked as if he was from an entirely different time. His silver armour, which was covered in a variety of faded rags, looked century's old. His weapon of choice was a thin black sword with a ridged edge.

'Can you move?' the man asked, pulling dagger after dagger as if from thin air, to throw at the monstrosity.

Lambert did not answer. She was transfixed on the monstrosity's movements. More and more green blood leaked out from the sword wound. It was clear to Lambert, that the monstrosity was suffering. It backed away, shrieking like a mad Beast.

Lambert was frightened, but still, she wondered who this man was and why, especial being from the South point, had he come to rescue her.

'Can you move?' the man asked again, in a raspy old voice.

Lambert could not move. She could not speak. She could barely shake her head in response to the man's question. All she could do was lay there, looking up at him, panting and shaking.

The man was no fool, he knew that they only had a short window of time, whilst the monstrosity was distracted, to gain some ground. They had to get as far away as physically possible from this chaos.

The man put his hands around Lambert and hoisted her up. It was not until her chest throbbed, that she realised the man was lifting her from the ground.

As they ran as far and as fast as they could through the wild thickness of the forest, Lambert looked back at the monstrosity. It was on all fours, roaring and bashing its spiked head against the leaf speckled forest floor. As long as that sword remained in its neck, it would be distracted and they would be safe.

Everything after that became a series of suffering breaths, agonising ripples of heart-wrenching reactions to the gash in Lambert's chest, and horrific head spins that ripped her in and out of consciousness. She was far from in a stable condition, yet this man, who cradled her, was doing all he could to save her life.

'Who are you,' she mumbled, as sickness crept up her throat and out of her mouth.

He did not answer. He was focused on the task at hand.

The world became foggy around Lambert then. She could not tell whether she was up or down, or whether she was dying or falling asleep. At least when her mind wandered and her head lightened, the pain in her chest subsided somewhat. Just before another drift from consciousness, she noticed something in the far distance. She could not tell if this was just an illusion brought on by an excessive loss of blood, or if she saw a grey cloud of smoke in the shape of a man moving weightlessly beneath a stretch of trees. She blinked, yet the figure remained under the light of the moon. If she didn't know better, she could have sworn it was looking back at her. The more she tried to focus, the more her vision blurred.

'Hold on,' the man said, cradling her tightly as he staggered up a slippery slope.

Every step he made was slow and precise, until he heard the monstrosity's cry, and began to rush. Sweat fell from his brow and landed on Lambert's head as he struggled onwards and upwards. The suffering discomfort of the man's erratic movements had caused another throat full of sickness to resurface.

When they had finally reached the top of the slope, the man began to pant rapidly, as if it was all too much for him. He put Lambert down on the soft ground and knelt over on his hands and knees. He was suffering. Though there was no blood or sign of a severe injury. He was as pale as milk and becoming paler by the second. Perhaps the monstrosity's strike had injured him internally. This was a severe turn for the worst, Lambert thought, folding every possible outcome over in her head. Without him, she was as good as dead. She could not move, nor hold on to consciousness for much longer. Even if the monstrosity did not follow their easily led trail, without assistance, she would bleed out in under an hour.

'I must leave you now,' the man said, struggling to breathe between words. 'The master approaches and I am not where I should be. You will be safe now, and so long as you never return to the Stronghold you will remain safe.'

He propped Lambert up under an old oak tree.

'To answer your question from before, my name is Swan Choker,' he continued.

She knew that name, she had heard it before, though she could not think of where she had heard it. She tried to ask him why she would not be safe in returning home, but no words came out, and before she could cough up another throat full of sick, he was gone.

Her eyelids became heavy. She could no longer hold them open. There was only darkness now. Only the futile thoughts of a lost future dancing around Lambert's mind. Her normally strong heart was now slow and diminishing. She was dying, she could feel it.

'Lambert...is that you?' a strong voice cried out.

'Mantis,' she mumbled, squeezing open the corner of her left eyelid.

It seemed as if no time had passed, but it had been hours. Her vision was blurry. All she could make out was the shimmering golden figure of Lord Mantis kneeling before her.

40. ~ LIMITATIONS ~

The clouds departed in the sky over the Oakwood forest. Lord Mantis, Lady Senna, Lord Noriega and Lady Lavender, along with two carriages full of medical supplies and combat-trained medics, found Dame Lambert slumped beside an old oak tree.

Mantis dropped his long sword and ran to his friend. She was barely conscious and as pale as the day she was born. The long silver softness of his shimmering hair ran through Lambert's blood as he took her in arms.

'Medics,' he called, rushing past the other Lords and Ladies, who looked on in shock. 'Medics.'

Four men dressed all in white, ran out of a carriage with a wooden edged stretcher.

'It will be your heads if you cannot save her,' Mantis threatened, as he placed Lambert on the stretcher.

The men did not remark. They only made haste and did exactly what they were trained to do. Save lives.

Mantis fell back to the group, scraped his sword up from the forest floor, and marched along with the heavy printed boot marks that made their way down the slippery slope.

'Mantis, don't go rushing off, we need to investigate the area,' Senna said, using her silver spear as a steady walking stick.

Unlike the other Lords and Lady's, even the Chieftain, who wore full armour, Lady Senna wore her lightest black leathers under her familiar red robes.

'This is where the sound came from. This is where we found Lambert. You can investigate all you want. I want some action,' Mantis said, with a laugh, swinging his sword from side to side.

Mantis was eager for the expected battle ahead.

The Chieftain, Lord Noriega, sniffed at the air. He approached Lord Mantis and sniffed the ground around the tracks.

'What have you found?' Mantis asked, looking over the tracks. 'These are the tracks of a man. They too large for Lambert.'

Mantis looked into the Beasts large brown eyes.

'But, where is he? Can you sniff him out, Noriega?' Mantis continued.

The Chieftain sniffed no more air, nor did he attempt to follow the tracks in search of the strange man. There were more pressing matters at hand. Only the Chieftain, with the advanced ears of a Beast, could hear the approaching step of the monstrosity.

'Are you listening to me,' Mantis said, struggling to hold his composure until he heard the monstrosity's cry for himself.

Everyone heard it, and every Lord and Lady in the group felt the chill of the monstrosity's presence.

The Chieftain growled and bared his teeth. Senna and Lavender, who gave each other nothing but a hard time, stepped closer together.

'What is it?' Lady Lavender asked, drawing a light-handed black blade from either side of her white robes.

She was terrified. She had not been in combat for almost two years and feared that her years of medical research had made her too weak for this wartime situation.

'You sound frightened, Lavender,' Mantis said, laughing in a way which suggested he does not fear anything. 'Do not worry your pretty little head over it. You need not get involved. Whatever is out there, is mine.'

At that, Mantis swung his sword around and shot down the slippery slope like an excitable infant.

'Mantis stop,' Senna screamed.

But there was no stopping him. The Chieftain snorted, liked the foul taste of monstrosity from the air and followed Mantis into battle.

He was the Beast Chieftain after all. He was not going to let a man, let alone an arrogant fool like Lord Mantis, take all the glory.

'Senna, tell me, what is out there?' Lady Lavender asked, hoping for an answer, hoping for a comrade who will help her.

Under normal circumstances, Senna would have called her a fool and mocked her cowardice, but Senna was kind at heart and one of the most knowledgeable people in Mangrove.

'Lavender, you must relax,' she said, gripping firmly onto Lavender's subtle right hand. 'What we face out there in the thickness of the forest is a monstrosity. They are quite a rare sight and they come in two forms. The lesser and more easily subdued are the giants, like the one under examination in your Division. Then, there are the likes of what we face. The misshapen, I call them. They, as you know, have quite the presence of fear and are known to come from the most powerful of cursed men.'

'How do you know all this?'

'I read,' Senna replied, pulling Lavender down the slope with her.

The medical research men remained at the top of the slope. Most of them could not move from fear and ones who could, would be attending to Lambert's extensive injuries.

Mantis was the first to come across the monstrosity. It was instantly clear to him. The disfigured, hunched creature, with looming fangs, was Lord Hawk. For a moment, neither of them moved a muscle. It was as if they were sizing each other up until the Chieftain darted out from behind a tree.

'I do not require any assistance,' Mantis said, keeping his gaze heavily fixed on the monstrosity.

Evan Mantis, the most reckless Lord in the Stronghold, knew that a single mistake in this battle would cost his life.

The wind whipped through the air, signalling a start to the combat. A flash of metal flickered in the light of the full moon and met with the Monstrosity's heavy claw. It was too much for Mantis, he could not hold the creature's strength, not even with a two-handed grip on his sword. Lunging forward with its wide mouth of sharp black fangs, the monstrosity went in for the kill.

'I expected more from you,' Mantis screamed out, dancing back to avoid a fatal bite.

The Chieftain circled and jumped for the monstrosity's back, digging his claws as deep into its back as he could. It did not matter how deep he dug in his claws, they were not deep enough to make the monstrosity flinch, let alone bleed. Mantis was unable to take a defensive stance, for if he did, the monstrosity would easily have enough time to deal with the Chieftain.

Mantis pushed forward, swinging from one side to another. A few blows landed, but they did not cut in, nor did they draw blood. They only cut through what remained of Lord Hawks chest plate.

Mantis knew that his blade was useless here, as were the Chieftains claws.

'Try this for size,' Mantis said, as he breathed in a lung of cold air.

He threw his sword as hard as he possibly could down the monstrosity's throat. It was a perfect hit. The monstrosity backed away. It choked and gasped. It clawed deep cuts into its already wounded neck.

At that moment, the Chieftain jumped from the monstrosity's back, but he was too slow. The Monstrosity swung around and slammed the Chieftain into a tree, snapping it in half.

Senna and Lavender arrived just in time to see the great lion Beast cry out and stumble to one side. Blood sprayed from his side as he hit the ground with a thud. He bared his teeth at the monstrosity, who was busy swallowing the longsword Mantis threw down its throat.

'You had better spit that up,' Mantis said, in seriousness.

Mantis realised the gravity of the situation. If he did not act fast, the Chieftain would be nothing more than a meal for the monstrosity.

Within the blink of an eye, Mantis had a black steel blade in each hand and had positioned himself between the Chieftain and the monstrosity. This was now a close hand battle and would test Mantis to his limits.

Mantis has never had a problem fighting, not anyone, or anything, at any time. He has not lost a fight in all the years, but it was clear that he was nervous about fighting this creature up close. This creature that was once Lord Hawk, his old master.

Mantis did not give it a second thought. When he saw the monstrosity swing its heavy clawed hand for his face, he twisted to one side and sliced deep into its arm. Black steel was sharp enough to break the monstrosity's skin, Mantis realised. With a slight smirk, he began to pummel the monstrosities chest with his small blades, easily dodging its heavy-handed attacks as he did so.

The Chieftain was now back to his feet and moving quickly to the opposing side of the monstrosity, where Senna and Lavender where anxiously stood. None of them made an effort to help Mantis from there on out. Not that he needed help, or that they were too frightened, they just did not want to get in his way. Mantis was on an entirely different level to them. He was a gold piece to their copper coins, a mountain to their molehill. He was a true warrior.

Just as Mantis was subduing the monstrosity, by pinning its right arm with both his black steel blades and yanking its left around its back with such might that its shoulder cracked out of place. The screeching howl it made was so loud, that Mantis heard nothing but ringing for a while after.

Mantis did not let up. He put all his weight behind the monstrosity's arms so that any attempt to move would require the monstrosity to either rip his arm free of the black steel blades or risk completely breaking its other arm. None the less, Mantis was determined to tear the demon Monstrosity that cursed Hawk in half.

Lady Lavender snapped out of her sorrowful stature and cheered for her fellow Lord. It was the least she could do really. Lady Senna smiled at what she was witnessing. She had a newfound admiration for Mantis, who has, on many occasions, made her skin crawl with his vulgar play on words.

But the Chieftain did not look pleased like the others. At first, he growled at the monstrosity, then he roared as only a proud lion Beast could. Though he was not all bark without the bite. He pounced for the monstrosity's weakened throat. A blur of sharp teeth and even sharper claws ripped away at the monstrosity's previous wounds until its throat hung wide open under its sloping jaw.

'Noriega,' Senna screamed, rushing over with a wave of her mighty spear.

But there was no time. An arrow the size of a small sword burst through the side of the Beast Chieftains stomach. It all happened so suddenly. The Chieftain squealed out in agony. He stumbled forward. His heart became heavy in his chest and the dim-lit forest faded into complete darkness. He did not fall, as one would expect after being punctured through with an arrow. He simply curled up into a comfortable ball and slipped into an unwelcomed slumber.

Nothing but a deadly silence surrounded the forest. There was life in the Chieftain still. The hint of a heartbeat rattled within his powerful chest. His breathing was so heavy, that if there was not an arrow sticking out from the side of his stomach, he would have been considered snoring.

Lady Lavender quickly ran to the aid of her companion, and with her medical wisdom, diagnosed the Beast as to have been hit with a poison arrow. It was poison from the blood of a black dessert frog. If he did not receive a serious course of potions, then he will not last out the night. Senna could not help but shed a tear, for Noriega. He was more than just the Beast Chieftain; he was a friend.

'We haven't the time for tears,' Mantis said, twisting the monstrosity's head from what remained of its neck. 'If you haven't noticed, an arrow has just put the lion to sleep. Perhaps we should be on our guard.'

Mantis proceeded to dig his longsword out of the Monstrosity. Although Mantis never appears to feel any emotion, he was broken inside, for in his hands was the deformed head of Lord Hawk, the only man, save for his father, who has ever truly understood him.

'Yes, you are right,' Lavender replied, leaving the Chieftains body in peace.

Lady Senna wiped the tears from her face and screamed out all the pain in her heart. Mantis smiled at her, for it was not the scream of someone scared of a fight, it was the scream of someone lusting for blood. Senna was someone on the verge of vengeance. She was someone who must, at all costs, fight for what she believes in.

41. ~ REVENGE ~

The next few moments, whilst Lord Mantis, Lady Senna and Lady Lavender waited in anticipation for another arrow to come flying through the tree line, were drawn out. It seemed like an age had passed them by. The wind began to blow in fierce burst through the forest, sweeping the length of the Lords and Ladies robes.

In the distance, they could see only darkness, but where they stood, now back to back, was the clearest and open part of the forest. They watched and waited for many moments, knowing that somewhere out there, someone was watching their every move.

'It is about time,' Mantis said, seeing a flash of steel through the trees to his right. 'Wait here and protect Noriega. I will be back soon.'

As the wind picked up with a tremendous ferocity that swept fallen leaves from their resting place, Mantis marched off.

Senna and Lavender looked at each other, neither surprised at how Mantis moved out without warning. Neither was sure of what to make of their situation, and neither truly able to give a reasonable command that would not put them or the Chieftain at further risk.

Moments later, Mantis had moved so far through the forest that he was no longer visible to those he had left behind. He came across a patch of clearly stepped on earth, next to an old oak tree, which from the marks left in the bark, had been climbed.

'Do not hide like a cat in a tree. Come out and fight me.' Mantis calmly said, looking up into the tree branches.

A mysterious woman hung down off pf a higher branch.

'So…you recognise me,' the woman said, in a creaky hiss of a voice.

She leapt from the tree and proceeded towards Mantis, who stood in complete stillness. That was until he burst into a seemingly uncontrollable fit of laughter.

The woman, who was a mere shadow of her former self, stood before Mantis with a face full of dissatisfaction as she waited in patience for him to stop laughing. Eventually, he did.

'Ella Crew…is it? If my memory serves me correctly, I left you to die in a carriage wreck,' Mantis said smirking.

'The very same,' she spat, in a full rage.

'The one-handed woman who kidnapped my little brother ten years ago, Ella Crew?' Mantis said. 'The one who was left to die alongside her sister and comrade in a carriage wreck.

'Yes...' she replied, angrily.

She looked just as she did then, down to the orange jewellery and the dress. It was as if she had not aged a day. She was the same, save for a few noticeable differences. Her left eye was no longer light and lime green like it once had been, but a deep sinking orange. Her skin was no longer covered in awful scarring but clean and in perfect condition. Though there was one thing that stood out and made everything about her seem entirely out of the ordinary. She now has two hands.

'How...pray tell, did you manage to survive that wreckage?' Mantis asked, lifting his long sword over one shoulder. 'And how did you regrow your hand?'

She gave only a snort of derision in response and turned away. Mantis decided that it would be most sportsmanlike to wait until his opponent was completely ready before starting combat.

After a short moment, Ella did something completely unexpected. She pulled the hand clean from her right arm and revealed an extremely sharp black steel spike beneath it.

'That is interesting,' Mantis said, almost sarcastically, as he approached her with a high raised sword. 'You must be made up like one of those marionettes I've seen lurking the streets.'

Mantis and Ella faced off under the dim light of the preceding full moon. They circled each other like a pair of Beasts ready to rip each other to shreds. Neither one of them willing to back down and both knowing full well, that this fight will not end until one of them is dead.

Mantis threw off his black robe in all seriousness, revealing the shimmer of his golden armour in all its glory. His face glowed with joy. It was as if he lived for life-threatening situations. Ella, on the other hand, wore no armour and her face was utterly twisted with anger.

'Do not hold back,' she snarled, stretching out her legs and arms in quick succession.

Mantis paid no heed to her words of warning; his mind was focussed on something back in the far distance from whence he came.

'Wait,' he said, listening intently.

Thud after tremendous thud echoed through the Oakwood forest.

'You didn't think I would come here all on my own,' she said, chuckling to herself. 'He is my good friend...we call him, Thunder. He is very unique, you could say.'

Mantis was concerned. It was written all over his face, but what could he do but trust his comrades to handle themselves. They were, after all, seated third and fifth in the King's council.

'Let us finish this quickly,' Mantis said, turning his attentions back to Ella.

Without a moment's hesitation, she charged. A barrage of swings and stabs were aimed for the obvious weak point of Mantis's head, for it was the only part of his body not covered by thick armour. Though Mantis could not understand why she struck for his face, as her black steel spike could easily pierce his armour. Perhaps she wished to cut the smirk from his lips. All the same, Mantis was not slow, nor was he a fool. He parried her attacks without much effort. Sparks danced in the air against the scraping of steel.

'You are not half as fast as they say you are,' Ella said, smashing the underside of Mantis's jaw with an uppercut.

He stumbled back a few feet but did not fall. And, without waiting for further punishment to befall him, he swiped his sword sideways with such strength, that the air could be heard ripping. Ella moved in time for the longsword to pass a hair's length from her face. Before she could respond with a follow-up attack, Mantis moved forward and booted her in the ribs, knocking the wind out of her.

'Is that all you have got,' Mantis said in the most mocking of tones.

He stepped slowly forward. The way he moved gave the impression that he was floating above the ground. He raised his mighty sword up and with a look of pure enjoyment, threw all his weight behind a forceful downswing. Ella looked; her eyes wide with unnatural confidence. She pushed herself to the left, allowing the length of the sword to carve through the tree trunk behind her. She pulled a small dagger from the inside of her black leather boot and dug it into Mantis's side. He pulled his sword free and rolled to one side with a groan. Ella threw herself at him, stabbing him over and over again. Blood ran out through the linings of his armour. But he was not discouraged, he was spurred on. He was thoroughly enjoying himself. Mantis bounded from the ground, kicked the dagger from her hand and began to swing his mighty sword violently from side to side.

The fight had gone for some time now and had taken them dangerously close to the edge of exhaustion. Mantis was having the time of his life. He loved nothing more than meeting his match. Though, he knew the end was near, for he was an advanced practitioner of swordplay and between all the cuts and scrapes, he had found an opening. It would seem that every time Ella launched an attack, be that with her bare hands or solid spike, she would leave her left side completely defenceless.

'Let us end this,' Mantis said, holding his sword high above his head with a two-handed grip. 'Come at me with everything you have. I shall do the same.'

'I will destroy you, Mantis,' she replied, matching his smirk with a disdainful glare.

The entire forest fell silent. It was as if time itself was holding its breath in anticipation for what was to come. They charged at one another, but as they reached the point of impact, Mantis doubled back and swung his sword around with incredible strength. A brief look of sadness flashed across his face as the head of his worthy opponent rolled to his feet.

Ella's body remained upright for the briefest of moments, suspended ephemerally in time. Then, she collapsed.

42. ~ SACRIFICE ~

Meanwhile…

Senna and Lavender watch as a mighty figure appear from out of the darkness and storm towards them through the thickness of tree cover. With each stomping footstep, more of it is revealed. It was a man. His head was bald, his beard was bushy and black, and he wore no clothes. None whatsoever. He was so large; he dwarfs even Giovanni. The Ladies stood in awe of the muscular man, yet they stood their ground, for they must protect their injured comrade at any cost.

Within a moment, he was before them, gazing down, with what can only be described as innocence in his green eyes. His expression was somewhat blank, like that of someone simple-minded. The number six, marked in ancient numerals, was visible across his hairless brown chest.

'Flank to the left,' Lavender shouted, using her years of battle experience to orchestrate a worthy assault.

Senna replied with a nod and moved swiftly to the left side of the man, who watched on without lifting a finger in defence. Maybe he was unaware that an attack was imminent, or maybe he was so powerful, that he felt little need of defence.

Senna swung first, slicing the sharp end of her spear across his side, leaving a deep gash. Blood freely poured out. The man slumped forward with a scream and held his wound.

From the right side, Lavender jumped to match the height of his head, and with a mighty crunch, berried both black steel blades into the side of his neck. She twisted and pulled down on the blades in the hope that she would cut a vital artery.

With a cry, the man swung his right arm around, missing Lavender by a mere inch.

'He is nothing to worry about, Lavender. 'Senna said, smashing him full in the face with the circular butt of her spear. 'Let us finish this quickly.'

The earth shook as the giant man fell back and began to cry. The Ladies could not help but feel sorry for the man. Although he possessed more extensive muscle mass than a full-sized Beast, he appeared to have the mental capacity of a mere infant.

'What do we do now?' Senna asked.

Lavender had never seen anything like this and was so utterly unsure of how best to proceed. She simply shrugged her shoulders. Senna began to approach the man, who was on his knees, holding his neck and crying out like a child in pain.

'Senna. Stop,' Lavender said, holding her arm back.

'It is alright. I do not think he is any danger to us.'

Senna laid a hand on the man's shoulder and slowly moved to his cheek, where she rubbed away the tears. The man looked at Senna and gave her a half-smile.

'Everything will be ok. We will not hurt you,' she said, kneeling beside him.

'What in the bloody hell are you doing Senna?'

Lavender was concerned, and she was right to be, for there was no denying the number six marked in the South point style across his chest. She imagined Senna being ripped in half or used as a plaything for the giant brainless man.

'Senna stop...'

'Look, Lavender. He is harmless,' she replied.

For a short time, the large man was harmless. That was until he caught a glimpse of the slowly receding moon in the corner of his eye.

The man's simple green eyes washed over with a pale white. He began to howl, which was followed by howls from wolves in the distance. Senna went to move, but there was no time. The man stood fast and grabbed her around the throat. She could not breathe. She could not break free from the strength of his grasp.

'Senna you fool.' Lavender screamed, stabbing hole after hole into the man's stomach.

She was knocked off of her feet and sent flying into an old oak tree. Luckily, her armour was very strong and made for such eventuality's. The impact could have been more devastating than a sore back and some future bruising If Lavender was not prepared for battle. Though Senna was far from safe. The Chieftain was out of action, and Mantis was dealing with a situation in the distance. No one was coming for her.

The man's bones began to stretch out. His jaw dislocated and dropped with the forming of large fangs. The entire composition of his face changed into something Beast like. Brown fur began to spurt out from every part of him. He tossed Senna to one side, as his back hunched over and forced him onto all fours. The pain within his ear curling howl could be heard for miles around.

A silence fell. It lingered for a moment. It would seem the transformation is complete. The man of muscular form is now a wolf creature with a mass larger than most Beasts?

Senna scurried away at the sight of the wolf. She rubbed the rawness of her throat and caught a long-awaited breath. She was shaken up.

'There is only one thing for it,' Lavender said, unscrewing the hilt of her blade to reveal a small metal syringe.

The creature looked through her with a cold lifelessness. It opened its slobbering jaw full of enormous fang, and charged, ripping earth up from beneath its newly formed claws as it bounded high into the air above Lavender. She was not frightened. She did not move. At the point from which there was no return, Lavender plunged the syringe needle into the giant wolfs underbelly, taking the full force of its heavy clawing impact. It landed hard and heavy on top of her.

Lavender's life was instantly crushed out. She could not breathe with such weight on her. She could not move. Every bone in her body was shattered to pieces. She had sacrificed all for the sake of the Stronghold.

'Lavender,' Lady Senna cried, rushing over to where only a black nail polished hand stuck out from under the wolf, who lay dead atop Lavenders broken body.

'Get off of her,' Senna screamed out, pushing and kicking as hard as she could to move the wolf. 'Get off…'

It was no use. The giant wolf was too large and too heavy for a horse to move, let alone a slender woman.

Senna gave up and slumped back with her head in her hands. She was devastated, distraught and filled with utter hatred for all those associated with the South point. She had finally, after a lifetime of pushing herself to achieve greatness, given up on hope.

Mantis returned to find Senna curled up in a ball of despair. She could not bring herself to look him in the eye. He was holding Ella's decapitated head by a tail of blonde hair. Her eyes remained open, leering at all who gaze upon her.

'What seems to be the matter, Lady Senna? Mantis asked as he laid an eye over the surroundings in search of Lavender.

'She is dead,' Senna burst, wiping the tears from her cheeks. 'She sacrificed herself to save us.'

'Well…I didn't think she had it in her,' Mantis said, smiling. 'What we need to remember now, is that she would not want her sacrifice to be in vain. We must ensure the Chieftains survival now…for Lavender's sake.'

He was sympathetic. It was as if he cared about her feelings. Mantis had never cared before, nor offered any words of a kind wisdom. Perhaps this was the turn of a new leaf.

'You're right,' Senna said, standing proud as if the weight of the world could no longer hold her down.

She could not give up, not yet anyway. She had to ensure that Lady Lavender's sacrifice would not be in vain.

Lavender will be remembered, not for making every encounter with Senna an unpleasant one, but for her years of service. She has saved countless Stronghold lives with her medical expertise and slowed the speed of demons with her potion work.

Sometimes life is funny. Things often change, but not always for the better. Lord Mantis and Lady Senna had to make the most of it or the worst of it. Mantis often said,' Sometimes you will be in impossible situations, most often, for no good reason, but it will make you think about the path you are on because sometimes, the people you hardly know will make the biggest impact on you.'

43. ~ DISCOVERY ~

Time ticked by at an unbearable pace. The bells of Mangrove chimed from the Citadel. Dawn was upon them.

Lord Mantis had been kind enough to comfort Lady Senna in the aftermath of the battle and resisted the compulsion to mock or berate her for being, as he would put it, a feeble woman.

Together, they managed the back-breaking task of dragging the Chieftains heavy body up the slippery slope to were the medics could treat him. Normally, this would be no less strenuous than Mantis's morning exercise, but he was losing more blood than he cared to notice. He was becoming weaker by the second. A dozen stabs of a dagger will do that to a man. Senna did what she could, but she was not cursed, nor did she possess anything near the strength required to move such a mass of weight.

None the less, they reached the top of the slope. Mantis took the brunt of the Beast's weight on his back, leaving Senna to carry his sword and steady their position from the rear.

The Chieftain was in a bad way, that much was clear from the blackness spreading from around his arrow wound. Steam rose with every hot breathe from his foaming mouth. His chest rose and fell in slow motion. It was almost as if the venom was sucking the life from within him. It was hard to tell how he was fairing, or if he had long to live at all. They were just glad to hear his heavy breathing, for if nothing else, it meant he was still alive.

Mantis placed Chieftains body down as gently as he could, though it was not gentle enough. The great lion growled and clawed at the air in its slumber.

'Mantis, after we administer some potion to Noriega, we must retrieve Lavender's body,' Senna said, walking with Mantis over to the medical carriage. 'It is only right that she receives a respectful burial.'

'You are a fool. Lavender does not wish to be buried. She is a medical researcher and wants nothing more than her body to be used for that exact purpose,' Mantis replied, grimacing from the pain of his injuries. 'How do you know that she is dead? She is no fool. Her body will be retrieved in whatever manner she has arranged it to be retrieved in.'

'What…you mean she wants to be an experiment.'

'Be quiet,' Mantis snapped, caution rising from within him. 'Do you hear that?'

'Hear what?'

'Exactly…there is no sound.'

Mantis was right to be concerned. The medics should have heard their voices and come out to treat them, but they did not. The only sound for miles around was the whistling of the wind and the carriage horse's soft pounding hooves on the wet ground.

'My sword,' Mantis said, almost snatching it from Senna's grasp.

'Mantis...wait,' Senna said, holding her spear defensively as she followed him to the side door of the carriage. Mantis did not reply. He was focused on the task at hand.

Slowly, he pulled down the handle of the carriage door and released the hatch. The door shot open. Four dead and bloodied medics fell out on top of him.

Upon Mantis's further inspection, it would appear that they had been slit at the throat and left to bleed out inside the carriage.

'Keep a sharp eye,' Mantis said to Senna, who gave a slight nod and turned her attention to her surroundings.

She was determined to make it out of the Oakwood forest alive, and nothing, save from an army, would stand in her way.

After a few minutes, Mantis returned from inside the blood-soaked carriage with a clear glass syringe. Potion, in large letters, was inscribed on the side. The yellow liquid bubbled as if being boiled within.

'Lambert is missing...perhaps she escaped,' Mantis said, rushing to the Chieftain.

Mantis did not hesitate, nor did he lose sight of the potion's importance. He stabbed the Chieftain straight in the ass and released the yellow liquid into his system. The Beast jumped awake and thrashed around in a circular motion, before falling back into a deep slumber.

'Only time will tell,' Mantis said, kneeling before the Chieftain with a hand on the Beasts mane.

That's when they heard it. The sound of approaching footsteps. Mantis and Senna turned at the same instant to see a flickering light approach from the not so far off distance.

'We are not prepared for this.' Senna whispered, bracing herself beside Mantis.

Though Mantis was in no fit state to protect himself, let alone Senna, from another South point onslaught. Mantis looked around in a panic, unsure of how best to proceed against another threat, one possibly more powerful than those they had already faced.

'Hide, Senna,' Mantis said, standing tall and proud in the face of uncertainty. 'Do it now and do it fast. Our only way out of this may be an ambush. Be prepared.'

'Are you sure?'

'No... not at all. But I don't see you coming up with any bright ideas.'

'Thank you, Mantis. Thank you for everything,' Senna said, before darting behind the side of the carriage and sinking away into the darkness.

It would not stay dark for long. The red sun steadily rose over the east.

Senna was not a moment too soon in hiding, for the tinge of a flaming torch lit up the surrounding area with a burst of flickering brightness. None other than Sir James strolled into sight. It was clear that he was not here to help. He was not dressed for it. He wore nothing but a pearl pleated red suit of leather and silk under an extravagant set of black robes.

'What are you doing here?' Mantis asked, loosening the firm grip he held around the hilt of his longsword as he approached his subordinate.

'Just following orders,' he answered, smirking at his Lord. Something was wrong, Mantis could feel it.

'Bloody orders. I have not ordered you to do anything.'

Mantis looked into James's green snake-like eyes, finding nothing but contempt.

It all changed then. The reality of the world turned on its head. A thunderous racket stirred the silence of the blissful morning sky. It was a sound that Mantis had heard only once before and one he would not soon forget. It was the sound of a Harpy swarm.

'I am not here under your command, Mantis. I am here under orders from the cursed King,' James said, laughing aloud.

'What in the blue hell are you talking about?' Mantis asked as a picture of betrayal crept over the forefront of his mind.

'It's simple old chum. The Cursed King is my true Lord. I am with the South point and I have been for some time,' James replied, revealing the mark of the number two on the palm of his spear hand.

All at once, they arrived. Hundreds of Harpies poured over the sky above, dipping and diving between one another. It would have been a sight of pure beauty if they were not armed to the teeth and dressed for war.

'You had better start explaining yourself, James?' Mantis roared, pointing the tip of his sword at the light greyscale of James's throat.

'Temper, temper.'

James clapped his ring-covered hands together. For a moment nothing happened. Then, an olive-skinned Harpy lady, much larger than any other, sank from the swarm in a delightful splendour. Though she was far from delightful, for Lady Senna was tied and gagged in the firm grip of the Harpies muscular grasp. She was unharmed, but for how long, was yet to be seen.

'What madness is this?' Mantis roared, filled with so many doubts, so many feelings of foolishness.

He squared his shoulders and lowered his sword, playing every moment of his time with James over in his head.

'You certainly are a fool, Mantis,' James said, overjoyed with the sound of his voice. 'I would have expected a little sneak like you to have figured it all by now. The truth is, the South point, along with Lady Kiera's Harpies, have the Stronghold wrapped around their little fingers. We are forging a new world. A world without mankind. A cursed world. We are leaps and bounds ahead of mankind's primitive nature. We have created so much…steam engines, marionettes, monstrosities. But all that is trivial. It is nothing more than a small part of a well-orchestrated plan to change the world. First, we will take the Stronghold, and then we will curse the world. We will have control. All you need to know, Mantis Black, is that one way or another, you will lose.'

'It all sounds very interesting, it does,' Mantis chuckled. 'But you should know that your plan will never come to fruition. A few cursed outcasts and a hand full of precious Harpy ladies will not last one day inside the stronghold walls. You have no real power. And, if you think you can kill me, James, then you are welcome to try.'

James responded with a gleeful laugh. The pleasure of his snake-like eyes held nothing back. He wanted a reaction. Mantis gritted his teeth, barely able to contain the blood lust within himself from slipping out in an uncontrolled act of violence.

'You are blinded by your self-worth, Mantis. Hawk was the same, and well, look at what happened to him,' James said. 'You would have figured it all out if you had only interacted with me as other Lords interact with their second commands. Because you have never trusted me, you have always kept me at a distance, never really knowing who I was or what I wanted. You never cared Mantis.'

'Do you ever shut up?' Mantis replied. 'I never trusted you. I kept you as my second command to keep an eye on you.'

'Oh, Mantis, please. You did not choose to keep me. I chose to stay with you. Your suspicions made for the ideal environment to put the cursed King's plans into action. All that you have seen…the marionettes, the attacks, the betrayals. They're all part of something greater. The real betrayal will be magnificent. It's just a shame you won't be around to see it.'

44. ~ BETRAYAL ~

The sun rose high into the morning sky, giving Mantis the advantage of being better able to see every move James made. He could kill James right there, but they were holding Senna hostage, which did not help his chances, for the Harpy, who looked just as brutish as she was beautiful, could easily move Senna into the path of his sword. They could kill her before he had a chance to take a single step forward. It was clear that Mantis was stuck between a rock and a hard place.

'Why don't you let her go and fight me like a man,' Mantis said, knowing that even with his injuries he could easily beat the likes of Sir James Sand in a fight. 'Or are you frightened?'

'I would love to kill you in a fair fight, Mantis, but I do not play fair and Just like your stupid little brother, I have you right where I want you.'

'So, what is to be done?' Mantis asked, feeling completely helpless for the first time in his life.

He had always had the upper hand in every situation. This was just so utterly unexpected, that he did not have a clue as for how best to proceed. He could run James down in a blaze of glory, but Senna would surely die. And, even if he could save her, how does one fight an army of Harpies.

'You are such a fool Mantis…and to think, I used to admire you,' James said, grimacing as Mantis laughed aloud. 'What is so funny?'

James was unaware that Dame Lambert was at his back. The Harpies were said to be of a single mind, and it was for this reason they did not see Lambert sneaking onto the scene. Every one of them was drawn to Mantis.

'You will not find it very funny, James.'

Mantis laughed. He was in such a hysterical state, that fresh blood poured from his stab wounds.

'Tell me what is so funny, or Senna will suffer the consequences. I swear it,' James screamed, holding the end of his spear over Senna's subtle neck.

'Alright. But I warn you, you will not find it very funny.'

With that, a pale-faced Dame Lambert, bandaged from head to the midriff, ran one of the medics thin-tipped swords through James's gut. He fell to his knees, cursing and screaming. The two brown horses rained to the carriage, reared up and rushed off in a frightened hurry.

'You are something special Lambert,' Mantis said, taking this opportunity to slash his sword through the Harpies left side.

The Harpy screamed out a horrible sound, like metal scraping against a stone.

Mantis wanted nothing more than to lay waste to James there and then, but he knew that if they mean to survive, they needed him for answers.

'Kill them. Kill them all,' James screamed out.

The rage inside him burned more painfully than the thin sword in his stomach. Hatred throbbed in the beat of his heart and pulsed through his veins.

Mantis stood over James and looked into his untrusting eyes one last time. Nothing was said. The actions in his eyes said more than words ever could.

Like a swarm of flies, the Harpies shot down, twisting and twirling as they fell from above. There was no time to waste, nor to release Senna from her bonds. Mantis flung her over his shoulder, gripped hold of Lambert's hand and made a run for it. He knew very well that they could not outrun the descending swarm, but he would be damned if they did not try. Only time would tell.

A muffling clatter, like rolling waves, reached ever closer to them. Screeching war cries bellowed out through the forest. Arrows struck into the side of trees, inching closer with every shot.

'We have to keep moving,' Mantis said, with urgency in his voice.

He tightened his grip around Lambert's hand and pulled her along, almost dragging her. They raced down slopes, clambered around tree cover and ran in whatever direction would be most difficult for the Harpies to follow.

An arrow cut into Mantis's shoulder. A second sooner and it would be stuck into the nape of Senna's neck.

Mantis stumbled, slowing their pace enough for the Harpies to reach a sword's length. Mantis doubled back on himself, tossed his long sword into the chest of the nearest Harpy and rushed over a rocky stream. The Harpies were in such a condensed bunch, that by killing the front runner, he had stopped them in their tracks. The noise of the Harpies wailing and screaming was intense.

Mantis was determined, not just for them to keep moving further into the forest, but to make it back safely. They had to inform the King of this treason and put a stop to the Harpies.

They came to a corner of the forest so thick with trees that even the smallest bird would find it difficult to move between the never-ending tangle of branches. But this was their only chance and they would be foolish not to take it.

They ran further and further in, taking no care whatsoever in avoiding the sharp branches that cut across their bare faces until they came across a large old oak tree with a hollowed-out hole in the side.

'In there, quickly now,' Mantis said, motioning Lambert inside.

There was no time for hesitation. She crawled in, only just able to squeeze through the small gap. All the while Mantis hurried the ropes from around Senna's arms, leaving her free to untangle the rest for herself from inside the hole.

'We won't all fit,' Lambert spluttered from inside the hole.

The Harpies were closing in fast. There was no time to waste.

'Senna, get inside and protect Lambert. I will draw them off. Hurry,' Mantis ordered, risking all for the sake of others once again.

He knew very well that he would not fit through such a small gap, and that he would most likely die protecting the girls. He was a true Lord. A man they could be proud to call their friend.

Senna gripped hold of Mantis's broad shoulders and pulled him close. She kissed his cheek, and spoke softly into his ear, 'We will see you again…wont we?'

A single tear rolled out of the corner of her right eye.

'You are a fool, Lady Senna,' he answered, smirking at her with a look of pride in his blacker than night eyes.

She took her place beside Lambert within the hollowed-out tree hole. There they would remain in absolute silence until the time was right. All they could do now was hope and pray for Mantis's safe return. Though by the look on his face, he means not to.

Mantis was now alone. He preferred it this way. It meant that when he had reached a sufficient distance from the hollowed-out tree, he could stop running and fight the Harpy swarm until his last breath, without worry for the safekeeping of others around him.

A river of screams edged closer. The Harpies were near and they would not stop until they had what they wanted. It was their way. Their single focus was drawn entirely on Mantis. He led them past the hollowed-out tree hole where Lambert and Senna hid from sight.

A rocky clearing opened up ahead of Mantis. At the very end, there was an ancient moss-covered wall from a time long forgotten. It was as fine a place as any to die, Mantis thought to himself, as he burst through the last line of trees and into the burning brightness of the red morning sun. He turned to face his foe, barehanded and surrounded. For a moment, there was only silence.

One Harpy with elegant blue eyes, loops of appealing blonde curls and the most bewitching set of sparkling silver wings stepped forward. She scrapped her spear tip across a rock and beckoned Mantis closer. He winked at the young Harpy and stepped forward. She gave what seemed to be a half-hearted swipe of her spear, grazing Mantis across his defending forearm.

'You are going to have to do better than that,' he said, snatching the young Harpies spear from her gentle grip and smashing it with tremendous force across the side of her head.

The sound of her skull cracking open like a rock to an egg sent her on looking sisters into a frenzy. Immediately, Mantis dropped the spear to his side. With a smile firmly affixed across his face, he closed his eyes for what was to come.

A dozen arrows crashed through his chest plate and into his heart, yet he remained standing. The tips of two swords met in the middle of his abdomen and realised a bath of blood over the surface on which he stood, yet he remained standing. It was not until he was sliced across the left eye with a silver war axe, that he eventually fell.

'Finish it,' he groaned, a line of blood leaking out over his pale lips.

Although the Harpies were known for being the most beautiful and elegant of all creatures, inside they were ugly. For anyone cruel enough to leave a dying man to suffer was not worth their weight in sand.

As Mantis lay there, watching hundreds of Harpies take flight around him, he thought of James betrayal. He thought of the South point being no more than a front for the rising Harpy empire. He thought of the treasonous manipulation of the Stronghold, and the cursed Kings plots to destroy mankind.

Before the world blurred out of focus and bruised into darkness, a ghostly figure of grey smoke emerged from the ancient wall. It reached out to him. A vision of his past flared into the front of his mind. And then he saw her, his lost love.

'Elinor...'

45. ~ DIVULGE ~

On arriving near the outskirts of the Mangrove Citadel, Captain Kara and I could hear a distant howling that drew our attention westward. At first, we considered it to be a large wolf, for it was followed by a flood of lesser howls that resonated through the forest. We could not ignore such a sound and so made immediate haste towards its direction.

During the time in which we had travelled together, Ice had taken an unusual disliking to Captain Kara, which was perhaps from her unfamiliar face. Every time Kara would look his way or step a foot too close beside the young Beast, he would bare his teeth and growl in discontent. This only became worse as we ventured further into the forest. It got to such a stage that I had Ice walk ten paces ahead of us, for if he saw it fit, he could cause an incredible amount of damage.

Within moments we had closed the gap between ourselves and the direction from which the war cries had come from. Only the sword in my hand and the hope in my heart kept me from sobbing at the thought of not being able to find Lambert. All I wished for was her safekeeping and a chance to once again hold her close.

Without warning, Ice growled and darted left towards what looked like an opening in the tree line. We followed him to find Lambert's curved sword half-buried amidst leaves and twigs.

'You are a wonderful Beast, Ice,' I said, looking the sword and the place where it was found over for any clues to Lambert's whereabouts.

The hilt was sticky with blood and under every fallen leaf, the sign of a struggle was evident.

Again, Ice growled. This time, he growled towards the large opening in the tree line. At first, I did not follow, but after concerning myself with the marks of something large and Beast like below my feet, I ran with him.

'Mace, we have to find Lambert and our best chance of doing that is not by following an aggressive Beast,' Kara said, unable to take her gaze away from the sky above as if saddened by the very sight of it.

Ice was persistent and if somehow by not following him, I was late to save Lambert from harm, I would not ever be able to forgive myself.

'We shall follow him, Kara.'

She looked at me as if I had insulted her and then looked back up at the sky in horror.

Something was wrong, I could feel it and so could Ice. It must be a Harpy thing, looking up at the sky that is. Perhaps she missed being in flight or seeing the view from above. Whatever her reason, I had not the time to stand around dwelling upon on it.

'Move out, Ice. Keep your growls to a minimum. We do not want to draw any unwanted attention to ourselves,' I said, kneeling to rub Ice across the flat of his head as an expression of gratitude.

'Well...what are we waiting for?' Kara said, marching towards the opening without a worry in the world for what might be waiting for us there.

For all we know, we could be walking directly into a trap, an ambush or something far worse, like a demon horde or a bloodthirsty monstrosity out for nothing more than a meal.

'Be cautious. We do not know what to expect,' I whispered, keeping a sharp eye on my surroundings as we stepped out from the thickness of oak trees and into the sun-glazed lustre of open land before us.

In the centre of the opening, there were clear signs of a struggle. Lambert's prints were easy enough to make out, as were the same claw marks from where we had found her sword. Lambert's marks were not alone. There were more besides hers and by the size of them, they belonged to a man.

We followed the marks close to where an incredibly large wolf lay dead. Next to the wolf was the severed head of a woman I hoped never again to see. The head of Ella Crew from the South point. The very same woman thought to have died in the carriage wreck when I was a boy. Though her face, for some reason, did not alarm me, nor did it bring back terrible memories of a time long past. I only thought of my brother and how he might have been the one to finish her off. His footmarks and the marks of two women, presumably Senna and Lavender, littered the damp earth.

'It looks like our comrades have been busy here,' I said to Kara, who took the time to investigate the wolf.

'I wouldn't speak too soon...look at this,' she replied from the other side of the wolf's massive frame.

I was disgusted at what I saw. Lavenders black nail polished hand poking out from the underside of the wolf chest.

'We must keep moving,' I said, almost in a whimper, as a single tear rolled over my cheek.

There was a story here that needed to be told and I hoped that the others would still be alive to tell it.

We made our way up a rather damp and slippery slope, where several other footprints had marked over.

Atop the slope, I paused. What I saw struck a deep nerve. The hairs on the back of my neck stood up on end, and my heart seemed to skip a beat.

Curled into a ball on one side of the slope, Noriega, the Chieftain, was breathing hard and heavy. A gaping black wound was left untended on his side. If there was not an arrowhead sticking out of the Chieftains side, I would have thought that he had been run through with a sword or spear.

On the opposing side of the slope, next to the marks of a horse and carriage, were four dead combat medics. Their throats were slit and their bodies piled atop one another as if tossed there aimlessly. Beside them, a Harpy lady with broad shoulders and beautiful orange wings lay face down in a puddle of what appeared to be fresh blood.

A thin man dressed all in red, save from a lengthy black robe stood in the centre of all this chaos. Although his back was turned, I had a pretty good idea who holds that posture. It could only be Sir James Sand. I was utterly positive that James did not leave with the original party of Lords and Ladies, and if he did not, then what reason could he possibly have for being here.

He turned to us, leaning to one side. His weight was balanced over his spear. A thin sword, not unlike the one's used by combat medics, rested neatly through his guts. A line of red trickled down his pearl pleated fabrics and into his shoes.

'What on earth are you doing here, Sir James?' I asked, trying my utmost to paint a rational picture of events in my mind.

James said nothing at all in response and looked me up and down with a contempt that grew with the meeting our eyes.

'Answer me,' I screamed.

James paused and turned back on me.

'Why is he here? You were meant to take him straight to the carriage,' James said, peering at Kara through the corner of his snake-like eyes

'Hush your wretched tongue, James,' Kara said. 'I can guess by the look of your bloody guts that your plans are not exactly progressing as you had expected.'

I did not know what any of this meant, but I knew that from the dead Harpy and the way James was talking, that Kara had betrayed me. I must be cautious. I find a cannot think rationally. There are too many questions that needed answering.

I approached Sir James, taking note of the many footmarks around him and one in particular, that belonged to Lambert. The footmarks lead off in the distance behind James.

I quickly correlated that each foot mark was a considerable distance apart, leaving no doubt in my mind that she ran from this area in quite a hurry.

'James, do you know where Lambert is?' I asked, acting almost oblivious to Kara and James's acts of betrayal.

I had to play as if I was obliviousness. I had to, in obtain even the slightest amount of information as to Lambert's current whereabouts.

James remained silent, only laughed heartedly in my face as if I were too dim whited to deserve a response.

'Is there something wrong with your head, Mace. James said, laughing as if possessed. 'You're worse than your bloody brother…this is a betrayal.'

I remembered then, exactly why I disliked Sir James. There was something all too incredulous about him. How Mantis had kept him as his second command all these years was beyond my reckoning.

Hearing the rasp of unsheathed steel, I turned my attention to Kara just in time to see her draw her shortest sword to Ice's throat. Though Ice was no fool. He had suspected Kara from the beginning and was on his guard. It shames me to think that I was so blinded in my efforts to keep Lambert from harm's way, that I did not take the heed of Ice's warnings. I have put us both directly in danger's path.

With a heavy clawed paw, Ice smashed the sword to one side and stood tall on his hind legs. He was the same hight as Kara's. I ran to Ice's aid as fast as I could. Ice was strong, but he would be no match for Kara in combat.

After a few steps forward, I felt a sharpness in my calf that instantly stopped me. When I turned to look, I noticed James's golden spear stuck through the side of my lower leg. The pain when James yanked it out, shot through me like a jolt of lightning. I could not move.

Ice held his own against Kara for as long as he possibly could, but it was not enough. He let his guard down only for an instant and she sliced his nose half off, saying in a voice of arrogance, 'You won't be sniffing any more tracks now. Damn Beast.'

I turned and sprang at James with my sword in one hand and Lambert's in the other. My heavy rage was bearing down on James's ability to concentrate. As suddenly as I had turned on him, James dropped his spear and cowered away. Further and further he coward back, until he had no choice but to turn tail and run. My advances, it would seem, were not for the weak-willed.

I had not the time to make chase. James will have to wait. I moved towards Kara now, who by this time had cut Ice across the eye and left the bottom of his right ear dangling like a wet rage.

She could have killed the poor Beast repeatedly, but did not and it was for this reason, that I questioned her.

'Kara, what is it you want with me?' I asked, my head spinning at the mercy of my better judgment.

Kara whirled around to the side of Ice in a quick motion and before I could react, she held a knife to his throat.

'You wish to know what I want with you,' she said, in a somewhat sad way. 'Well, there is a carriage waiting for you at the foot of the Mangrove Citadel that will take you directly to the South point. The cursed King awaits the pleasure of your company. I want you to put your hands behind your head and sit your pretty little bottom down inside that carriage.'

'And if I refuse.'

'Listen carefully, Mace. I will only say this once. If you do not do exactly what I say, I will kill your Beast, and then you will be taken by force to the South point. It will all be very unpleasant and unnecessary,' Kara said, as a thunder of cheering and chanting rang out overhead.

The sound grew louder and closer with every beat of my pounding heart.

'You're probably wondering what that sound is…are you not?' Kara said. 'Well, if you like Harpies you're in for a treat. My sisters are swarming this way in their hundreds.'

A thin trickle of blood streamed from Ice's throat. There was nothing I could do but what she asked. If I did not, Ice would be slit across the throat, and that is something I could not live with.

'Alright, alright. I will do as you wish. Just please let Ice go,' I said, hoping that Ice would find it in his heart to forgive him, for if it was not for my reckless stupidity, he would not be in such a predicament.

'That's the spirit, Mace,' Kara replied, moving the knife away from Ice's throat.

I dropped mine and Lambert's sword to the damp earth and embraced my Beast. Though as I held Ice, I felt something was not right. I cast an eye over my sorrowful surroundings and realised that the Chieftain was no longer curled up by the slope. He was gone, and to confuse matters further, Kara began to sob as if in regret of her actions.

'You do not have to do this,' I said, stepping towards her.

'Don't you take another step,' she roared, 'I am truly sorry, Mace, but this is something I must do.'

Tears began streaming down the side of her face. She was a mess of emotion.

'Before I go answer me this. Has King Enzo truly been killed and has he truly been replaced with a godforsaken marionette?' I asked.

If I did not ask and sent Ice running back to Stronghold with nothing but his stubby tail between his legs, there would be no telling the torment he may endure at the hands of a marionette King.

'Yes, it is true,' she said. 'The King is dead. A marionette sits in his throne. It's all my fault. I have betrayed you, and I have betrayed the Stronghold. Ever since I was little, I have been involved in this betrayal.'

'I don't understand...'

'Mace you fool. The King is dead because of me, and the cursed King has control, because of me,' she said, sobbing with her head down. 'The only thing that was not part of this plan was the creature of grey smoke, that knew exactly where I was and pulled me from the top of the red tower...I was coming to get you either way. don't you see?'

I had never heard weeping like that before. Kara fell to her knees. Her head, full of dark brunet hair, sank low. She looked hard into the earth beneath the weight of her hands.

'I wish it was not true...' she continued.

'Then why, if you wish it all untrue, did you do such a thing in the first place?' I asked, approaching her in the hopes that I could convince her to put right what she has done wrong.

'There is no time for answers. Just that I have my reasons. Now take this, keep it safe,' she said, tossing a small black box, not unlike those used for engagement rings. 'When the time is right, you must make haste. Make haste anywhere but where the South point can get their hands on you. You are the key to their success. Even with the Harpy empire behind them, they will fail without you.'

She looked up at me. She was a sorry state.

'Sorry...' she mouthed to me in silence.

Moments before hundreds of harpies swarmed into sight, swinging swords and spears as they spiralled above in complete synchronicity, I pushed the box into the most secure side pocket of my robes and fastened it with the attached bronze button. The Harpies took little notice and continued circling above. They were magnificent in flight, each one of them had an unchallenged elegance that would shatter the hearts of weaker men.

'Sisters...take Lord Mace to his carriage at once,' Kara commanded in a violent tone of voice that suggested there would be no love lost between us.

The Harpies did not hesitate. All at ones, they poured from the sky in a circular motion.

'Ice, you must do exactly what I say,' I whispered hurriedly into his ear. 'Take these and run as fast as you can to the East bay. Wait for me there.'

With that, I put one hand on Ice's head and with the other, I placed both mine and Lambert's swords between his razor-sharp teeth. Ice left in a hurry, a low wailing of sadness left his lips. I wished him all the safety of the gods as I was dragged off my feet and up into the bright sunlit sky above.

46. ~ PENITENCE ~

There was a time when soaring through the morning sky between the arms of two Harpies would have been nothing more than a delightful dream, but now I was higher than I had ever been, with a view far more glorious than I had ever anticipated gazing upon, and yet I wish only to feel the ground beneath my feet. Ahead of me is the Mangrove Citadel and behind me, in the ever-shrinking distance, stood the Stronghold, the place in which I cannot return.

We rose higher and higher into the cloudless emptiness above. We rose to such a height that I could hardly breathe in the frozen air. It stung against my skin and set my eyes to tears as it passed over my face. There was a point in which we had flown to such a height that I could no longer distinguish between the trees and trails of the forest.

After a short time above the world, the two Harpies that held me on either side cried out in excitement. I could see by the look of delight on their faces, that souring free in the sky and being weightless above all else, meant more to them than any treasure this world had to offer. It was hard to believe that such enchanting creatures of passion could be at the heart of the Strongholds undoing.

Without warning, like a ripple from a stone thrown to water, they all cried out, folded their wings flat to their backs. They plunged with such force to the foot of the Citadel that my head felt as if it might tear from my neck. The ground grew with every wincing glance forced open under the pressure of pounding wind. A horseless carriage of grey came into focus.

'Hold,' the Harpy to the right screamed out, spreading her wings full to drag against the momentum at which we fell.

I noticed that the hundreds of other Harpies that had remained in a close group, were no longer in view, and when I looked back, I saw that they had begun circling above.

Every instant seemed an age as we glided peacefully down to meet with the carriage that was waiting for my arrival.

A hooded man, dressed in a robe of colourful variety, sat cross-legged atop the carriage roof. I quickly assumed him to be the driver, and by how my life had played out these last few days, I would not be surprised if it was the Cursed King himself atop that carriage.

Closer and closer we drew to the ground until we had landed safely without harm on the firm grass-covered ground below. I was glad to be back where I belonged, on solid earth, though I would not have time to enjoy it. The moment my feet touched the ground, I was dragged forward and thrown into the back of the carriage.

It was bare inside and reeked of a foulness I knew not the smell of and wished never to find out. Only a cold slab of slanted metal, that was moulded across the back wall, and a thick barred window frame would keep me from madness along the road ahead.

The door slammed hard behind me and with it, the sound of a large lock being fastened into place.

'That's very kind of you to bring him to me. I am guessing that's the boy, Lord Mace, and none other in the back of my carriage,' the man from atop the carriage said as he jumped from the roof to make pleasantries with the Harpies.

It would appear that his attempts in conversing with them were not his first and would have been a failure at best.

The more commanding of the two Harpies said in a tone of frustration, 'Did I not make my myself clear the last we spoke. Never address me unless I address you first.'

At that, both Harpies turned their noses up at the man, spread their wings in fullness and joined their sisters in the circular flight overhead.

'Damn it,' he said, calmly stretching a single-arm behind his head. 'Well...there be nothing here of much use. Best be on our way.'

He gave an indifferent shrug and entered the driver's side door of the carriage. With the turn of a key, came the clanking of unoiled clogs, the rattle of metal pipes and a billowing black cloud of smoke that almost entirely engulfed the carriage.

We were now moving and this gave me the perfect opportunity to open the black box that was gifted to me by Kara, the controversial Harpy Captain, who's moral conundrum led her to regret her betrayals. She had what some would call a moment of clarity.

Inside the box, there was nothing more than a seemingly unused silver key and a slip of parchment with the words, safe and open, written on it. It was written in such an exaggerated neatness that I stared at it for several moments. To what this all meant I had not the slightest of clues and thought only to do what one does with a key and test it upon a lock.

Peeking out from the corner of the metal bars, I could see a lock the size of a man's head dangling from the latch of the door. Pushing my arm through the bars I reached a fingers tip from the lock and pushed the key firmly in place. During the deepest of breaths, I prayed to the gods and turned the key in a clockwise motion. It popped open and when pulling it back from the door frame, I counted back from three, two and on one, I leapt from the carriage in a single bound. The driver did not appear to notice and with the carriage door swaying in time with every turn of the wheel, he continued travelling at an average pace along the path.

I was alone and with luck would remain alone until I arrived at the East Bay, where I hoped to find my loyal snow bear, Ice, and the sea Lords awaiting my arrival.

On retrieving the key from the lock, I rushed behind the nearest tree and began constructing an evasive plan. The driver will soon discover my absence and send word for my immediate capture. I cannot travel through the forest, where the Harpies will have a constant vantage point from above, nor can I take paths in or around the Citadel, where the false King now holds sway over the land and would surely have a warrant for my arrest. There leaves only one option, the web of old underground aqueduct systems that may or may not have been blocked from use.

I had not the luxury of waiting around to configure a more elaborate plan of escape. In peeking around the side of the tree to ensure a safe clearance, I darted across the carriageway and made immediate haste towards the Citadel wall in search of the aqueduct's entranceway.

'You look a little lost,' the carriage drivers voice called out from behind me and with it, the sound of a thunderous roar.

It hit me so fast in the back that it knocked me off my feet and onto my front. I had never felt such a shock in all my life and when checking what I thought was an arrow wound, I discovered a gaping hole from back to front. I rolled over to find the driver stood over me with a grin plastered across his gaunt face. In his hand, he held a weapon the likes of which I had never seen.

'Damn this hand cannon is mighty powerful,' The man said, clocking his thumb over a miniature copper hammer to the rear of the weapon that aligned the revolving centre cylinder with the long silver aiming barrel at the front.

In a single motion, he moved his index finger from the dark wooden handle and placed it gently over a crossbow styled trigger. For an instant, my heart stopped beating and I would have screamed out if I was not paralysed in excruciating pain.

With a mocking smile, the man held the hand cannon to my forehead and in utter delight, he ordered that I return at once to the carriage.

I could not answer him. I could not breathe, and the blood within my lungs was at such fullness, that it leaked out of my mouth.

'It is not over,' a soft voice raged as if from within my mind.

At the same instant, a flash of red washed the reality of the world away and left me in darkness.

'It is not over,' the voice raged on.

Again, a flash of red flooded across the front of my mind, this time surrounding me in all its glory.

Somehow, I understood. Somehow, I felt the full unrelenting anger of my cursed soul. It was as if another consciousness was inside of me, stronger than me, edging ever closer to control and I no longer had the strength to hold it off.

47. ~ REDEMPTION ~

I woke to the sound of heavy breaths that were not my own, and the feel of cold stone beneath my bare hands. The smell of something rotten lingering in the thick air and the memory of a dream so real, so powerful, that for a time I dwelled upon it. I believed it true.

I felt lost, alone and in my heart's absence, a sense of bitter indignation from having been treated with such unfairness, overcame me in such a way, that I could not bear to continue along this path.

I was nudged to the ribs and with a jerking motion, I leapt to my feet. The white lion, the Chieftain, Noriega he was here. He stared back at me. The Chieftains weakness was clear, as was the blackened wound from a sword-sized arrow embedded in his side.

'Noriega, what are you doing here?' I asked, stroking a hand across his thick mane of fur.

I glanced over my surroundings. It was clear enough by the long arching support pillars that shouldered a maze of streams and passageways, that we were in the Aqueducts. We were deep below the Mangrove Citadel.

'If I am not mistaken, that slanting centre stream leads directly to the East bay. It is with great sadness that it has come to this, but I must seek guidance from sea Lords,' I said in uncertainty. 'They are now the Kingdom's only hope for retribution.'

I moved from the stone surface on which I now stood and in an absence of care, I slipped and tumbled down a steep set of stairs and towards a pit of absolute darkness. As I gripped hard to the last step in the hopes that I would not fall to my doom, I was caught off guard by the gleam of something moving quickly below me, and then again to my left.

I pulled myself to safety and regained my footing. With the Chieftain beside me, we began following in the direction of the streams flow, paying little attention to the increasing number of figures that flashed like candle lights. I ensured every step of my foot was placed firmly in front of the next. I did not wish to fall to the bowels of the earth.

Within moments, we had reached a point in which we could go no further and all that stood between us and freedom was a sheer stone wall.

A feeling of unease came over me. I felt as if I was being watched.

Suddenly, I was ripped from my feet. The Chieftain flung me atop his back and sent us hurtling at full speed through the archways of the Aqueduct. It was with such speed and force, that I could scarcely catch a breath or take a view as to what horrors we fled. Then I saw it, and as I did the tips of its sharp teeth pierced my armour and gouged deep holes into my flesh. The creature had four legs below its body and was no larger than a common dog. It was altogether fish-like, with several gill slits in the side of its scaled head, with large elongated fins, that ran down its blue back to its grey tale.

It was no surprise that the Chieftain was moving with such haste. The creatures were hungry and we were surrounded. They dove from the high arches, scrambled across walls and sprang at us from every possible angle. They squealed as they bit down into the Chieftains flesh, yet he remained focused.

Before long we had reached the bright light of the East exit.

'This cannot be how it ends,' I said.

All at once the creatures, hundreds of them, desperately scrabbled for us, biting and clawing. It was as if they could not follow us into the outside light and this was their last chance to feed before returning hungry into the depths of the earth.

A claw scraped against my throat. I immediately drew away and with blazing anger in its murky green eyes, the attacking creature ripped the innermost pocket of my robe to reveal the purple-tinged piece of eight within. At the sight of the coin, every one of them stopped where they stood and stared as if transfixed by the shallow glare of the coin's light. I had not the first clue as to what possible control this most interesting of ancient coins had over the fish-like creatures, but as long they were not consuming the flesh from my bones, I was more than content.

The Chieftain roared with all his might as he leapt high over a fallen pillar and fell to one side. A few steps further and we would be out of this wretched Aqueduct.

It would seem the White Lion had taken all the steps he could take. His life was now in my hands. I did not intend to leave him, not here, not alone in the dark to be devoured by strange creatures. If it was the last thing I ever did, I would see the Chieftain to safety.

With all my efforts, I could not move him and it was with my final exertions that something incredible happened. The piece of eight that I held in a tight grasp began to pulse with purple light. It burned the blue from the palm of my gloved hand, singeing into it the ancient symbols of the octagonal coin. With a slow step, the creatures came upon us and as they did, I snapped a dozen of their necks.

I could not stop them all and before long I could not move through the thickness of their forward marching.

There was something very different about the creatures. They were not attacking, nor did they appear fearful of the outside light as they once did.

They were simply marching forward in a mindless motion and when I stopped snapping the necks of those steering too close to the Chieftain, we were both pushed from our feet in a mighty sweeping motion and carried off on a wave of the creature's backs.

I stared into the eight-sided coin that rested on the palm of my gloved hand, mesmerised by the purple glow and the power it held over these strange creatures.

So many questions sprang to my mind as we exited the Aqueduct and met with the enchanting picture of purity that was the setting sun. A glimmer of hope crept over me, setting his eyes to belated tears.

After a while, the wave of creatures had climbed over the Eastern hills and there it was, before my very eyes, the East bay, a place most never would wish to come, for fear of what they do not understand.

It was a sight to behold. High towers filled with arrow men littered the many miles of crisp golden sand, whilst cheering and chanting could be heard from the vast fleet of black ships surrounding the edge of the bay. One ship, with twin masts and a multitude of cannons, cross ropes and harpoons stood out from the rest. It was this ship I believed to be the sea Lords mighty vessel of mass destruction. It dwarfed over the smaller black ships as if they were mere ants to a giant foot. It had the appearance of being sculpted from ice. Under the sun's rays, it glowed in an illuminated orange light. I was too far a distance to make out the thousands of faces that walked its decks, yet I had a feeling, that if my snow bear was anywhere, he would be on that ship.

With a worried sigh, I took the Chieftains mighty paw, held it tight, and in pulling myself to an upright position, I felt a tremendous wave of heat roll overhead.

I peered up through the squinting slits of my eyelids and was overjoyed. The bird of fire, though minuscule in comparison to its former self, blazed with tremendous speed across the cloud-speckled sky above. It was a sign of hope.

A.G SMITH

TO BE CONTINUED...

THANK YOU FOR READING

If you have enjoyed reading this book, please leave a review on the site you purchased it from.

Printed in Great Britain
by Amazon